PROPER[illegible]

The Anatomy of Victory

The Anatomy of Victory

Battle Tactics 1689–1763

Brent Nosworthy

HIPPOCRENE BOOKS
New York

Hippocrene Paperback Edition, 1992

For information, address Hippocrene Books, Inc.
171 Madison Avenue, New York, NY 10016.

Library of Congress Cataloging-in-Publication Data

Nosworthy, Brent.
The anatomy of victory : battle tactics, 1690–1763 / Brent Nosworthy.
Bibliography: p. 353
Includes index.

1. Military art and science—Europe—History—18th century.
2. Military art and science—Europe—History—17th century.
3. Tactics—History—18th century. 4. Tactics—History—17th century. 5. Battles—Europe—History—18th century. 6. Battles--Europe—History—17th century. I. Title.
U39.N67 1989
355.4'2'09032—dc20 89-35732
CIP

ISBN 0-87052-014-8 (pbk)

This book is dedicated to Alice, Tristan and Mom, whose patience and understanding provided much needed encouragement while I was writing this book.

CONTENTS

Part II: Evolution of Tactics and Grand Tactics *1714–1756*

Part III: Doctrine and Training in the Seven Years' War Period

ACKNOWLEDGMENTS

I would like to thank Roger T. Kennedy, George Nafziger, and Brian Piper for supplying me with a number of interesting research items. Stephan Patejak for editorial assistance, and Storn Cook for the diagrams. I would also like to thank the staff of the research libraries whose efforts greatly simplified the task of uncovering invaluable materials: 43rd Street Annex, New York Public Library, New York, New York; Rare Book Room of the McClennen Library, McGill University, Montreal, Quebec; and Bibliothéque Nationale de Québec, Montreal, Québec.

Introduction

THOUGH A GREAT MANY BOOKS HAVE BEEN WRITTEN ABOUT WARFARE during the eighteenth century and the Napoleonic Era, surprisingly few of these deal with how armies actually fought on the field of battle.

Anyone interested in military history during this general period will encounter little difficulty finding adequate information about most other aspects of warfare. The so-called higher levels of warfare, generally referred to as the "operational" and "strategic" levels, are particularly well covered. Library shelves are filled with histories of the period's major wars, and even the individual campaigns within each war. Using these works, it is relatively easy to assemble a detailed account of a particular commander-in-chief's strategic objectives, and the day-to-day movements of his army.

It is ironic that the area many readers would find the most interesting, how armies fought one another during the various battles, combats and skirmishes is usually only covered in sketchy detail. Though we are given general information, such as the types of formations the troops employed and some of the methods they used to fire their weapons, the picture blurs as soon as we increase the degree of magnification.

For example, how did an army attack? Did it just advance straight forward, or did it attempt to break its opponent's will by firing before it began its assault, or during the actual advance? Once the advance began, did the men just march, or were the troops and officers trained to divide the assault into recognizable phases, changing their actions according to the enemy's response? What were the officers and NCO's doing as they approached the enemy?

With a little thought, this list of questions can be greatly expanded. In fact, if we were working for a defense consultant and were asked to analyze the doctrine and practice of any modern army, our analysis could literally fill volumes.

This leads to the first basic question: was it simply a question that warfare on the battlefield during the seventeenth and eighteenth centuries was considerably simpler, and there just wasn't that much to write about? If we judge by the amount of space allocated to these issues in works where, given the subject matter, we would expect them to have been addressed, we would have to conclude many authors have, indeed, decided that warfare of that time was much simpler.

The answer is, of course, that most writers in the last century have come to believe, consciously or unconsciously, that the information needed to answer these questions has died with the men who participated in these wars. They believe, in this sense, that the "soft" concerns such as beliefs and training were like the flesh on dinosaurs, having long ago disappeared, leaving only the "bones," which in this case are the notable occurrences of famous battles and such.

Undoubtedly, the scarcity of material has come about, in part, because there is a tendency for eye witnesses and participants, and later, historians to focus on the extraordinary or distinctive events in any action or battle, rather than those that were viewed at the time as being common practice. When a chronicler sat down to write an account of a battle, most often he unconsciously presumed that those reading the account knew generally how troops fought in battle. Though this may have been true for the reader of his time, it certainly isn't true for a reader of ours.

But the tendency to ignore the "commonality" of action also has another origin, one whose origin lies at the very heart of how we perceive events and then communicate them to others. What makes a battle a battle? We tend to think of any battle in terms of its distinguishing qualities. The description of any combat tends to provide us with the composition of the contending armies, their initial positions, the layout of the terrain, and the original intentions of both commanders. It then goes on to describe the events and how each led to the eventual conclusion of a battle. These are the qualities that distinguish one battle from another.

Implicit in most descriptions of battles is the notion that the various units within the two armies are "neutral" elements, to be governed and manipulated in the upcoming battle purely by the orders received on that occasion and their responses to the ebb and flow of conditions as they occurred during the conflict.

The problem with this type of approach is that it diverts our attention from the various minor processes that were at work. What it also doesn't provide, and which is essential for any true understanding of how combat was resolved, is the body of thoughts, expectations, and training of the participating troops at the start of the battle, what today is called "doctrine." In other words, what the troops on one side would do if they were totally successful in getting their own way.

The result of this tendency, unfortunately, has been the chronic underestimation of the importance of tactical systems in contributing to the events and the outcome of battles and other types of engagements during this period.

The lack of detailed knowledge about each tactical system, and precisely how it differed from its counterparts, has led some to assume either that the various armies either employed the same tactical systems, or if there were differences, they were not significant. It has led others to believe that even if notable differences in tactics did exist, tactics by its very nature was only a minor consideration and did not greatly affect the overall outcome of any engagement.

The belief regarding the "sameness" of tactical systems can be substantiated or repudiated only by a detailed examination of the various tactical systems used by the armies of the period. If notable differences between tactics can be shown to exist, this view ceases to be accurate.

The other belief that tactics by its nature is never significant involves a completely different set of analyses, and it is unfortunately insufficient to show that distinctive systems did, in fact, exist.

The goal of the present work, *The Anatomy of Victory: Battle Tactics 1689–1763,* is to reconstruct each of the major tactical and grand tactical doctrines as they existed during the period under consideration, and to explore how these doctrines evolved to produce what could be called "Fredrician warfare."

In addition to the types of questions mentioned earlier, such as how did the armies attack and defend, and how did they advance, this work will also concern itself with how an army deployed on the battlefield, and how these procedures slowly were modified. The types of formations used on the battlefield and how troops went from one formation to another or from position to position is also of central importance.

This type of discussion will not only deal with "tactics," which in its original sense means to deploy troops on the battlefield, and move them from position to position, but extends also to "grand tactics," referring to more general movements made to execute the commander's battle plans.

Any work dealing with how warfare was fought on the eighteenth-century battlefield, has to confront an ingrained bias that has molded much of how we look back at the events under consideration. This is the myth that during the eighteenth century and even the Napoleonic period, the armies once on the battlefield did not really "maneuver." In its most popular form this has been expressed as "the drill regulations were useful solely on the parade ground, but had no applicability on the battlefield." Whereas, this type of statement was sometimes true, it certainly doesn't hold true as a blanket statement covering all times and all nationalities.

There are three major reasons why this belief has become so firmly rooted in the English-speaking world. The first two of these have come about because of the cultural and historical perspectives of the English and American population.

The English military tradition, and this has thoroughly permeated even the so-called ivory tower of historical research, is that the true way of fighting a battle is to explore the lay of the land, and provide for the best possible defense. Once the battle starts, the character of the typical "John Bull" would guarantee that at forty to eighty yards the enemy's will would be ultimately broken, such as repeatedly happened during the Peninsular Wars.

The English tradition views "linear warfare" as essentially valid during its period of popularity. However, it views all of the theoretical embellishments pursued by continental armies as distinctly "not British," and hence not really useful. "Practical" linear warfare is to hold one's position tenaciously, and not try to outmaneuver the opponent. The ultimate argument offered for this point of view is that the British did, after all, win the Battle of Waterloo, and didn't this show the poverty of military thinking of the previous hundred years?

For Americans, the perspective is slightly different. Those of us who are Americans are made to believe, from elementary school days onwards, that the methods of linear warfare used by continental troops were innately inferior to the skirmishing tactics of the pioneer sharpshooters: "We beat the British, didn't we?"

The American tradition implies that linear warfare only existed because of the mutual consent of all the parties that partook in the game. It arose out of a preoccupation with symmetry and other characteristics of the Age of Enlightenment. Once linear warfare was exposed to an army that was not limited by its rules and conventions, such as during the American War of Independence, its shortcomings were immediately made obvious.

Unfortunately, onto these two culturally generated biases, history has itself added a third. When smooth-bore muskets started to be replaced by rifled weapons in the mid-nineteenth century, that aspect of Napoleonic warfare that continued to remain useful was "open order" fighting, that is, fighting by skirmishing. Even many high-ranking military authorities who had served in the Napoleonic wars, given the new weaponry being introduced, found it necessary to decry former practices. The chief target of such tirades became the older method of using "closed order tactics," i.e., tight and geometrical formations, during combat. And, of course, they *had* outlived their usefulness, once the range and rate of fire of small arms were significantly increased.

The only unfortunate aspect of these developments was how, coupled with the other culturally oriented biases already discussed, they permanently influenced how future generations would look back at warfare during the eighteenth century and Napoleonic times. When compact formations ceased to be practical, soon almost everyone forgot they had ever been functional at all.

These three intellectual motifs have led to the pervasive modern view that the warfare during the seventeenth and eighteenth centuries, and even to some extent during Napoleonic times, was a baroque system whose ultimate origins lay in the intellectual limitations of that age. To express it simply, "They wouldn't have fought that way, if they knew what we know."

One of the major goals of this work is to demonstrate that most of the tactical and grand tactical systems used during the period under discussion had their basis in the nature of the weaponry then in use, and as often as not, represented optimal solutions to the problems being faced.

As the title indicates, the purpose of this work is to explore how warfare was conducted on the European battlefield during the 1690–1763 period. On the face of it, this may appear to be a rather strange time frame: not conforming to the major landmarks, traditionally used to define this general era in history. The usual practice has been to divide this epoch into a number of periods, the boundaries of each having been defined by political events. Usually this event took the form of the start or end of a major war, as in the case of the War of the Spanish Succession, War of the Austrian Succession, Seven Years' War, and so on.

Unfortunately, the military historian has taken the political historian's demarcations at face value. This approach, though useful for political analysis, can be misleading when studying a nonpolitical event or subject, such as art history or the conduct of war. The problem is that it cultivates the expectation that warfare, in our case "battle tactics," was significantly different during each of the major wars within this general period.

It is much more useful to consider the time extending from 1690 to 1763, at least as far as how warfare was resolved on the battlefield, as a single general period that was slowly evolving. The basis for this continuity lay in the fact that, despite minor improvements here and there the weaponry remained largely the same throughout the period.

The period which we are going to examine is defined by the adoption of the flintlock musket and the socket bayonet. At no point after their adoption were there any dramatic changes in military technology which would have forced a concomitant transformation of the art of warfare, of the magnitude that had, for example, occurred during the Thirty Years' Wars (1618–1648).

Warfare, during this period is usually referred to as "linear warfare," and with good reason. As we shall see, troops before the battle were arranged in lengthy lines, and usually met one another in frontal assaults.

The period ends with the conclusion of the Seven Years' War. The seeds of a new system of battlefield warfare, what could be termed the "impulse system"—one closely associated with the Napoleonic period—had its origins before the close of the linear period. However, it would only be after the termination of this general conflict that military thinkers would have the luxury of being able to digest the lessons of the last war, evaluate the more successful experiments, and effectively assemble the conceptual components of the new system.

PART I

Linear Warfare 1689–1713

Introduction

THE USE OF FIREARMS CONTINUED TO GAIN IN IMPORTANCE DURING THE seventeenth century. By 1600, approximately two out of every three infantrymen were equipped with a matchlock musket, and the cavalry also depended on firearms, the lance having disappeared from Western Europe.

Previously the infantry, following Swiss practices, had been formed into massive formations known as *tercios*. However, Maurice of Nassau during the Dutch Revolt started to successfully use smaller infantry formations, and systematized the manner in which his infantry delivered their fire and reloaded.

Warfare quickly underwent a series of reforms during the first half of the Thirty Years' War, especially as practiced by the Swedish army. The heavy Spanish-style muskets requiring a fork rest were replaced by light muskets. Relatively lighter "leather" guns were also introduced for close infantry support.

Though the Dutch had been the first to use thin formations, wider than they were deep, the Swedes started to use even thinner formations both for cavalry as well as infantry. These thinner and smaller formations were strung along the length of the battlefield at intervals, instead of the large checkerboard formations still employed by the Imperialists.

Gustavus, impressed with the Polish cavalry he fought against in the

1620's, stopped his cavalry from relying exclusively upon their firearms during the attack, and reintroduced shock tactics among the Swedish Cavalry.

During the remainder of the seventeenth century, a number of new factors modified the way battles were fought. Increasing numbers of the infantry were armed with the matchlock musket, and the percentage of foot soldiers carrying a pike steadily declined. Though obviously this increased the individual battalion's firepower, its ability to defend against cavalry was correspondingly weakened.

The fight to drive the Turks back out of southeastern Europe also provided a new watershed of experience. The European cavalry, no match in hand-to-hand fighting for their nimble Asiatic adversaries, had to rely on orderly, densely packed formations and the use of firearms to defeat their enemy. This produced a reliance on a slow, orderly advance against the enemy cavalry that would be later used against other European armies.

After 1670, the French cavalry, which did not participate in the Turkish wars, discontinued their total dependence on the older system of firing at the enemy from a stationary position, and developed a relatively fast charge. Though this quicker charge lacked the order and cohesion of its Germanic counterpart, it suited the French cavalrymen's love for the impetuous assault and provided tactical basis for the string of successes enjoyed by French cavalry up until the War of the Spanish Succession at the turn of the next century.

Originally, infantry battalions six to ten ranks deep were perceived as "solid bodies", and were deployed in lines with wide intervals separating them and their neighbors. These battalions, now consisting of only five or six ranks, started to be looked upon as "linear" bodies and were positioned much closer together. Increasingly, battalions, instead of being thought of as independent units which could stand on their own, were viewed as being part of a much larger formation, the line. The reduction in the number of ranks, the Turkish wars, and the increase in the number of battalions to be deployed on the battlefield, as well as some new tactics developed to exploit the wide spaces on either side of a battalion, all contributed towards this tendency.

Though the flintlock musket, which ignited its charge with a spark caused by flint striking steel instead of a cumbersome slow-burning fuse, was theoretically available by the latter years of the Thirty Years' War, it started to be slowly introduced into military applications in the 1670's and 80's. However, it was only by the end of the first decade of the eighteenth century, that the matchlock was totally replaced.

Roughly at the same time, a number of attempts were made to devise and introduce a workable bayonet that could be attached to the end of a musket to allow the infantry to defend themselves against cavalry without having to rely on cumbersome pikes. The introduction of the socket bayonet appears to have made tremendous progress during the 1690's, though as with the flintlock, its adoption continued during the War of the Spanish Succession.

The changeover to the socket bayonet and the flintlock musket ultimately had a number of tactical repercussions, though the time it took for these to be felt varied between armies. The musketeer's rate of fire slowly increased from an average of about one shot per minute to about two. This increase, coupled with the adoption of the bayonet, made the infantry less dependent on the use of pikes, and much less vulnerable to cavalry.

On a purely tactical level, the adoption of flintlock affected not only the way infantry in a number of armies would systematically deliver their fire, but also the types of formations the infantry would be able to use. Up until the late 1680's, most armies deployed their infantry along six ranks. Though three ranks had been known as early as the Thirty Years' War, they originally were reserved only for special situations. With the introduction of the flintlock, the three-rank battalion became much more widespread, and even the conservative French officially deployed in five ranks, and in practice were usually forced to use four.

The effect on the way a battalion could now deliver fire was just as profound. In the British, Dutch and Prussian armies a new fire system known as "platoon firing" was developed. It offered a number of advantages over the older systems: it was much less disorganized and easier for the officers to control, it guaranteed delivery of fire along the entire battalion front, but most of all, of all known systems it most effectively permitted continuity of fire.

In these armies, the general method of attacking was to advance to within middle range of the musket and then deliver a fire. If after several volleys, the enemy showed no signs of weakening, the infantry was to advance a little further towards the enemy before stopping once again to resume firing. This general grand tactic was based on the belief that the effective use of firepower was essential in breaking the enemy's will to continue fighting, and circumvented the need to close to contact, thereby reducing the number of casualties friendly troops would be likely to suffer.

The development of "platoon firing" with its reliance on a succession of firefights was not adopted in all armies. In many armies, such as the French, Bavarian, and Swedish, the *á prest* or "go through" attack, used with great success by the French in the late seventeenth century, continued to be popular. In this offensive doctrine, the friendly infantry advanced along lengthy lines towards the enemy, and every effort was made to prevent these troops from stopping and firing. The theory was that the enemy, attacked by determined troops, would lose their courage and would break prior to both armies coming to contact.

As a result, in these armies little attention was paid to the new methods of delivering fire. The French, for example, for the most part continued using their "fire by ranks" system of firing, where the men in a rank after firing would march to the rear of the battalion where they would reload.

This tactic, which had been successful during Turenne's and Luxembourg's time (c. 1650–1695), was geared to the capabilities of the musket, in its matchlock form. As the infantry in various armies switched to the more effective flintlock, it would become increasingly difficult to work this tactic successfully, and the infantry would tend to stop and break out into impromptu firefights at increasingly longer ranges. Even by the early 1690's it still was not uncommon for opposing infantry to fire at each other from 20 to 50 paces, while by Frederick the Great's day (mid-eighteenth century) this distance was almost always between 50 and 100 paces.

During the 1690 to 1714 period, a transformation in cavalry tactics was also under way. At the beginning of the period the Germanic armies, influenced by experiences in the Turkish wars, placed emphasis on the maintenance of the strictest order in the ranks and closed to the enemy at a slow to medium trot. They reserved their pistol or carbine fire until the last 20 paces or so. At the beginning of this period the French, on the other hand, used a more aggressive charge, without as much emphasis on order. Up until 1700 the French were generally successful against their enemies. However, around this time a retrograde movement occurred in the development of French cavalry tactics, and the German-style use of firearms during the assault gained a short-lived popularity.

Around this date, two military leaders independently started to forge new cavalry tactics, where importance was completely placed on the sword, foregoing the use of the carbine or pistol. Marlborough, commander-in-chief of the Allied armies in Flanders during most of the War of the Spanish Succession, required his cavalry to advance at a brisk trot, while still maintaining complete order. Charles XII, King of Sweden, adopted even more aggressive tactics. His cavalry advanced at the gallop with their sharp narrow swords, thrust at the enemy cavalry.

The change in weaponry also had a higher level effect. On a more conceptual level, the transition to true linear warfare, something that had been slowly occurring since the Thirty Years' War was finally completed. With the disappearance of the pikes in each battalion as well as the tendency to deploy the infantry along longer battalion frontages, there was much less basis for thinking of the formations as "solid" bodies. This was reinforced with the lessons learned from the Turkish wars which promoted the use of continuous lines to prevent the enemy from working their way into the formations.

CHAPTER 1

Seventeenth-Century Warfare

ARMS AND ARMOR

IT IS RATHER UNFORTUNATE THAT THE POPULAR VIEW OF WARFARE DURING the War of the Spanish Succession has Marlborough and Prince Eugene entering the scene and quickly institutionalizing a series of changes in weaponry, drill, tactics and grand tactics that within a few years leads to crystallization of "linear warfare." This view maximizes the differences between the way troops conducted combat at the end of Turenne's time, in the 1670's, and the way Blenheim was contested in 1704. In fact, it barely acknowledges the similarities between warfare as it was during Marshal Luxembourg's time, in the 1690's, and that at the start of the War of the Spanish Succession ten years later (1701–1713).

When all the details are considered, and each aspect of warfare is checked against that of its immediate predecessor, a more evolutionary view emerges. Warfare during the War of the Spanish Succession was a lot closer to its counterpart of ten years previously than has been generally acknowledged, and, as we shall see, retained some surprising similarities with that of Turenne's time. Looking the other way in time, warfare during the War of the Austrian Succession, about 25 years later, hadn't changed as much as might be expected, and remained very similar to that at the start of the eighteenth century. This observation, of course, ignores the Prussians who at this latter point were very busy redefining the whole process.

For this reason, we shall start our treatment of battlefield tactics by taking a quick look at how combat occurred on the seventeenth-century battlefield. In the early 1600's, each European army invariably consisted of infantry, cavalry, and some artillery. The cavalry of the period tended to consist of three major types: cuirassiers, mounted arquebusiers, and dragoons. The lance, so characteristic of mounted warfare during the late Middle Ages, had all but disappeared from Western Europe by the turn of the seventeenth century, and though there were many different types of cavalry, almost all of these were armed with a sword and some type of firearm, such as a carbine or pistol.

The cuirassiers were protected by "three-quarter" armor, extending from the helmet on the head, down to the knees. The breastplate was proof not only against pistol shot, but even musket shot at longer ranges. No longer carrying the lance, they were armed with a brace (pair) of pistols, and a sword. The mounted arquebusiers, sometimes called "carabiniers," wore only a breastplate and a morion helmet. They were armed with a short wheel-lock musket, one or two pistols and a sword.[1] At this point, dragoons served as a type of mounted infantry, who in theory, were on horses in order to be quickly deployed where needed, either during the campaign or on the battlefield. A majority of dragoons were armed with infantry-style matchlock muskets, but a portion carried pikes instead.

There were two types of foot soldiers in the infantry: pikemen and musketeers, both of whom were named after the weapons they carried. The pikemen were chosen from the tallest and strongest men; in addition to the pike, they also were armed with a sword and were protected by an open helmet, armor on their chest (a demi-cuirass or plastron), thighs (cuisse) and arms (brassards) and wore a heavy buff or leather coat and large leather gauntlets. The musketeers also wore a sword or rapier, and sometimes a dagger, but were only protected by a strong leather coat which was nearly sword-proof and a flat-rimmed "pot-helmet."[2]

Originally, the pikes carried by the pikemen were the same length as in late-medieval times, that is, about 15–18 feet long, excluding the point. However, given that infantry by this point were no longer threatened by cavalry armed with the lance, this length was found to be excessive, and as early as the start of the century, the pikes were often cut down to about 11 feet, excluding the point.

The pikes were made of ash, or sometimes oak, and were headed with steel. The forward end of the pike was also protected by metal plates about four feet long designed to prevent the enemy from easily cutting the weapon in half. The rear end of the pike was also sharpened so that the pike could easily be shoved into the ground under the soldier's foot when it came time to level the pike to ward off enemy cavalry.[3]

The remaining infantry were armed with a "matchlock," a muzzle-loading musket carried and fired by the individual soldier. Usually weighing between 14 and 20 pounds and five feet in length, it was fired by a rather crude mechanism that required the musketeer to go through a battle carrying several feet of slow-burning fuse. The "match," as the fuse was called, was attached to the "cock," which was the name given to the striking part of the firing mechanism. When the trigger was pulled, the cock, and consequently the match, plunged into the priming pan which was located just above the touch hole, at the base of the barrel. The fuse ignited the priming powder in the pan which, in turn, flashed through the touch hole, detonating the main charge (hopefully!).

In the late sixteenth century, the Spanish introduced a heavier version, which was capable of firing a two-ounce ball a considerable distance. In the days when most infantry and all cavalry wore armor of some sort, this was seen as quite an advantage. However, these large muskets naturally were heavier and more cumbersome, and required the musketeer to rest his weapon on a wooden fork whenever he pointed it in the enemy's direction.[4] This trend was reversed during the Thirty Years' War, when a lighter, less awkward weapon was introduced.

Despite these modifications the matchlock remained a cumbersome weapon throughout the entirety of its career. Its weight, coupled with the awkwardness of the match, meant that the musketeer had to devote all of his attention to the act of loading and firing. The slow-burning match was very susceptible to any type of inclement weather, such as wind and rain, and was extremely difficult for untrained troops to master. During battle conditions, its misfire rate was as high as 50 percent. Judging by its rate of fire, range, and accuracy the matchlock was a primitive weapon. Requiring at least forty-four separate movements to load, according to the *Exercise of Foot* (1690), an average of one shot per minute was considered serviceable, And, although its effective range was approximately 250 yards, anything approaching accuracy was usually limited to ranges of less than 60 yards.

The matchlock could *not* be used under battle conditions for aimed fire, at least in the modern sense of the term. To get an idea of the accuracy of the average military matchlock, we just have to consider the accuracy of the flintlock, the weapon which later replaced it on the European battlefield at the turn of the eighteenth century.

Under ideal conditions with a perfect specimen, the flintlock could be fired accurately at ranges never more than 100 yards, but these two requirements were rarely, if ever, found on the battlefield. The following excerpt, although already widely quoted, is necessary as a vivid reminder of what the contemporary officer thought of the accuracy of the type of musket used by the military:

> "A soldier's musket, if not exceedingly badly bored, and very crooked, as many are, will strike the figure of a man at 80 yards—it may even at 100 yards. But a soldier must be very unfortunate indeed who shall be wounded by a common musket at 150 yards, provided his antagonist aims at him; and as to firing at a man at 200 yards, you might just as well fire at the moon and have the same hopes of hitting your object. I do maintain, and will prove whenever called upon, that no man was ever killed at two hundred yards by a common soldier's musket by the person who aimed it at him . . . and in general service, an enemy fired upon by our men at 150 yards is as safe as in St. Paul's Cathedral."[5]

Weapons with much greater accuracy did exist. The rifled wheel lock used for hunting by much of the nobility maintained accuracy well past 200 yards. However, as suitable as this weapon was for general hunting purposes, it was not practical on the battlefield. Having an intricate and involved loading procedure, it required about two minutes to load and fire. During the same period of time a skilled flintlock musketeer could discharge as many as five shots.

Even discounting its slow rate of fire, the rifled wheel lock remained totally impractical for military considerations. Being painstakingly and individually made by master craftsmen, it was far too costly for military use where thousands, if not tens of thousands, of muskets were needed at a time. A colonel, at the beginning of the period we are dealing with, usually owned his own regiment, and consequently looked to this property, if not as a source of income, then at least as something that wasn't a potential source of financial liability. He had to be constantly on guard against extravagant expenses. A regiment could be supplied with matchlocks for a tiny fraction of what it would cost to supply an equivalent number of wheel locks.

The artillery of this period was of the classic smooth-bore variety. On the battlefield, most artillery pieces were "guns" firing a low straight trajectory, the most common ammunition being solid shot. During the Thirty Years' War, the artillery was used most effectively during the opening phases of the battle, during the enemy's approach. The weight of the pieces made redeploying during the action extremely difficult. As a result, cannons were generally left in their original positions, which meant they would be unable to fire as the general course of action moved away from them as the battle unfolded.

Turner, writing in the late seventeenth century, provides us with approximately how quickly the various types of cannons then available could be fired. "Whole cannons" (i.e., firing 48-pound balls) could be fired about eight times per hour; demi-cannons (24-pounders) about ten per hour; quarter-cannons (12-pounders) about 12 per hour; and field pieces (3-pounders) 15 times per hour. The limiting factor here, simply wasn't just how fast they could be loaded and fired, but how often these pieces could be fired without taking an undue risk of bursting the barrels because of overheating.

However, the real limitation with seventeenth-century artillery lay in its weight. A "whole cannon" weighing about 6000 pounds, in a 12-hour period would fire 3600 pounds of lead and 2400 pounds of powder, giving a total weight of 12,000 pounds. When it is remembered that one horse could draw about 272 pounds, it is obvious 44 horses were required to draw this one cannon and the ammunition required for 12 hours' service. The weight of the pieces, and the number of horses required to draw them made artillery of the seventeenth century difficult to deploy, and they were rarely deployed after the start of the battle. This, coupled with their low rate of fire, limited their effectiveness. Turner concurred with Montluc who, writing in the second half of the sixteenth century, had concluded that as far as artillery was concerned, "Il fait plus de peur, que du mal," that is "it frightens more than it hurts".[6]

FORMATIONS

The solution to the problem of accuracy was discovered very early in the muzzle-loader's career, by the middle of the sixteenth century. The arquebusiers and later musketeers were massed together into relatively large groups of men, and made to withhold their fire until ordered by their officers to commence firing. Though the individual weapon was not aimed, by having the officers channel the general direction of the formation's fire, it was possible for them, in effect, to select a general area as a target. Massed fire allowed a large number of balls to be hurdled at the same area, increasing the odds of hitting some of the enemy's forces in a particular area. It did not matter that an enemy soldier was unlikely to be hit by any one musket when there were between 300 and 600 muskets being fired in his general direction in a short period of time.

In order for this massed fire to be effective, it was necessary for officers to control the troops' firing position, their direction of fire (hence the target to be fired upon), when they should begin firing, as well as the exact procedure used to reload. To achieve this control, it became necessary to have the arquebusiers arranged in an orderly formation. Had the men simply been thrown together in any haphazard fashion, it would have been virtually impossible for the officers to ensure that the troops were pointing their muskets in the desired direction or that they fire in unison at the designated moment. Having a large number of men deliver their fire at the same moment had a greater psychological impact on the enemy, who would become more aware of their casualties than if the same number was inflicted over several minutes.

When arranging the musketeers into a workable formation, the officers soon discovered there were three main concerns. The width of the formation should be as wide as possible so that the greatest number of firearms could be brought to bear against the enemy at any given moment. Counterbalancing this, the formation had to have "sufficient weight," to resist the enemy when it closed to fight with either "cold steel" or the "push of pike."

This was because, given the time necessary to reload the weapon, there had to be enough rows of men to guarantee that there was always at least one row ready to fire, if necessary. For example, in the days when it took about a minute to reload, if the officers wanted fire to occur every six seconds, the men would have to be arranged so there were ten rows. On the other hand, as the musket became easier to reload and the rate of fire increased, the number of ranks needed to deliver the same volume of fire per unit of time became smaller. In our example, only six ranks would be needed to have fire delivered every six seconds, when it took only 30 seconds to reload.

There is a tendency for the modern to view this practice of arranging the troops in symmetrical formations, of perfectly ordered ranks and files, as purely a military version of the then current philosophical world view, known as the "Age of Enlightenment." It is difficult for us to see that warfare then, as it is now, was firmly grounded in pragmatic efforts and experimentation. The *raison d'etre* for the use of the ordered rows of men lay in the nature of the weaponry then in use. It was purely pragmatic considerations that induced all European armies to adopt essentially the same basic structure when deploying their troops: the men were physically organized into a series of "ranks" and "files." The general practice was to have each man stand behind the man in front (if there was one), and aligned to his neighbors on his left and right. A "rank" referred to each row of men running from left to right along the width of the battalion; a "file" to each row of men running from back to front along its depth. Two other terms, which will be used intermittently throughout this work, should be explained here: "file leader" and *serre-file*. The first man in any file was referred to as the file leader. Generally, there was a row of subaltern officers (what today we call NCO's) or commissioned officers running along the length of the battalion behind the last rank of men. Subalterns would position themselves in a file, that is, they would stand in line behind the eight to ten men directly in front of them. In this case, these subalterns or officers "closed that file" and were described by the French term *serre-file,* referring to that fact.

The actual size of an infantry formation varied widely according to nationality. In the early 1600's, as far as grand tactics was concerned, there were two schools of thought prevalent in Western Europe. The first and more traditional school was known as the Spanish school; the second, called the Dutch school, was created by Maurice of Nassau during the Dutch Revolt (1566–1609).

The Spanish school used massive infantry formations, called *tercios.* On the battlefield, the large tercios were usually grouped together in an arrowhead formation (one up front, two in the rear on either side), although a diamond-shaped one, with four tercios in each group, was also used occasionally. These formations were relics from the days when the critical moment of the battle was resolved when opposing groups of pikemen or landeskneckts met and decided the day with fighting at close quarters. Though these massive formations were partially reduced in size near the end of the Dutch Revolt, they still remained quite large. Tilly's infantry formations at Breitenfeld (September 17th, 1631) were about 1500 men, and probably deployed along a frontage of 50 men with a depth of 30. These large and ponderous formations would move slowly forward. It was extremely difficult to maneuver them in any other direction, and they would attempt to crash into the enemy's formations.

The adherents of the Dutch school favored much smaller infantry formations, where there was a much larger ratio of frontage to depth, maximizing the number of musketeers that could be brought to bear at any given moment. These wider, thinner formations were in fact the predecessors to the linear formations that would evolve during the second half of the seventeenth century.

In the days of pikes and the matchlock musket, the men were spread out more than they later would be by the time of the Seven Years' War or later. Each file of men was usually separated by two to three feet; each rank was generally separated by 12 to 13 feet (twice the length of the sergeant's halberd), except when the battalion neared to about 50 paces from the enemy, the distance between ranks would be considerably reduced, to one or two paces (five feet). If only purely offensive or defensive factors had been considered, the men would have been positioned more closely together; however, there were two major considerations which demanded that the above minimum distances be kept. In these times, the soldiers marched without "cadence" that is, though each man was supposed to take the same-sized step, called a "pace" (the length of a "pace" varied from army to army, period to period, but it was almost always between two and three feet), no effort was made to have the men stick out their left or right feet at the same time. This was a very inefficient way of marching, and the only way to maintain order for more than a few moments was to keep a reasonable distance (about 12–13 feet) between each rank as the battalion marched or maneuvered.

The reason why the files needed to be separated by two to three feet had more to do with the nature of the matchlocks the musketeers carried, than with the way they marched. In the days before the flintlock, each musketeer went into battle carrying a lit "match" (fuse) attached to his musket. Gustavus Adolphus would introduce the use of cartridges which prepackaged a standard amount of gunpowder for each charge during the Thirty Years' War (1618–1648). However, this innovation was not universally adopted by all European armies due to the expense of the cartridges which had to be provided by the regimental commanders. As a result, it was very common for soldiers to be carrying loose gunpowder not only in powder horns, but even in their leather-lined pockets even up to the middle of the War of the Spanish Succession (1701–1713). And, it doesn't require much imagination to envision what could happen if the troops were pushed too close together, and someone was careless or preoccupied.

When writing his *Military Discipline* (published 1680) Harford noted that he personally had seen such catastrophes occur quite often. Referring to the bandoliers the musketeers of his period wore over one shoulder, he noted:

> "when they take fire they commonly would wound and kill him who wears them and those near him; for likely, if one bandoleer takes fire, all the rest do in that collar [portion of the musketeer *manche*]."[7]

With the adoption of paper cartridges, the space between the files of infantrymen could be reduced to half or less than the former distance. The French, however, were not as quick to perceive that the files could be closed, and maintained a two-foot distance well past the end of the War of the Spanish Succession.

TACTICS IN THE EARLY SEVENTEENTH CENTURY

In all Western European armies of the period, there were two types of infantry, musketeers and pikemen. The pikemen occupied the center of the battalion, and were usually deployed on a depth of at least ten ranks. The musketeers were placed on either side of the pike nucleus on a similar depth. The pikemen when called to defend their formation against cavalry or other pikemen would lower their weapons facing outwards and place the butt end into the ground near their feet. They held this weapon with their left hand so as to be able to use their right hand to grasp their sword, should this be necessary.

The pikemen were direct descendants of the Swiss pikemen who enjoyed so much success against men-at-arms (what today would be commonly referred to as "knights") during the latter part of the fifteenth century. During the early sixteenth century, the pikemen had proven themselves still capable of great victories, but as small arms became increasingly effective, the pike's role and employment on the battlefield started to change.

However, despite these changes, the pikemen continued to play a vital role until the late 1600's. First, they were to protect the musketeers from the enemy cavalry. The musketeers, though also armed with swords, would have been overthrown in an instant, if they were left unsupported by friendly pikemen. At this point, they lacked the independence they would later develop when bayonets were attached to the end of their muskets to keep enemy horsemen at bay. The second function of the pikemen was to resolve the combat whenever two opposing forces of infantry succeeded in closing with one another. The pikes, between 15 and 18 feet in length were far more effective than swords in this capacity. For this reason, at the start of the Thirty Years' War, the pikemen still represented between 25 and 35 per cent of the total infantry establishment in any of the combatant armies.

During the course of the previous century, it had been discovered that arquebusiers, armed with an "arquebus"—the primitive forefather of the musket—when available in sufficient quantities and properly supported by friendly pikemen could do significant damage to an enemy pike column. Maurice of Nassau was the first to introduce a sophisticated organization to the musketeers (it was also about this time that the musket was replacing the less-effective arquebus) making them employ a uniform series of steps to load and fire. To achieve a continuous fire along a front, the musketeers used the "caracole" system of delivering fire. In the infantry version, each musketeer after presenting his arm and firing would march down the space separating him and his neighbor to the rear of the body of musketeers. Here, he would reload his piece and walk gradually to the front as each successive row of musketeers fired. By the time he reached the front again, he was ready to fire, and the whole process repeated itself.[8]

When threatened by enemy cavalry, the musketeers would run to the protection offered by the pikemen. Several musketeers would stand between each pair of pikes, close to the pikemen holding these long weapons. In theory, the pikes projecting 12 to 15 feet in front of the musketeers prevented the horsemen from reaching the musketeers and allowed them to reload and fire at the threatening cavalry.

In the Imperial army against which the North German states and the Swedes fought, the cavalry consisted of "cuirassiers" (so named because of the heavy breastplate they wore), dragoons who were, at least in theory, mounted infantry; *arquebusiers à cheval* or carabiniers, and Croatians. The Imperialist cuirassiers were protected by heavy armor from the top of their head to their knees (so called "three-quarter armor"). They were armed with two long pistols (0.60 meters long) and a long sword designed for the thrust and the cut. The carabinier wearing an iron helmet and demi-cuirass carried a wheel-lock carbine, two pistols-and a sword. The dragoons had an iron helmet, wheel lock musket and a sword; while the Croatians were armed with a wheel-lock carbine, a small ax and a long hunting knife.[9]

The cavalry of the early 1600's, under normal circumstances, was placed as equally as possible on both flanks of the infantry. Like its infantry counterpart, it was deployed in ponderous formations made up of six to ten ranks. Up until the mid-sixteenth century, the most effective cavalry had been armed with the lance; however, from this point on, it was gradually replaced by a heavy wheel lock "pistol," whose stock rested on the right of the cavalryman's chest when fired.[10] The German *reiters* were the first to use this weapon systematically, and it was they who devised the "caracole" system of delivering fire. In this system, the cavalryman, though also armed with a sword, relied on firing his weapon at short range.

There were several versions of the caracole system. In one, the cavalry would approach the enemy using a number of half halts, half wheels, etc. to draw the enemy's first fire. When it had succeeded in doing this, and closed to short range (probably 20 to 50 paces), the first rank of cavalrymen would fire at roughly the same time. They would then circle around the formation, usually one behind the other, until they were at the rear, where they would reload their weapons. Sometimes, though, the cavalry would start to reload as they were circling around to the rear.

Another version of the caracole was used to attack an enemy formation that was slightly to the flank of the cavalry squadron. The first rank would file off one by one to the left or right, depending upon the enemy's position, until all of its men were in front of the enemy. They would then stop and face the enemy and deliver fire. After this, they would file off and proceed to the rear of their cavalry formation. Each succeeding rank would perform exactly the same maneuver. Although this maneuver appears to be complicated and time consuming, at least the enemy's return fire could never affect any of the other cavalry ranks who would still be to the flank.[11] As soon as the front was clear, the second rank would fire and then go to the rear behind the first rank, which would still be in the process of reloading. Each successive rank would repeat this process. By the time the last rank fired and cleared off, the first rank presumably would have finished loading their musketoons (a short musket used by some cavalry), and would be ready to fire again. At this point, the squadron could either repeat the entire procedure, or if the enemy was seen to be weakening, they could draw their swords and advance on the enemy.[12] The cavalry used essentially the same methods to attack the enemy infantry. The carabiniers usually attacked first and the cuirassiers, if any, followed in support, to take advantage of the disorder the first might cause.

The artillery of the period, still very massive and immobile, was relatively ineffective. Once an artillery piece was taken off its cart, given its weight, it had to remain in position throughout the remainder of that operation, which meant it had a limited scope during a battle, and if the combat was lost it invariably fell into enemy hands.

This was roughly the art of warfare as Gustavus Adolphus found it at the start of the Thirty Years' War.

GUSTAVUS ADOLPHUS

To a large extent, warfare after 1630 was either modelled on, or a response to, the transformation of war as effected by the Swedish warrior-king Gustavus Adolphus during the Thirty Years' War (1618–1648). Although Gustavus himself was clearly inspired by Maurice of Nassau (1567–1625), an earlier Dutch military leader, his army introduced or popularized a number of innovative reforms which would eventually be adopted, some quite quickly, others more belatedly, by many other major European armies.

Like Maurice of Nassau, Gustavus advocated the use of smaller formations. There were a number of reasons why the smaller formations proved to be more useful. They were easier to "deploy," that is, arrange in order suitable for fighting, on the battlefield, especially in rough terrain. From a tactical point of view, these smaller units were better suited for moving around the battlefield, and also better able to mutually support each other. When both armies enjoyed an equality of numbers, the army using the smaller-sized formations would occupy a wider front than the opponent, thus being able more readily to attack the other's flank. Moreover, when a smaller unit was defeated and routed, the overall impact was less serious than when the same fate befell a larger type of unit.[13]

Owing to the increased effectiveness of both his infantry and cavalry tactics, Gustavus was able to have his men deploy in less ponderous formations. The Swedish infantry now started to deploy along six rather than the customary ten ranks; while the cavalry deployed first along four, then along only three ranks. By 1631, the infantry would occasionally deploy along three ranks while delivering their volleys.

During the early 1600's, the manner in which both the infantry and the cavalry fought on the battlefield started to change. "Push of pike" as the contest between two opponents both armed with the "queen of weapons" (the pike) had become less frequent. By the opening of the Thirty Years' War, the increased effectiveness of musket fire meant the issue was increasingly resolved before the troops were able to approach close enough for hand-to-hand fighting. A "charge," which had previously meant a rush by a group of infantry to come to grips with their enemy counterpart, now often came to mean a fire-fight at close range lasting until one side or the other gave way, rather than an actual collision. Additionally, cavalry, especially Swedish cavalry, attacking in co-ordination with friendly infantry, also enjoyed greater success against enemy pikemen.[14]

The pikemen originally carried a 15 to 18 foot pike; however, this extreme length had become less necessary once the lance disappeared and pike versus pike confrontations had become less frequent. As a result, some pikemen now carried a shorter 11-foot version.

Gustavus took steps to make the musketeers more effective. Since the time of the Battle of Parma, circa 1590, it had become common practice for musketeers to carry a heavy firearm, firing balls weighing as much as two ounces. This weapon, which eventually became known as a musket, was quite heavy to hold for any extended time and so was rested upon a "fork." Gustavus instituted a number of reforms that greatly increased the effectiveness of small-arms fire on the battlefield. He lightened the musket and made it simpler to load; and his musketeers experimented with "volley fire" delivered by a portion of a formation, while the remainder readied themselves for the next fire. The heavy Spanish-type musket requiring a wooden fork had been popular in many armies at the beginning of the Thirty Years' War. However, the use of the fork made loading the musket, a lengthy and sophisticated procedure under the best of conditions, an even more complicated affair. The musketeer, only having two hands, had to hang the fork from his elbow or stick it into the ground while using the wooden ramrod to load his musket.[15] The Swedes solved this problem by lightening the musket so that the fork was no longer necessary. This new weapon fired a 1.25-ounce ball (12 per pound), and its dimensions shrank to roughly the same dimensions found until the musket was replaced by breech-loading weapons in the nineteenth century.[16] This innovation was quickly copied by other armies and by 1650 was universally employed.

Originally, Gustavus drew his infantry up into formations six deep, compared to the ten-deep formations of Maurice of Nassau. He disliked deeper formations, arguing, among other things, that the men in the back of these ponderous formations couldn't even hear the commands.[17] The normal procedure at this time was for the infantry to fire by caracole, one rank at a time. Gustavus first experimented with having two ranks discharge their muskets at the same time, introducing the concept of the "volley." By the time of Breitenfeld (September 17th, 1631), the Swedish infantry developed the practice of "doubling the files," thereby halving the number of ranks to three. At this point, the Swedes were using a number of different firing systems: firing two, three, and even six ranks at a time. Occasionally, fire was also delivered by fractions of the formation's front, that is by platoon or division.[18]

The adoption of cartridges also greatly simplified the loading procedure, and as we will see in the next chapter, made firing more accurate. Up until this time, the musketeer used a "bandolier" to hold a number of charge-cases to hold pre-measured amounts of powder. The ball was still separate. These bandoliers were abandoned, and Gustavus had his musketeers carry a pouch holding paper cartridges housing the charge and ball in the same package.[19] It is estimated that this innovation allowed his men to fire three to four times more quickly than their Imperialist foes. To provide some measure of protection against cavalry, his musketeers were originally provided with "Swedish feathers," iron-pointed stakes serving as a rest for musket and fence against horsemen, but these were discarded when more rapid marches were required in subsequent campaigns.

As far as cavalry was concerned, Gustavus discarded the use of the caracole system, and reintroduced cavalry shock tactics into Western Europe. Gustavus' cavalry reforms were based on necessity: the Swedish cavalry when faced with their mounted adversaries during the Polish War (1621–1629) were at a sizeable disadvantage. Generally mounted on smallish horses, the Swedes were unable to fight the Polish cavalry on equal terms. The Poles were still armed with medieval-style lances, rode larger horses, and only used their pistols prior to their attack conducted at a fast pace, with outstretched sword or lance. Since many Swedish cavalry carried only a single pistol, while the Germans invariably carried two, Swedish cavalry were also unable to perform the caracole tactic as effectively as their German counterpart.[20]

After several years of avoiding large scale cavalry engagements, Gustavus devised a method of improving his cavalry's effectiveness. The size of the average horse made it impossible for the cavalrymen to be more heavily armored, so Gustavus instead decreased the amount of armor in order to gain greater freedom of movement for his horsemen. At the same time, he changed the tactics that were to be used. The series of half wheels, half halts, and caracoles, which cavalry using the caracole system employed to draw the first fire of the enemy, were strictly forbidden. Gustavus maintained that the quicker a line of cavalry rushed the foe, the less it suffered from its fire.[21] His cavalry was to attack at the gallop. Only the front rank was allowed to fire one of their pistols, but this had to be reserved until they saw the whites of their enemy's eyes. At Lutzen (November 16th, 1632), Gustavus forbade even the first rank to fire until the enemy had fired first. As soon as the first rank fired the entire squadron was to rush in at the gallop.[22]

The use of the caracole meant that the cavalry had to be deployed in a relatively large number of ranks; this was to insure that there was a continuous fire while the rear ranks were reloading their pistols. When Gustavus abandoned this sytem, and had his cavalrymen fire only once before charging the enemy, he was able to deploy his cavalry in fewer ranks, since a continuous fire was no longer needed. At first, he reduced the number of ranks to four; the first three were to charge the enemy, the fourth was held in reserve. By his death in 1632, the Swedish cavalry was being deployed in only three ranks. Starting in 1627, the Swedish cavalry began to frequently be more successful against the Polish cavalry. The lightened load meant the Swedish mounts could gallop much more quickly than their Polish counterpart, who with their heavier armor were probably moving at something like a medium trot. Entering the Thirty Years' War in 1630, Swedish cavalry soon gained some notable triumphs, as at Breitenfeld, and within several years some aspects of these reforms started to be copied in other armies.[23]

Gustavus placed great emphasis on the role of artillery, and attempted to improve the capabilities of this arm. At the Battle of Dirchau (August 8th, 1627) extra light "leather" cannons were introduced, which fired 4-pound cannon balls.[24] The bore was formed by an iron tube reinforced by iron rings, reinforced by ropes of boiled leather. These pieces, weighing less than 120 pounds, could be dragged by only two horses, which meant they could be attached to individual infantry regiments. About five later heavier regimental pieces were introduced which could fire further. These guns were less likely to overheat than the regular ordnance and could be fired more rapidly. It is estimated that they had a rate of fire 50 per cent more than the infantry of the time.[25]

Most of Gustavus' individual reforms were ultimately accepted throughout the remainder of Europe, though some such as "platoon firing" not before 60 to 70 years had elapsed. Nevertheless, the Swedish military machine had succeeded in redefining the overall manner in which armies fought on the battlefield by the time of Gustavus' death in 1632. Some armies, such as the Spanish, would attempt to resist change, and fight using the same tactical systems employed prior to the start of the Thirty Years' War. However, most military leaders in other armies soon started to absorb the lessons provided by the Swedish army.

THE POST-THIRTY YEARS' WAR PERIOD

Unlike the Imperialists, who deployed their infantry in a relatively small number of *tercios* during the Thirty Years' War, the Swedish infantry was stretched across the field in two rows. These rows were not the "lines" used in a later period, since the formations in each were not positioned along one straight line. At Breitenfeld, for example, the exact positioning of each infantry unit was determined by the use of a "brigade" structure, an invention of Gustavus. There were three battalion-sized units to a brigade, and the middle one was advanced in front of the other two.[26]

These battalion-sized units along each line were separated by a distance that was roughly the same as their individual frontage. This space, or "interval" as it was called, was to allow the battalions deployed along the second line to advance when necessary to support those in the first. The author of the "Swedish Discipline" claims for it: "one part so fences, so backs, so flanks another, is so ready to second or relieve another, that though men may indeed be killed, very hardly shall the whole order be routed."[27] Another reason for these intervals arose out of existing musketeer tactics: depending upon the situation, a battalion's musketeers would be placed in front, to the side, or behind the battalion's pikemen. The interval between battalions allowed the musketeers to move from one position to another much more freely. In this system, the army was divided into two rows, separated by 300 paces. The men in the forward group were to engage the enemy, while supported by those in the second "line." The men in the rear row, serving as a reserve force, proved to be very convenient in beating off any enemy that managed to enter the spaces between the infantry in the front line. Initially it was common for a number of battalions to advance out of the second line to support those in the first when necessary. In the true "linear warfare" which would slowly emerge throughout the remainder of the seventeenth century, the importance of this relationship would gradually diminish, slowly being replaced by an increased emphasis on the role of the battalion in its line, and the use of the entire second line as a reserve. By the time linear warfare fully evolved, battalions from the same regiment would be placed in the same line, and lower ranking general officers of the second line would no longer be free to use individual battalions to support the front line as they saw fit. However, even by the end of the Thirty Years' War, this trend still lay in the future, even if the basis for this development had already been sown.

The post-Thirty Years' War period was an era of gradual transition with few distinctive milestones. Nevertheless, by the 1680's, it was clear that warfare had undergone a pronounced metamorphosis. Part of the transition was simply the growing acceptance of many of Gustavus' reforms. The heavy musket, with its reliance on a fork to aim, completely disappeared. So did infantry armor, and the use of three-quarter armor by cavalrymen. Where cavalry armor survived, it was reduced to simply a breastplate, known as a "cuirass." In the French army, at least, the use of light artillery survived, where 4-pounders known as *pieces suédoises* continued to be used intermittently until the mid-eighteenth century.[28]

In terms of tactics, the depth of the formations was at least slightly diminished. The German armies followed Gustavus' lead and deployed their infantry in a battalion along six ranks, while the French only reduced the number of ranks to eight (the Imperialists after Breitenfeld reduced theirs to ten). When it came to the cavalry, the Germans again proved themselves to be more progressive, discarding the caracole method of fire soon after the Thirty Years' War. The French retained this sytem until the 1670's. Though none of the generals of the next generation had Gustavus' combined genius for developing both new weapons and the corresponding tactics, during the numerous wars of the mid- and late-seventeenth century, advances gradually were made beyond those developed by the Swedes during the Thirty Years' War.

The infantry, now carrying the lighter musket which could be loaded more quickly, played a more prominent role during the battle than previously. And, to an ever-increasing degree, the use of firepower became the central issue when deploying the troops prior to the battle. Emphasis was placed on deploying the infantry along longer and longer lines so that a greater amount of firepower could be delivered by the same number of men, and as this happened these formations became thinner. It has been estimated that the average infantryman fired less than eight times during the typical battle, and the decisive blow was still usually delivered by the cavalry. Infantry firepower was powerful enough, however, to have an important impact on the defense, being effective enough to stop the advance of enemy cavalry.[29]

By the 1670's, tactical use of musketeers within a battalion in a continental army had changed. Earlier in the century, the musketeers would position themselves to the side, front or rear of the battalion's pikemen, depending upon the situation. The assumption underlying this practice was that the formation's pikemen provided a solid corps upon which the musketeers could always be regrouped. This was still feasible in Gustavus' days since even in the Swedish army at least a third of the infantry were still armed with the pike (the proportion was higher elsewhere). With the passage of time and successive wars, the proportion of pikemen to musketeers within the battalion continued to dwindle as the importance of firepower was recognized. This, in turn, influenced the handling of the musketeers who were deployed in fewer ranks, so that having a greater width their fire would extend over a greater front. At the same time, the practice of moving the musketeers to the front or the rear of the battalion fell into disuse, and they were permanently placed on either side of the pikemen, unless attacked by enemy horsemen, in which case they found protection between the pikemen's staves. The older practice was discarded as it was recognized that it was necessary to always maintain the best possible order to deliver an effective fire at a moment's notice.

NOTES

1. Wagner, Eduard, *European Weapons and Warfare 1616–1648*. Translated by Simon Pellar. London, 1979, p. 32.

2. Longueville, Thomas, *Marshal Turenne*. London, 1907, p. 43. Wagner, *op. cit.*, p. 86.

3. Marham, *The Soldier's Accidence,* cited in *Ibid.*, p. 42.

4. Lloyd, Earnst M., *A Review of the History of Infantry*. London, 1908, p. 91.

5. Held, Robert, *The Age of Firearms: a Pictorial History*. Northfield, Illinois, 1957; citing A Plan for the Formation of a Corps Which Has Never As Yet Been Raised in Any Army in Europe By "A colonel in the German Service in the British army serving in Germany and Austria," pp. 113–114.

6. Turner, James, *Pallas Armata: Military Essays of the Grecian, Roman, and Modern Art of War*. London, 1683 (reprinted New York, 1968); p. 193.

7. Hardrord, *Military Discipline*. London, 1680. cited in Longueville, *op. cit.*, pp. 41–42.

8. Canonge, J. F, *Histoire et art militaire*. Paris, 1900–08, Vol. 1, p. 264.

9. *Ibid*. Vol. 1, p. 264.

10. Longueville, *op. cit.*, p. 40.

11. Wagner, *op. cit.*, p. 83.

12. Roemer, Jean, *Cavalry: Its History, Management, & Uses*. New York, 1863, p. 324.

13. *An Epitome of the Whole Art of War, Etc*. London, n.d. (circa 1690), p. 39.

14. Lloyd, Ibid., p. 135.

15. Held, *op. cit.*, p. 43.

16. Lloyd, *op.cit.*, p. 112.

17. Roberts, Michael, *Gustavus Adolphus: A History of Sweden 1611–1632*. London, 1958, p. 257.

18. Ibid., pp. 259–260.

19. Lloyd, *op. cit.*, p. 112.

20. Roberts, *op. cit.*, p. 247.

21. Roemer, *op. cit.*, p. 324.

22. Lloyd, *op. cit.*, pp. 109–110; Roberts, *op. cit.*, pp. 255–257.

23. Roemer, *op. cit.*, p. 324.

24. Roberts, *op. cit.*, p. 248.

25. Lloyd, *op. cit.*, p. 112.

26. *Op. cit.*, p. 111.

27. *Swedish Discipline*. p. 79; cited in Lloyd, *op. cit.*, p. 111.

28. Canonge, *op. cit.*, Vol. 1, 275.

29. Colin, Jean Lambert Alphonse, *L'infanterie au XVIIIe siècle: La Tactique*. Paris, 1907, *op. cit.*, pp. 21–22.

CHAPTER 2

New Influences on the Battlefield

THE SEEDS SOWN DURING THE THIRTY YEARS' WAR SLOWLY STARTED TO bear fruit. However, in the years after 1660 a number of new, widely divergent factors started to influence how warfare on the battlefield was fought. These factors ranged from the increased effectiveness of cavalry due to the decline in the use of the pike to the various advancements in weaponry introduced around 1670, and the resulting development of new methods of delivering fire. These factors also included the use of some new tactics found to be necessary during the Austro-Turkish Wars.

INFANTRY'S ABILITY TO DEFEND AGAINST CAVALRY

As long as 50 per cent or so of a battalion's men were armed with the "queen of the infantry," to use Montecucoli's term, the pike was quite capable of keeping large numbers of the horsemen at bay. Two to three hundred pikemen organized into a compact and orderly formation were able to surround themselves with levelled pikes making it impossible for any horsemen to approach without first inflicting significant casualties using small arms or accompanying artillery.

However, by the second half of the seventeenth century, the number of men in a battalion armed with pikes dropped to between 15 and 33 per cent. As this happened, the pikemen gradually lost their ability to defend the remainder of the battalion against cavalry. By the last quarter of the seventeenth century, many military experts realized that the pike was not living up to its *raison d'etre*. Puységur, a veteran of all the wars involving French forces between 1676 and 1720, recounted at the end of his career that infantry on either flank of the pikemen were invariably run down, and that the small nucleus of pikemen in each battalion when attacked on the flank and rear would also eventually be defeated.[1] The problem was that there was as yet no reasonable alternative to the pike. For a variety of reasons, the versions of the bayonet then known were not suitable for widespread usage.

To understand the limitations of the pike, it is necessary to look at how the French infantry behaved when attacked by enemy cavalry in the last decades of the seventeenth century. By this point, only about 15–20 per cent of the French infantry were armed with the pike. A battalion at its full theoretical strength of 650 men would deploy along five ranks, each rank theoretically consisting of 130 files. The central 24 files would be armed with the pike; there would be 48 files of musketeers on each flank of the pikemen, with ten extra files of grenadiers on the battalion's extreme right. Each of the 48 files of musketeers was referred to as a *manche,* or sleeve. Contemporaries thought of a battalion as looking like a man viewed from above: the smaller group of pikemen were thought of as being the head, with the longer appendage of musketeers on either side being the arms or sleeves. The term *manche* continued in use in French military circles long after pikes disappeared, while the equivalent English term "sleeve" ceased to be used in this context.

All that the enemy cavalry had to do to obtain a very good chance of overturning an infantry battalion was to disregard the effect of the infantry fire, something that was still considerably easier to do than it would be 30–40 years later, and attack along the entire front of the battalion. The squadron attacking directly into the front of the pikemen would, of course, be stopped. This was not always the case for the remainder of the enemy cavalry forces who would be met by infantrymen only able to defend themselves by swinging their muskets or relying upon their swords. The pikemen, still threatened by cavalry to their front, would be unable to go to the assistance of the musketeers on either side of them.

The earlier practice of the musketeers either moving behind the pike formation, or if need be, placing themselves between the rows of lowered pikes was no longer as feasible as it had been earlier in the seventeenth century. Now there were, counting the grenadiers, 530 musketeers versus only 120 pikemen. This meant, if the musketeers attempted to shelter themselves among the pikemen, on the average there had to be four or five musketeers between each pair of pikes. The disadvantage of this was that the pikeman could lose sight of what was in front of him, and also not be able to move his pike to the left or the right, as might become necessary depending upon the actions of the enemy attacking him. All this meant it would be easier for a cavalryman to successfully push the pike to the side and enter the space thus created, the single most important precondition for overthrowing the pikemen. Having a depth of only five ranks, the pikemen no longer had the same degree of solidity as when their predecessors were deployed on eight, ten, or more ranks.

As the relative number of pikemen diminished, a number of tactical, grand tactical and technological experiments were devised to counter this problem. One anti-cavalry tactic known to be successful was called "fraising the battalion." In the case of the French infantry, each of the battalion's 13 companies consisted of 40 musketeers and ten pikemen. The company's ten pikemen were normally sent to join the pikemen of the rest of the battalion; however, when the battalion was "fraised," the pikemen remained with their parent company. Each company was deployed next to the adjoining company to form a battalion in a five-rank line; however, in this case, the first, second, fourth, and fifth ranks were musketeers, while the pikemen were deployed along the third rank.

When this formation was attacked by enemy cavalry, the ranks and files would close up and the men would present their arms. The pikes held by the men in the third rank being 14 feet in length would extend beyond the first rank by more than seven feet. Unlike the situation where the pikemen were placed in the center of the battalion, and the musketeers would run between their pikes for shelter, there were now only 2 musketeers between each pair of pikes. This meant the musketeers were much less interference, and allowed each pikemen a lot more control of his weapon. This formation allowed reciprocal protection between the musketeers and the pikemen. The officers at the front of the battalion and the first ranks each placed a knee on the ground and prepared to fire on their attackers, should the battalion's commander order them to do so. Protected from the cavalry by the pikes, the musketry tended to fire with greater assurance; the pikemen, seeing the approaching cavalry challenged and hurt by the continuing fire, tended to be more confident and were less likely to weaken.

Although from a tactical point of view the practice of fraising a battalion offered a battalion its greatest hope of resisting a cavalry onslaught, it was rarely used on the battlefield after 1650. The reason for this was the effect this maneuver had on a battalion's subsequent efforts to move or change formations, and even more important its use meant that only two ranks of musketeers were ever in a position to fire. Pikemen were notoriously clumsy when moving across country containing hedges, ditches or trees, and the use of this formation while moving would have needlessly disordered the battalion. For these reasons, "fraising the battalion," by Puységur's time, was strictly forbidden in the French army.

So far, we have implied that an extensive body of cavalry had an advantage over the battalions of infantry they faced. To a degree this was true, and this accounts for the success of cavalry in seventeenth-century warfare and its use in dealing the final death blow. Despite this, the commander did have at least one viable option against a possible cavalry attack. This ploy, was to intersperse his cavalry along the battle line. There were two ways of doing this. Gustavus Adolphus, and later Turenne, made a practice of interspersing platoons of infantry armed with muskets between their squadrons of cavalry. However, this was to assist the cavalry with immediate fire support, rather than to protect the infantry from the enemy cavalry. It was also a common practice to position a large body of cavalry between two bodies of infantry, possibly with additional cavalry on the flanks of the infantry. The goal here was to have cavalry sufficiently close to friendly infantry to intercept enemy cavalry that would otherwise have been free to attack them.

Robert Munro witnessed the successful use of this tactic by the Swedes at Breitenfeld (1631). He provides a descriptive account of the advantages of cavalry and infantry working together to defeat an enemy cavalry attack:

> "the horsemen on both wings charged furiously one another, our horsemen with a resolution abiding unloosing a pistol on the enemy until the enemy had discharged first, and then at a near distance our musketeers meeting them with a salvo, then our horsemen dis-

charged their pistols, and then charged through with swords and at their return the musketeers were ready again to give the second salvo of musket against them."[2]

In the last years of the seventeenth century, other efforts were made to find a tactical solution to the musketeer's vulnerability to enemy cavalry. In the French army, for example, some pikemen were placed on each of the battalion's two flanks, Louis XIV in a May 15, 1693, instruction required the major to have one-quarter of the pikemen (six files) march between the ranks to the right of the battalion; at the same time another quarter of the pikemen would proceed to the left of the battalion, leaving 50 per cent of the pikemen (12 files) in the center. Two files (ten men) of grenadiers were positioned immediately to the right of the right group of grenadiers, while two files of "fusiliers," men who carried the recently adopted flintlock, were on the right of the left group. This formation, designed to provide pike protection along the length of the battalion rather than being localized in the center, was not widely used on the battlefield. Its performance wasn't significantly better than the traditional formation with the pikes in the center, and by this time the socket bayonet, a highly effective anti-cavalry weapon in the hands of experienced infantry, had made its way into front-line troops in large numbers.[3]

None of these tactics completely solved the problem as the number of pikemen continued to decline and infantry became increasingly vulnerable to cavalry. Some military thinkers experimented with new weapons that they hoped would thwart enemy cavalry. During the 1600's, a number of devices were experimented with. Their goal was to enable the musketeer to face cavalry without relying upon pikemen. For example, "Swedish feathers" were first adopted, then discarded by Gustavus Adolphus.[4] *Chevaux de frise* offering another means of protection against cavalry, were widely used, especially against Turks. Barriffe, writing before the English Civil War, mentions that heads of pitchforks were sometimes unscrewed and the stems fixed in the muzzle of the musket.

The middle of the seventeenth century saw some infantry being outfitted with a dagger later known as a "bayonette," or more precisely as a "plug bayonet," since its end was plugged into the mouth of the matchlock's barrel. Its blade and handle were each a foot long, and the handle was shaped especially to be fitted into the musket. These rather crude defensive weapons made their first appearance around 1640, but were only used on a wider scale about thirty years later. In France, a regiment of fusiliers formed in 1671 was provided with plug bayonets and their use soon spread; Puységur in the late 1600's, for example, sent out parties armed with these bayonets instead of swords. English troops at Tangiers had been armed with them eight years previously, and a Warrant of 1672 directed their issue to dragoons.[5] However, it was only after the "Glorious Revolution" of 1688 that they became generally available to the common English infantrymen.

Although the need for a bayonet had been recognized since the last years of the sixteenth century, the plug bayonet in practice proved to be of limited use, serving exclusively as a defensive weapon against possible attacks by enemy cavalry. When threatened by the opposing cavalry, the men in the first rank would crouch down and place the butts of their muskets into the ground with the bayonet angled towards the enemy. The remainder of the ranks would continue to fire upon the advancing horse.

The plug bayonet lent itself to a purely defensive role, being useful only when the infantry were attacked. More offensively oriented tactics were prohibited by the very nature of the weapon. The infantryman could not fire his musket while the bayonet was inserted into the barrel. If the musket were fired under these conditions, the barrel invariably burst, causing injury and sometimes death to the unfortunate holding the weapon, as happened at the battle of Killikrankie in 1689. Consequently, if the plug bayonet was to be used while advancing, the infantrymen would have to go through the complicated cycle of putting the bayonet in the barrel, charging the enemy, taking off the bayonet, reloading the musket, firing, reattaching the bayonet on the musket, charging, etc. When one considers the awkwardness of plugging and unplugging the bayonet while the soldier's hands were encumbered by coils of glowing slow match, the impracticality of performing this type of operation under battle condtions becomes apparent.

A new form of bayonet, the socket bayonet, started to be introduced around 1690. Unlike its predecessor, it did not fit into the mouth of the barrel, but could be attached to a ring above or below the barrel. Although there were many varieties of socket bayonets, each army tending to sport its own version, they all shared the same basic features. Usually around 16 inches long, the triangular blade ran into a tubular sheath which fitted over the muzzle of the musket. This metal sleeve had a slit in it allowing it to fit over a stud brazed onto the muzzle. Twisting the bayonet a quarter turn locked it securely into place. Usually, the bayonet fit on the side or underneath the opening of the muzzle, although the French fitted their bayonets on top, interrupting their line of sight.

The main virtue of this newer variety of the bayonet, unlike the older plug type, was that the infantrymen could have the bayonet affixed to the muzzle and continue to fire. Consequently, the likelihood of infantry being caught unawares by cavalry was greatly reduced. Despite these advantages, the bayonet continued to be mostly used defensively. The Prussians, for example, never fixed the bayonet while firing. Carrying the bayonet from a leather sling worn over the shoulder, they only attached it to the musket when threatened by cavalry. Unlike its use in later times, the bayonet was rarely, if ever, used against enemy infantry. The weight of the early muskets continued to make thrusting motions difficult. However, it is more likely that the presence of the infantryman's sword served as a greater deterrent to its use. When presented with the opportunity of closing with enemy infantry, the average soldier appeared much more eager to discard his musket and draw his sword. Bayonet charges became more common during the course of the eighteenth century as the common foot soldier was stripped of his sword.

The use of both types of bayonets quickly demonstrated that men armed with this weapon were able to fend off repeated cavalry attacks, as long as the men in their ranks were well closed and maintained strict order. In fact, soon after the adoption of the bayonet, experienced officers realized that self-confident infantry that didn't panic would rarely, if ever, be broken by a frontal assault of cavalry. The adage "if infantry understands its force, cavalry can never break it" became commonplace.[6] Exactly how infantrymen used the bayonet to defend themselves is discussed in a later chapter.

By the close of the Thirty Years' War, the pike ceased to be an offensive weapon. Gustavus Adolphus made an effort to revive the pike as an offensive weapon, but given the degree of coordination required between pikemen and musketeers, these tactics do not appear to have long survived their author's death in 1632. After this date, infantry versus infantry confrontations tended to be resolved exclusively by means of the matchlock, and one side or the other broke after being hit by sufficient fire. Two bodies of men no longer closed to resolve the issue with push of pike; the effectiveness of musketry made this redundant. And there was little incentive for the musketeers to engage in a melee since their primary weapon, the musket, still lacking a bayonet of any sort, was not very suitable for close combat.

These considerations meant that infantry, though the backbone of an army both in numbers and overall use on the battlefield, ceased to be used to deliver the *coup de grâce,* which to an ever-increasing degree was left to the cavalry. Gradually there developed an unconscious attitude among the infantry that if they succeeded in breaking the opposing enemy in front of them, the final act of destruction would be performed by friendly cavalry. The enemy infantry after being sufficiently softened up by the friendly infantry would be attacked by the cavalry and ridden down and dispersed. The universal adoption of the bayonet ultimately caused these attitudes to be abandoned. The flintlock musket, which replaced the older matchlock version about the same time, was now equipped with a sword-like appendage which the foot soldier could use with great effect in hand-to-hand combat. Battalion commanders faced with a stubborn opponent who refused to give way, could once again attempt to have their men march up to the enemy and overthrow them with the use of cold steel.

This was more feasible than it would be in later years when the troops armed with the flintlock would acquire more effective methods of delivering fire, and be able to destroy their opponents before these latter were able to actually close to very close range. However, during the War of the Spanish Succession, when almost no one was armed with a steel ramrod and many were still loading their flintlocks without the use of cartridges, when a general lack of training denied higher rates of fire, and when many used antiquated firing drills such as the original fire by ranks (i.e., caracole), there was a real possibility of reaching an enemy and resolving the issue with the threat of the bayonet (two groups of infantry, rarely, if ever, actually crossed bayonets in open terrain). The action of the infantry on the French right at the Battle of Malplaquet (1709) illustrates how long it took for some attitudes to change. Here, the French infantry having decisively beaten back the Dutch attack, failed to initiate a counterattack which would have decided the battle in France's favor.

EXPERIENCES IN THE TURKISH WARS

In the second half of the seventeenth century, a new set of military experiences started to make itself felt on the art of warfare as it was then perceived. This took the form of the wars against the Turks. These contributed to how both the infantry and the cavalry were to fight in later wars, even in Western Europe. The Turkish army provided a different type of foe than was found anywhere in "civilized" Europe. The individual soldier, whether mounted or on foot, was invariably brave and very adept at individual combat, especially when compared to his Western counterpart.

During the sixteenth and seventeenth centuries, the finest cavalry was the Turkish. The horsemen rode on steeds which, though not overly large, were nimble and so well trained as to be perfectly under control. The hollow saddles and broad stirrups they used provided them with a firm seat on the horse, and made it difficult to unseat them in combat.[7] There was no standard armament for the Turkish cavalry. Almost all carried a *yataghan,* a short slightly curved razor sharp saber, although some wore straight swords up to six feet in length. However, whatever else the rider carried seemed to be up to individual preference. Some of the Spahis carried *sagayes,* or javelins, while others carried carbines and pistols. The Asiatic troops often were still armed with bows and arrows, while others used long pikes, hammers or pole-axes. Some of the Turkish cavalry wore defensive armor akin to European light horse in the early seventeenth century, consisting of chain mail, a scullcap of iron, brassards, and gauntlets. Often, shields made of wood or rushes and covered with leather were used.[8]

Turkish cavalry did not use any ordered formations during combat. The basic Turkish tactic when fighting Europeans, or anyone else, was to attack in large groups, and break through their opponent's formations, by sheer energy and "savagery." They would attack enemy formations in wedges, and if one wedge was unsuccessful they tried another and another. Given their extremely high standard of horsemanship and swordplay, they sought to reduce the fighting to a number of individual combats, in which they would be the likely winner. In these, the greatest reliance was placed on the sword, and the other weapons were usually thrown away at the start of a melee.

If they succeeded in penetrating a hostile line, they would quickly overpower those around them, their sharp weapons inflicting mortal wounds, cutting off the limbs of their foe. As soon as their opponents started to give way, they would "spread out like a fan." Some would continue the assault in front, while others turned the flank and attacked the rear.[9]

Initially, the Europeans met this threat by relying on their heavier armor. However, this meant that they were only capable of advancing slowly. Being unable to fight their adversaries on a man-by-man basis on equal terms, they were forced to maintain the strictest order within their formations, making sure that their men were pressed closely together. However, as the seventeenth century waned, both cavalry and infantry armor virtually disappeared. This meant that the Europeans had to rely increasingly on tight formations when fighting the Turks.

In the case of the cavalry, the men were to advance in perfect order, maintaining little or no space between each rider. This made it necessary to move at a controlled speed, a "gentle" trot, so that order could be maintained. Small arms were not as common in the Turkish army, and the Turks were quite frightened by organized fire. As a result, German cavalry fighting the Turks developed the practice of firing their carbines at the Turks before attacking them with the sword. These two traits: moving relatively slowly to maintain perfect order, and the use of firearms in the final moments while closing with the enemy were carried over to fighting other Western European armies.

As we have seen in Western Europe in the 1648–1690 period, it was common for infantry to fight deployed in line in battalions separated by "intervals" from one another. This practice was modified when fighting the Turks. It was imperative that the formations be continuous, to not allow the Turks the opportunity to enter the ranks or to slip between the battalions and circle to the rear of the formations where they would soon wreak great havoc. This consideration gave rise to the practice of stringing battalions in line, one beside the other, which was known as a "curtain," or *en muraille*.

The French cavalry never had to fight the Turks, and were free to develop a separate tradition. They were, in fact, the last major army to use, on a wide-scale basis, the caracole system that had been universally employed at the start of the Thirty Years' War. In fact, Puységur recalls that the French cavalry were still using this system at the outbreak of war in 1670. It was during this war that French cavalry discontinued the use of the caracole as the general method of fighting. This change undoubtedly was due to the efficacy of the tactics employed by the cavalry they now faced. Their adversaries had long adopted Gustavus' policy of charging the enemy cavalry sword in hand, though as we have just seen, this was usually after the first ranks delivered a single volley and invariably was conducted at a controlled trot.

From the time of Turenne's last campaigns, in the early 1670's, through Luxembourg's campaigns, in the 1690's, the French cavalry attacked enemy cavalry by attacking quickly, sword in hand. This technique was known as a *charge en foraguers,* and although performed at speed, little attention was placed on cohesion, and the troops were generally disunited and disordered when they made contact with the enemy. Nevertheless, this was generally sufficient to overthrow the solemn-moving German troops, influenced by their Turkish experiences, up until the English and German cavalry were reanimated by Marlborough and Prince Eugene.[10] It shouldn't be thought that the French always employed the same set of cavalry tactics. As with almost everything else in the French army, there was little standardization, and as we will see in a later chapter, there were some military thinkers who advocated the German method of having the front ranks of cavalry fire their musketoons before engaging the enemy with the sword.

THE FLINTLOCK AND THE SOCKET BAYONET

Many of the liabilities inherent in the matchlock musket and the plug bayonet were either totally eliminated, or at least greatly reduced with the introduction of their successors: the flintlock musket and the socket bayonet.

The flintlock musket was an outgrowth of two precursors, the miquelet and the snaphaunce, both a significant improvement over the matchlock in that they each produced a spark to be ignited in the flashpan by means of friction caused by a flint (or pyrites) hitting the battery. Both of these predecessors to the true flintlock made their appearance in the late 1500's. The flintlock musket was in a sense an amalgamation of the distinctive features of these two guns. There was increasing pressure as the seventeenth century progressed to replace the matchlock with the flintlock. General Monck writing in 1646 recommended it for picked shots for infantry, as well as cavalry and dragoons, and in 1660 as commander-in-chief ordered matchlocks in his regiment, the Coldstream (2nd Regiment of Foot Guards), be exchanged for snaphaunce muskets.

The flintlock became common in the English army and among many German regiments during the late 1690's, the Brandenburg army being among the first states to completely change over to the new type of musket, officially making the conversion in 1689.[11] In the next year, the Danish contingent employed in Ireland in 1690 was armed with the flintlock, as were the British Guards and half of the musketeers of other regiments.[12] The new weapon met with greater resistance in the French and Hapsburg armies, where colonels were as much preoccupied with the expense of re-equipping their regiments as they were concerned about the faulty mechanisms, common among the early models. As a result, in the French army even though the flintlock musket was officially prescribed by a December 15, 1699, ordinance, it was not until 1703 that the flintlock was commonly employed. The last matchlocks were totally withdrawn from the line troops only in 1708. The even more conservative Hapsburgs possessed large quantities of matchlocks as late as 1710.

The flintlock's advantages when considered individually might not appear significant. Only when they are examined collectively is it apparent how much more practical the flintlock was compared to the matchlock. The flintlock was a more reliable firing mechanism than the matchlock, especially when used by unskilled troops, with the result that the misfire rate fell from about 50 to 33 per cent. The process of reloading a flintlock only required 26 motions, approximately 60 per cent of the 43–44 required by the matchlock. The result was that the rate of fire effectively doubled. It was now possible for a skilled infantryman to average two rounds per minute during the initial stages of a firefight. Lastly, the flintlock now around 12 pounds, was marginally lighter than the matchlock, which usually weighed more than 13 pounds. This weight difference coupled with the absence of a match allowed those carrying a flintlock to march farther and faster.

The flintlock musket was not appreciably more accurate than the matchlock it replaced, and if it enjoyed a long lifespan, continuing to be used throughout the eighteenth century and for the first half of the nineteenth century, it was because it was relatively inexpensive, and usually enjoyed a relatively high rate of fire. In the days before society and military training imbued men with enough initiative to roam the battlefield in small groups, a high rate of fire was one of the most important factors in determining a victor on the battlefield. During the two minutes or so required by the rifleman to load and fire his weapon, the fusilier or musketeer at the beginning of the War of the Spanish Succession could fire between two and five shots, depending upon whether he was armed with a matchlock or flintlock, the method of delivering fire used, and his level of training.

It is natural for us to wonder why it took the flintlock so long to be accepted among the military. Part of the reason is attributable to the ferocity of the Thirty Years' War, and the degree to which this conflict consumed the resources of the combatant states. Under the circumstances, it just wasn't possible to allocate the required financial and manufacturing resources needed to rearm the large number of foot soldiers carrying firearms with the new-style musket.

In France, Louvois was initially against flintlocks for infantry, and ordered inspectors to break up any they found in the regiments, and replace them with matchlocks at the captain's cost. But in 1670, a small proportion was allowed and in the following year a regiment of fusiliers was formed to serve as guards for artillery and were armed with the flintlock.[13] In other countries, there was less resistance to the flintlock, and by the early 1690's large numbers had been introduced. The French, however, tenaciously clung to the traditional weaponry, despite the feelings of the men themselves.

The French army of Flanders succeeded in defeating the Allied forces of William of Orange at the Battle of Steenkirk on August 3, 1692. Not however, before the French infantry experienced severe losses from enemy infantry, most of whom were equipped with the new flintlock. The French, abetted by the hedges and other obstacles on the battlefield were only able to overthrow the Allies "sword in hand." After the battle, the victorious French infantry threw away their matchlocks and pikes, picking up the enemy's muskets lying about the battlefield.

The correspondence between the King and his generals, principally Marshal Luxembourg, in the months after this battle helps to shed light on the reasons why the French were so slow to officially discard the matchlock and pike. It has often been implied that this slowness was the result of French military conservatism, however, the following exchange shows logistical reasons were at least as much responsible.

The Comte de Lux, an aid-de-camp to Luxembourg, informed the King that during the battle ony the fusiliers (those armed with a flintlock) within each battalion were able to produce effective fire. Moreover, those inexperienced soldiers who were armed with matchlocks were unable to load and fire under battle conditions. The King responded by asking the senior generals whether the matchlock should be completely abandoned and replaced by the flintlock. He also asked if the pikemen who armed themselves with flintlocks after the battle should be rearmed with the pike.[14]

Luxembourg responded, in turn, on August 17th: ". . . However, my advice is that for a siege, the muskets (matchlocks) are worth more and the fusils (flintlocks) for the war in a campaign, as much because the soldiers fire more often in an action as because in the detachments one takes what one can from fusiliers." In a second letter dated August 21st, Luxembourg advised Louis that his senior officers felt that in a campaign each company should have as many flintlocks as matchlocks. Marshal Catinet, commander of the army of the Alps made the same recommendation, noting that it was essential that the pike be retained.

Interestingly enough, it was only at this point (September 7th) that Louis started to object to this change. The King's argument was that increasing the number of flintlocks per company was not the solution to the lack of French firepower, since invariably all these new flintlocks would end up in the hands of the veteran soldiers. The inexperienced soldiers and recruits would continue to be equipped with the matchlock, which they could not use effectively.

On September 28th, Luxembourg continued the exchange declaring that his officers felt they would be hard pressed to find enough flintlocks for the infantry, so they now recommended only 20 men be given them per company. Finally, on October 1st of the same year the King decided on the following distribution of matchlocks and flintlocks in each company of 55 men:

Field Company	**Garrison Company**
2 sergeants	2 sergeants
3 corporals (fusils)	1 corporal (fusil)
5 anspessades (fusils)	2 anspessades (fusils)
10 pikemen	
13 fusiliers	16 fusiliers
21 musketeers	33 musketeers
1 drummer	1 drummer

This meant there were 21 musketeers armed with a matchlock and 13 fusiliers with a flintlock in each field company, and 16 fusiliers and 33 musketeers in a company on garrison duty. In each field company, the captain was able to give a carbine to one or two of the most adept soldiers.

Puységur points out there was another reason why the pike lingered on in France. During the Nine Years' War, socket bayonets were placed on all the muskets within the *du Roi* Regiment. Unfortunately, because there was no single standard barrel size, many did not fit tightly enough, and either fell off when the musket was fired or caused the barrel to burst.[15]

These problems notwithstanding, by 1692 the King had ordered the universal adoption of the socket bayonet. However, this too ran into difficulties. The captains were responsible for the acquisition of the bayonets and they only purchased a fixed number each year. A circular distributed among the higher officers on November 11th, 1692 read:

> "the intention of the king was that the soldiers on campaign are furnished with socket bayonets to place in the end of the fusil or musket on the day of battle, His Majesty desires that you advise the captains, so that they will give them to those of their soldiers who do not have them."[16]

By the opening of the War of the Spanish Succession, it became obvious to both the King and his senior officers that the pike was no longer as useful as formerly and that the Imperialist forces enjoyed more effective firepower. It was also noted that the pikes were particularly cumbersome in broken terrain. Consequently, Marshal Villeroi commanding the army in Italy was allowed to eliminate all the pikemen in his army by an order dated January 16th, 1702. Unfortunately, this order was not immediately carried out, Villeroi being captured soon after by Imperialist forces. The Duke de Vendôme who then took over command decided upon the elimination of the pikes, but there now proved to be an insufficient number of flintlocks available to implement this new policy.[17] The lack of flintlocks proved to be a chronic situation, and it was only in 1708 that the pike was completely eliminated from the battlefield.

Another important technological change during this period was the more general adoption of the paper cartridge as a means of prepacking gunpowder and ball into a single package, allowing the soldier to more easily load and fire his musket. Although a work entitled *Pallas Armata,* published near the end of Turenne's time, described horsemen as using cartridges for the charges in their pistols, it is difficult to establish to just what extent cartridges were adopted in various mid-seventeenth-century armies. According to this work: "Horsemen should always have the charges of their pistols in patrons (boxes), the powder made up completely in paper and ball tied to it with a piece of thread". It is probable that cartridges first gained popularity amongst the cavalry, since its benefits were more readily apparent to those who had to reload on horseback. However, the usual infantry practice continued to be carrying charges of loose powder in bandoliers hanging in a belt slung over a shoulder.[18]

The other new weapon that ultimately would prove to have a great impact was the socket bayonet, which became more commonly available during the same period the flintlock was replacing the matchlock. According to one source, Vauban the famous fortification engineer was instrumental in the introduction of the socket bayonet. In 1687, Louvois consulted Vauban about issuing the French infantry plug bayonets. Vauban apparently proposed a socket bayonet which had some practical application. A French regiment, more than ten years previously had attached a sword with copper ring (instead of a guard and another at pommel) to the end of each musket.[19]

Although the socket bayonet first appeared in continental Europe in the 1680's, it was only in 1697 that it was completely adopted by the English and Germans. The French proved to be again the more conservative. Even though an ordinance of Dec. 15, 1699, called for the use of both the flintlock and the socket bayonet, in the case of the socket bayonet, it was only universally adopted in 1703.[20] In England, the number of pikemen had dropped by that time to a mere "piquet" of 14 men per company and similar reductions soon occurred in the French infantry.

GRENADIERS

One last development should be mentioned. The use of grenadiers to throw small bombs started to fall into decline during the War of the Spanish Succession. Its abandonment was not the result of any decline in utility. It resulted from the newly developing perception that the use of grenades was needlessly dangerous to the friendly troops near those throwing them. When all musketeers carried the matchlock musket, this consideration was not a practical issue: a grenadier with his lit match (fuse) posed no more danger than an ordinary musketeer. Of course, there was a real danger that the lit match carried by either could ignite the quick match in other grenades or the loose powder in an infantryman's pockets, but there was no remedy since the matchlock was still the mainstay of the infantry.

The danger posed by the grenadier's match only became a consideration when the advent of the flintlock musket meant the elimination of the musketeer's match. Now the grenadiers were the only ones with lit matches, and ultimately the use of grenades with their attendant dangers were not considered as wise an investment as the same number of men armed with the effective flintlock. The grenadiers changed their roles, but retained their title.[21] This is not to suggest that the practice of using grenades vanished overnight with the introduction of the flintlock. In addition to siege warfare where they could be quite useful, grenades still were occasionally used on the battlefield.

The Battle of the Schellenberg (July 2nd, 1704) provides an example of infantry still using grenades. De la Colonie, who was acting commander of a French battalion of grenadiers at this battle describes how, after the English attack on the French/Bavarian parapets was repulsed, grenades were used to unsettle the attackers while they prepared for a second offensive.

> "At last the enemy . . . were obliged to relax their hold, and they fell back for shelter to the dip of the slope, where we could not harm them. A sudden calm now reigned amongst us, our people were recovering their breadth . . . but our whole attention was fixed on

the enemy and his movements; we noticed that the tops of his standards still showed at about the same place as that from which they made their charge in the first instance, leaving little doubt but that they were reforming before returning to the assault. As soon as possible we set vigorously to render their approach more difficult than before, and by means of an increasing fire swept their line of advance with a torrent of bullets, accompanied by numberless grenades, of which we had several wagon loads in rear of our position. These owing to the slope of the ground, fell right amongst the enemy's ranks, causing them great annoyance and doubtless added not a little bit to their hesitation in advancing the second time to the attack."[22]

Clearly, grenades were still being used on the battlefield, albeit in special situations.

NOTES

1. Puységur, J. F., *Art de la guerre par principes et par règles,* 2 vols. Paris, 1748, Vol. 1, pp. 69–70.

2. Robert Munro, *His Expedition with Machey's Regiment.* 1637, p. 65, cited in Lloyd, *op. cit.,* p. 110.

3. Belhomme, V. L., *Histoire de l'Infanterie en France,* 4 volumes. Paris, no date, vol. 2, p. 320.

4. These consisted of a rest for the heavy musket with sharp metal spikes on top of its forks. When its base was inserted into ground and the spikes made to slope towards the enemy it functioned identically to a bayonet. Longueville, *op. cit.,* p. 40.

5. Lloyd, *op. cit.,* p. 135.

6. Puységur, *op. cit.,* vol. 1, p. 71.

7. Roemer, *op. cit.,* p. 328.

8. Warnery, Major-General, *Remarks on Cavalry.* Translated by G.F Koehler. Whitehall, 1805, p. 7.

9. Roemer, *op. cit.,* p. 328.

10. Dundas, David, *Principles of Military Movements Chiefly Applied to Infantry.* London, 1788, p. 4.

11. Meyer, M., *Technologie des Armes des à Feu.* Translated by M. Rieffel. 2 vols., 1857, vol. 1, p. 114; cited in Lloyd p. 136, *op. cit.*

12. Walton, Clifford, *History of the British Standing Army (1660–1700).* London, 1894, p. 433; cited in Lloyd, *op. cit.,* p. 136.

13. Lloyd, Ibid., p. 133.

14. Belhomme, *op. cit.*, vol. 2, p. 311.

15. Puységur, *op. cit.*, vol. 1, p. 72.

16. Belhomme, *op. cit.*, vol. 2, p. 313.

17. Belhomme, Ibid., p. 359.

18. Longueville, *op. cit.*, p. 41.

19. Lloyd, *op. cit.*, pp. 135–136.

20. Rousset, C., *Histoire de Louvois.* 4 vols., 1872, vol. 3, p. 326; cited in Lloyd, *Ibid.*, pp. 135–136.

21. Susane, L. A., *Histoire de l'Ancienne Infanterie Françoise.* 8 vols., Paris, 1849, vol. 1, p. 280.

22. De la Colonie, Jean-Martin de, *The Chronicles of an Old Campaigner: 1692–1717.* Translated by Walter C. Horley. London, 1904, p. 185.

CHAPTER 3

Infantry Fire Systems

THE PRACTICE OF HAVING MORE THAN ONE RANK FIRE AT THE SAME TIME can be traced back to the late sixteenth century. Henry of Navarre is known to have encouraged his troops to use a primitive version of "volley fire." However, at the beginning of the Thirty Years' War, the caracole remained the usual method of delivering fire: one rank firing at a time. Gustavus sensed the limitations of the traditional methods and also experimented with the concept of the "volley."

> "to [two] Rancks, having made readie alike, they advance ten paces before the bodie, being led by an Officer that stands in even Front of them . . . The second Rancke being close to the backe of the foremost, both gives fire alike, priming and casting about their Muskets they charge againe where they stand, till the other two Ranckes advance before them, and give fire after the same manner, till the whole Troop hath discharged, and so beginne againe as before,

> after the order of the through-countermarch; ever advancing to an enemie, never turning backe without death, or victorie."[1]

This type of fire, in addition to hurling twice as many musket balls in a single moment, allowed the formation to slowly advance between volleys. Also, because the men didn't have to march to the rear, but instead loaded in place, some time was saved when recharging their muskets.

Gustavus and his officers were quick to realize the importance of having several ranks deliver a "salvo" or "volley" at the same moment. Not only did it affect the number of enemy casualties suffered in a short period of time, but often determined to what extent a friendly force was able to resist an enemy attack. "Volley fire" is used here in its modern sense, referring to any organized discharge conducted by a portion of or an entire battalion. However, the term in the seventeenth century applied only to a *feu de joie* fired at festive occasions or at affairs of state. The infantry fired with their muzzles elevated and without bayonets. It derived its name from the trajectory of the bullets which reminded some of a flight of birds, hence *vollé* meaning "flight."[2]

Sir James Turner, writing in the *Pallas Armata,* describes the effect of a battalion volley (all six ranks at once) on the enemy's morale:

> "you pour as much lead into your enemies bosom at one time as you do the other way (firing with only 3 ranks) at two severall times, and thereby you do them more mischief, you quail, daunt, and astonish them three times more, for one long and continued crack of thunder is more terrible and dreadful to mortals than ten interrupted and severall ones."[3]

Most of these innovative practices were not immediately adopted by other major Western European armies. The concern was that the use of three-rank volleys gave only two opportunities to fire, and the battalion could find itself denuded of fire should it be attacked after the second volley but before the men in the first three ranks had been able to reload. In the days when it could take up to a minute to reload, if two three-rank volleys were delivered in quick succession, this could be a real danger.

This explains why the French infantry, for example, by mid-seventeenth century were still using essentially a caracole system, known as "fire by ranks" *(feu de rangs).* This is a confusing term, since the next major method of delivering fire that would replace it would be known by the same name.[4]

The only trace of a Swedish influence in this fire system was that it could be performed while the infantry battalion slowly advanced towards the enemy. The first rank would advance three paces to the front and then fire. Its men would then turn around by the left (because after firing, the musketeers passed their matchlocks to their left side and would start to reload as they walked) and pass between the files of the other ranks to go to the rear where they would recharge their firearms. Each of the rear ranks then successively did the same. A similar process could be used to fire while retreating, except that each rank would now no longer advance before firing, so that the front of the battalion slowly moved away from the enemy. Notice, that in this French version, each rank only advanced three paces and the advance was considerably slower than in the Swedish version where each rank advanced ten paces before firing.

This system had a number of drawbacks and couldn't long survive the introduction of the flintlock musket. Its most serious drawback was that its use invariably disordered the battalion, since the men, by definition, had to be in motion. This was an extremely important factor when the battalion was threatened by nearby enemy cavalry, and would mean that the infantry would have to stop firing to receive the enemy's advance. A related disadvantage was the effect that it had on the battalion's disposition in line. Since the men had to walk down a file to go to the rear, the files had to be separated by at least a pace while the soldiers were firing. This was another reason why the battalion would have to stop firing if approached by the enemy, so that it could close its files to receive the attack. One last disadvantage was that it further detracted from the soldier's ability or inclination to aim; the whole process was about standing in a queue and reloading the musket, the soldier's view of the enemy changed as he walked to the rear and then slowly advanced. However, this last consideration rarely came into play, since all volley fire was unaimed.

During this period, French infantry occasionally used two other methods of delivering fire: "firing by files," and "firing by divisions." Fire by files was executed by groups of two files at a time. The ten men (if there were five ranks) would advance six paces to the front, spread out into a line and then fire. They would then return to their original places in line and two other files would advance and fire. The fire by division was similar in execution to fire by files, but was conducted by four or six files. These files advancing to the front would deploy along two or three short lines.[5] Firing by files and firing by divisions were almost always reserved for special situations where the battalion was deployed behind a parapet, hedge, battlement, or sunken road. They were rarely used on the open battlefield because their use demanded the troops maneuver in the face of the enemy, something experienced officers sought to avoid.[6] All three of these firing systems had been developed while infantrymen were armed exclusively with the matchlock. As the flintlock musket started to be introduced, some officers experimented with new methods of having the infantry deliver their fire.

During the same period, the Dutch continued to use the older version of the caracole where the men in the front rank after firing marched to the left or the right of the battalion, depending whether they were closer to the left or right flank, and then walked around to the rear. By this time, most military men thought this to be archaic, since it was easier to have the men walk through the three-foot gaps between the files.[7]

In 1686, Demorinet in his *Le Major Parfait* describes a new firing method; one that, in one form or another, would soon be used in the French army up to the late 1740's. However, from another source, Turner's *Pallas Armata,* published in 1683, we are told that this system had been devised by Martinet, a *maréchal de camp* in the French army, probably in the 1670's.

> "Of the six ranks of musqueteers he would have the first five to kneel, the sixth to stand and fire first, then the fifth to rise and fire next, and consecutively the rest, till the first rank have fired, after which he will have the foremost first ranks to kneel again, till the sixth discharge, if the service last so long."[8]

This technique was probably that used by most French infantry during the early 1700's, regardless of the depth of the infantry. When the infantry had a depth of four or five ranks, two or even three ranks were sometimes made to fire at the same time.[9]

Each file in a French battalion dressed strictly from the front, that is each man in the file stood directly behind the one in front. This made it impossible for more than the first three ranks to close up and fire in a concentrated volley. The front rank would kneel, the second would crouch, and the third stand. The fourth and fifth could do nothing but stand idly by.[10] One criticism that some officers leveled against this method of delivering fire was that the men remained in the same position after firing. Though this was perceived as a bonus in that the battalion was less likely to be disordered, remaining in the same position often jeopardized the men's morale. In the older caracole systems, the formation either advanced or retired as the fire was delivered by each rank.

One question must strike many modern readers. Why didn't all the men in a battalion just fire at the same time? To do so, would have denuded the *manche* or battalion of its fire capability while its men reloaded. This could have been fatal if the enemy was near and able to seize this opportunity to attack.

Though the practice of having men in the first ranks kneel was a novelty in France during the 1690's, it had been used among some German armies for at least 20 years, the practice having apparently originated with the Swedes during the Thirty Years' War. Besides removing the men in the front ranks from the line of fire of those in the rear, it also reduced the number of casualties suffered by those with their knees on the ground from small-arms fire.

In 1743, the Chevalier d'Alsfeld attacked a detachment of British infantry near Saint-Etienne de Liter. These latter knelt down as soon as the French assumed their firing positions; after the French discharge the British soldiers immediately got up without having taken any casualties.[11] Some felt that it was even better to go one step further and have the troops lie on the ground. This way they were sure not to suffer any casualties. However, this tactic could only be used with troops whose courage was unquestionable. Otherwise, it would be difficult, if not impossible, to get them to stand up afterward. By the end of the Battle of Parma (1734), for example, many of the infantry were to be seen crawling along the ground, ignoring all of the officers' efforts to get them to stand up again. The Scottish highlanders used a similar tactic to evade the enemy's fire. They would run towards their opponents with sword and buckler in hand. As soon as they saw the enemy infantry assuming a firing position, they would fall flat on their stomachs and wait till the enemy had fired. Then virtually unscathed, they would get up and resume their attack. This is exactly what the Black Watch did as they attacked the French infantry in the entrenchments around the Fontenoy redoubt.[12]

During the seventeenth century, the French infantry when placed in entrenchments or other strengthened positions were sometimes ordered to fire individually, without waiting to fire in a volley. In these situations, speed was of the essence, and French volley fire could not be relied upon. The French infantry at the Siege of Etampes in 1652 provides an excellent example. The main body of the French infantry had been involved in an action early one morning. Later that day, the enemy, seeing that the entrenchments contained less then the usual amount of men, decided to sally out and attempt to retake a portion of the siege works. Fortunately for the French, the point about to be attacked was reinforced by the timely arrival of 200 musketeers from the French guard regiment, the only reserves available locally. Marshall Turenne specifically ordered these troops to fire on their own, and he enjoined them to aim their fire as much as possible. This they did, and the affair became notable as a result of the large number of casualties inflicted by such a small number of men.[13]

The Siege of Turin in 1706 provides an example of exactly the opposite, where French troops in entrenchments were constrained by having to wait for orders to fire, and were easily overthrown by the attackers. The Imperialists attacking the French lines were initially driven off by a very lively fire, and retired greatly disordered. These were eventually rallied by Victor Amadeus, Prince Eugene of Savoy, and Leopold of Anhalt-Dess'au and made to attack a second time. Interestingly enough, for reasons that are unclear, the French who were successful in their first defense were now ordered to withhold their fire until point-blank range. The Imperialists, no longer subject to any fire at a long or medium range, now had a much easier time advancing. When the French fire was finally delivered, the attackers, relieved that the worst was over, rushed in to fight hand to hand. Dispirited, the French hardly resisted, and were soon driven out of the entrenchments.[14]

ENGLISH FIRE SYSTEMS: LATE SEVENTEENTH CENTURY

During the 1670's the English infantry probably used firing techniques very similar to those just described for the French infantry. However, the flintlock musket encountered less resistance in England than in France, and provision for the new firing methods was officially introduced in the "Abridgement of the Military Discipline," published with English royal authority in 1686.

This is an interesting document showing that English tactics were very much in a state of transition and is a curious collection of both old and new practices. On the one hand, this work recognized the arrival of "firelocks," i.e., flintlock muskets, and bayonets as well as the new version of firing by ranks that would replace the older "caracole" form. It also continued to sanction the use of this older form while the infantry either advanced or retreated. Provision was made for firing in either three or six ranks.

The "Abridgement" implies that infantry could be deployed in either three or six ranks, with the pikemen always in the middle of each battalion. It also describes a grab bag of different firing techniques.[15] In mentioning both the three- and six-rank formations, the work appears to have handed the decision over to the regimental commander, when each formation could be used. It is possible that the military authorities responsible for the work envisioned the musketeers being deployed along six ranks during the attack against enemy infantry when, given the practices of the time, firepower was considered less important than an unshaken resolve to engage the enemy. The use of three ranks was reserved for those situations where it was important to bring as much firepower to bear as possible. The method of fire that would be used depended upon whether the infantry was stationary or either advancing or retiring, as well as the number of ranks in the battalion. If the infantry was stationary and deployed in three ranks, the men in the first rank knelt, those in the second stooped, while the third rank stood upright. After the rear ranks fired, the front rank stood up, presented their arms and then fired in turn.

When the musketeers were stationary and arranged in six ranks there were two similar methods of firing by ranks available. The first resembled firing by ranks on three ranks, in that the front ranks knelt, the middle stooped, and the rear stood. Firing could then be conducted by individual ranks, or pairs of ranks.[16] The other method was identical to that described by Turner in his *Pallas Armata*. The men in the first five ranks knelt, while the sixth stood. After the sixth rank fired, those in the fifth stood up and fired, then the fourth rank, etc. As in the French version, the commanding officer could order two ranks to fire at a time. Here, when the fifth and sixth ranks stood up and fired, the third and fourth would then do the same, etc.[17] Presumably, the officers made certain that the fire rolled from rank to rank, when firing occurred by single rank, no faster than once every five or ten seconds, to insure that the men in the sixth rank had reloaded by the time the first fired their weapons.

Provision was also made for firing while either advancing or retiring. In either case, the same general method was used. This was the caracole system which has already been described. The "Abridgement" suggests that this fire was withheld until there was a minimal distance between the opposing forces, since the pikemen were to "charge" the enemy when the last rank had fired. This firing system could also be used to fire while retreating, except that each rank now no longer advanced before firing, each successive rank of men firing from their original position in the queue, so that the front of the battalion slowly moved away from the enemy.

The *Epitome of the Whole Art of War, Etc.,* published around 1690, describes essentially the same systems, but sheds some additional light on other practices. What is especially revealing is the emphasis the "Epitome" placed on the need to have men in the battalion protect their flanks and rear. This is not surprising in light of the large intervals that were maintained between battalions at that time. Officers were enjoined to keep a space in the middle of the pikemen, to allow for the baggage, colors (flags), and musketeers.

If a battalion was threatened by cavalry, the pikemen were to form a square. The battalion's grenadiers were to be divided into four groups and positioned at each angle, deployed in three ranks. The second and third ranks of grenadiers were to fire in unison with the corresponding ranks of musketeers, who were still deployed on both sides of the pikemen. When the first rank of musketeers were ordered to fire, the first rank of grenadiers threw their grenades before unslinging their muskets and placing a plug bayonet in the muzzle.

If the enemy managed to enter the area between the battalions, the men in the battalion were ordered to "face square." The musketeers on the flanks would be ordered to face to the flank. The three rear rows of men would face the rear. The pikemen did the same. Those on each flank of the body of pikemen faced to the side, while the three rear rows faced the rear. In this situation the first rank of musketeers facing in each direction would kneel. As soon as the men in the second and third ranks fired over those kneeling in the first rank, these latter would immediately stand up, without waiting to be ordered and deliver their fire.[18]

The "Epitome" also provided for the contingency where it was necessary to fire out of the sides of the battalion. This was nothing more than the "caracole" system, moving from flank to center, instead of front to rear. In this case, a six-pace interval was left between the musketeers and each side of the pikemen. The musketeers to the left of the pikemen faced to the left, those on the right faced to the right. The first file (a row, running from front to back) of musketeers presented their weapons and then fired. After firing, they turned around and walked between the ranks towards the pikemen, where they then turned around again and started to reload.

We should mention, that the English by this point had cultivated the French practice of using "grenadiers." These were tall and strong men who in addition to the musket were armed with small bombs, called grenades, which they hurled by hand. The grenadiers had their muskets slung over their backs while they threw the grenades, rank by rank. The grenadiers also carried a hatchet which they would wield whenever they attacked fortified positions.[19] Given the French influence in the court of King James II, it is not surprising to find that these Gallic experiments were quickly accepted into the English army, something that would rarely, if ever, occur in either direction during the next century.

The Glorious Revolution changed England's international alignments, and French military influence was quickly replaced by Dutch. The Earl of Marlborough (later Duke) commanding the troops sent to Flanders in 1689 asked the Secretary of War, William Blathwayt:

> "I desire that you will know the King's pleasure whether he will have the Regiments of Foot learn the Dutch exercise, or else to continue the English, for if he will I must have it translated into English."[20]

This "Dutch exercise" was almost in all certainty "platoon fire."

PLATOON FIRING

There is some evidence that Gustavus Adolphus may have invented a primitive version of platoon firing during the Thirty Years' War. However, it remained for the Dutch in the late seventeenth century to devise a similar system upon the widespread introduction of the flintlock in their army.[21]

By the middle years of the War of the Spanish Succession, the flintlock had completely replaced the older and more primitive matchlock musket in virtually all European armies. However, the effect this change had on tactics was split along national grounds. The French and Bavarian armies do not appear to have modified the way they used their small arms to any significant degree, and continued with their by now traditional tactic of limiting the use of infantry firearms while on the offensive, and attempting to endure the enemy's fire until they approached to close quarters.

On the other hand, the English and Prussians were more willing to explore the advantages offered by the increased firepower provided by the new firearm, and were willing to experiment with the Dutch fire system, and develoved a completely different style of offensive based upon this new fire system. Though the Swedes also experimented with "platoon firing," when on the attack they usually used the same basic tactics as the French, that is, they withheld their fire and attempted to close with the bayonet or drawn sword.

Fortunately, Captain Parker of the Royal Irish Regiment (18th Foot) provides an interesting description of platoon fire, as practiced by his regiment at the Battle of Malplaquet in 1709. Interesting enough, this regiment was led by the then acting commander, Richard Kane, who would 35 years later (1745) provide a very detailed description of British platoon firing then in use. The major difference between platoon firing as conducted circa 1709 and that detailed by the later description was the use of drums to transmit orders.

The British tactic was to advance until the enemy started to fire, usually at between 70 and 100 paces, and then stop the advance and return the fire, one rank firing at a time. In the British army of 1709, platoon firing was conducted as follows. Each battalion was divided into four "grand divisions," each of which divided, in turn, into four platoons. Counting two of grenadiers, this meant each battalion contained 18 platoons. For the purposes of fire, these were organized into three "firings." The platoons in each firing were not side by side but were distributed along the length of the battalion. The firings were paced so that, at any time half of the battalion's men stood ready with loaded muskets on their shoulders.[22]

By 1745, only the last two ranks of men participated in these firings; the men in the first rank were kept as a reserve, either as a fourth firing or for use only in critical situations, depending upon the inclination of the colonel.[23] This reserve was especially useful in the final moments before enemy infantry or cavalry closed to contact. It is not clear whether this practice of keeping the front rank as a reserve fire was used during the War of the Spanish Succession.

Throughout most of the firings, the colonel, sword in hand, and a drummer were positioned eight to ten paces in front of the battalion between the two central platoons. Whenever the firing containing the two central platoons was to occur, the colonel and his drummer nimbly had to move temporarily behind these platoons in order to avoid being accidentally shot. As soon as the platoons fired, the colonel and the drummer would quickly resume their normal position in front of the line.

In the engagement described by Parker, the Royal Irish Regiment, in British service, encountered the Royal Regiment of Ireland in French service. Firing commenced at about 100 paces, the French opened fire, delivering the fire from one of their ranks. The British stopped their "gentle" advance and the first firing delivered its fire, in turn. Immediately, the six platoons in the second firing readied themselves to fire and the battalion started its slow advance once more. As the British battalion advanced, the French fired a second rank. Once again, the British regiment stopped and returned fire using the second firing. As a result of this salvo, the French were observed to "shrink." They managed to have a third rank fire, in a "scattering manner," but they soon retreated into a nearby wood in great disorder.

When the Royal Irish Regiment in British service advanced to where the enemy had been standing, they found 40 men killed or wounded on the ground. They themselves had four men killed and six wounded. If this incident was truly representative of the respective capabilities of the fire systems used by either army, we could conclude British platoon firing was 400 percent more effective than firing by ranks (the newer version which had the firing start with the fifth rank). Considering De Saxe's comment that he had observed volleys, delivered at relatively close range but which had failed to kill four men, the performance of the Royal Regiment of Ireland was probably not only typical for the French, but for the infantry in Austrian and German states' armies of the period, as well.

In his memoirs Captain Parker went on to attribute at least some of the greater effectiveness of British/Dutch platoon fire to the difference between the British and French flintlocks then in use. The British fired a heavier ball weighing an ounce apiece, while the French fired a ball weighing two-thirds of an ounce. It must be remembered that these weapons imparted a much lower velocity to their projectiles than a modern rifle. This means the weight of the ball played a more important role in the extent of damage caused than it does today, where high speed projectiles can make even very lightweight bullets lethal.[24]

Parker goes on to say that the British platoon firing was much more effective than French fire by ranks. But why was "platoon firing" more effective? After all, if a French battalion was deployed along, let's say, four ranks so that when each rank delivered its fire, 25 per cent of the battalion's muskets was fired, wouldn't this have the same effect as when a British battalion, with four separate "firings" delivered a volley, assuming both battalions were the same size?

LeBlond in his detailed analysis of the various fire systems available at the start of the Seven Years' War appears to provide the answer. The platoon system as used by the Dutch and British solved a number of problems that had previously plagued commanders and was indeed, superior to any other method of delivering fire for at least three reasons. Unlike firing by ranks (either version), platoon fire allowed the fire to be directed, if necessary, obliquely to the left or to the right, and not just perpendicular to the front of the battalion.

Unlike the French who were deployed in four and five ranks, the British deployed in three ranks, which were brought closely together. The fewer number of ranks, and the fact that the men in each rank were not directly behind one another, but "interlocked" meant that the soldiers were able to more readily swing their weapons a little to the right or the left to achieve oblique fire. This was impossible for the French infantry, given the number of ranks and the distance between each (assuming they hadn't yet been closed up to march *à prest*).

Another reason for the effectiveness of platoon firing was that it guaranteed that 25 per cent of the battalion's men participated in each firing (this is assuming that the first rank was being withheld as a reserve). This is to be compared with 8.3 per cent (1/12 of the battalion) for the French army when, after 1707, it performed its own version of platoon firing. Breaking up the battalion into four firings meant that, given the same number of men per battalion, there was likely to be three times more casualties per individual firing, a fact that would tend to wreak havoc on the enemy's morale. In theory, the French would fire three times more often than the British during the same time (of course, each firing was one-third the size), but these casualties were broken up into smaller parcels, causing less of an effect on morale.

However, the greatest advantage of platoon firing was that it best solved the problem of continuity of fire. Breaking up a battalion's fire into four firings was more manageable than breaking it up into twelve as in French platoon firing, and continuity of fire more was likely to occur. Platoon firing allowed each soldier to stand up and start to reload immediately after he fired. He did not have to change positions or wait until other ranks behind him had finished firing.

This was not the case in the stationary version of firing by ranks that some French regiments used where firing started with the fifth rank and proceeded to the first, one rank at a time. In this latter system, after a certain point the fire had to be interrupted while some ranks reloaded. As soon as the last rank fired, it would immediately start to reload and would be ready to fire again by the time the first rank had fired. However, the first rank was to return to a kneeling position as soon as it had fired, in order to let the sixth rank fire again. The theory in the French army was that the front ranks of troops would reload while in their kneeling position. This would have been extremely difficult for even highly trained troops, especially under battle conditions, given the length of the musket's barrel and, if the battalion had been closed up at shorter ranges, the closeness of the files. Given the level of training then current among French troops, this was an impossible task, and the fire of the rear ranks was periodically interrupted while those in the front reloaded their weapons.[25]

At the start of the War of the Spanish Succession, the French continued to use the same fire systems that they had employed twenty-five years previously: fire by rank, fire by files, and fire by division. In various accounts of battles, the French are usually described as "firing by ranks." However, by this point "fire by ranks" could refer to two different firing techniques, either the caracole-like system where the troops walked to the rear of the battalion after firing, or where the first four ranks knelt down and the rear rank fired first while standing, before each of the other ranks would stand up in turn and then fire. Because the French would normally advance to the attack without firing, either system was used only if their advance ground to a halt.

During this time, some French regiments seem to have experimented with another "fire by rank" system. Here firing would start with the first rank, who would fall down in a prone position as soon as they fired. The second would then fire and fall down. This process was repeated until the last rank in the battalion fired, whereupon all the ranks stood up and started to reload their weapons. This system was probably rarely used, and the reasons why it has been described probably stem more from its unusualness rather than any widespread usage. This system is obviously inferior to the other two versions of the "fire by ranks." Unlike the traditional caracole system where each rank could start to reload as soon as its men got to the rear of the battalion several moments after they fired, here no one could start to reload until the last rank had fired. It is impossible to reload a muzzle-loading weapon while lying on the ground. At the same time, the battalion was increasingly vulnerable to attack as each rank fired, since the men couldn't present their bayonets while on the ground. Lastly, this system demanded that the ranks remain "open," that is that they be separated by a wide distance, to accommodate the length of a soldier while in his prone position.[26]

Even after the start of the War of Spanish Succession, French regiments sometimes continued to use the original "fire by ranks" method (the caracole). However, if this occurred within 50 to 60 paces of the enemy, the officers would have closed the spaces between the files to a minimum, and as a result the men would not be able to proceed to the rear walking between the files of men. Some officers prevented the ensuing confusion by having the men in the rear ranks move to the right, creating enough room for those who had just fired to gain the rear of the battalion where they would reload. Whenever the officers didn't take this precaution, the men in the first rank would simply walk to the left or the right of the line, thus gaining the rear by the battalion's flank. This was a much less desirable alternative, since the fire of the rear ranks was interrupted as they waited for the men in front to move out of the way.[27]

One remark that was often made about the French infantry's fire deserves some attention. It was often observed, despite the performance of the Royal Regiment of Ireland at Malplaquet, that the initial fire of the French could be severe, in fact more effective than the initial fire of the British. This at first appears to be an anomaly, since none of the various fire systems the French experimented with were as effective as the British/Dutch platoon firing. What contemporaries were probably referring to was those situations where the French fired by ranks, but with two or three ranks firing at the same time. This would have produced a greater volume of lead thrown in the first two or three volleys than anything the British or Dutch could have returned during the same short period of time. Given the continuity problems intrinsic to this fire system, that output would have quickly fallen off as delays occurred in subsequent volleys.

The Allied use of platoon firing, especially in defensive situations, was noticeably impressive, and the French soon attempted to follow suit. When Marlborough forced a passage of Marshal Villeroi's line on July 28th, 1705, the French battalions at the point of the attack used platoon fire. This, incidentally, is the first mention of French troops placing their knees on the ground, a practice already in use for about thirty-five years by German troops. Many of the less experienced officers involved in this combat demonstrated that they had not mastered the intricacies of platoon firing. As a result, on August 10th of the same year Marshal Villeroi ordered that 50 pounds of gunpowder be delivered to each battalion so that each could conduct two firing practices.[28]

During the winter of 1707 the method of executing platoon fire was officially regulated in the French army. It was to be performed successively by fractions of a battalion called "quarters of a *manche*" (about one-twelfth of a battalion: a battalion equalling ten subdivisions plus the grenadiers and the piquet). The rightmost platoon in the battalion opened the fire, followed by that of the left, then the center, and so on. The platoon that was to fire advanced six paces to its front with its ranks closed; the first two ranks placed their knees on the ground in order that all four ranks could fire at the same time. After firing, the platoon turned around and returned to its original position in line to reload its muskets. When this fire was to be made behind an obstacle or an entrenchment, the ranks were halved and the platoon fire made on two ranks. During a campaign, the battalions often deployed only in four ranks, and sometimes only three. In these cases, usually only the first rank placed their knees on the ground.[29]

In the French army platoon firing was limited to defensive applications such as firing behind entrenched positions, and so on. All indications are that the French never duplicated the success enjoyed by many of the Allied armies when using this firing system. One disadvantage of the French version of platoon firing was that each captain chose the moment when his men fired, thus breaking the battalion's fire into 12 or so divisions; this meant each firing was relatively weak, and the number of firings made fire control more difficult. The colonel also found it much more difficult to stop the firing, since the troops were intently following their captains' commands.

By 1709 the British had devised, albeit still in a rough form, the most effective controlled fire system that would be used any time during the history of the smooth-bore musket. Though the French had experimented with their own version of platoon firing in defensive situations, they would continue to use some form of fire by ranks throughout the Wars of the Polish and the Austrian Successions. In fact, they only officially adopted platoon firing as the primary method of delivering fire in 1755.

Although the French understood clearly the concept and importance of "weight of shot," they do not appear to have appreciated platoon fire's ability to more readily produce continuous fire. Similarly, they appear to have not appreciated the limitations of fire by ranks in this same area. In all fairness to the French military commanders of the time, their overall offensive tactics attached little importance to firefights conducted at a distance, every effort being made to approach the enemy and overthrow them with the threat of the bayonet or drawn sword.

FIRING ON FRIENDLY TROOPS

No discussion about fire combat is complete without mentioning that friendly troops occasionally fired on friendly troops. This embarrassment was caused by a number of factors: lack of visibility caused by smoke from all the firing, the fact that volley fire was essentially unaimed, as well as the similarity of many of the uniforms. There was a great variety of color on the same side, and often the enemy was dressed in a similar color scheme. The usual practice was to judge the allegiance of a mass of troops by the direction it was facing. Sometimes this was difficult to determine, and sometimes it was outright misleading. This often led to "embarrassing cases of mistaken identity."

De la Colonie, the acting commander of a battalion of French grenadiers in Bavarian service at the Battle of Ramillies, had occasion to fire on several Allied squadrons who were attacking French cavalry fugitives caught in a mire. Dressed in blue and red, his men were mistaken for an Allied regiment, and the enemy signaled them to stop firing. The French grenadiers continued their fire, and the enemy recognized this mistake.[30]

The Battle of Oudenarde provides a similar error with much more significant results. The Maison du Roi were able to escape because of the mistake of an enemy officer, who delivered an order to them, thinking them to be British because of their red coats. Captured, he understood his survival depended upon the escape of his captors, who along with him would have been annihilated otherwise. He warned them that they were going to be surrounded, and they all retired in disorder, avoiding capture or annihilation.[31]

Notes

1. *Munro II,* p. 190. Cited in Roberts, *op. cit.,* p. 258.
2. Grose, Francis, *Military Antiquities.* London, 1786–88, vol. 2, p. 280.
3. Turner, *op. cit.,* p. 237.
4. Le Blond, M., *Elémens de tactique.* Paris, 1758, pp. 409–410; Colin, *op. cit.,* p. 25.
5. Colin, *op. cit.,* p. 25.
6. Le Blond, *op. cit.,* p. 410.
7. Turner, *op. cit.* p. 237.
8. *Ibid.,* p. 238.
9. Le Blond, *op. cit.,* p. 406.
10. Chandler, David, *The Art of Warfare in the Age of Marlborough.* Guildford, Surrey. 1976, p. 115.
11. Le Blond, *op. cit.,* pp. 418–419.
12. Skrine, Francis Henry, *Fontenoy and the War of the Austrian Succession.* London, 1906, p. 168.
13. Ramsay, A. M., *L'histoire de monsieur de Turenne,* vol. 2. p. 17. Cited in Le Blond, *op. cit.,* p. 411.
14. LeBlond, Ibid., p. 417.
15. Grose, *op. cit.,* vol. 2, pp. 277–285.
16. Epitome, *op. cit.,* p. 33.
17. Grose, *op. cit.,* vol. 2, p. 279.
18. Epitome, *op. cit.,* pp. 19–22.

19. Grose, *op. cit.,* vol. 2, p. 277.

20. William Blathwayt, cited in Chandler, *op. cit., The Art of Warfare*. p. 116.

21. Le Blond, *op. cit.,* pp. 405–406.

22. Maude, F. N., Lieut. Col., *Cavalry, Its Past and Future*. London, 1903, p. 78.

23. Kane, Richard, "A New System of Military Discipline for a Battalion of Foot on Actions With the Most Essential Exercise of the Cavalry," in *Campaigns of King William and Queen Anne from 1689 to 1712*. London, 1745, p. 112.

24. Chandler, David, ed., *Robert Parker and the Comte de Mérode-Westerloo: The Marlborough Wars.* London, 1968, p. 89.

25. Le Blond, *op. cit.,* p. 406.

26. Chandler, *The Art of Warfare, op. cit.,* pp. 115–116.

27. Le Blond, *op. cit.,* pp. 409–410.

28. Belhomme, *op. cit.,* vol. 2, p. 413.

29. *Ibid.,* vol. 2, pp. 432–433.

30. De la Colonie, *op. cit.,* p. 314.

31. Saint Simon (Duc de), *Memoirs of Louis XIV and the Regency,* vol. 2. Translated by Bayle Saint John, London, 1901, p. 37.

CHAPTER 4

Deployment on the Battlefield

MARCHING CROSS-COUNTRY

THOUGH AN ARMY WOULD ULTIMATELY DEPLOY ALONG A WIDE FRONT (with or without intervals) prior to any engagement with an enemy force, it adopted a much narrower front as it crossed the countryside during the campaign. During the Thirty Years' War, the practice of dividing the army into a number of separate columns evolved. This was intended to ease the problem of congestion and reduce the time required to travel any distance.

Initially, each of these columns consisted of a series of regiments or brigades, one following the other. The men in these regiments or brigades were formed in dense solid squares, and were larger formations than would be used on the march by the early 1700's. The roads in

Western Europe at this time were not as wide as they would be during the second half of the eighteenth century, and the width of these large formations made traveling long distances difficult and extremely time-consuming.

The exact formations used in these situations varied from army to army, commander to commander. This system was modeled on the Spanish school of tactics which emphasized the use of large formations. Although the system was thoroughly obsolete by the late 1600's, "An Epitome of the Whole Art of War, Etc.," provides two detailed methods of marching across country.

The marshal of the camp drew up the men in battle array, according to the order assigned by the commander-in-chief. If the army was marching through open terrain, unobstructed by forests, villages and so on, most of the infantry were grouped together in great bodies (i.e., tercios) of two or three regiments. The large pieces of artillery traveled on the flanks, guarded by several battalions of infantry. The cavalry rode, in turn, on the flanks of the artillery, in "little squadrons" of two "cornets," or companies. Further on the flank came the baggage, ammunition, and field cannons. Finally, on the extreme flanks marched another column of infantry, this time drawn up in "small bodies."[1]

The accumulated experience of the late 1600's showed that for an army to minimize the chances of being surprised by the enemy, and to be able to deploy quickly once on the battlefield, a number of precautions were necessary while on the march. As a result, the various procedures to be followed while in column of route had become more elaborate by the end of hostilities in 1713.

What follows is a description of these procedures as formulated by Lieutenant General de Quincy in the early 1720's. It appears to be an amalgam of traditional French practices with that of several innovations made by Louis of Baden during the War of the Spanish Succession.

Louis of Baden emphasized the importance of "exactitude" while on the march. He systematized both the troops' position within the columns and their roles. Also, in an effort to minimize the disorganization caused by the heavy and light baggage, Louis of Baden regulated its position within the columns of march. Prior to this, the equipage of various types was assembled for the march much more haphazardly, and the army's progress was constantly being impeded by the disruptive impact of the baggage, provisions and camp followers.[2]

According to de Quincy's principles, as long as the army was traveling through clear terrain and not in the presence of the enemy, the commander was able to divide his army into as many columns as he saw fit.

In any other situation, he was to have as many columns as there were to be lines on the battlefield. When the army was to deploy along two lines and a reserve, for example, they would march in three columns.

The battalions and regiments in each column were in the same order in the column as they would later be in line on the battlefield. The troops destined for the right half of the battlefield would take the right road, those for the left would take the left-most road. Similarly, within each column, the troops to be stationed on the right of a line would march in front, those intended for the left would be in the rear. This arrangement was absolutely necessary if the cavalry and infantry were to be deployed without lengthy delays.[3] Several squadrons of dragoons were placed at the head of each column. These were accompanied by a number of laborers and a wagon filled with tools to prepare the roads for the column that followed.

By 1700, the size of the typical formation in these columns of route had shrunk considerably. Instead of marching in wide frontages, each battalion was divided into "divisions," one following the other. In the French army, at this point, the term "division" did not stand for a fixed number of platoons; it referred to whatever fraction of a battalion the regimental commander or army commander-in-chief decided was most convenient in that situation. Typically, a division was made up of 18, 20 or 24 files, and it was common for a battalion in column of route to consist of six divisions, plus a grenadier company.

The roads along the countryside would often narrow to where it wasn't possible to maintain ten files side by side. One of the main dangers in this situation was the elongation of the column which would ultimately lead to disorganization, with resulting delays. To help reduce this problem, the conventional wisdom of the time was to maintain 12 small paces between each division in the column, and six paces between each of the five ranks in the division. This gave each division, counting the space behind it, a depth of 36 "small paces" (24 inches). This distance allowed the men in each division who couldn't be placed on the road to march between the five normal ranks. If the six-pace distance had not been maintained when the narrow point of the road was reached, the increased number of ranks would either be brought too close together, or the 36 paces per division would have to be expanded. If the ranks were brought too close together, it would become difficult to keep each straight, and order could not be maintained for any period of time. On the other hand, if each division occupied a greater depth, the entire column was elongated accordingly.[4]

The artillery, large baggage and provisions would march along the center road. Because of the weight of the equipage making up this column and the difficulty of negotiating the various obstacles encountered during any journey, this road would receive a greater amount of attention from the troops assigned to engineering duties.[5] The small baggage was under the command of a "baggage master" and a number of archers. It was escorted by several soldiers and a sergeant and was positioned in both the left and right columns, unless there were a number of parallel roads in the area. Then, if the enemy was distant, it could travel independently, escorted by some detachments.

Originally, the baggage belonging to each infantry or cavalry regiment was identified by a streamer with distinctive colors. This allowed the officers' valets to quickly locate their masters' baggage. However, for unexplained reasons this practice fell into disuse by 1701. The order of both the light and heavy baggage was determined by the rank and seniority of the officers to whom they belonged. That belonging to the commander was placed in front, followed by that of the lieutenant generals, then came the baggage of each of the regiments. This latter was arranged according to the seniority of the individual regiment.

If the army had a *corps de reserve,* it would often be stationed with the central column of artillery, baggage and provisions. It would be placed in front of or at the rear of this column, depending upon whether the army was moving towards or retreating from the enemy. The numerous sutlers and camp followers were always troublesome on the march, often impeding the army's progress or causing havoc and ill will in the various villages and towns they passed. To remedy this chronic problem, the provisioners and camp followers were ordered to march behind the central column of artillery and baggage where they could no longer pillage and cause disorder. The senior officers were enjoined to apply this rule without exception.[6]

Whenever the army had to march through broken country where it would frequently have to pass through narrow passages (such as clearings in woods, etc.), or "defiles" as they were called, a number of other precautions were taken. The dragoons at the front of each column were now supported by a large detachment of grenadiers followed by a brigade of cannon. This artillery would be deployed in open terrain in front of the defiles, if the enemy was near, to help guarantee that the remainder of the column could clear the passage and be able to deploy into line, if necessary.

As soon as the army entered the general vicinity of the enemy, a number of other modifications became necessary. The small baggage moved to the rear of the left and right columns. The *corps de reserve* was now definitely positioned in front of the central column. The artillery would mostly remain in this column although a brigade or two of artillery was now to be placed in front of the other two columns, preceded by some infantry.

When the enemy was known to be on the flank of the intended path of advance, the central column consisting of the artillery and baggage would move to one side, so as to be protected by the other two columns of line troops. For example, if the enemy was to the right, the artillery column would work its way to the left. This allowed the army to quickly deploy into line without being obstructed by all of the wagons and artillery trains. The two lines would quickly form, the infantry by quarter-wheeling towards the enemy; the cavalry achieving the same effect by performing a series of motions called a "caracole." The artillery would then work its way into position by passing through the intervals in the lines and station itself in front of the first line. For this maneuver to work smoothly, it was necessary that sufficiently large gaps were left between various infantry and cavalry formations while they were still in column.

To prevent the equipage being stolen or destroyed by any enemy force that managed to go around the lines of friendly troops, it was to be guarded by troops taken from the *corps de reserve*. However, these detachments were to remain in an ordered formation so they could be recalled by the commander to rejoin the battle, if the need arose.

When the army had to retreat in the face of the enemy, the responsibility of keeping the enemy's forces at bay fell to the rear guard. The artillery, baggage, and provisions led by several squadrons of cavalry were placed in front of the line troops. One or two brigades of artillery remained with the rear guard, and were deployed if the enemy approached. They were also used to cover the passages of any defiles or rivers that had to be crossed. In these cases, the artillery was positioned on any high ground covering the area the enemy had to cross in order to attack. At the same time, numerous detachments were stationed in other strong positions near that river or defile. As soon as the column cleared the defile, the artillery and the detachments would themselves retire.[7]

DEPLOYING INTO LINE

Up until 1745, all European armies deployed into line from open columns, using one of the two processional methods of deployment then available: either deploying while marching from the left side of the battlefield, or deploying while marching from the right. Both of these were "parallel" methods in the sense that the army ultimately had to march parallel to the intended line before or while deploying. Forming line while the army marched along the battle line from the left was by far the more common of the two methods, since all of the battalions were ready to deploy into column at the same time; though in the early 1700's this was still a theoretical, rather than a practical, capability.

For an army to use this method of forming line, it would have to approach the intended battlefield from the rear. The infantry usually marched in two separate columns; the infantry that was to be deployed along the first line of battle in one column, the infantry of the second line in the other. Each multi-battalion column had to advance until it reached the left side of the prospective battle line, i.e., its lead battalion had reached where the line was to form. The column then turned 90 degrees to the right and marched parallel to the intended line. It continued until it reached the right of the intended line. When the leading battalion had reached the right of the battlefield, the troops in each battalion were ordered to "close ranks," that is, reduce the six-pace distance between ranks to a little over a single pace. Once this was done, all of the battalions were ready to be deployed. When a cannon shot signaled the army to begin deploying, each division in the column was to quarter-wheel to the left, thus forming a continuous line. This process was, in theory, performed simultaneously by the two lengthy infantry columns which maintained a distance of about 300 paces throughout the procedure. In practice, it was anything but simultaneous, usually requiring at least one or two hours to form a line of any length.

Forming line after the army marched to the right side of the field was less common since it was even more time-consuming. The army would still march across the area where the line was to be formed, but in this case each battalion formed line in succession before the next battalion could advance to where it was to deploy. In this case, the army once again approached the battlefield from the rear, but now on the right side, rather than the left. When the lead battalion was even with the intended battle line, it turned 90 degrees toward the left.

The first division quarter-wheeled to the right and then marched one "interval" forward (it marched forward a distance equal to its front). The next division marched straight ahead until it was even with the left side of the first division now in position along the line; this division now also quarter-wheeled to the right and advanced until it was in line with the first division. The third division advanced until it was even with the left side of the second division, then it quarter-wheeled to the right and then advanced, etc. This process continued until the last division advanced to the left edge of the line being formed quarter-wheeled and then advanced into line.

As soon as the first battalion had deployed, the second marched past the first battalion to where its first platoon or grenadiers were to deploy and it then performed the same actions as the first battalion. Each remaining battalion in the column followed suit one at a time until all of the battalions had been deployed into line.[8] As was the case with forming line from the left of the field, this process was usually performed by two lengthy infantry columns which maintained a distance of about 300 paces throughout the procedure. This allowed the two columns to be deployed into the first and second lines, respectively.

Prior to the mid-eighteenth century, an army rarely, if ever, deployed a complete line from the same column. In practice, the army was divided into a number of columns, up to nine or ten. This was, in part, the acknowledgment that the procedures used to deploy were still very time-consuming, and it was best to form portions of the line from two or three different columns, so that a number of battalions would be in the process of deploying at the same time. At the Battle of Blenheim, for example, the Allied army deployed into battle order from nine separate columns.

Despite these measures, forming line throughout this era remained very time-consuming. This resulted in most battles only getting under way in the afternoon. To return to Blenheim once again, Marlborough's attack was delayed to around one o'clock, allowing at least four hours for complete deployment of Eugene's columns, the leading elements of which had first entered the battlefield between 7:30 and 9 o'clock.

Another reason for these multitudinous columns was the diversity of grand tactical formations used by the armies of the period. It was not uncommon for a number of lines to be stacked one after the other in part of the battlefield, especially if the force was to assault a strong position, as in Cutts' assault against the village of Blenheim where there were four lines of infantry followed by two of cavalry in the rear. Similarly, at the combat of Wynandael (September 28th, 1708) the French deployed four parallel lines to attack the Allied force drawn up in two.

PROBLEMS IN DEPLOYMENT

This was how armies formed line in general terms. However, in the days before soldiers marched in cadence, changing from one formation to another was accomplished only with the greatest of difficulties. This was especially the case in the French army where maneuvering was made much more difficult by the depth of each battalion, the result of the five-rank line. In those armies where infantry was deployed in only three or four ranks, the deployment process avoided certain problems encountered by deeper formations.

Most descriptions handed down to posterity have scrupulously avoided the mire of detail necessary to describe the actual deployment procedures used during this period. Fortunately, one source is replete with the Byzantine "evolutions" ("maneuvers" is a later term referring to the new methods introduced by Frederick the Great) necessary to have troops go from column into line. This is Marshal Puységur's *Art de la Guerre par Principes et par Règles* published in 1748, several years after his death, and much too late to have any practical effect on French military thought. By the next year (1749), the introduction of the relatively simple Prussian principles of march and maneuver made Puységur's suggestions, with their reliance on open ranks and complex timing constraints, obsolete. The true value of Puységur's work is that it serves as a type of fossilized catalogue of the various debates that raged throughout French military circles during the period, solutions that were offered to solve these problems, and the actual practices that were used on the battlefield for the period between 1701 and 1740.

Puységur pointed out that in the French infantry at the time of his writing (circa 1735) there was still no single method of deploying a battalion into line. In fact, there were a large number of different systems, varying from regiment to regiment. For a long time the lack of a uniform distance between ranks complicated matters. As long as various regiments adopted different distances between ranks, no single method of forming line could be used, and it was only after this distance was officially fixed at 13 feet that any attempt at standardization could be made. The 13 feet between ranks was a convenient distance, being exactly twice the length of the halberd carried by a sergeant, and so was easily measured. Prior to this, the halberd was not used to measure distances between ranks. There was no way of accurately measuring the distance between files; each file continued to be separated by about two feet while marching and maneuvering, but was closed up before advancing on the enemy.[9]

Before looking at the mechanisms used to deploy French infantry in line, let's first see how the men changed direction while marching either as they crossed the countryside or as they went from column to line. This was done by having each of the divisions execute a quarter-wheel turn when it reached a predetermined point. This process was sometimes also known as a "conversion." There were two ways of conducting a quarter-wheel: in the first each rank quarter-wheeled one at a time, in the other the ranks within a particular division quarter-wheeled at the same time. The first, with each rank quarter-wheeling independently, was used when the width of the ranks making up the column was relatively narrow. Having all the ranks quarter-wheel at the same time was reserved for wider columns.

Regardless of which method was being used, it was of fundamental importance that all of the divisions within the column wait until they had advanced to the same "pivot" point before beginning the quarter-wheel. This allowed each of the successive divisions to follow the head of the column, and guaranteed that once all the divisions had quarter-wheeled, all the divisions were directly behind the leader.

When a quarter-wheel was to be performed by individual ranks, each rank would only start to turn when it reached the pivot where the turn was to take place. The man on that flank would almost stand still as the men on his other side described the radius of a circle (turning up to ninety degrees).

Each quarter-wheel had to be performed in the time taken for the troops to march six small paces. It was very important that it be performed in exactly this amount of time. If the quarter-wheel was performed more quickly, the ranks within the column would crowd together. If the quarter-wheel was performed more slowly, the column would elongate, and the men in each rank would have to rush forward to regain their proper distances. If this happened too frequently, the column would start to lose its proper proportions and become disordered.

When the rank consisted of 12 files the man on the extreme flank had to march 18 paces. When the rank contained even more files, the end man had to go an even greater distance, and it was more and more likely the turn could not be made in the prescribed time. This usually forced the column to slow down for awhile after making a quarter-wheel turn.

According to Puységur, it was impractical to have a column quarter-wheel by individual ranks when each of these were 20 or more files wide. Here the end man would have to rush 30 paces in the time it took to make six normal paces. As a result, if the column had been formed by dividing the battalion into five or less divisions (24+ files per rank), whenever the column was to change directions all the ranks within a division would have to quarter-wheel at the same time. Puységur estimated that the time required to quarter-wheel all five ranks was twice as long as turning one rank, i.e., equivalent to marching 12 paces. Since each division was to be separated by 12 paces, the next division in the column would have advanced to the pivot point just as the one in front was completing its turn. However, the proper distances would be restored as soon as the second division completed its quarter-wheel turn, since the first division would now be 12 paces in front.

In the French army of this time, the depth of a battalion posed a major problem when deploying. The process of simultaneously quarter-wheeling a number of divisions roughly at the same time was only possible when a division's front was greater than its depth. Otherwise, it would be very difficult for each division to quarter-wheel, and even if it succeeded, there would be large gaps between the divisions when in line. Unfortunately for the French, their practice of utilizing deep formations was coupled with that of dividing a battalion into a relatively large number of divisions when in column (often between six and ten).

In theory, a French battalion deployed in five ranks, each of about 120 files, had a frontage of 120 small paces (240 feet) and a depth of 24 small paces, there being roughly six small paces between each rank. Additionally, a 12-pace distance was always maintained between each division in the column, so that each division had a total depth of 36 small paces, regardless of its frontage. So, if a battalion in column was divided into six divisions, it had a frontage of 20 paces, and a 12-pace frontage when it was divided into ten divisions.

The practical effect of these narrow divisions was to force the French infantry to use a very clumsy sequential method of deploying. The troops in the first division would deploy, quarter-wheeling each rank one at a time. However, if each division in the battalion was 12 paces wide, the first rank in the second division only started to quarter-wheel when the fifth rank in the first division started its quarter-wheel. Those in the third division had to wait for the last rank in the second, and so on, meaning there was a cumulative delay as each successive division started to deploy. If each division was 18 paces wide instead, the first rank in the second division started to quarter-wheel when the fourth rank in the first began its quarter-wheel, and so on, resulting in a little less accumulated delay between divisions.

It is painfully apparent that the officers had to calculate the exact moment each division had to start its maneuver, depending upon the width of the column. If they started quarter-wheeling divisions in the rear too soon they would bump into those in front, and if they waited too long they incurred more delay than was necessary.

When a battalion had been divided into six divisions in column (20 paces frontage) all the ranks in the same division could start their quarter-wheel at the same time: the division would quarter-wheel as a unit. This was quicker than the ranks quarter-wheeling one at a time, but this posed a new problem. Often, the officers would misjudge the proper distance to be maintained between divisions, and they would advance their division too close to the one in front. When this happened, the men in each rank, assuming they were quarter-wheeling to the left, had to shuffle to the left as they quarter-wheeled to get back to their division's proper places in line. Now, of course, each division behind them was also too far forward, and they would have to perform the same irregular quarter-wheel to make up for this one officer's misjudgment. This could prove to be very tedious if the column was at all lengthy.

There were even greater problems to be solved when a battalion "broke," that is, divided itself into divisions as it went into column. There were two methods of forming column: the divisions could quarter-wheel all together to the right to immediately form column, or each division could quarter-wheel one at a time, starting with the one on the right.

Obviously, it was preferable to form column by having all the divisions quarter-wheel at the same time. In theory, the entire column could be formed in the time required to perform a single quarter-wheel. However, it wasn't always possible to do this. If the battalion commander decided that the battalion was to form a narrow column, where each division was to be only a tiny fraction of the battalion's front, column could only be formed by quarter-wheeling each division one at a time.

Since the distance between ranks had to remain constant, the depth of each division remained at 36 paces, regardless of its frontage. This meant that if the battalion was to be broken up into many divisions, its depth in column would necessarily be greater than its width while in line. In this situation, if all the divisions were quarter-wheeled at the same time, the rear ranks in each division would bump into those in the next division as they wheeled.

For example, if the battalion was divided into four divisions, each would have a frontage of 24 files, thus 24 paces. All of the men in the first rank could complete their quarter-wheels without anyone along the rank bumping into the men in the next division. However, with each succeeding rank an increasing number of men on the far flank would bump into the next division. In this example, this would be one soldier on the far end of the second rank, two soldiers in the third, five in fourth, and seven or eight along the fifth rank. These soldiers would have to double behind the men in their rank who were closer to the pivot. They remained behind them until their rank was clear of the flank man in the other division. At that point, they could return to their proper places in their rank. However, in practice this always caused extensive confusion.

Some battalion commanders worked around this problem by advancing the last three ranks to immediately behind the second rank whenever they wanted to form column using simultaneous quarter-wheels. However, as easy as this sounds, it was in fact very complicated, and Puységur recommended against its ever being used.

To avoid these problems, the battalion commander, when dividing his battalion up into a large number of divisions (more than four), had to have each division quarter-wheel one after the other into column. Forming column this way, the commander was free to divide the battalions in as many divisions as he wished.

Although this avoided the problem caused by narrow frontages relative to greater depth, it created a whole new series of problems. The concern now became having each division start its quarter-wheel at exactly the right moment. If there were delays between quarter-wheels, the depth of the column would expand. Though the few extra paces may not seem important when looking at a single battalion, this could be a very large problem when a number of battalions in a row were forming a lengthy column. In this case, if each battalion in column was needlessly expanded, the column would start to stretch a very noticeable distance.

It is difficult for the modern mind to understand exactly how serious a problem this was. Each battalion in line had a frontage of approximately 240 feet; however, when in column of ten divisions (plus the grenadiers), it occupied a minimum of 840 feet. In the case in which there were 30 battalions in line, by the time the last battalion started to march into column the first battalion would have already marched 28,200 feet, roughly the amount it was expected to march for the entire day. Truly, the lead of a long column would be entering the next camp just as the end of the column was setting off from the old.

In practice, a column was usually even more elongated than the proportions suggested by these calculations. The men in the first ranks of each division had to begin their quarter-wheel at exactly the right moment; otherwise there would be more distance between them and the previous division than was necessary. To achieve this, the officers had to pay the greatest attention to the motions of the preceding divisions, and men's movements had to be "like clockwork." Of course, this rarely happened in the French army of that time.

These were the types of problems that officers faced as they ordered their men to form line or column. These problems were the most severe in the French infantry where the use of five ranks separated by six paces made quarter-wheels much more difficult. Though the thinner lines used in most other armies simplified matters, prior to the advent of cadenced marching all officers faced similar issues and difficulties while maneuvering.[10]

NOTES

1. Epitome, *op. cit.,* p. 35.
2. Quincy, C. S. (Marquis de - Lt. Gen. d'artillerie), "Maxines et Instructions sur l'Art Militaire," in *Histories de Règone de Louis le Grand,* vol. 7. Paris, 1726, p. 37.
3. Ibid., vol. 7, p. 34.
4. Puységur, *op. cit.,* vol. 1, p. 95.
5. Quincy, *op. cit.,* vol. 7, p. 34.
6. Ibid., vol. 7, pp. 37–38.
7. Ibid., vol. 7, pp. 36–39.
8. Generalstab, Grosser, *Die Kriege Friedrichs des Grossen: Seibenjähriger Krieg.* vol. 1. Berlin, 1890–1913, vol. 1, pp. 130–133.
9. Puységur, *op. cit.,* vol. 1, p. 72.
10. Ibid., vol. 1, p. 78–85.

CHAPTER 5

Battle Order and Grand Tactics

BATTLE ORDER

PRIOR TO THE START OF A BATTLE, AN ARMY'S COMMANDING OFFICER AND his general officers (what today we call "generals"), would arrange their troops on the battlefield according to a number of theoretical principles, as far as the terrain and circumstances would permit. During this time, the term "linear warfare" is most frequently used to describe this arrangement of troops and their subsequent methods of fighting.

In this model, the troops are seen as being deployed along two, sometimes more, lengthy but continuous lines, with the infantry in the center and the cavalry, whenever possible, on the flanks. The prevalent "received wisdom" is that linear warfare somehow coalesces with the universal adoption of the flintlock musket and the socket bayonet in the first decade of the eighteenth century and, as a guiding principle for deployment and grand tactics, essentially remained in use until the French Revolution. In actuality, the theory used by general officers by the start of the War of the Spanish Succession to arrange their troops into battle order was virtually identical to that employed during the Nine Years' War (1688–1697) and very similar to that in Turenne's last campaigns (1672–1675). In fact, there are a greater number of similarities between these doctrines, as described in 1680 and 1725, than there were differences.

By the second half of the seventeenth century, it was common to draw up an army along three parallel lines, one behind the other. The infantry were to occupy the central portion of each line, while the cavalry were placed on either flank, whenever possible. In the French army, it was also the practice to place any carabiniers, fusiliers, and general's guards near the wings, slightly in front of the other troops. The artillery was positioned in front of the first line: the heavier pieces in the center, while the light pieces were on each flank.

The first line, was called the "vanguard," the second line, the "main battle," while the third was referred to by two different terms, depending upon its relative size. If the third line contained approximately the same number of men as the first two lines, it was called the "rear guard"; if it was appreciably less, it was known as the *corps de reserve* instead. Most of the infantry was placed in the "vanguard" and "main battle," and not in the rear guard. This was because it was believed that the infantry would be useless in this position, not being able to reach any critical point on the battlefield in time to make a difference.

The first line tended to have more men than either "main battle" or "rear guard," and had to be long enough not to be easily outflanked. The second line was to be almost as strong as the first, while the third line, either as the rear guard or *corps de reserve* was weaker than the two lines in front of it.

Sometimes, a line would have to bend to the rear, either to conform to the terrain or to protect the end of the line from the enemy. In these cases, the line angled backward 90 degrees or less from the alignment of the front line. If the line angled less than 90 degrees, it was termed *en crochet* (literally meaning "crooked"), while if it was at right angles to the front line it was termed *en potence*.

The infantry battalions and cavalry regiments in each line invariably were deployed so that there was a sizeable space between each unit in the line. Until at least the 1680's, this space was equivalent to the width of the infantry battalion or cavalry regiment, plus eight paces or so on either side. In other words, if a battalion had a width of 50 paces, the spaces on either side would be between 66 and 70 paces wide. Most often, the battalions or cavalry regiments in the second line were each positioned so that they stood opposite the interval in the first line. Using the same logic, the battalions in the rear guard or third line were placed opposite the spaces in the second. This system was known as the "cross" because of the shape when one considered a battalion in the front line, the two to its rear in the second, and the battalion directly behind it in the third.

There were other arrangements of battalions that were occasionally used such as the *cinquin* (the fifth), the *sixain* (the sixth), and the "checker." However, the "cross" was the most widely used, since it offered the most compact arrangement of troops. It also minimized the size of the intervals between each group of battalions, an especially important consideration for those in the vanguard (first line).[1]

To the modern reader, these large spaces between each of the units in a line probably appear as a potential liability that would allow enemy infantry or cavalry to enter the lines and attack the flanks of each battalion or squadron. However, there were a variety of reasons why this arrangement was used. The most important perceived advantage was that it allowed the units in the second and third lines to advance through the spaces and attack the enemy or support the friendly units in the first line. Also, should the whole or parts of the front line be defeated and break, this arrangement allowed panicked men to filter to the rear without having to run through the formations in the second line, an event that would have invariably led to the disruption and breaking up of these formations.[2]

Another reason for these spaces, less commonly understood, was that given the elementary methods of maneuver available in the seventeenth century, such spaces were necessary for formations to maneuver. This was especially important for cavalry when it attempted to face the rear, as would be necessary if it either attempted to leave the battlefield or meet an enemy approaching from its rear.[3]

In most armies, the position occupied by a regiment was governed by its seniority. Certain parts of the battle line were regarded to be positions of "honor." For example, to be positioned in the vanguard (the first line) was more honorable than to be placed in the following two lines, and to be in the "main battle" was more honorable than being in the rear guard.

In the French army, however, the Guards, though the most senior of all regiments, were always placed in the "main battle," and not the vanguard.

These considerations were also applied to a unit's position along the line. In the French army, for example, the most senior regiment within a line was placed on the far right. The next most senior regiment in that line was placed on the left flank. Subsequent regiments were alternated on the right and left until the most junior regiment by default occupied the middle of the line.[4]

How consistently these rules were applied varied from army to army, and in some armies, such as the British, it was tempered by the practical realization that when it came to actually deploying troops, it wasn't always possible to position a particular regiment according to their exact position of honor. The French, on the other hand, followed this policy to its logical conclusion, and beyond. It was only in such dire emergencies as Steenkirk (August 3rd, 1692), where they were totally caught off guard and had to position the regiments in the line in the order of their appearance, that they deviated from such a fundamental tradition.

By the outbreak of the War of the Spanish Succession, a number of changes had been made to the accepted theory as to how troops were to be arranged on the battlefield prior to the start of the battle. An army continued to be deployed along a series of parallel lines, with the infantry in the center and the cavalry on the flanks. However, the practice of referring to the successive lines as the "vanguard," "main battle," and "rear guard" fell into disuse, and the lines were now referred to by their order, such as the "first line," "second line," etc. Also, the notion of having a third line that might run across the battlefield was also discarded. Any third line was now always considered to be a *corps de reserve* and only positioned at certain critical areas behind the second line.

The use of various battalion arrangements, such as the *cinquin,* the *sixain,* and the checker, was completely abandoned. By this point, the battalions in the second line were always placed directly behind the intervals in the first. The distance separating the first and second lines was now more closely regulated: the battalions in the second line were to be deployed 300 paces behind those in the first. One finds this 300-pace distance between the first and second lines in use until the close of the Napoleonic Wars. The reason lay in the practicality of this distance. The distance was not so great that the battalions in the second line couldn't quickly move to support those in the first when the necessity arose.

Frederick the Great initially experimented with an 800-pace distance between lines, but practical experiences during his first campaign (1740) taught him this distance was too great, since the second could not support the first in time, and the traditional distance (300 paces) was restored.

On the other hand, the 300-pace distance was sufficient to guarantee that the men along the second line were outside of effective musket range, even when the enemy had come into contact with the troops in the first line, thus minimalizing the number of casualties suffered by the second line as it waited to come into action. It was also distance enough to allow individual battalions to maneuver out of the second line as they were ordered to support those in front. Given the processional methods of forming column then in use, this was a more important consideration than it would be latter in the eighteenth century, when more efficient maneuvers would allow units to pull out of line even when less space was available.[5]

The French army was traditionally predisposed toward the offensive, and usually attacked its opponent. The doctrine underlying the deployment of French troops reflected this fact. Both the majority of the troops, and the best corps were to be placed in the first line. It was universally recognized among French military authorities that the success or failure of the French attack often lay in the first assault.

In theory, the wise spaces between each battalion were only slightly reduced. The distance between each unit was now to equal the width of the unit, and was known as an "interval."

Much of the nineteenth and twentieth century literature gives the impression that by the War of the Spanish Succession, infantry battalions and cavalry regiments were deployed one beside the other with little space between. Though we can generalize and say that the traditional full-sized intervals were less common during this war than they had been in 1670, and those intervals that were found tended to be narrower than previously, this development was not because all senior officers had reversed their beliefs regarding this issue. In fact the traditional belief, that battalions should be separated by a distance equal to their frontage, continued to be accepted on a theoretical basis in the French army, at least, until 1753.

There was an emerging school of thought which advocated placing the battalions virtually side by side, without these wide spaces. One of its origins was in Southern Germany, where continuous lines were necessary when fighting the Turks (Austro-Turkish War 1682–1699). It gained advocates in France, and emerged during the 1680's.

Originally, an infantry battalion was regarded as a solid body, and because of its depth and its pikes was capable of standing on its own in clear terrain. The decrease in the number of ranks as well as the decline in the number of pikemen made military thinkers view a battalion as a linear formation which had to be supported by another formation.[6] The fact that, during the War of the Spanish Succession, battalions tended to be deployed more closely together was as much a function of the larger armies then coming into use, and the commander-in-chief finding himself with a much greater number of battalions to deploy along the battlefield, as it was a conscious change in the doctrine underlying how the army should deploy under ideal conditions. Puységur (d. 1736), a major proponent of the use of continuous lines in the French army, found it necessary to reiterate his arguments until the end of his career.

The artillery was always placed in front of the first line. The heaviest pieces were placed in the center. In those armies where the lines were deployed with battalion-sized intervals between each battalion or cavalry regiment, a smaller piece, the 4-pounder *cannon suédois,* was placed in these intervals. The officers controlling the artillery were instructed to utilize the available terrain; if heights commanded either flank, quantities of artillery were to be placed on whatever heights were available to enfilade the enemy's position, and, if possible, to disorder its troops and prevent them from deploying their own cannon.[7]

In the French army, the *corps de reserve* was to be stationed 500 to 600 paces behind the front line. Prior to the War of the Spanish Succession, in the French army the reserve tended to contain only cavalry. However, experiences during the last quarter of the seventeenth century showed the importance of having reliable infantry battalions available for use at critical moments during the battle. At several times during the War of the Spanish Succession, especially when two French armies were combined to fight a single foe, a large reserve containing both cavalry and infantry was available. In these cases, the *corps de reserve* was divided into three sections. If the number of general officers was large, it was commanded by a lieutenant general who had *maréchaux des camps* under his orders.

So far, the doctrines governing how the troops were to be deployed have been described as though the opposing armies were engaged on completely flat ground. Of course, this was purely a theoretical situation. The terrain on which the battle would be fought would not only affect how the troops were to be deployed, it would also influence how the battle was to be fought; that is, the grand tactics the commander-in-chief would use to best his opponent.

Another factor that could affect both the method of deployment and the type of grand tactics to be used during the combat was the ratio of men in the friendly forces to those of the opponent. If the two armies were roughly equal, although the commander-in-chief was to occupy the most advantageous terrain possible, it was not considered necessary to make special preparations to entrench or fortify one's position. However, it was *always* considered vital to *appuyer,* that is, lean or anchor one's flanks on some natural position, preferably a river or marsh, a ravine, or impassible woods, but an ordinary village would do, if nothing else was readily available. A number of battalion would be posted in such a village where they would entrench themselves.

If one's army was appreciably weaker than the enemy being faced, it was necessary to *appuyer* one's flanks on more defensible terrain. Each flank should now rest on a river, stream, ravine, or impassable woods. Simple villages would not ordinarily serve to anchor a flank in this type of situation. However, in those cases where the army was faced with a superior force and it was impossible to anchor a flank with natural terrain, carts or wagons could be used as a last resort. These were flipped over in a line of sufficient depth, the wheels were removed, and they were garrisoned by a sufficient number of musketeers to protect that flank.[8]

This was how an army was, in theory, to be drawn up prior to the start of the battle. It is interesting to note these tenets were not strictly followed in any of the four major battles (Blenheim, Ramillies, Oudenarde, and Malplaquet) occurring in the Flanders theatre during the War of the Spanish Succession. In each of these situations, the commanders of each army had to significantly modify how their troops were to be laid out according to the demands of the terrain being contested and other circumstances peculiar to the situation at hand.

At Blenheim, for example, instead of finding the infantry in the center with the cavalry on the flanks, in both armies we find large bodies of cavalry interspersed along the line with the infantry. In the case of the French, this was largely the result of fortuitous circumstances. Much of the French and Bavarian infantry was placed in or near the three towns (Blindheim, Ober Glauheim, and Lutzingen) spread out along the battlefield. Most of the first line between these towns was held by cavalry, which was quite unorthodox, even for that day. The overall French/Bavarian army actually consisted of three constituent armies, those of Marshal Tallard, Marshal Marsin and the Elector of Bavaria. These three forces were maintained as separate bodies, each occupying a different portion of the battle line. Tallard's horse had previously acquired an infectious disease, probably glanders, and couldn't be mixed with the other French-allied cavalry.

Similarly, the Allied force at Blenheim was actually two armies, one technically commanded by Eugene of Savoy, the other commanded by Marlborough, although effectively there was a much greater degree of cooperation on this side than on the French. Another factor that contributed to the Allied army's departure from the theoretical manner in which an army was to be deployed, was Marlborough's use of cavalry/infantry cooperation and support on the battlefield. At both Blenheim and Ramillies, the decisive blow was administered by a force containing both cavalry and infantry, deployed so as to support one another. At Blenheim, the infantry crossing the Nebel between Blindheim and Ober Glauheim was in lines with wide intervals between each battalion and behind two other lines of cavalry to the front. A portion of the Dutch infantry was similarly deployed between the villages of Taviers and Ramillies at the Battle of Ramillies.

In many respects, the large-scale organization of troops on the battlefield was much more diverse in this war compared to what it had been previously, and what it would be later during either the War of the Austrian Succession or the Seven Years' War. Much of this can be attributed to the fact that in the larger battles, the combatant armies often were made up of two, and even three (the French at Blenheim), constituent armies. In these cases, often the commander of each constituent army would continue to deploy his army as though it was an independent entity, i.e., his infantry in the center, with the cavalry on either flank. This had not occurred as frequently in earlier wars when the armies had been much smaller. Turenne's armies, for example, usually totalled between 15,000 and 30,000 men; both French and Allied armies in Flanders were usually closer to 60,000.

GRAND TACTICS

Most of what has been discussed so far falls under the heading of "tactics." Tactics in a military sense is the study or discipline covering the deployment of troops on the battlefield, and movement from one position to another. It also encompasses how these troops actually use their weapons and how they attack and defend themselves. Anther term, "grand tactics," is also frequently used. This refers to the use, movement and deployment of larger bodies of troops. Grand tactics is essentially the "stratagems" (used in the non-military sense) the commander employs to bring his forces to bear and defeat the opponent; "tactics" are the methods the individual bodies of troops use to participate in the broader grand tactics.

Grand tactics in the classic linear system was relatively simple, and tended to lack the full range of options that would characterize warfare by the end of the eighteenth century. Once the army succeeded in deploying on the battlefield and occupied all the advantageous terrain and the roads leading to the lines of communications, if the enemy was found to be unprepared, the army was to go on the offensive immediately, and charge the enemy before it was able to respond effectively. This was the accepted rule in all armies, but French authorities felt the precipitous assault, when made feasible by the overall situation, was particularly in line with the general character of their troops.[9]

The assault was usually delivered by the entire length of the line of battle, contrary to the practice that Frederick the Great would later establish where he would "refuse," or hold back, part of the line, so as to move as many troops as possible to the point in the enemy's line under attack. It was felt that the broader-based attacks were superior to limited attacks, based on the assumption that the greater the number of troops in the advancing line, the more vigorous the assault. At the same time, a lengthy line was more likely to be able to outflank the enemy. This was of great importance because if the enemy could be taken in the flank, this would ordinarily decide the first shock.

The second line of infantry was to start moving roughly at the same time as the first, to always remain within supporting distance. The cavalry on both sides was to begin its attack at the same moment as the infantry. Initially, it was to advance at the same pace, though as it neared the enemy it adopted a faster pace and pulled away from the adjoining friendly infantry. Usually, the cavalry on each flank was to first attack the enemy cavalry opposite it, then after overthrowing it, if necessary, to turn and attack the enemy infantry. However, it was hoped that the defeat of the enemy cavalry would induce the hostile infantry to voluntarily quit the field. Unless the attacking army was in the process of attempting to surprise the defender, the artillery in front of the first line would cannonade the enemy. Usually after an hour or so of artillery fire, the attacker would begin the assault.

During the actual conflict, the primary duty of each general was to support whatever troops were in trouble with fresh troops from the second line, and then to rally wavering troops. The army's commander-in-chief was to continue the assault as long as there was a good chance of winning the combat. If checked, the attack would be renewed as soon as the troops were rallied. Because an army might engage its adversary along its entire front, it wasn't uncommon that the attacker would be successful along portions of the line, while repulsed in others. The army's commander was to consider the situation, weighing advantages and disadvantages, before deciding upon the next course of action. He was cautioned against pulling back victorious forces to assist those not faring as well. Instead, he was to call upon the formations in the second line or even the *corps de reserve,* if necessary. These were to march up to the needed position and replace any squadrons or battalions that had been bested, and whose desire to fight was now suspect.

In theory, battalions were to be separated from each other by an "interval", i.e., a space equaling their individual width, so that reinforcements could be positioned more readily. In those cases where these intervals were actually maintained, the second line could be advanced in front of the first to either continue the attack or defend against an enemy offense. The first rank, given time to rally, was to reestablish itself behind the second and then serve in a supporting capacity.[10]

If the attacking army was so weakened or the defender's position discovered to be insurmountably strong, the commander was to turn all his attention to devising an orderly retreat, and issue his instructions to this effect to the various general officers under his command. These generals were, in turn, to take the necessary steps to prevent the enemy from interfering with the retreat.[11] If, on the other hand, a group of battalions succeeded in pushing back the enemy, they were to reorder and support any battalions in the same line in need of help before rushing off to pursue the defeated enemy. A small body from each end of the battalion could be employed in this pursuit, or even one or two entire companies. Scattering, these would chase the enemy, to prevent them from easily rallying.[12] Some squadrons of the cavalry, if available, were also to be sent to follow enemy fugitives. In addition to pushing the defeated enemy, they were to take prisoners and reconnoiter to see if the enemy managed to rally to return to the attack.[13]

So much for the attack on open ground. If the enemy was comfortably ensconced in a solid defensive position, the attacking general was to devise means of evicting the defenders from their strong points, on a position-by-position basis. It was advisable to use veteran troops in these attacks, since the likelihood of the forces actually closing to hand-to-hand combat was very much greater than in a fight on open terrain, where one side or the other invariably broke before the two forces met. Attacks on these "improved" positions were always to be preceded by lengthy artillery fire. This often led to individual regiments opposing one another to contest the ownership of a particular important position, rather than a general engagement where all of the troops were involved in the combat down the entire length of the line.[14]

In practice, the actual grand tactics that were used tended to be dictated by the circumstances surrounding the particular engagement, the peculiarities of the terrain, the composition of friendly forces and how they matched up against the opponent, and so on. The French, for example, who had a reputation for going on the offensive and overthrowing the enemy with their first attacks, and whose doctrine demanded they follow this tradition, were on the defensive in all four major battles conducted in the Flanders theatre during the War of the Spanish Succession. The initiative displayed by Marlborough and Prince Eugene in almost every case forced the French to depart from their practices and respond to the enemy's initiative instead.

At the same time, the increased size of the armies made conformity to traditional grand tactics increasingly problematic. It was much more difficult to have a line of battalions strung over several miles move in any type of coordinated fashion than it had been when the front had been about half this size. At Blenheim, for example, the Allied extreme left under Lord Cutts fought completely independently of the Prussian, Danish and Imperial troops led by Prince Eugene on the right.

No look at grand tactics during the period would be complete without looking at Marlborough's practices. The Duke, strictly speaking, did not invent any new grand tactical elements. His genius lay in his ability to use existing techniques in a novel fashion which usually successfully confounded the enemy. Invariably, Marlborough seized the initiative and attacked. However, his attacks were not monolithic affairs where the entire battlefield was regarded as a continuous front and all the troops in the front line acted as a single unit. Marlborough's battles are more readily broken down into a set of phases and subphases, each falling into a greater overall "plan" than those of his contemporaries.

Although a number of attacks could be initiated at the same time, each served a distinct grand tactical purpose. They were not intended to all be all-out affairs where each would overthrow the enemy at that point. Many of the attacks were to serve as probes to determine the enemy's strength in a particular sector or an attack could serve as a method of containing an enemy. Once again, we don't have to go any further than Blenheim to find examples of these grand tactics. Cutts' assault on the village of Blindheim served both as a probe and a containment device.

The Duke of Württemberg's attack with Danish and Hanoverian cavalry on the village of Ober Glauheim served in a similar capacity. Once these were carried out and the French forces were effectively fatigued and pinned down, Marlborough was able to bring in his reinforcements and vigorously attack the enemy's force lying in the open terrain between these two villages. Often, these probes had another, more subtle, objective: to serve as a feint to deceive the enemy regarding the Allies' true intentions. The enemy being misled would often respond by focusing their attention to a secondary part of the battlefield, sometimes even weakening the very area where the Allies planned to attack.

Ever since Gustavus' days commanders tried various means of achieving some sort of close support between infantry and cavalry. Most often, this took the form of either interspersing platoons of infantry among cavalry squadrons or mixing several squadrons of cavalry along an infantry line. Marlborough used a slightly different method. At both Blenheim and Ramillies, he placed both infantry and cavalry in a "column" formed by a number of lines placed one behind the other. Lord Cutts' forces consisted of four lines of infantry and two of calvary at the rear. At Ramillies, four regiments of infantry were placed in line behind two lines of Dutch cavalry positioned between Taviers and Ramillies.

The impact of these mixed formations with the infantry/cavalry support they fostered was quite dramatic. At Blenheim, five English squadrons who had overthrown part of the French Gendarmerie, being pursued by a larger cavalry force, were succored by their own Hessian infantry in the second line. Later, Allied infantry again went to the cavalry's aid as the cavalry attempted to establish itself on the French side of the Nebel. The same type of timely support is also seen at Ramillies where the Maison du Roi was only stopped by four infantry regiments after it had overthrown two lines of Dutch cavalry.

Marlborough also placed great importance on the use of an informal reserve. Rather than allocating a significant percentage of his forces to a formal reserve positioned in a third line, he instead took large numbers of battalions and squadrons from the first and second lines and injected them into the thick of the fighting at the critical moment. The advantage of his system was that it tended to confuse the enemy, giving little hint as to where and when the real blow was going to fall.

BATTALION FORMATIONS

So far the discussion has focused on the arrangement of the infantry battalions and cavalry regiments making up the army as a whole. But how was the individual battalion and cavalry regiment organized and deployed?

During the War of the Spanish Succession each French infantry battalion was composed of 12 companies, each of 45 soldiers, and a company of grenadiers, for a total of 585 men. Officially, each company was augmented by five men in 1712, but because of the difficulty of locating the needed men, this never took place. As a result, a battalion usually had a field strength of 500 men during the campaign.[15]

Temporarily disregarding the presence of the central nucleus of the battalion's pikemen, the arrangement of the musketeer companies in a French infantry battalion during the last years of the pike was similar to that which would be maintained well past the Napoleonic Wars. The logic underlying the arrangement of these companies was provided by the concept of the "place of honor," which continued in most armies to be an important consideration governing the sequencing not only of companies, but of battalions, regiments and even brigades until the end of the Seven Years' War (1756–1763). The place of honor was on the right side of any line, whether one was considering the entire battlefield or only a single battalion. Consequently, those with the most power, i.e., with higher rank or more seniority within the same rank, positioned themselves and the men they commanded on the right side.

By the late seventeenth century, this principle was applied in a most sophisticated fashion. When the battalion was to be deployed in line, its companies were placed one beside the other in order of the rank and the seniority of the officer commanding them. This meant that if the battalion contained the colonel's company, this was to the right of the remaining musketeer companies commanded by officers of lesser rank (usually captains). The remaining musketeer companies were arranged according to the seniority of their captain, so that the most junior captain's company found itself at the left end of the line.

The exception to this was the grenadier company which was always positioned on the right flank of the battalion, to the right of the colonel's or most senior captain's company. Since 1693, the practice developed of extracting a "piquet" of 50 men with a captain, lieutenant, and a sub-lieutenant to serve as a second grenadier company, to be located on the battalion's left flank. As long as pikes continued to be carried, once on the battlefield the pikemen were grouped together and placed in the center of the musketeers, with an equal number of musketeer companies on each side.

This scheme possessed at least a theoretical flaw: by definition almost all of the experienced officers were all on the right side of the battalion, with the least experienced on the left. As the seventeenth century neared its end, a number of officers noticed this problem and took steps to place some experienced officers on the left side of the battalion, also. According to Puységur, throughout the entire 1670–1720 period this potential problem was addressed by some battalion commanders who used a number of modifications of the above arrangement. Marshal de Catinat, commander of the French forces in Italy during 1692, for example, in his instructions for his army, used the standard sequence with the exception that the second most senior captain was to be placed on the battalion's left, with the remaining captains in order of seniority, from right to left.

Other officers went further and emulated what was standard practice in England and some German states. The most senior officer's company would continue to be the right-most (again, excepting the grenadiers who maintained their position on the right flank), only now the company commanded by the next most senior officer was placed on the left flank. The company commanded by the third most senior officer was placed to the left of the first company and the fourth company was placed to the right of the second. This system of alternating companies to the left and to the right guaranteed that experienced officers leading the companies would be placed on both flanks of the battalion. This arrangement, though used by only a minority of officers in the French army around 1670 would become more popular later on, and would completely supplant the strictly seniority-oriented system described above by the 1720's.

Usually when any of the modified versions of the standard order were used the captains' companies remained in the normal order despite the fact that a captain's commander might be at the other end of the battalion.

In the days before 1703, and even after, there was little standardization, and layout could vary from regiment to regiment or army to army. The following is a description of the placement of officers and subalterns (NCO's) in the French army, where the captains were alternated according to seniority. The battalion's commander was positioned in front of the center of the battalion, far enough away from the ranks to be seen by all the men. He was accompanied by two sergeants and two grenadiers or fusiliers who stood behind him (in some regiments he was accompanied by the three flags). The most senior captain was on the right of the battalion, the second most senior on the left. Both were two paces in front of the first rank and each was accompanied by two grenadiers or fusiliers. A row of officers and sergeants ran along the rear of the battalion consisting of three captains, four lieutenants, two under lieutenants and six sergeants; these were known as *serre-files,* meaning they "closed the files." The third captain was in the center of this row, and the two least senior captains were behind each flank. Two lieutenants and one "under-lieutenant" were placed in a row between the central captain and each flank. The remainder of the captains were placed in a row in front of the first rank of soldiers. The last two files at the right and left end of the battalion had two grenadiers or fusiliers behind them, for additional support.

It is not exactly true to say that a captain, even if he remained in front of his normal command, actually commanded a "company." It is more accurate to say he was in charge of a predetermined number of files. This was necessary since during the course of a campaign the companies within the same battalion could vary greatly in strength. Once they were deployed in line, sergeants serving in under-strength companies would withdraw men from their larger counterparts and insert them into their own, so that each company would have the same number of files.[16]

In the days of pikes, the flags tended to be placed in the first rank of soldiers. However, when the pikes disappeared the flags were placed deeper in the formation.[17] The flags, which were to be held as high as possible, were then placed between the second and third ranks of soldiers. Experience had shown it was better to bring all three flags together and position them between the third and fourth ranks, with several sergeants to guard them. The drummers were placed immediately behind the flags.

The positioning of the officers and the subalterns was designed to allow them to see in all directions, so that there was no blind spot, and so they could see all that approached the battalion. It also intended to allow the officers and subalterns to supervise the men during the advance or while firing and to prevent or correct any confusion that might arise.[18]

Puységur felt that this scheme had defects, arguing that whereas the officers in front of the battalion were close to the men in the first rank, those in the rear were too far removed from the men in the following ranks to be able to effectively manage them. This usually resulted in the men quickly being left to their own devices and meant the end of organized fire. He also pointed out that the row of *serres-files* did not have sufficient strength to prevent the men from breaking in a crisis situation when the line started to break.[19]

In the French army, the gradual introduction of the flintlock musket had some effect on tactics, though it wasn't as marked as in the British army where it would ultimately lead to the adoption of a completely new method of delivering fire. On May 15th, 1693, Louis XIV issued instructions which officially sanctioned two tactical changes. Henceforth, a battalion was to deploy along five rather than six ranks. In practice, during the realities of the campaign, battalions weakened by casualties had been deployed along five, and even four ranks since Turenne's time. One is tempted to explain the reduction in ranks by the increased effectiveness of the new flintlock musket. This would have been true, except that, as we have already seen, by this date (1693) most regiments in French service were still primarily armed with the matchlock. The reduction in ranks (from six to five) was more probably an after-the-fact admission that the existing fire systems, in use during the late 1680's, were more efficient than their predecessors, each portion along a battalion's front requiring fewer men to produce the same volume of fire per unit time.

The King's instructions also mandated a change in the handling of the pikemen, who were no longer to be kept completely in the center of the battalion. Before moving to approach the enemy, the major was to ensure that a quarter of the pikemen marched to the right wing of the battalion, and another quarter to the left wing. Two files of grenadiers were placed on the right wing of the pikemen on the right, and two files of musketeers taken from the piquet were positioned on the flank of the left group. This measure, which proved ineffective, was an attempt to strengthen the flanks of the battalion which had proven to be very vulnerable to enemy cavalry in the days before infantry battalions were placed end-to-end so as to eliminate the flanks of the intermediately positioned battalions in the line. Several other tactical changes, though not officially sanctioned by a royal ordinance, appear to have also taken effect, or at least gained acceptance in a portion of the army.

FRENCH CAVALRY

A squadron consisted of four companies, each of 35 *maitres,* giving a squadron a total of 140 men deployed in three ranks. This size was chosen since it was felt a larger grouping would be difficult to put into motion; a smaller squadron, on the other hand, was considered to be too weak and capable of little resistance. The squadron was deployed in three ranks, each trooper occupying a width of one pace. Maintaining this distance was critical, since crowding the troopers too closely together interfered with their movements, while too great a space permitted the enemy to enter and thus overturn their ranks when they met during combat. The most experienced cavaliers and best horsemen were placed in the first rank and another twenty in the flank files at either extreme of the squadron. This was to insure that the squadron would deliver the most lively attack possible. The twenty expert riders on the flanks were called "commanded" men and were often assigned special tasks during the battle, such as to work around the enemy's flanks, etc.

The squadron commander placed himself in the center of the squadron with the back of his horse positioned partly in the first rank of troopers. His slightly advanced position allowed him to observe both flanks. Each of the four company captains was similarly placed with respect to his company. Their horses, though mostly in the first rank, were positioned so that their necks were sticking out of that rank. The lieutenant and cornet in each company were placed along the first rank. If a squadron was commanded by a major of the regiment and the major stayed with the squadron during the battle, his place would be taken by the aide-major who would accompany the colonel and temporarily function in his place. After issuing his last orders to his squadron, the major would ride over to the colonel and place himself in the rank of captains. In this case, the aide-major would go to the second squadron and place himself in a similar position.[20]

BRITISH LAYOUT

On the parade ground, around 1686, a battalion was taught to deploy along the six ranks in open order, with four paces between each rank. The senior company, the one led by the most senior captain, was positioned on the right, the next on the left, then the third senior company next to the first company, and so on. This continued until all companies were placed with the least senior in the middle. If there was a company of grenadiers, it was drawn up on the right of the battalion three deep, about two or three paces' distance to the right of the battalion's drummers. Its grenadiers' drummers were to its right.

Once in position, the musketeers would turn to the left or the right and march towards the ends of the battalion, while the pikemen in each company marched between the ranks towards the middle. As they reached their proper position, they turned and faced forward. This allowed the battalion to assume the, by now, traditional form of three "sleeves," the pikes in the middle with a musketeer sleeve on either side.

Some of the sergeants were positioned on the flanks of each rank, the remainder were posted three paces behind the last rank. The drummers were on the flank of the sergeants along the first rank. The lieutenants were positioned in a row two paces in front of both musketeer sleeves. The captains were two paces in front of the lieutenants. The ensigns were along the same row as the lieutenants but were only positioned in front of the pikemen. The battalion's commander was in the center of the formation, six paces in front of the first row of pikemen.

When the regiment consisted of a single battalion and the colonel and the lieutenant colonel were both present, the lieutenant colonel was to the left of the colonel. The major, who always remained on horseback, was in front of the sergeants on the right flank, a little to the front of the line of captains. The adjutant, also on horseback, occupied a similar position on the left of the battalion.[21]

With the disappearance of the pike near the turn of the eighteenth century, each battalion in British service came to be arranged slightly differently. The battalion tactically was divided into four "grand divisions," instead of three as during the era of pikes. The grenadier company was divided into two and placed on either flank, and each "grand division" was divided, in turn, into four platoons.

The ensigns, the officers carrying the regiment's standards, were positioned on the second rank to the right and left of the two center platoons. The drummers were assigned three positions: to the right and left and behind the two center platoons. All the drummers were aligned with the sergeants.

Before advancing, the major ordered the NCO's and officers to take their positions with their platoons, and as soon as the order to march was given, by drum or by the colonel, the lieutenant colonel and officers marched through the intervals to the rear of the battalion. The officers spread themselves evenly along the length of the battalion, forming a line four paces behind the third rank of infantry. The lieutenant colonel, or in his absence the most senior captain, stationed himself eight paces to the rear of the last rank in the center. These officers were to make certain that the soldiers were doing their duty.

Some of the battalion's sergeants were placed in the intervals in the rear rank; the others were placed on the flanks and in a separate row behind the battalion between the last rank of men and the row of officers in the rear. The major and the adjutant, after having seen that the battalion was properly ordered, posted themselves on either flank to continue to observe the battalion's motions. They had to be very careful, however, not to ride in front of the battalion, especially when it was about to deliver fire.[22]

NOTES

1. la Vallière, François, *The Art of War Containing the Rules and Practice of the Greatest Generals in the Maneouvres.* Philadelphia, 1776, pp. 176–178.
2. Quincy, *op. cit.,* vol. 7, p. 57.
3. Puységur, *op. cit.,* vol. 1, p. 128.
4. La Vallière, *op. cit.,* p. 177.
5. Puységur, op. cit., vol. 1, p. 154.
6. Anonymous, "Essay on the Art of War." London, 1761, p. 423.
7. Quincy, *op. cit.,* vol. 7, pp. 58–59.
8. Ibid., vol. 7, pp. 57–58.
9. Ibid., vol. 7, p. 59.
10. Puységur, *op. cit.,* vol. 1, pp. 151–152.
11. Quincy, *op. cit.,* vol. 7, pp. 62–63.
12. Puységur, *op. cit.,* vol. 1, p. 152.
13. Quincy, *op. cit.,* vol. 7, p. 62.
14. Ibid., vol. 7, pp. 57–59.
15. Ibid., vol. 7, p. 65.
16. Puységur, *op. cit.,* vol. 1, p. 72.
17. Daniel, (Père), *Histoire de la Malice Françoise,* 2 volumes. Paris, 1724, vol. 1, p. 238.
18. Quincy, *op. cit.,* vol. 7, pp. 65–66.
19. Puységur, *op. cit.,* vol. 1, p. 72.
20. Quincy, *op. cit.,* vol. 7, pp. 63–65.
21. Grose, *op. cit.,* pp. 277–278.
22. Kane, *op. cit.,* pp. 113–114.

CHAPTER 6

Offensive and Defensive Tactics

OFFENSIVE TACTICS (FRENCH, BAVARIAN, AND SWEDISH)

ONE OF THE MAJOR REASONS FOR THE FRENCH FAILURE TO DEVELOP AN effective fire system appears to be the general temperament of the officers and soldiers in the French army. As was the case in Napoleonic times, the French army was noted for its *elan* during the first assault. And so, there was considerably less interest in experimenting with new firing methods in order to utilize the flintlock's advantages.

Part of the reason for these attitudes was undoubtedly the long string of victories achieved by officers such as Marshal de Turenne. Such triumphs were still fresh in people's minds, especially among ranking officers, many of whom spent their formative years during the glorious campaigns of 1670–1675. Many of these victories, from the infantry point of view, were based on the ability to advance toward the enemy in an ordered formation, to resolve the affair with cold steel, or at least with the threat of hand-to-hand fighting, which was almost always sufficient to cause one side or the other to break.

Throughout the last quarter of the seventeenth century, the method of attack used by Monsieur de Greder the commander of the regiment later to be led by Maurice de Saxe, is exemplary in this regard. He ordered his men, who at this point were still furnished with matchlocks, to shoulder their arms while approaching the enemy. In order that his men would not have any choice in this matter, Monsieur de Greder forbade them to even light their lengthy coils of match, thus making it physically impossible to use their firearms during the march. He concentrated on having his men march in the best possible order, and as soon as the enemy started to fire, usually at 25 to 75 paces, he would throw himself, sword in hand, in front of the regiment's colors and cry "Follow me!" This method of attack invariably succeeded for him, and using this technique Monsieur de Greder and his men defeated the Frisian Guards at the Battle of Fleurus (July 1, 1690).[1]

Although few other colonels went to this extreme, French grand tactics at the turn of the eighteenth century was based on the same general principles. In the French army, at least, the tactics used during the attack changed little during the 1690 to 1713 period. During this time, the flintlock replaced the matchlock, and the pike had completely disappeared. These changes in technology caused the number of ranks to be reduced to five, then unofficially to four, and the space between files would similarly be tightened. But, in the French army, at least, the immediate impact of the adoption of the bayonet was first applied to the defense. The method of attack remained virtually unaltered during the War of the Spanish Succession, despite some periodic experiments with the increased firing efficiency. This is the reason why the French entered the War of the Spanish Succession with the archaic fire-by-ranks system, and why they were so slow to change. Their main preoccupation was with the attack, and they considered firepower to be less important here than in defense, where it was obviously essential. From our perspective, knowing about the effectiveness of the musket later during both the Fredrician and Napoleonic wars, we may initially have some difficulty understanding this. However, prior to the universal adoption of the cartridge, the flintlock musket, and the iron ramrod, as well as the policy of continual practice to train the troops to load and fire effectively, musket fire was often surprisingly ineffective even at close range.

At the Battle of Freiburg (August 3rd, 1644), Turenne's forces, after debouching through a forest and being unable to advance further because of the presence of a large mixed force of enemy infantry and cavalry, with their backs to the forest traded small-arms fire with a sizeable enemy force for several hours, separated by only 40 paces.[2] Though musket fire had undoubtedly improved by the turn of the century, by this point these types of experiences had etched themselves on the French military consciousness. They had dampened their desire to look for effective methods of delivering small arms fire, and instead fostered the desire to quickly attack and resolve the issue with the threat of cold steel. Looking at the conduct of other armies during the War of the Spanish Succession, one sees that this view certainly wasn't limited to the French, and was adopted by other major armies when on the offensive.

When faced with an enemy equal in size in open terrain, the French army normally was to go on the offensive and attack its opponent. Although these were the days before an army followed a single body of doctrine to provide its tactical and grand tactical dictates, the following represents a consensus on how the attack was to be conducted in normal circumstances, and is a synthesis of the various descriptions provided on the conduct of French troops during the 1690–1713 period: De Catinat's instructions (1693); the King's instructions of May 15th, 1693, and March 2nd, 1703; De Saxe's *Reveries* (written 1732, published 1757); Quincy's *Maxims et Instructions sur l'Art Militaire* (1726); and Puységur's *Art de la Guerre par Principes et par Régles* (1748).

The infantrymen attached their bayonets to the end of their muskets prior to the advance; each soldier resting his musket on his left shoulder. When the moment came to attack, usually the entire first line would start to advance at the same time. The cavalry would start to advance at the same time as the infantry and ride with sword in hand. The second line of infantry was to start advancing at the same time as the first, in order to insure that the original distance between the two lines was maintained. If too great a distance was allowed between the two lines and the first line was overthrown, the second would not be able to advance in time to support it. This was one of the factors leading to the French defeat at Ramillies. Here, the second line of infantry failed to follow the first, and as a result was unable to come to the assistance of the right wing when it was broken by the Allied attack.[3]

The advance was to proceed cautiously at a slow pace to minimize disorder, and was led by officers with spontoon in hand. All of the officers were on foot, except for the major who was always on horseback and the colonel who could either be mounted or on foot. The function of the colonel was to make the decisions, and the major to insure that they were carried out. The major was placed on one side of the battalion and the colonel on the other. One of these officers had to be on horseback to ride back and forth making certain the orders were being carried out, and that the required intervals were maintained.[4]

The men were under the strictest orders not to fire until ordered to do so, when very close to the enemy.[5] While marching, the soldiers were all supposed to take the same size steps. In the last decade of the seventeenth century in the French army, this was the "great pace" equalling 36 inches. During the War of the Spanish Succession, Puységur, at the least, preferred the smaller "small pace" of 24 inches, believing smaller steps allowed the men a greater chance of retaining their order.

The men were to advance in the strictest silence, only the colonel or major being allowed to speak. From time to time the men were to take the "small pace" if they were in advance of their neighbors and wanted to "dress" the line, i.e., have it reassume correct alignment. As the officers marched they were to turn around from time to time, to make certain they maintained the proper distance from the men in the ranks following. If they pulled too far ahead the men would start to speak, losing their concentration, which would soon lead to the battalion disordering itself.

Contrary to practices in later warfare, the trumpets or drums in the French army often remained silent. Although the sound of "martial airs" would have been useful to buoy the morale of the attacking troops, most senior officers realized it was far more critical that their men hear their orders without any ambiguity. These were the days before standardization of trumpet calls or drum-beats made it possible for these instruments to be used to provide signals on a widespread basis. Moreover, because of the lack of cadence, the music really didn't assist the actual process of marching as it would later, when everyone was to march in step.[6]

This was in contrast to the practice in the Swedish army where the men marched in cadence and to the accompaniment of drums, which were used to communicate orders.[7] This leads one to wonder whether the adoption of cadence was a necessary precondition for the use of musical instruments as means of delivering orders. The French adopted the use of music in this role in 1749, the first year they contemplated using cadence on a universal basis; the British had started several years earlier, in the early 1740's.

Throughout the era the musket was in use, the ordering of a battalion's ranks and files was referred to as its "dressing." During the advance, the officer's main duty was to make certain that the men maintained their proper dressing. This meant that the company officers attempted to have the men in the company keep each rank as straight as was humanly possible and the soldiers in each file in their proper position following their file leader.

The more senior officers, on the other hand, made every effort to keep their battalions aligned with the remainder of those in the line, and preserve the prearranged distance (called the "interval") between each battalion. Alignment was "made by the right," meaning that the troops to the center and the left always attempted to keep even with those on the right.[8] The lieutenant general commanding the second line made certain that the center and the left of this line remained straight and that its distance remained about 300 paces from the first.[9] In the days before the introduction of cadenced marching (where every man sticks out his left foot at the same moment, and marches a predefined number of steps per minute) this was extremely difficult, and it was necessary for the lieutenant general commanding that portion of the army to frequently order a halt so that the men in the various battalions could reorder themselves.

Before advancing, each battalion had been deployed in "open ranks," each rank being separated by about four paces. When the attacking force had advanced to within 100 paces, the officers would work to close the ranks to two "great paces" (six feet).[10] At this point, the files would also be closed together a little more, but not so much that it would hinder the movement of a soldier's elbows which would have affected his ability to easily march, load, or fire.[11]

Initially, the men would advance marching at the average speed. However, as soon as the enemy started to fire or started to march forward, they would march *à prest,* that is, they would quicken their pace to reduce the time they would be fired upon and, they hoped, catch the enemy before he was able to reload. Often, this doubling of pace effectively meant a run "because the attack which is made running is the most terrifying."[12] Before changing their pace, the officers would further close the ranks to a distance of one great pace (three feet) or even the small pace (two feet). It was a universally accepted maxim within the French army not to bring the ranks closer than this distance; otherwise, the troops would start to bump into each other, the ranks and files would become confused, and a "murmur" of complaints would be heard throughout the battalion.[13]

As soon as ranks had been closed, the officers at the front of each battalion would prepare themselves for the "charge." They had to position themselves closer to the soldiers in the first rank or, if it actually came to hand-to-hand fighting, they would run into the enemy line unsupported by their own soldiers. Consequently, before ordering the soldiers to march *à prest,* all officers other than the battalion's commander would march closer to the front of the first rank. In fact, in many battalions the officers would position themselves partially inside the first rank, halfway in, halfway out, edging in between the files of soldiers. In either case, it was always necessary that they remain in front of enough of the troops to see the length of the line both to the right and the left.[14] The battalion commander still positioned himself in front of the battalion two paces beyond the front rank.

Up until the last years of the seventeenth century, it was customary in French service to have the soldiers march "presenting arms," as soon as they started to march *à prest*. This meant holding the flintlock or matchlock vertically about six inches in front of the soldier's face, so that he could go through the entire ritualistic firing procedure, step by step according to the manual of arms. However, during the War of the Spanish Succession, it gradually became the practice to have the men hold their arms *en chasseur* (like a huntsman), holding the musket with one hand near the lower barrel and the other on the lower stock, with the flintlock pointed diagonally upward and sideways, as a hunter would casually carry his hunting piece in the forest, hence the name.[15]

It was almost universally accepted among experienced officers that the soldiers were not to fire their weapons during the advance. Catinat, writing around 1690, describes this rationale:

> "One prepares the soldiers to not fire, and endure the enemy's fire considering that an enemy that fires is assuredly beaten when one will have his fire entire. It is good to inject this into the spirit of the soldiers and the sergeants, in order to hold themselves together.".[16]

This quotation implies that all commanders were enjoined to never order their troops to fire when attacking the enemy. Though some officers fervently believed in this theory, others believed that offensive fire should be reserved till the last moments when the attacking force had approached to 20 to 30 paces from the enemy's defensive line, where they would be able to fire at a point blank range, and then rush in with bayonet or sword. The following is a detailed account of both the defender and the attacker withholding their fire until at a very close range:

> "At the Battle of Calciante (April 19th, 1706), Monsieur de Renventlau, who commanded the Imperial army, had ranged his infantry on a plateau and had ordered them to allow the French infantry to approach to twenty paces, hoping to destroy them with a general discharge. His troops executed his orders exactly.
>
> The French with some difficulty climbed the hill which separated them from the Imperials and ranged themselves on a plateau opposite the enemy. They had been ordered not to fire at all. And since Monsieur Vendôme did not care to attack until he had taken a farm which was on his right, the troops remained for a considerable time looking at each other at close range. Finally they received the order to attack.
>
> The Imperialists allowed them to approach to within 20 to 25 paces, raised their arms, and fired with entire coolness and with all possible care. They were broken before the smoke had cleared. There were a great many [Imperialists] killed by point blank fire and bayonet thrusts and the disorder was general."[17]

Lieutenant General de Quincy, writing in the 1720's, after digesting the experiences of the War of the Spanish Succession, felt that it was appropriate for some of the troops in the advancing battalion to be ordered to fire. However, these were limited to the grenadiers and the platoon of musketeers on the left flank. The remainder of the troops were to withhold their fire.[18]

If the attackers had sufficient spirit, and the defenders stood their ground, the attacking army ultimately would close to hand-to-hand combat. Before the introduction of the socket bayonet, the soldiers as they neared the enemy would shift the weight of their musket to their right hand, so that they could draw their sword with their left. These were the days before muskets were equipped with shoulder straps (except for those of the grenadiers), so usually in the final moments, the soldiers would throw their muskets away and concentrate on attacking with their swords. When the flintlock was introduced, it came equipped with a shoulder strap, so the infantrymen could sling their muskets over their shoulders even if they elected to attack with the sword instead of the bayonet. It appears that as long as the soldiers were equipped with the sword they preferred its use to the more clumsy action of musket and bayonet.

In those cases where the attackers elected to use their bayonets, they were to lower their bayonets and point them and then lunge at their opponents as they surged ahead. The theory was that in a melee, should one occur, the first rank of attacking infantrymen would be pushed and supported by the "weight" of the three or four ranks behind them, and they would have nowhere to go but forward. It must be pointed out that in open country rarely did two opposing forces actually continue to stand in the final moments before closing; almost invariably one side or the other broke before contact had been made.

From Puységur's work, we know that the French of a later period were trained to take advantage of any wide spaces they might find between enemy battalions. The commander of a battalion that found itself facing the interval separating the enemy battalions was to notify the companies on either side to fall on the flank of the enemy to their left and right as soon as the battalion reached the enemy line. The center of the battalion was to continue marching to protect the other battalions from a counterattack that might be made by the enemy's second line. Meanwhile, the enemy battalion in the first line attacked by another battalion to its front was expected to be quickly overthrown, and the detached companies were to immediately return to their parent battalion.[19] To what extent these tactics had been developed on the battlefield at the turn of the century is debatable.

This was theoretically how the French army was to attack. It is known that a number of other armies used very similar tactics when attacking. De la Colonie provides an account of virtually identical tactics on the part of the Bavarian forces at the affair of Heyzempirne [March 3rd, 1703].

"The Elector was soon ready, and both armies opened a desultory cannonade whilst deploying. Our force scarcely had time to get into battle array before the Elector set us moving at a steady pace with well-closed ranks, due regard being given to the maintenance of an equal pace throughout. When we moved thus a sufficient distance, our two wings, consisting of cavalry, advanced at a rapid trot, whilst the infantry quickened their pace, in order to dash upon the enemy without firing, reserving this until they were in a close contact. The first shock was a very sharp one, that gave one the impression that the animosity between people of the same nation was more obstinate than if they had been strangers to one another. Victory hung for a long time in the balance between the opposing cavalry, so stubborn was the fight, for the Emperor's cuirassiers are really among his very best troops. Our infantry did not experience the same resistance: they stood the first effect of the enemy's fire, charged home with bayonets fixed, and crushed all resistance. Soon afterwards the enemy's cavalry gave way and their rout became universal."[20]

The Swedes also were known for their spirited attacks. The Swedish infantry regulations of 1701 called for the infantry, deployed along four ranks, to advance firmly toward the enemy, without any fire conducted at longer ranges. This tactic was known as "ga-pa," which literally meant to "go on," referring to one of the main principles of this technique, to concentrate on the forward motion, and disregard the casualties inflicted by the enemy's fire.

Though similar in overall philosophy to its French counterpart, the Swedish method differed in that it purposely called for a momentary halt to the advance in order to use the infantry's firearms. At roughly 50 paces the advancing Swedish infantry would stop momentarily and the two rear ranks would deliver their fire. The advance was immediately to be renewed, the two front ranks were to reserve their fire until they saw the proverbial whites of the enemy's eyes. The Swedish soldiers resigned themselves to their possible fate during the last moments of the encounter by accepting the fatalism of their religious beliefs: "God would not let one be killed till one's appointed hour had come."[21]

Charles XII, whether giving into his natural impetuosity or a sincere desire to discover better tactics, appears to have departed from the tactics as called for in the 1701 regulations, on a number of occasions. Whether his beliefs were influenced by French thinking and example is unclear. In any case, his attitudes were nevertheless very close to those of Monsieur de Greder.

During the course of the Great Northern War, Charles started having his infantry engage the enemy counterpart in the final moments with sword in hand, a tactic popular among the French in the 1690's. Marshal de Saxe describes one notable attempt to have his [Charles'] own regiment implement this tactic:

> "[Charles XII] had spoken of it [this tactic] several times, and the army knew that he favored the system. Accordingly, in a battle against the Russians, at the moment it was about to begin he hastened to his regiment of infantry, and made a spirited harangue, dismounted, posted himself in front of the colors, and led them to the charge himself. But as soon as they came within about 30 paces of the enemy, his whole regiment fired in spite of his orders and his presence. And although he routed the Russians and obtained a complete victory, he was so piqued that he passed through the ranks,

remounted his horse, and rode off without speaking a single word."[22]

The Swedish offensive tactics were very similar to those used by the French at this time.

BRITISH, DUTCH AND PRUSSIAN OFFENSIVE TACTICS

The offensive tactics described so far were applicable to the French, Bavarian and Swedish armies. However, the British, Dutch and Prussians were busy developing a separate set of offensive tactics.

In addition to differences in the methods of delivering fire, the British used an entirely different set of offensive tactics. Unlike the French and Bavarians who usually attempted to ignore the enemy's fire and come to contact, British tactics, during fighting in open ground, relied on a series of firefights to reduce the enemy's will to fight before finally moving in.

A Spanish general, the Marquis de Santa-Cruz, best described the rationale underlying the Anglo-Dutch firefight tactics. He concluded that if infantry advanced against enemy infantry without firing, and the enemy being attacked was equally determined to fight and delivered an orderly fire, the attackers would always be at a disadvantage:

> "If as soon as you are disposed to fire upon the enemy, you do not, you deprive yourself of the advantage of many killed, and intimidating many others by the whistling balls, and by the spectacle of their comrades killed or wounded: you do not profit by this result, that this dread and this spectacle would make on the enemy, especially on their recruits and their new soldiers, which are more troubled by the danger and having their hands and their arms also trembling that their pulse is agitated, firing as much at the sky as the earth, whereas still not being afraid by any losses, they will lay their fire with less trouble, and you will then close with the *arme blanche,* when by their fire our army will be already much diminished and intimidated."[23]

This was exactly the philosophy of the British and the Dutch. The usual British plan was to advance the battalion until the enemy in front of it opened fire. This would often occur between 100 and 50 paces.

As soon as they were under fire, provided they were within 100 paces, the colonel would order the battalion to halt and the first "firing" was to make ready. It would fire as soon as ordered to do so by the colonel, and then immediately start to reload while the men in the next firing prepared to fire.

If the enemy broke as a result of this first fire, the colonel would order the march and have his men pursue the retiring enemy. If the enemy stood or advanced to meet the attack, the men in the next firing would fire upon the colonel's command. As soon as this fire occurred, the men in the third made ready to fire, while the men that had just fired started to reload.

The colonel would have this fire continue until either the enemy broke or he felt it was necessary to resume the attack. In this last case, the men who would have been ordered to fire next were to make certain they were prepared to fire, if necessary. This having been done, the battalion was ordered to advance. If the enemy continued to stand, the battalion would once more be brought to a halt. The colonel would then have the battalion conduct platoon fire once again, a single firing at a time, and he was to make certain that the firing occurred as fast as was possible.

If the enemy broke at this point, assuming that they were retiring quickly in broken order, the colonel was to have the battalion continue to fire until the enemy was out of range. Under no circumstances was the battalion to follow the enemy if the speed required to catch up to the enemy would threaten to disorder the battalion. In this case, the destruction of the fleeing enemy was left to any cavalry in the vicinity.

The preceding description is based on Richard Kane's "A New System of Military Discipline for a Battalion of Foot," published in 1745.[24] Captain Robert Parker provides us with a vivid description of virtually the same system used by the Royal Regiment of Ireland (the 18th Foot) at the Battle of Malplaquet (September 11th, 1709) in the woods of Sart on the French left.

> "Upon this Colonel Kane [Richard Kane was actually brevet lieutenant-colonel, acting in the absence of Colonel Sterne], having drawn us up, and formed our platoons, advanced gently towards them, with the six platoons of our first fire made ready. When we advanced within a hundred paces of them, they gave us a fire of one of their ranks: whereupon we halted, and returned the fire of our six platoons at once, and advanced upon them again. They then gave us the fire of another rank, and we returned them a second fire, which made them shrink; however, they gave us the fire of a third rank after a scattering manner, and then retired into the wood in great disorder: on which we sent our third fire after them, and saw them no more. We advanced cautiously up to the ground which they had quitted, and found several of them killed and wounded: among the latter was one Lieutenant O'Sullivan, who told us the battalion we had engaged was the Royal Regiment of Ireland. Here, therefore, was a fair trial of

> skill between the two royal regiments of Ireland, one in the British, the other in the French Service; for which we met each other on equal terms, and there was none else to interpose. We had but four men killed and six wounded: and found near forty of them on the spot killed and wounded."[25]

The Allied infantry (British, Dutch, Prussians, etc.) did use a form of the *à prest* attack, but only when the enemy being attacked was ensconced in an entrenchment or otherwise-strengthened position. One of the best examples is Lord Rowe's attack at the opening of the Battle of Blenheim. Dismounting, General Rowe led his brigade in complete silence towards the enemy position. The troops had been ordered not to fire until he plunged his saber into the town's defenses. The French troops, mostly seasoned veterans, withheld their fire until the British were 30 paces off, then their volleys decimated the British. Rowe miraculously reached the palisade and stuck his sword into the wood, whereupon the British returned the fire. The British assault against a much larger force in the highly fortified village was ultimately driven back. This same type of attack had been used by the Allies against another fortified French/Bavarian position at the Schellenberg (July 2nd, 1704) with similar results. To return momentarily to the Allied attack on Blenheim, Lord Cutts received orders from Marlborough to cease attacking the village. In order to hold the attention of the numerous French battalions in the village, the British infantry advanced periodically toward the enemy parapets, but now fired only by platoons.[26]

On the defensive, the British, as well as most Allied infantry, used platoon fire. Dutch infantry regiments, using this type of orderly volley, having been placed behind several lines of Dutch cavalry, were able to stop a successful charge by the French Maison du Roi at Ramillies, when they broke through the Dutch cavalry. This set the stage for the Dutch/Danish cavalry counterattack that decided the battle. Several years later we find another Allied force (Dutch, Hanoverian, British, Prussian) under General Webb repulsing a numerically superior French infantry assault at the combat of Wynandael (September 28th, 1708) using platoon fire.

To summarize the differences between the two major theories of offensive tactics, the French, Bavarian, and Swedes believed that firepower was not effective in the attack. According to this view, stopping to fire stagnated the attack and disordered the troops. This system was dependent on the bravery of the troops conducting the attack, and their desire to come to grips with the enemy. As a competitive system, it was based upon the fire-effectiveness of the small arms used during the second half of the seventeenth century. The other view, held by the British and Dutch, was that if firepower was conducted by well-trained troops, was well directed, and delivered in a regular pattern, it could be extremely effective, reducing the enemy's will to fight before it was necessary to close to very close range. This set of tactics sought to take advantage of the capabilities of the flintlock musket introduced in quantities during the 1690's.

ATTACKING IN BROKEN TERRAIN

When infantry attacked an enemy in open terrain, the two bodies of opposing infantry rarely, if ever, actually came to grips. One side or the other retired in disarray before the moment of contact. The Prince de Ligne, for example, in Austrian service during the Seven Years' War where he saw extensive action, only observed a single case of a bayonet fight in open terrain. This occurred at Moys on September 7th, 1757, when an Austrian and Prussian force surprised each another after climbing opposite sides of Jäckelsberg hill.[27]

"Closed order combat," as it was sometimes called, was frequent enough in any type of broken terrain, such as woods, copses, hedges, thickets, villages, and entrenched positions. De la Colonie provides one of the most detailed accounts of hand-to-hand fighting in these circumstances. The bulk of the French and Bavarian forces at the Schellenberg were stationed behind a parapet near the banks of the Danube river. The assault was led by English infantry and dismounted dragoons. According to De la Colonie:

> "Rage, fury, and desperation were manifested by both sides, with the more obstinacy as the assailants and assailed were the bravest soldiers in the world. The little parapet which separated the two forces became the scene of the bloodiest struggle that could be conceived . . . . It would be impossible to describe in words strong enough the details of the carnage that took place during the first attack, which lasted a good hour or more. We were all fighting hand to hand, hurling them back as they clutched at the parapet; men were slaying, or tearing at the muzzles of guns and the bayonets which pierced their entrails; crushing under their feet their own wounded comrades, even gouging out their own opponent's eyes with their nails, when the grip was so close that neither could make use of their weapons. I verily believe that it would have been quite impossible to find a more terrible representation of Hell itself than was shown on this occasion."[28]

The defenders proved desperately obstinate and the Allied attack eventually collapsed and was forced to retreat behind a reverse slope some distance in front of the parapet.

DEFENSIVE TACTICS

These were the dynamics of attack. There was also a set of tactics to be used when a line of infantry was to be on the defensive, and await the other's attack. The same set of defensive tactics tended to be used by all Western European armies during this period.

The army on the defensive, like the attacker, would deploy itself along two lines, usually separated by 300 paces. However, it would make every effort to take advantage of the terrain it occupied.

Care would be taken to insure that each battalion was in complete order. The army would then await the enemy's advance in silence, so as to hear the orders issued by the senior officers. At this point, two slightly different tactics were available to the army on the defensive. It could start to fire when the enemy had advanced to about 50 paces, or it could withhold fire until the last possible moment. In the French army, when firing at this longer range, this fire was almost always by either of the two "fire by rank" systems discussed earlier. The Swedes, British, Dutch, and Prussians used the more efficacious "platoon firing" system.

The whole purpose of starting to fire at the longer range (50 paces) was that the defenders hoped to disorder the attackers during the final moments of their advance, thus softening up their assault and possibly making them vulnerable to a countercharge. The attackers usually responded to being fired upon at this range by marching *à prest,* that is, they quickened their pace to reach the enemy before they could reload. In the days before cadence, marching even the 50 paces separating the two forces meant the attackers would be at least slightly disordered. The distance between the individual files in a cavalry squadron or an infantry battalion would start to become uneven, some becoming too close together, while others would open up. This, in turn, usually had the effect of the men in a battalion crowding inward upon its center, producing wider intervals, i.e., spaces, between the battalions than was originally desired.

The defending army, because it hadn't moved, would remain in perfectly good order. Each of its ranks would be perfectly straight, and the men in each file would be directly behind the file leader. The attacker's disorder, besides increasing the chances of the attacker turning around before coming to grips with his opponents, gave the defender an advantage if the two forces actually met.

The other tactical option open to the defending army was to withhold its fire to the very last moment when the enemy had advanced to about 20 paces. This was predicated on the belief that by firing at such close range, a great number of casualties would be inflicted in an instant, and the attackers would either turn around and flee, or be beaten back by a last-second countercharge. This tactic recognized that, given the weaponry then in use and the standard of training then prevalent, only one ordered volley could be delivered during the opponent's advance. Subsequent volleys would only contain a fraction of the number of shots of the first.

In using either option, many German armies would order the men in the first rank or two to place their knees on the ground. This was to allow the men in the rear ranks a better opportunity to fire. Once the first rank fired, it would rise to receive the enemy's bayonet or sword charge.[29] The British, Dutch and Prussian troops often used the new and more effective "platoon fire" when they were forced to fire in defense. When the French were on the defensive they tended to use "fire by ranks" in a normal open field situation, and voluntary fire when behind entrenchments.

CONFUSION AND RALLYING

Such was the prevalent theory on how the men were to act while on the attack or the defense. In actuality, a number of factors tended to interfere with a smooth and easy implementation of these tactics, whether offensive or defensive. The single greatest obstacle for the attacker was simply marching across the short distance separating the two armies in the days before marching in cadence. The men, marching in lengthy lines, quickly became entangled and the senior officers had to call frequent halts to the attack, so that order could be restored.

Marshal de Saxe provides us with a good description of how these problems occurred:

> "The battalions, then, march ahead, and this very slowly because they are unable to do anything else. The majors cry "Close," on which they press towards the center; insensibly the center gives way, which makes the intervals between the battalions. There is no one who has anything to do with these affairs but will agree with me.
>
> The majors' heads are turned because the general, whose head is also turned, cries at them when he sees the space between the battalions

> and is fearful of being taken in the flanks. He is thus obliged to call a halt, which should cost him the battle; but since the enemy is as badly disposed as he, the harm is slight."[30]

Henri-François de Bombelles, writing in 1754, claimed that the deep formations being advocated by many French officers at this later period were completely unnecessary when attacking the enemy. He observed that in his experience, the required depth was always inadvertently achieved even when the infantry attacked in a line of three or four ranks.

> "Its [the enemy's] presence so frightens most of the less experienced men, so that when approaching [the enemy] they slide behind any of their comrades who are brave enough [to stay in position], where they believe they are more secure; then one easily perceives that the wings of the battalion shrink in upon the center and that instead of being four [ranks] in depth, one often finds . . . eight at the moment which they charge the enemy. Thus one must never apprehend that a battalion loses depth, and one must estimate oneself happy when one can maintain it in good order on four ranks of depth . . ."[31]

This confusion affected the attacking force in another very important way: the officers' control over their men became weakened, giving the men the opportunity to give in to their personal best interest, which was to fire at a longer range. Because of the high rate of misfire, the smoke, and the general confusion that accompanied the firing of muskets, the first volley was by far the most damaging. The troops in the attacking line or column hoped that the defenders would deliver this volley at a middle or long range, where it was less crippling. The longer the defender could withhold his fire, the greater the strain this usually caused in the approaching enemy. When the defenders managed to withhold their fire, very often sporadic firing would commence here and there along the advancing line, bogging down the attack to a standoff firefight conducted at medium range. This violated the entire spirit of the attack and gave the initiative and the advantage to the defender.

This problem was the most acute for new or mediocre troops, who had the greatest difficulty in marching effectively. These were the troops who also were the poorest at firing, and so were at a disadvantage firing at this lengthy range (i.e., middle range). They would tend to fire at too great or too close a range, and after awhile realizing they were getting the worst of the firefight, they would turn their backs and flee.[32]

Although everything about the attacker's tactics was geared to reaching the enemy and breaking his will to stand and defend himself with the bayonet, in practice the conflict was ordinarily resolved before the two parties came to grips. Most attacks ended with one side taking away the other's desire to continue the fight, rather than its physical destruction. Writing in 1732, De Saxe commented that most infantry attacks were resolved one way or the other when the forces had approached to about 50 or 60 paces of each other. It was at this point that the defeated side most often would "take to its heels."

Though the defenders did not have to worry about the confusion caused by changing positions, they had to make certain that the rank and file held their fire until they were ordered to fire. It wasn't always possible for the officers and subalterns to completely control their troops. The sight of the enemy foot slowly but determinedly advancing was usually enough to make the more inexperienced soldiers want to open fire. Sporadic fire would often break out up and down the line as the more nervous gave way to their impulses with the approach of the enemy. The danger in this situation was that it was contagious, causing almost everybody in the line to eventually open fire before the commanding officer gave his instructions. When this occurred the defender forfeited the (relatively) deadly first fire which was supposed to be conserved until the closest possible range, usually between 30 and 70 paces.

Even a controlled volley, when held to the last possible moment, sometimes did not produce the expected results, as we already have seen at the Battle of Calciante, where the Imperial army firing at French troops at a distance of 20 paces still were unable to cause sufficient casualties to stop the enemy from advancing to the attack and overthrowing their positions. There is also De Saxe's celebrated observation that he had seen battalion volleys delivered which had failed to kill even four men.

> "Powder is not as terrible as is believed. Few men, in these affairs are killed from in front or while fighting. I have seen entire salvos fail to kill four men. And I have never seen, and neither has anyone else, I believe, a single discharge do enough violence to keep the troops from continuing forward and avenging themselves with the bayonet and shot at close quarters. It is then that men are killed, and it is the victorious who do the killing."[33]

Though De Saxe's *Reveries on the Art of War* was first published in 1757, it was written in 1732 and reflects the author's experience during the War of the Spanish Succession. His observation that few men are killed from in front while fighting is accurate for turn of the eighteenth century warfare, especially when we compare the situation with later wars, in which De Saxe himself would participate, when the troops were more thoroughly trained in loading procedures and firing techniques. This is not to say that large numbers were not killed during the course of the battle by infantry fire; they were in any hotly contested battle. Rather, the number of men killed in any single volley or a given attack was less than it would be 50 years later.

RALLYING

We tend to think that a formation only had to be rallied in those situations in which it had been beaten and forced from its position. Actually, a number of factors might force the officers to regroup the men and restore order. As we have already seen, often just moving forward would sufficiently disorder a formation that the lines would have to be "dressed," and the unit reorganized. A formation would also become disordered if it had to quickly force a passage through rough terrain; this could be something as seemingly innocuous as a ditch or a hedge. The Prince de Ligne, serving with the Austrians during the Seven Years' War, describes how the men in the Andlau regiment at the Battle of Leuthen, unable to deploy into line because of the presence of houses, stood "thirty deep," that is in large unorganized masses. They were so uncontrolled that when they fired, they frequently shot the men in De Ligne's regiment, who were the neighboring formation, in the back.[34]

A formation would also be disordered when it advanced against an enemy and was victorious, even in clear terrain where the enemy dispersed upon its approach, and no contact was actually made. This was because some of the officers and even more of the men would join in the pursuit and chase the retiring enemy. This they would do at a trot without any regard for order or maintaining either ranks or files. Of course, if contact had been made, which normally would only occur in broken terrain (entrenchments, hedges, etc.), the battalion would definitely be disordered, win or lose.

This was a potentially dangerous situation, and the officers and subalterns had to immediately work to restore order, for as long as they were disordered they were highly vulnerable to attack and to being easily overthrown. A battalion charging with leveled bayonets with closed ranks and files would invariably overthrow an opponent whose formation was disorganized (no coherent ranks and files) or whose battalion advanced in partial succession and not all together.[35]

In theory, if a battalion succeeded in pushing back the enemy in front of it, it was to detach a small group of men, possibly several companies taken from each end, to pursue the retiring enemy so that it could not easily rally.[36]

Once the victorious battalion was reordered, it was normally supposed to support any of its neighbors still in contact or threatened by the enemy, rather than immediately advancing and ignoring events along its own line. If these neighboring battalions had already been defeated, it was to attack the enemy pursuing the retiring battalion(s). Only when the other battalions were free were the battalions as a group to start to advance and attack the enemy to their front.[37] If the battalion was disordered because it had been pushed back or had quickly retired, this process couldn't start until a certain distance had been traversed.

Puységur tells us that the very penchant the French had for the aggressive initial assault would often rebound against them if this initial attack proved to be unsuccessful. The problem was that in the heat of a combat, the officers, having a misplaced sense of honor, would leave their designated positions within the battalion's formation. Too many French officers, fearful of "losing their honor," would run to the front of their formation during a fray, leaving the rank and file behind. This would create obvious difficulties if the battalion was defeated. First, the officers would suffer a disproportionate number of casualties; furthermore, the process of rallying was made much more difficult.

Even if the battalion had been successful over its adversary, the officers position in front was a problem. As the army advanced over the dead and dying, the more unscrupulous soldiers would drop out of formation to plunder enemy casualties. If the battalion was attacked under these circumstances, even though the officers succeeded in rallying a number of men around the colors, they would still be defeated if a significant number of others had dropped out or fled.[38] The only solution was to insure that the officers maintained their positions at all times. The officers and subalterns in the rear rank had a better chance of stopping fugitives or potential plunderers than if they ran to the front. Unfortunately for the French, this problem was never adequately addressed prior to 1750.

What happened to a formation in the reverse situation, when the morale of its men started to give way? In very desperate situations, many of the men would run away if they could get by the subalterns and the officers stationed behind the rear rank to prevent exactly this occurrence. If enough men managed to run away, the battalion would lose its cohesion and break. Before a formation broke, it would usually first start to "waver." What occurred was very similar to what has been described happening during an advance, that is the frontage would shrink as men grouped behind those brave enough to hold their position. Sometimes, as at Steenkirk, in 1692, entire battalions would cower behind others, such as when the men in the right battalion of the Bourbonnois regiment, unable to endure the deadly fire of the English Guards and a Danish regiment, doubled behind that of the left battalion.[39]

More frequently, however, the men would run behind those in the same company, thus shrinking the battalion's frontage. This is the reaction found among many of the Austrian battalions who, at Mollwitz, were beleaguered by superior Prussian fire despite the fact that they were crouching behind a wall made up of their knapsacks, while the Prussians were firing in an upright position in the open. After a while, many infantry regiments had shrunk out of musket range and several refused to re-enter regardless of how much they were goaded by their officers. Several did advance again but individual soldiers edged away so that a regiment "stood forty to eighty men deep" with paths through the ranks every two or three yards and was thus completely vulnerable to infantry, if only the Prussian cavalry had not been previously driven from the field.[40] At Leuthen where the confusion was even greater, the battalions formed on even greater depth. According to the Prince de Ligne, "Behind the windmills they are a hundred men deep."[41]

This leads to two last comments about the dynamics of the usual infantry assault against an enemy infantry position in clear terrain. First, though troops on both sides would often unwisely start firing at 70 to 80 paces, before the enemy was within an effective range (for this period), many conflicts were still resolved at a 20 to 40 pace range. Secondly, the theory for both attack and defense was predicated on the assumption that friendly troops would only be able to get off one effective volley.

Both of these characteristics differ from those occurring fifty years later, during the Seven Years' War, where murderous fires would occur at the 40 to 60 pace range and given the new higher level of training, commanders felt confident that their men would be able to deliver several volleys during an engagement, especially when they were defending. This did not mean that the French *à prest* or Swedish "go on" attack was abandoned. In fact, we find these principles to be the basis of a major tactical philosophy that continued down until the end of the Napoleonic Wars. In 1799, we find Suvorov advocating the use of the "through attack," where the enemy's fire is ignored and the troops attempt to close to cold steel. At the same time, this offensive philosophy is at the heart of "deep order" tactics that would be developed after the War of the Spanish

Succession by the Chevalier de Folard, Mesnil-Durand, etc. In a sense, it is also the basis for the columnar attacks often used by the French during the Revolutionary and Napoleonic Wars.

NOTES

1. de Saxe, Maurice, *Reveries on the Art of War.* Translated by Thomas R. Phillips. Harrisburg, Pa., 1944, pp. 34–35.
2. Longueville, *op. cit.,* p. 70.
3. Quincy, *op. cit.,* vol. 7, p. 60.
4. Ibid., vol. 7, pp. 67–68.
5. Colin, *op. cit.,* p. 25.
6. Puységur, *op. cit.,* vol. 1, p. 151.
7. Hatton, R. H., *History of Charles XII.* London, 1968, pp. 116.
8. Belhomme, p. 306; Quincy p. 65.
9. Quincy, *op. cit.,* vol. 7, p. 60.
10. Belhomme, vol. 2, p. 320; Quincy, pp. 66–67.
11. Ibid., vol. 2, p. 306.
12. *Essai sur L'influence de la poudre à canon.* Mauvillon, Leipzig, 1788, cited in Colin, *op. cit.,* p. 35.
13. Quincy, *op. cit.,* vol. 7, pp. 66–67.
14. Quincy, *op. cit.,* vol. 7, pp. 66–68; Puységur, *op. cit.,* vol. 1, p. 151; Belhomme, vol. 2, p. 308.
15. Quincy, *op. cit.,* vol. 7, p. 67.
16. cited in Colin, *op. cit.,* p. 25.
17. de Saxe, *op. cit.,* p. 33.
18. Quincy, *op. cit.,* vol. 7, p. 67.
19. Puységur, *op. cit.,* vol. 1, p. 153.
20. de la Colonie, *op. cit.,* p. 13.
21. Hatton, *op. cit.,* pp. 115–116.
22. de Saxe, *op. cit.,* pp. 43–44.
23. cited in Le Blond, *op. cit.,* p. 416–417.
24. Kane, *op. cit.,* pp. 113–120.
25. Chandler, Robert Parker, *op. cit.,* p. 89.
26. Taylor, Frank, *The Wars of Marlborough 1702–1709.* 2 volumes, Oxford, 1921., vol. 1, p. 216.
27. Duffy, Christopher, *The Army of Maria Theresa.* New York, 1977, p. 79.
28. de la Colonie, *op. cit.,* pp. 184–185.

29. Puységur, *op. cit.,* vol. 1, p. 152.

30. de Saxe, *op. cit.,* pp. 31–32.

31. Colin, *op. cit.,* p. 54, citing Bombelles, *Traité des evolutions militaires.* Paris, 1754.

32. Puységur, *op. cit.,* vol. 1, p. 152.

33. de Saxe, *op. cit.,* pp. 31–33.

34. Carlyle, Thomas, *History of Frederick the Great,* 6 volumes. New York, 1872, Vol 5, p. 203.

35. Puységur, *op. cit.,* vol. 1, p. 72.

36. Ibid., vol. 1, p. 152.

37. Ibid., vol. 1, p. 152.

38. Ibid., vol 1, pp. 72–75.

39. Fortesque, Sir J. W., *A History of the British Army,* vol. 1. London, 1899, vol. 1, book 5, p. 364.

40. Carlyle, *op. cit.,* vol. 3, p. 245.

41. Ibid., vol. 5, p. 203 citing Prince de Ligne's Diary, vol. 1, p. 63.

CHAPTER 7

Cavalry Tactics: 1690–1720

DURING THE THIRTY YEARS' WAR, THE SWEDISH CAVALRY STOPPED USING the caracole tactics that had been popular since the second half of the sixteenth century. Gustavus Adolphus, influenced by his contact with Polish cavalry, who still attacked with the lance, reintroduced shock tactics to Western European cavalry. The Swedish cavalrymen now would fire their pistols and then close with the enemy, charging at the gallop with outstretched sword.

After the Thirty Years War, possibly because much of the fighting was against the Turks, against whom continued order was a vital necessity, Swedish cavalry tactics began to be slightly modified as they were adopted by other armies. Although many German armies discontinued the use of the caracole, the charge against enemy cavalry was conducted with more control, and less abandon. At the same time, the cavalry would usually fire their pistols before closing in with the sword.

Puységur in his *Art de la guerre* provides us with an excellent description of German cavalry charge tactics during the War of the Spanish Succession, as he witnessed first hand on one memorable occasion. The German cavalry force awaited the French advance, swords hanging from their wrists and their musketoons hanging from their bandoliers. The French advanced, building up to a fast trot, all the while sword in hand. The troopers in the opposing squadron maintained perfect composure until the French had advanced to about 50 feet (eight *toises*) and then both officers and men, using only their right hands, grabbed their musketoons, took aim, and then fired at will. This fire was aimed or "voluntary" fire, as opposed to volley fire. Volley fire was, by definition, unaimed, since the men were compelled to fire at an exact moment rather than when they had an adversary "in their sights," so to speak.

As soon as each trooper had discharged his firearm, he dropped it, and grasped the sword hanging from his right wrist, and then waited for the French cavalry to close in. When properly performed by resolute troops, this tactic could inflict considerable casualties among the first rank of the attackers, as was the case on this particular occasion.[1] However, even some of the officers who accepted this tactic admitted that it had one potential weakness. If the defender's files were not completely ordered and well closed, the defending line would fold. The men could not help but see the enemy quickly approach while they were standing still, and the men in the end files would often flee in the final moments. If the ranks were not sufficiently compact others would follow and the line would be overthrown.[2]

From our modern vantage point, we tend to view the use of firearms when fighting enemy cavalry as a feeble tactic, one that would invariably lead to the destruction of those using it. We have this view because we are aware of the cavalry developments that would lead to the defeat of the French cavalry employing these tactics by the Allied horse at Blenheim, not to mention those that later would allow Frederick the Great of Prussia to create the finest cavalry of the entire epoch. Be that as it may, the tactic of firing at an enemy before charging was a competitive one, at least up until the outbreak of the War of the Spanish Succession.

To understand this, we must remember that this was before charges were conducted at the gallop. The enemy would advance at a normal or even a slow trot; at the very fastest, at a quick trot. These advances lacked both the physical and psychological impact of the later charges made at full speed, and it was far easier to succeed in getting man and horse to await the moment of impact. Also, because each squadron in an advance was separated from its neighbor by 50 to 60 paces, there was a greater tendency for individual troopers to fan out in the final moments before the collision, thus softening the impact of the oncoming horsemen.

The rationale was that even if the defending forces stood still, the enemy would be checked by the falling horses and men in the first rank who were unfortunate enough to be hit by the fire. Those in the French army that advocated this tactic felt that it promoted individual combat, something the French cavalry eagerly looked forward to.

The inherent problems of firing during the advance arose out of the nature of the carbine carried by the cavalryman of the period. Loaded, the carbine or pistol carried a single shot, and to reload the cavalryman had to stop. It was an inaccurate weapon, even compared to the musket of the time, which itself was highly inaccurate. The trooper had to advance very close to the enemy at whom he wished to fire, and he then had to slow down to a walk to have any chance of having the musket ball travel in the intended direction. To give an idea of the practicable range of the carbine fired by mounted troops, in 1672 a treatise recommended the carbine be fired at a range of 12 feet.[3] And, of course, the accuracy was even less if the cavalrymen were equipped only with pistols. Also, ever since the first ineffective trials at the beginning of the sixteenth century by *arquebusiers à cheval* (horsemen carrying matchlocks), the use of firearms by men mounted on horseback had always appeared to be intrinsically at odds with equestrian imperatives. Unlike infantrymen, who could deliver volleys by two, three, and possibly four ranks simultaneously, a squadron could only deliver fire by its first rank.

Moreover, the very process of firing seemed to disorder the squadron. If the carbines were fired too early, the resulting dense smoke would confuse the cavalry, and make it easier for the enemy to start to outmaneuver them.[4]

In any squadron there always seemed to be three or four skittish horses; merely cocking the carbines tended to throw some in confusion, making it extremely difficult for the trooper to present his piece and take any sort of accurate aim.[5] This became much more of a problem as the campaign progressed, since the use of an ever increasing number of remounts became necessary. These remounts were not always as well trained as the troop's original horse and more inclined to be gun-shy.

Cavalry engagements, where the attack or defensive relied upon firearms, sometimes were lost because of the confusion caused by a single new horse.[6]

The appropriateness of cavalry using small arms was eventually challenged by the English and Dutch during the War of the Spanish Succession, and even more by Charles XII of Sweden during the Great Northern War (1700–1721), who discovered that the morale benefit gained by the adoption of a tight formation in motion more than offset the few casualties suffered if the enemy cavalry slowed down or stopped to fire their firearms.

This is why a cavalry regiment relying upon firearm tactics at the last moment almost invariably was defeated by a cavalry regiment using vigorous shock tactics. Cavalry using the carbine or pistol had to slow down immediately prior to making contact with the enemy. This meant that the regiment advancing at the brisk trot met the enemy moving at a relatively fast pace, while their opponents were virtually standing still. The few casualties caused by the carbine or pistol fire were not sufficient to compensate for this loss of momentum and resulting loss of morale.

It must be emphasized that during this period whenever troops were to retain their order they could only advance at the quick trot, at the very fastest. Whenever we hear of charges being delivered at the gallop in the pre-1743 period, it is almost certain that these were delivered without any semblance of order. By the time the troopers reached the enemy, the charge would be simply a collection of individual cavalrymen hitting the enemy line at slightly different times. This type of attack was sometimes referred to as *à la hussard,* i.e., after hussars' fashion, and was usually reserved by ordered cavalry for those situations where the enemy was already broken, such as when Lord John Hay's Dragoons (the "Scots Greys") charged two battalions of the Le Roi (King's) regiment on the French left at Ramillies as the remnants of the French army started to make its way off of the field. At this point in the battle, all of the English cavalry trying to run down fleeing French fugitives conducted all of their charges at the gallop. This, however, was because they ceased to meet any organized opposition.[7]

The description provided by Colonel Mack (General Mack of Ulm infamy) about the Austrian cavalry's charge capabilities in 1769 certainly applies to any cavalry prior to 1744, when the Prussians lengthened their charge at a gallop to 200 paces. No squadron could maintain its dressing after charging 50 paces at the gallop. By this point, 25 per cent of the horses in the front rank would have loosened themselves from the first rank by breaking out in front.[8]

To execute a charge at the fastest possible speed, i.e., at the fastest speed of the slowest horses in the line, with the files pressed close together, "knee to knee," was an extremely difficult feat, one that was essentially impossible until the training reforms introduced by Frederick during the early 1740's.

The difficulty was not in having the cavalry advance at the gallop. As Lieutenant Colonel Maude has pointed out:

> "Any man might mass a horde of mounted individuals and let them loose at racing pace in the direction of the enemy, and the thing has often been done, but ages of experience had shown that even a hundred yards was always sufficient to destroy all cohesion, and the mass invariably degenerated into a horde of individuals whose impact, when it ensued, produced no more effect on the densely packed body of cuirassiers riding in truth knee to knee, and whether at a walk or trot, than a charge of case against a modern ironclad."[9]

Up until the mid-eighteenth century, horsemanship was seen as a means of gaining the advantage in individual combat, which in armies such as the French was viewed as the object of any cavalry engagement. Reliance upon a charge in good order conducted at the trot imparted several interesting features to the average charge. The first and most important was that there was a very good chance that the two groups of opposing cavalry would actually meet. When this occurred, one of two things usually happened. The cavalry action would be reduced to a number of individual combats, where each contest was settled by the combatant's horsemanship and his ability with his sword.

De la Colonie, for example, mentions that at the affair of Heyzempirne (March 3rd, 1703) the cavalry action was a stubborn one with victory hanging in the balance for a long time. He then provides us with a lengthier description of a similar situation at Schmidmidel (1703). Here, the Bavarians started to advance as soon as the enemy cavalry set into motion, making certain they were moving at the moment of contact:

> "The fury of both sides was so great that the collision was violent in the extreme, and we remained locked together in the confusion of the melee for some considerable time."[10]

The other event that often occurred when the opposing cavalry forces met was that they "threaded" one another, referring to when the two groups of horsemen would pass through each other's formation and come out on the other side. Often, after passing through they would continue forward until either they were overthrown by ordered enemy in the next line, or fresh squadrons of friendly horse came up to support them. Obviously, this "threading" happened when both groups maintained the trot even at the last moments and were unable to slow down for individual combat.[11] We know from De la Colonie that this is what happened to at least a portion of the cavalry at Schmidmidel:

> "The cavalry on both sides, after having driven its way through the opposing forces, whilst their infantry were still engaged, retired, re-formed, and actually met once again in the charge; but after a long and hard fight each side retired for a second time to their own part of the field, both losing a great number of men. . . . I lost the horse I rode during the fight; he died that day from saber cuts to the head—steel is more murderous than fire in these cavalry fights, though the iron framework in my hat saved me once again from many hard blows."[12]

One last important point about "threading." As nineteenth-century cavalry authorities later pointed out, it could never occur if either one of the opposing forces had remained "knee to knee" at or immediately before the moment of contact. Later in the century, when it became possible, as a result of new training techniques, to conduct a knee to knee charge at the gallop, "threading" became increasingly less frequent. Invariably, one side or the other, faced with a wall of fast-moving horses, would now break prior to contact.

In this period, maneuvering during the course of the battle was not completely unknown, but it tended to take the form of shifting cavalry units from one part of the battlefield to another, as was the case at Ramillies when Marlborough ordered reinforcements to be shifted from the Allies' right to the other side of the battle to aid the Dutch regiments of horse which were locked in fierce combat with the French and Bavarian cavalry under the command of General Guiscard. In almost all of these cases, the cavalry regiment was withdrawn from its place in the battle order and moved behind the friendly lines and reinserted at some other position in the battle order. Once the cavalry was deployed with enemy cavalry more or less to its front, it would ultimately advance directly to engage the enemy. In this respect, the actions of the two opposing regiments was reminiscent of two knights at a medieval joust: the two regiments almost invariably moved toward each other in a straight line. Except for English cavalry under Marlborough, it was uncommon to find a cavalry regiment maneuvering against an enemy cavalry regiment to gain a local tactical advantage offered by a rear or flank attack.

FRENCH CAVALRY

During this period the French cavalry did not universally adhere to a single body of cavalry doctrine. Unlike fifty or sixty years later, an official regulation governing charge doctrine did not exist. The exact manner in which a cavalry or dragoon regiment approached the enemy and then conducted its combat varied from regiment to regiment, and could be influenced by the commander-in-chief of the army, or even the King. The colonel of each regiment was free to decide how his troopers were trained and, when that regiment acted independently, what type of tactics they would use in the field. As a result, there is not the same consistency of doctrine as found among the English cavalry during the same period.

The decision to attack the enemy, or receive it in their original position, if there were squadrons from more than a single regiment in line, was usually a grand tactical one, made by the "general of cavalry" or a lieutenant general. This meant that the squadrons in the same line would all move to the attack or all await the enemy's advance together, and the tactics that would be used in a particular situation were governed by the overall grand tactical instructions of the commander-in-chief or lieutenant general commanding that body of cavalry. The commander of the French/Bavarian cavalry drawn up between the villages of Ramillies and Taviers, for example, was ordered by Villeroi not to advance toward the enemy until the enemy cavalry was first enfiladed by friendly artillery in Ramillies. This, in effect, meant it was strait-jacketed, and had to wait for the enemy to come to it, in order to fulfill the standing orders. When it was finally attacked, the French/Bavarian cavalry barely had time to set itself into motion to avoid being caught at a disadvantage.

We know from Puységur that French cavalry upon occasion were using the caracole as late as 1672. After this date, the French cavalry developed a more aggressive quality, and enjoyed their greatest successes when they attacked at speed, sword in hand. Though these charges were furious, little attention was paid to the order of the formation after the horses were made to advance at a fast trot. These successes notwithstanding, the French cavalry charge tactics underwent a transformation between 1690 and 1695. An increasing number of French officers began to be impressed with the German method of receiving a cavalry attack, that is, firing the pistol at the last moment before coming in contact with the enemy horse. These officers believed that the cavalry should either stand still and fire at the last moment before the enemy contacted them or they should advance and fire when close, before charging in with cold steel.

This view gradually came into vogue at the French court, and during the 1690's we see a number of examples of official acceptance of the new tactics. For many years each company within a cavalry regiment included two "carabiniers." They would be positioned at the head of the squadron during combat and would fire at the enemy while still at long range. However, late in 1690 the King ordered that a separate company of carabiniers be formed in every regiment. The next year, the cavalry regiments being up to "book" strength, the King ordered the carabinier companies withdrawn from the individual regiments to form a "carabinier brigade." The King responded to his officers complaints that they could hardly recognize its men, given the number of different uniforms worn in the brigade, and the corps was transformed into a permanent regiment with its own colors, known as the Royal Carabiniers. Obviously, when fighting on the battlefield, its men relied primarily on the weapon after which they were named.[13] These firearm tactics were not confined to the Royal Carabiniers. In 1695, during the siege of Namur, Louis XIV ordered that his cavalry should use their firearms during the final moments of the charge.[14]

By the advent of the War of the Spanish Succession, senior French cavalry officers appear to have been split between the two major cavalry philosophies. Traces of this dispute, which continued into the 1740's, are found to be in Puységur's work, and the French cavalry used both tactics on the battlefield.

One of the most notable cavalry failures occurred at Blenheim, when eight squadrons of the Gendarmerie attempted to overthrow five squadrons of English horse that had just crossed the Nebel in order to reinforce Cutts' force which was busy attacking the village of Blindheim. The eight French squadrons enjoyed both the advantage of numbers, and the advantage of position. Having the greater front, they were likely to outflank their opponents. The English were still reorganizing after a difficult crossing and were downslope.

The eight squadrons of Gendarmerie initially advanced as if they were going to charge the English; however, to the latter's astonishment, they halted when they advanced to within pistol range and discharged a feeble volley. This was noticeably ineffective and, worse, still interfered with the momentum of the charge, nullifying any advantage derived from the slope. Palmes and Sybourg, commanding the English squadrons, reorganized their troops and commanded the squadrons on either wing to fan out and attack the Gendarmerie on the flank. The center three squadrons charged straight forward and the Gendarmerie recoiled and were totally routed. Much has been made of this type of failure, and the French cavalry of the time is often depicted as fighting in this fashion, and always encountering similar results. Though this incident probably represents the nadir of French cavalry achievement during the entire 1670 to 1748 period, most other French cavalry actions, though often ending in failure, were better conducted and utilized more realistic tactics.

We don't even have to leave the Battle of Blenheim to see this. During the last moments of the cavalry action, most of Tallard's cavalry, seeing the onslaught of the massive amount of Allied cavalry advancing together in two lines, hastily fired one volley at a very distant range and precipitously fled from the field. Because of this, there has been a tendency to equate the first actions of the French cavalry that day, i.e., the Gendarmerie's ignominious charge, with the last. However, separating these two incidents were a number of other cavalry actions, which unfortunately have not been handed down to posterity with the same degree of detail, partially because of inconclusiveness, and partially because the English at times had the worst of it. The first line of Tallard's cavalry (to the left Blindheim village) had been engaged a number of times prior to the final Allied cavalry assault. The Marquis de la Vallière, whose regiment was in the center of the first French line, claims to have repulsed seven Allied attacks.[15] Regardless of how many there actually were, at least one was ridden home since the Marquis received several saber wounds on the head.

This tells us that these Allied troops were slashing with their swords rather than thrusting. Also, since it is improbable that at this stage of the battle the Marquis was wounded while fleeing, both sides either moved to contact or "threaded" one another and the French retained their position after the charge. Trevelyan, a twentieth-century historian, attributes the slow but sure Allied cavalry success at this stage of the battle (as the Allies were crossing the Nebel above Blenheim) not to a noticeable inequality of cavalry tactics, but instead to Marlborough's clever use of infantry to closely support his cavalry at critical moments.[16] The French cavalry even when successful were forced to ride into formed infantry battalions whose fire inevitably turned them back.

One other observation is necessary concerning the French cavalry's performance at Blenheim. As much as one-third of Tallard's cavalry horses had been inflicted with glanders, and many of the troopers were probably riding on recently acquired remounts. These inexperienced horses were notorious for being skittish and gun-shy and had a tendency to flee at the outbreak of any nearby fire. Five or ten inexperienced remounts per squadron could have an enormous effect on how the entire formation would perform under fire.

The Battle of Ramillies provides additional evidence of a French cavalry determined to fight and overthrow their enemies. At the start of the battle there were 78 squadrons of French and Bavarian calvary opposing 48 Dutch and 24 Danish squadrons. The Danish squadrons quickly destroyed 14 squadrons of French dragoons, leaving the remainder of both forces to attack frontally. This charge (Dutch) and countercharge (French) was ridden home by both sides. The Dutch squadrons were drawn more closely together, while there were noticeably large spaces between the French squadrons. As a result, the Dutch were able to pass through these intervals and attack the French of the first line in the rear.

Nevertheless, the Maison du Roi constituting the first line succeeded in breaking through two lines of Dutch cavalry in places and were only stopped by the platoon firing of Dutch infantry judiciously placed by Marlborough in line at the rear of the cavalry. There is no evidence of firing from the saddle or of premature flight on the part of the French.

The ultimate discomfiture of the French and Bavarian cavalry in this portion of the field had more to do with grand tactical considerations than it did tactical deficiencies, or lack of performance. Marlborough, a commander greatly superior to Villeroi, was able to twice reinforce his cavalry in the later stages of this cavalry contest, giving his hard-pressed cavalry a tremendous advantage which they pressed home. After two hours of charging and counter charging, the French, now faced with an additional 39 Allied squadrons and the 24 Danish squadrons which had finally managed to change their face and attack the French cavalry's right flank, turned and fled. Regardless of the final outcome, this engagement shows greater determination and tactical dexterity than usually associated with the French cavalry when we think of them firing from the saddle.

An insight into the mechanics of French cavalry charge tactics is provided by Quincy's *Maxims et instructions sur l'art militaire*. When writing this work, Quincy set about describing the French army, its training and its tactics as they existed during the mid-1720's. These stemmed from experiences provided by the late war, i.e., the War of the Spanish Succession. According to his account, there usually were 20 "commanded" troopers on each wing (side) of the squadron. A squadron at its full establishment of 140 men had a frontage of approximately 46 files, being deployed in three ranks. The "commanded" men were positioned in the extreme six to seven files on each of the squadron's flanks. These "commanded" men were at the disposal of the squadron commander, to be used whenever he felt it appropriate. They had a number of responsibilities beyond those held by the ordinary horsemen in the center of the squadron, and in this sense, they were the mounted equivalent of infantry grenadiers.

Those "commanded" men that were deployed along the first rank held their musketoons high as the squadron approached the enemy. They were allowed to fire during the charge; this was voluntary aimed fire where each soldier was instructed to aim at enemy officers. The remainder of the commanded men in the two rear ranks held their swords in their right hand, their musketoons hanging from their bandoliers.[17] At the moment of contact, the commanded men were to follow a semi-circular course in order to attack the enemy squadron in its flank. The use of the commanded men in this last role would be practiced with great effect in a slightly different form by Prussian cavalry during the Seven Years' War.

These tactics, described by Quincy in 1724, were merely a formalization of tactics that had slowly evolved over the previous 150 years. In the late sixteenth century, the practice developed of grouping 50 or so *carabins,* as those cavalrymen armed with arquebus were then called, together in each company of *chevau léger* who, despite their name, were heavily armed and attacked the enemy using shock tactics. The *carabins* formed a small, narrow formation to the left of the squadron of the *chevau léger.* They would advance to within 200 paces of enemy lancers, or to within 100 paces of enemy cuirassiers, and then stop and caracole fire at this relatively long range. If the enemy itself was using firearms they were to skirmish and prevent them from firing on *chevau léger,* who would use this time to charge the enemy.[18]

This practice continued to be used in a modified form throughout the seventeenth century, even after the *carabins* disappeared around 1660. Now, instead of a company of *carabins,* the piquet served in a similar role, riding at the side of the squadron, using their firearms to harass the enemy while the main body of the squadron advanced to attack the enemy, sword in hand.[19] The tactics described by Quincy are obviously an offshoot of this tradition.

RESURGENCE OF COLD STEEL TACTICS

During this period the French and the various armies of the German-speaking world placed an increasing reliance upon the use of firearms during a cavalry assault. However, a reaction to these dilatory techniques that would have a great impact on future cavalry developments was about to get underway in England under the leadership of the Duke of Marlborough, and in Sweden under its extremely aggressive young monarch, Charles XII.

Under Marlborough, much of the Allied cavalry was revitalized. Tremendous attention was given to the quality of horses selected, and to maintaining their condition throughout the campaign. Crisp offensive tactics emerged. The use of firearms during an assault was expressly forbidden. Kane recalled that the Duke allowed the English cavalry only three charges of powder and ball during an entire campaign, and these were only to be used when the horses were grazing. The English cavalry operated by tactical units formed from two squadrons drawn up in two lines, each three ranks deep. This assault was to be made at a fast trot so that the troopers in each rank could maintain order, and the troopers met the enemy sword in hand.[20] Initially, the British cavalry had no body armor, but in 1707 Marlborough gave his cavalry a cuirass in front.

Another feature of Marlborough's cavalry was its tactical reliance upon infantry for support. Conceptually, this was not new, the idea having been popularized by Gustavus at Breitenfeld more than seventy years earlier. However, Marlborough was given new incentive to try this tactic, by the adoption of the socket bayonet, which greatly increased the infantry's ability to repulse cavalry on open ground. During both the battles of Blenheim and Ramillies, the Allied cavalry was able to escape dangerous situations by falling back on a nearby infantry reserve which would invariably drive off the pursuing French cavalry with orderly and highly effective volleys of platoon fire. At Blenheim, as the Allied forces crossed the Nebel between Blindheim and Ober Glauheim and forced their way up the slope, the presence of Allied infantry very probably was the deciding factor. Once the cavalry crossed the stream, the infantry was placed as a reserve in its rear, with intervals between the battalions. These allowed the cavalry to retire through them when broken by the French cavalry. The pursuing French cavalry would then suffer the effects of the infantry's volleys and be forced back, bloodied quite a bit more than the Allies they were chasing.[21] A similar tactic stopped the Maison du Roi at Ramillies after it had broken through lines of Dutch cavalry on the French right. Obviously, this tactic contributed to the Allied cavalry success which effectively won both of these battles for Marlborough.

The rejection of the cavalry's use of firearms on the battlefield and employment of a fast, aggressive charge relying on the sword assumed an even more pronounced form in Sweden. Here, Charles XII was to have a lasting effect on the way European cavalry would fight in future wars. Although his efforts were first copied, in part, by the French and the Spanish, they would be most adroitly used by the Prussians under the tutelage of Frederick the Great who, using Charles' principles, would raise cavalry tactics to an as yet unknown height.

Scorning the effect of carbine or pistol fire during the charge, Charles XII was the first monarch to forbid his cavalry to use their firearms in battle. His cavalry, mostly dragoons, was to charge the enemy at full speed, and in order to be lighter, all personal defensive armor was forbidden. This Swedish monarch knew the pyschological effect of breakneck speed on his cavalry. In the words of a nineteenth-century officer:

> "More velocity of motion quickens the natural vivacity of mankind, which, often amounting to reckless fury and headlong enthusiasm leaves no time for thought or calculation of danger; that at such moments of madness, death loses its terrors and victory presents itself in dazzling colors to the soul of the wildly rushing warrior."[22]

At the conclusion of the fast-moving charge, the Swedish cavalry was to thrust at, rather than slash at, their opponents. Charles XII considered this important enough that the type of swords issued to the cavalry, straight, long and narrow, could only be used in the prescribed manner.[23] A slashing motion with a straight sword, as opposed to a slightly curved saber, has little effect.

A new formation was devised to facilitate the aggressive Swedish cavalry charge. Instead of advancing in straight lines, as was the universal practice in other Western European armies, the Swedish squadrons adopted an arrow-shaped formation. The cornet, the center-most man in the squadron, was slightly in front of the others. The men on each of his two flanks rode "knee behind knee," so that they would both be about six inches behind him. Each man along the "line" was arranged in the same manner, so that the entire squadron was placed in echelon to the left and the right of the cornet.[24] Although this formation could not be physically stronger than the more conventional line, it probably had a more devastating psychological impact on the opposing cavalry. Almost certainly there would be a tendency for the men in the middle of the enemy cavalry line, opposing this Swedish formation, to edge towards the flank. This would open up the enemy formation, cause disorder, and allow it to be more readily overthrown. The Swedish cavalry enjoyed a number of notable victories using these tactics, and were even successful in capturing several entrenchments and batteries.

LIGHT CAVALRY

In the last quarter of the seventeenth century light cavalry was introduced to Western Europe in the form of Hungarian hussars. These fought in an irregular fashion and at this point, though not of great use on the battlefield, were highly useful to conduct raids and generally wreak havoc on the enemy's operations throughout the campaign. The value of these hussars lay in the swiftness of their horses and the skill of the horseman who rode them. The Hungarians in these regiments were known for their hardiness and the fury with which they conducted their attacks. Like the Turks, on whom they modeled their fighting, they were expert swordsmen who cut up Western cavalry in seconds if ever given the opportunity of entering their ranks. Although they also carried firearms, these were usually reserved for long-range skirmishing to harass ordered enemy formations.

Regular cavalry had to be especially careful to maintain order at all times when faced with this type of enemy, and at no time was this more important than when conducting a retreat in their presence. When regular cavalry was foolish enough to make a sudden disorganized retreat, the hussars would immediately fall on all sides of the retiring troops, and would often be able to enter the ranks. If this happened the retreat would soon dissolve into a general rout.[25] Hussars were usually not able to make any type of impression against cuirassiers or other heavy cavalry that remained firm and resolved and retained their order. De la Colonie provides us with a vivid description of typical Hungarian hussar tactics when faced with regular cavalry:

> "The hussars are, properly speaking, nothing but bandits on horseback, who carry on an irregular warfare; it is impossible to fight them formally; for although they may when attacking present a solid front, the next moment they scatter themselves at full gallop, and at the very time when they might be thought to be entirely routed and dispersed, they will reappear, formed up as before."[26]

When the hussars were forced to disperse by enemy heavy cavalry, they would take shelter behind friendly line cavalry, if any were available in the vicinity. The hussars could not frontally assault heavier cavalry as long as that cavalry maintained its order and rode knee to knee. One frequent hussar tactic was to advance against heavy cavalry preceded by a number of men who scattered themselves along the enemy's front and skirmished at a distance while the remainder attempted to gradually work around the enemy's flanks into the rear.

The one advantage that light cavalry had over heavy was that they could turn and otherwise manage their horses more readily. If the opposing cavalry, harassed by the skirmishers in front and threatened by others to their flank, made a "false move" such as wheeling about, the hussars would throw themselves on the flanks and immediately attack.[27] The disordered cavalry, attacked on all sides, would find it difficult to reorder in the presence of a relentless enemy. The light cavalry had to move continuously and avoid the volley fire of the heavy cavalry which would stop and attempt to drive off the hussars with ordered fire. Competent light cavalry would make this very difficult and were able to cause a greater number of casualties with their aimed skirmish fire.[28]

General Grandmaison, a former lieutenant colonel in the Volontaires de Flandres, recounts how in a later war French cavalry was discomfited by aggressive hussars:

> "Our French cavalry, may remember, that in the affair of Troia, near Prague, the hussars suffered themselves to be killed, by pistol shots, in the midst of our ranks, while they were cutting to pieces, with their sabers, officers and men; and had it not been for the assistance given by our pickets of infantry, the cavalry of Mr. Broglio's (i.e., De Broglie) army, would have been beaten by the multitudes of Hungarians."[29]

Experience gradually demonstrated that the correct tactic was for the regular cavalry to attack them vigorously and not let them skirmish at a distance. As the hussars retired, part of the opposing cavalry was sent after them to prevent them from quickly reforming in that area. Of course, light cavalry was always able to escape the pursuit of the heavy cavalry, its horses being much faster.[30]

Although several regiments of hussars were formed in French service, in most Western European armies the duties that would later become the responsibility of light troops were conducted by the dragoons. The Spanish, British, and Dutch only employed several independent companies of Walloons. The Imperialists (forces of the Holy Roman Empire) did have a number of hussar regiments, but these appear to have been held in check by French and Bavarian dragoon regiments.[31]

Light cavalry was extremely useful in dogging the movements of heavy cavalry. They could do a lot of damage in a lengthy retreat of enemy regular cavalry unsupported by infantry. Following the enemy cavalry, they would inflict casualties with constant skirmishing, using aimed fire. As soon as the enemy cavalry would turn and approach them they would scatter, only to quickly reform and start annoying the enemy anew.

CAVALRY ATTACKING INFANTRY

The French were in greater agreement among themselves about how to use cavalry to attack enemy infantry than they were about how to attack other cavalry. The cavalry would advance, usually at the trot, toward their pedestrian opposition, and when they were within 20 to 30 paces they would fire their carbines. Next, they would quickly advance with their swords drawn and hope their horses would be able to enter between the various files of foot soldiers. The theory was that the carbine fire would succeed in causing sufficient casualties that some parts of the line would waver, thus momentarily disordering themselves and opening up some of the files. It was also hoped that the threat of the advancing cavalry would unnerve the enemy infantry and undermine their officers' control over them.[32] Often, as the cavalry neared, untrained or untried infantrymen would give in to their natural impulses and start to fire before being ordered to do so. When this happened, the infantry being attacked usually would find themselves without any reserve fire, the morale of the men in the ranks would give way, and the line would invariably start to waver. Even in situations where the infantry managed to maintain volley fire, often they would fire so rapidly that it had little effect.[33]

This is essentially what happened when the French Maison du Roi attacked the British infantry at the Battle of Dettingen (June 27th, 1743). The British infantry in the first line delivered their volley too soon, and the French cavalry, seeing the disorder, pressed home their attack, which resulted in portions of this line and the two behind it being repulsed and disordered. The French cavalry, confused with success, galloped up and down the parts that had remained firm. The fourth British line was unaffected, and was able to advance and deliver a devastating fire. This broke the Maison du Roi's charge, who now in tatters precipitously retired to its own lines: "Our front lines (the English infantry which was reforming) made lanes for them, terribly maltreating them with musketry on right and left as they galloped through."[34]

The experienced cavalry officer knew that the defending infantry would usually be able to cause numerous casualties among his assaulting force. However, it was a truism among cavalry officers that not all who were hit were disabled. In fact, many horses once hit, especially in the breast area, became furious and moved ahead in situations where otherwise they would have stopped. At the same time, if the cavalry were spirited, once the defenders had made their volley [infantrymen of this time often were only able to participate in one organized volley in the final moments against cavalry] and relieved that the greatest danger had passed, they would continue the attack with even more impetuosity than before.[35]

On the negative side, the experienced cavalry officer knew that a trifle could mean the difference between a success and failure. Several horses might be afraid of the enemy fire. This proved to be an even greater problem with remounts introduced during a campaign to replace others that had been killed. Other horses might demonstrate an unwillingness to step over carcasses of other horses. In either case, the resulting disorder was difficult to repair under fire and usually led to the failure of the attack.[36]

Let us now look at how an infantry battalion was to receive this attack. This was virtually the same in all armies whose men had adopted the flintlock equipped with the socket bayonet. When a battalion was faced with the prospect of being attacked by enemy cavalry, the spaces between the files were narrowed, so that there were two files to every three feet. Because the infantry was normally deployed in five ranks and the effective width of horseman and rider was also about three feet, this meant that each enemy horseman faced ten infantrymen, when attacking French infantry deployed in five ranks.

The infantryman's musket was about five feet long and the bayonet another foot and a half. Subtracting four inches for the overlap of the bayonet over the musket's barrel, the total length of a musket equipped with a bayonet was about six feet, two inches. If it is assumed the soldier's forward hand gripped the musket about 24 inches from the base of the stock, that would mean that a musket on the average extended about four feet beyond the soldier's reach. On the other hand, the cavalryman facing the outstretched bayonets was armed with a saber approximately three feet in length. This gave an infantryman an advantage of about one foot in extension.

Unfortunately not all of these infantrymen were able to participate in the defense simultaneously. For a start, the first two ranks usually knelt, in order that the rear ranks would be able to continue to fire. This meant that for the most part those with one of their knees on the ground were unable to effectively thrust their bayonets at the body of a horseman, given the height of the rider. At the same time, those in the rear ranks were similarly out of reach. The heel of the rear foot of a man in the fourth row was usually at least 30 inches behind that of the temporary file leader in the third rank (the men of the first ranks were kneeling). This meant that the point of his bayonet was 30 inches behind the file leader, and he couldn't effectively reach any horsemen unless the latter managed to enter the ranks.

Notwithstanding the fact that a rider primarily faced the bayonets from the men standing in the third rank, infantry armed with musket and bayonet most often were able to withstand a cavalry onslaught. For one thing, the bayonets belonging to the men in the first two ranks were far from useless, acting as a deterrent to the horses. It must be pointed out in this regard that horses, like men, do not willingly impale themselves on a row of pointy blades. And, if the men in the ranks stood firm, the bayonets every 18 inches or so were enough to thwart the horse, and if the horse was stopped, so was the rider.

The task of defending against cavalry was made considerably easier if the infantry was well trained. In this case, an economical but well-timed fire during the last moments of the enemy's advance would soon cause a "rampart" of fallen men and horses, obstructing those in the rear from passing. The fallen horses could not be easily pushed out of the way and served to turn the following horses. When this happened, the cavalry's attack usually failed, since success was based as much on the horse's wanting to advance as it was the rider's. The soldiers were advised to "fire in the nose" of any horse that still wanted to advance into the line of infantrymen.

The Battle of Fleurus (July 1st, 1690) provides an excellent example of what determined infantry could do against a numerically superior force of cavalry, even when supported by infantry:

> "for after they (the Dutch foot) were abandoned by the horse, they also sustained the charge of French cavalry and infantry, and being attacked in front, flank and rear, all at once, yet remained firm, unbroken, and impenetrable: they let the enemy's horse approach within pistol shot of them, and then discharged with such an unconcerned and steady aim, that the whole squadron together seemed to sink to the ground, scarce thirty of the whole squadron number escaping: and this course they so accustomed themselves to observe, that at length they laughed at the enemy. The French, on the other side were so confounded with the exactness done upon them, that they fled as soon as the Dutch began to present their muskets, now durst they any more come near them, but suffered them to retire in good order, without offering to pursue them."[37]

Puységur summed up the experienced infantry's advantage over cavalry: "If infantry understands its force, the cavalry never breaks it."[38] This remained true throughout the cavalry's career on the battlefield.

This is not to say that the results of cavalry attacking infantry were predictable. The outcome was as much the product of the training and the determination of the infantry receiving the attack. For example, a Swedish detachment of 200 infantry was able to resist the repeated efforts of Prussian dragoons at Plettenburg on open terrain during the War of the Austrian Succession. This even though the dragoons managed to saber several of the men in the ranks, and dragged one officer out of the ranks by grabbing onto his queue (styled long hair). At the end of the affair, the 200 infantry had killed and wounded 128 men.[39]

The War of the Polish Succession (1733–1738), on the other hand, provides an example of an opposite outcome. Monsieur Jacob, a partisan commanding several companies of light troops, captured 300 Austrian grenadiers who had managed to form square prior to the attack. His sudden appearance with only 80 dragoons and his reputation were sufficient to cause the Austrian force to surrender. Needless to say, the Austrian higher authorities were not amused with this incident and the Austrian commander was tried by courtmartial.[40]

NOTES

1. Puységur, *op. cit.*, vol. 1, pp. 120–121.
2. Ibid., vol. 1, p. 152.
3. Kemp, Anthony, *Weapons & Equipment of the Marlborough Wars*. Poole Dorset, 1980, p. 58.
4. General de Grandmaison, *On the Military Service of Light Troops in the Field and in Fortified Places*. Translated by Major Lewis Nicola. Philadelphia, 1777, p. 92.
5. Warnery, *op. cit.*, p. 16.
6. Grandmaison, *op. cit.*, p. 92.
7. Trevelyan, George Macaulay, *England Under Queen Anne*. 3 vols. London, 1932–34, vol. Ramillies, p. 116.
8. Maude, *op. cit.*, p. 124.
9. Ibid., p. 69.
10. de la Colonie, *op. cit.*, p. 138.
11. Maude, *op. cit.*, p. 150.
12. de la Colonie, *op. cit.*, p. 138.
13. Père Daniel, *op. cit.*, vol. 2, p. 244.

14. Warnery, *op. cit.,* p. 13.

15. Verney, Peter, *The Battle of Blenheim.* New York, 1976, p. 141.

16. Trevelyan, *op. cit.,* vol. Blenheim, p. 387.

17. Quincy, *op. cit.,* vol. 7, p. 64.

18. Père Daniel, *op. cit.,* vol. 1, p. 169.

19. Ibid., vol. 1, p. 244.

20. Chandler, *The Art of War, op. cit.,* p. 53.

21. Trevelyan, *op. cit.,* vol. Blenheim, p. 387.

22. Roemer, *op. cit.,* p. 328.

23. Warnery, *op. cit.,* p. 17.

24. Chandler, *The Art of War, op. cit.,* p. 57.

25. Grandmaison, *op. cit.,* pp. 89–90.

26. de la Colonie, *op. cit.,* p. 159.

27. Maude, *op. cit.,* p. 81.

28. Grandmaison, *op. cit.,* pp. 92–93.

29. Ibid., p. 90.

30. Ibid., pp. 89–92.

31. Ibid., p. 7–8.

32. Puységur, *op. cit.,* vol. 1, p. 152.

33. Grandmaison, *op. cit.,* p. 109.

34. Cited in Carlyle, *op. cit.,* vol. 3, p. 529.

35. Puységur, *op. cit.,* vol. 1, p. 152.

36. Grandmaison, *op. cit.,* p. 109.

37. "The Field of Mars: Being an Alphabetical Digestion of the Principal Naval and Military Engagements", 2 vols. London, 1781, vol. 1, "FLE".

38. Puységur, *op. cit.,* vol. 1, pp. 70–71.

39. Duane, William, "The System of Discipline and Manoeuvres of Infantry Forming the Bases of Modern Tactics", (For use by the National Guard and French Armies, 1805), contained in *The American Military Library of Compendium of the Modern Tactics Embracing the Discipline, Manoeuvres, & Duties of Every Species of Troops.* Philadelphia, 1809, vol. 2, pp. 49–50.

40. Grandmaison, *op. cit.,* pp. 107–108.

PART II

Evolution of Tactics and Grand Tactics *1714–1756*

Introduction

TACTICAL AND GRAND TACTICAL DEVELOPMENTS: POST–1714

IN THE YEARS FOLLOWING THE PEACE OF RYSWICK (1697), THERE WAS little or no evolution in official military training and doctrine in most of Western Europe. However, starting in the mid-1720's, several interesting theoretical developments, proffered by the likes of the Chevalier Folard and Maurice de Saxe in the French army, started to attract some attention.

Both Folard and De Saxe questioned the wisdom of accepting linear tactics as the only method of resolving combat in all situations. Both authors criticized linear tactics as being an inflexible system that generally reduced a battle to the conflict between opposing first lines, making it difficult, if not impossible, to introduce reserves into areas of critical importance. By always placing cavalry on both wings, the linear system also systematically worked against any type of close cavalry/infantry support; cavalry and infantry initially each fought its own separate battle. The Chevalier de Folard, advocated the use of heavy "columns of attack," interspersed along the line to break through the enemy line of infantry. These would advance without firing, and would overthrow the enemy with their "weight." De Saxe, in turn, believed a number of men from each battalion should serve as light troops and be deployed in front of the line to harass the enemy with aimed, as opposed to volley, fire. Both De Saxe and Folard sought various means of placing cavalry near the infantry lines to make cavalry support of infantry possible. However, these systems failed to gain either official recognition or practical application, and prior to 1750 had not succeeded in making any impact on the instructions and regulations governing French tactical doctrine and practices.

The 1740–1763 period is defined politically by Prussian efforts to become a major European power and its subsequent struggle for survival as the existing powers retaliated. From a military historical perspective, it is significant for two seemingly contradictory reasons. It was during this time that linear grand tactics, having crystallized during the Nine Years' War and the War of the Spanish Succession, was brought to its most sophisticated form by Frederick the Great. At the same time, in France, the seeds were being sown for a new grand tactical system, the "impulse" system, which would supplant the linear grand tactics by the turn of the next century.

With the outbreak of the next major round of hostilities in 1740, the armies of the major European powers intended to fight these new wars using virtually the same tactical and grand tactical systems developed by the end of the War of the Spanish Succession, more than 25 years earlier. The infantry in most armies continued to deploy in four ranks and, in theory, were to rely on the advance to contact without firing, while the cavalry's use of small arms fire prior to final contact was still acceptable in many armies. However, almost as soon as the war started, the evolutionary process recommenced. Faced with near-disaster at Mollwitz, Frederick was the first to effect changes, especially concerning the training and conduct of his cavalry. Recognizing that the value of cavalry was in the offensive, Frederick took a number of measures to revitalize Prussian cavalry tactics. The use of firearms by line cavalry was abandoned, and the charge at the gallop was introduced by gradual increases in the distance it had to gallop.

Even more fundamental than this was the increased emphasis that was placed on training, which ultimately produced riders capable enough to perform these increasingly complex tactics and maneuvers. The Prussian cavalry learned how to attack with large numbers of squadrons acting together in unison, and when necessary, to quickly perform maneuvers like a change in front or a rapid deployment into line from column in the presence of the enemy. The triumphant charge of the Bayreuth dragoons at Hohenfriedeberg conceptually had an enormous impact on Frederick, and in an effort to reproduce this type of effect at will, he started to secretly advocate cavalry "columns of attack." To protect the secrecy of this tactic, which he regarded as a state secret, he reserved its use for only those situations where a cavalry charge against infantry would settle the battle. The Prussian hussars also underwent a transformation. Originally light horse in the traditional sense, in the late 1740's under von Winterfeld, they started to adopt closed order practices on the battlefield.

The Prussian infantry had received effective training since Frederick William's time, and during the latter part of his reign the practice of marching in cadence had been introduced. During his son's reign (Frederick the Great), this innovation was to bear fruit and make possible a whole new spectrum of maneuvers and tactical capabilities, so that linear tactics would be brought to its final and most perfect form.

The foundation of this accomplishment lay with the emphasis placed on uniform discipline and practical versus ceremonial training in the Prussian army, without which none of Frederick's innovations would have been possible. These better-trained Prussian troops were able to deploy in tighter ranks and files, and were no longer forced to constantly change back and forth between open and closed ranks while marching or maneuvering. At the same time, their well-rehearsed platoon fire system, delivered the most effective fire then known to any army. Having also brought cadenced marching to a hitherto unknown level of excellence, Frederick was able to create a number of maneuvers that offered alternative methods of forming battle order to the lengthy processional methods then used throughout Europe. In fact, it was the Prussian infantry's ability to perform the basic maneuvers quickly and under pressure that allowed Frederick to employ his "march by lines" and "attack in echelons," which together would be known to posterity as the "oblique attack." Influenced by the example of Charles XII of Sweden and theoretical writers like the Chevalier de Folard, Frederick exhorted his infantry to withhold its fire during the advance and to charge the enemy with lowered bayonets. Despite his infantry's firepower, Frederick thus adhered to the predominant theory on how to conduct an infantry attack. Up until 1758, his men were instructed to advance on the enemy without firing. However, by then the general increase in infantry firepower, effected by the near-universal adoption of the iron ramrod, made this difficult. The best-trained troops by this point were able to fire up to five volleys per minute, if only for a short span of time. This compares with two rounds per minute earlier in the century.

The precision of the Prussian troops and their ability to consistently beat the larger Austrian army impressed the French military authorities, who started to introduce some Prussian practices in the years of peace prior to the start of the Seven Years' War. This was especially true during the 1749–50 period. Older French methods of delivering fire were finally abandoned, and platoon firing, very similar to the British version, was introduced along with a number of other new fire systems. Like the Prussians, the French started to augment the one or two traditional "evolutions" used to go into line and then back into column with a number of specialized maneuvers. However, during the next several years the French military authorities seemed to retreat from the new Prussian influence and began to officially accept many aspects of the teachings of tacticians such as De Saxe and Folard. It was during this period that the column of attack and the column of retreat were introduced. Moreover, the French repertoire of maneuvers developed during this period were not based on any Prussian models and represent a separate tradition.

Most of the other armies proved to be more conservative. Throughout the Wars of the Austrian Succession, the Austrians fought as they had earlier in the century. The cavalry advanced towards the enemy at a trot and fired their carbines before closing in with the sword. The infantry, like the Swedes and French during earlier wars, was expected to advance without firing and overthrow the enemy with the threat of the bayonet. In December 1744, following the Prussian initiative, the Austrian authorities introduced the iron ramrod into service. The only significant change in Austrian infantry tactics occurred in 1757 when the Austrian infantry started to be deployed in three rather than four ranks. Somewhat more reform was made in Austrian cavalry tactics. In 1751 the use of firearms during a charge was prohibited and during the last 20 or 30 paces the horses were to be brought to the gallop.

In the British army, the infantry use of platoon firing continued to be an intrinsic part of both offensive and defensive doctrine. Unlike the infantry in most other armies, the British were expected to stop and conduct a number of volleys during the advance, to weaken the enemy's will to hold his position. As in many other armies, the British cavalry was forced to respond to the new standard set by Frederick's cavalry. The charge at the trot was replaced by that concluding at a gallop.

CHAPTER 8

Theoretical Developments in the French Army: 1724–1732

THE HUMILIATING DEFEATS OF BLENHEIM, RAMILLIES, AND OUDENARDE made the more adventurous of the French officers challenge the existing traditions and search for new methods. A number of theoretical developments started to influence portions of the French officer class from the mid-1720's onward. These bodies of doctrine were "theoretical" in the sense that they represented the views and beliefs of individual officers, and in their purest forms never gained official sanction. This meant they were never tested on the parade ground or in the training camp, and were never exposed to the ultimate crucible, the battlefield, to anywhere near the same degree as an officially endorsed doctrine and tactical system. However, the impact these theoretical systems later had on tactics and grand tactics during the Seven Years' War, and to an even greater extent during the Napoleonic Wars, makes it important to understand them.

THE CHEVALIER DE FOLARD

An experienced, if eccentric, officer and a veteran of both the Nine Years' War and the War of the Spanish Succession, the Chevalier de Folard later served with the Swedish forces for several years (1717–1719). Influenced by the aggressive tactics of the Swedes, their legendary successes, and some of the novel formations they experimented with, Folard wrote several works during the 1720's that greatly influenced French military thought throughout the next forty years.

His first work, *Nouvelles découvertes sur la guerre,* was published in 1724. His major work was *Histoire de Polybe . . . avec un commentaire,* published three years later in 1727. Like most officers in the French army, Folard believed that during the attack the French infantry was to rely on the *arme blanche,* and not their firearms: "True valor consists not in combats which are made at a distance; but in shock and sudden attacks. That is the only road which brings us to victory."[1]

Unlike his contemporaries, who felt that the attack *à prest* should be conducted by battalions deployed in normal lines, Folard advocated the use of very large columns during the assault. Folard felt that there were a number of inherent weaknesses in linear tactics. Reliance upon lengthy lines of battalions made it difficult for each formation to move, even over clear terrain. The lack of depth of a battalion deployed on four or five ranks made it impossible for it to fight independently; it always had to have another formation beside it to cover its flanks. He also argued that this thinness also led to its being easily pierced or broken when confronted by a stronger enemy formation.

For Folard, "The true force of a corps lies in its weight; or in the depth of its files, in their union, in their pressing [together], and that of its ranks at sword's point. That weight renders the flanks strong, or almost as strong, as the front. By that method a battalion is to resist, to overthrow every battalion which does not fight on this principal . . . One ought to regard it as a maxim, that every battalion which attacks, ranged on a very great deal of depth and little front, although weaker, ought to overcome a stronger one ranged according to the ordinary method, although one extends beyond its wings."[2]

These large columns were to consist of from one to six battalions, each containing 400 fusiliers and 100 men carrying partisans. On open ground the front was to consist of from 20 to 30 files, though rough terrain could force a reduction in the depth and the front could be increased up to 60 files. The column's strength was seen as arising from physical hardness, itself the result of density of men. The column was intended to pierce the enemy formations. Consequently, the men were to be brought as close together as could be done without preventing them from marching or using their weapons.[3] There were to be no intervals between the various battalions forming the column. The hundred men carrying pikes or partisans were to be placed in the outer files to be able to defend against cavalry; the officers were to be positioned at the head and along the flanks of the column. The grenadier companies were to be stationed outside the column, at its rear or along its side.

As far as Folard was concerned, this column was superior to any formation, cavalry or infantry, the enemy was capable of throwing against it. It had nothing to fear from cavalry on its flanks, since every second soldier was armed with a pike or partisan, and the remainder had bayonets at the end of their muskets. At the same time, Folard argued that this mass was capable of offering the most effective musket fire, though exactly how this could be is not clear from his arguments.[4] If, on the other hand, this column was surrounded by enemy infantry it could split into two, along its length, and simultaneously attack the troops which had enveloped it.[5] The other major advantage Folard believed his formation possessed was increased mobility and maneuverability. Having a shorter frontage, Folard reasoned it could advance more quickly than battalions deployed in line. Also, being able to split up into its component parts, it could transform itself into other formations quickly or so Folard believed.

Folard devised a completely new grand tactical system within which his columns were to operate. In addition to disliking the traditional linear formations because of their lack of depth, he also criticized the lack of cooperative interaction between the cavalry and infantry. When cavalry was placed on both flanks, the battle tended to devolve into separate cavalry and infantry engagements. He observed that usually if one's cavalry was defeated, by default one's infantry was then forced to retreat and cede the day's contest. Linear tactics made it difficult to reinforce faltering troops with others already deployed in line. Any time one attempted to pull troops from the line to reinforce elsewhere, the enemy would foil these efforts by opening a local offensive, making withdrawal impossible.[6]

In Folard's system, the army was to be drawn up in the traditional two lines, separated by the usual 300 paces. However, to allow mutual support of the two arms, a cavalry brigade was alternated with an infantry brigade along each line. This was to insure that, whenever the enemy attacked, he encountered both infantry and cavalry acting in concert. In the second line, an infantry brigade was placed where a cavalry brigade had been placed in the first line, and vise versa. Each infantry battalion was deployed in eight ranks. However, the wings of the cavalry brigades as well as the center of each line were protected by columns of three or four battalions with a depth of 12 to 16 ranks.

> "The wings being so well flanked, they have nothing to fear even if the enemy outflanks them or envelops them with a great number of squadrons."[7]

It was especially important for the center to be reinforced, for it was here that Folard felt the battle was going to be won or lost. The squadrons in a cavalry brigade were each to be separated by platoons of 25 grenadiers. A reserve consisting of dragoon regiments was placed in a third line, and was divided into three groups, placed at the center and on the two flanks. Hussars were placed "interline," that is, between the two lines, on the flanks and at the center.[8]

When the battle started, the massive columns were to advance and rupture the enemy's line in several places. If a breech occurred, the column was to divide into two parts and roll up the enemy line. As the first line advanced, the grenadier platoons interlaced with the cavalry squadrons were to remain slightly behind the cavalry, and the moment the enemy was reached these were to rush on the flanks of the enemy and fire. Folard felt that even if the friendly cavalry advanced ahead, or worse, were defeated, the grenadier platoons were not endangered, being able to join the nearby infantry columns or retreat to the second line.[9] It is interesting to note that this doctrine presupposed that the cavalry would never advance toward the enemy at faster than a medium trot, since otherwise the grenadiers could not have kept up. The second line was to advance to assist the first line as soon as the action in front became lively; they were not to wait until the friendly troops wavered, which experience had invariably shown to be too late.

Whenever the infantry was forced to fire because rough terrain made closing upon the enemy difficult or impossible, the troops were to use platoon fire, which Folard recognized as superior to fire by ranks then used by French infantry.[10]

Because Folard was absolutely convinced that his heavy columns would defeat the enemy, he never really seriously considered how his formations would be able to deliver fire. To ward off this criticism, he claimed that the men along each edge of these formations would be able to converge their fire toward the same target. Considering the problems of command control, not to mention that every other man along these edges would be armed with a pike, this was a ridiculous claim, and merely shows that Folard never seriously analyzed the role of firepower in his system.

Folard, like most his French contemporaries, was aware of the importance of advances such as the adoption of the flintlock and the use of the bayonet. He did not fully appreciate the ultimate significance of the subtle changes that had occurred in tactics during the War of the Spanish Succession. His intermixing of cavalry and infantry along a line, for example, presupposes that the cavalry would fight as in the early 1690's, that there would be no effort to attack at a very quick trot. Similarly, Folard underestimated the advances that were being made in fire tactics. He recognized that the Dutch system of platoon firing was superior to any other known type, but he failed to realize that increased training would transform this superiority, which made itself felt occasionally in the early 1700's (as by the Royal Regiment of Ireland at Malplaquet), to a constant dominance as on the fields of Dettingen and Fontenoy, during the next series of major wars.

Though Folard's use of a concentrated mass of troops against an enemy line would later prove to be a fundamental element of "impulse" (i.e., "Napoleonic") grand tactics, the formations he advocated were excessively unwieldy. As was demonstrated repeatedly in training camps during the early 1750's, they could neither be formed nor moved easily.

MAURICE DE SAXE

Maurice de Saxe, one of the three hundred or so illegitimate children of King Augustus the Strong of Poland, entered French service in 1720. By the time he was twenty he had seen service with the Allies against the French, fought with his native Saxons against Charles XII and the Swedes, and served with the Imperial army in its great drive against the Turks.

Like the Chevalier de Folard, he was disillusioned with the existing system of French tactics. Late in 1732, De Saxe became ill and was forced to convalesce. Fascinated by the strange state of mind induced by fevers accompanying his illness, he decided to take advantage of this creative mood and write a short work about what he considered to be the ideal military system, if he was totally free to change the existing technology, doctrine, and social system upon which the existing military machine was founded.

It is unfortunate that many who read De Saxe's *Mes Reveries* are unaware of the circumstances under which the work was written, and take all of its proposals at face value, as though De Saxe seriously believed that these could implemented in European society as it existed. It is much more fair to compare *Mes Reveries* with Jules Verne's *20,000 Leagues under the Sea,* in that the work served to display a wide and varied array of novel ideas and inventions of a fertile and imaginative mind. And, as with Jules Verne's classic work, many of the ideas that appeared the most outlandish when the work was originally published, (breech-loading muskets, recruiting through conscription, etc.) did, in fact, come about at a much later time, as more sophisticated technology and social systems evolved.

De Saxe has often been criticized for his advocacy of a return to pikes, and the use of defensive armor. Because of these two tenets, there has been a tendency to lump De Saxe's ideas with those of Folard as all being part of the *ordre profond* school of thought. However, De Saxe and Folard's works represent two widely divergent bodies of thought, and by the time he wrote *Mes Reveries,* De Saxe was highly critical of Folard's use of massive columns, the most fundamental principle in the latter's military philosophy.

De Saxe's proposed system is an eclectic mixture of traditional and innovative elements. Ideas such as the reintroduction of pikes, fraising the battalion, and the adoption of a *de facto* checkerboard pattern by doubling the battalions appear to be anachronistic, harkening back to the warfare of his grandfather's time. On the other hand, many of his ideas represented the very latest developments among the French officer intelligentsia. The use of light troops to weaken the defender prior to the main attack is an example of this.

As far as the number of ranks in each battalion, De Saxe adhered to what by the early 1730's had become common practice in the French army, advocating the infantry in his "legions" be deployed in four ranks. When threatened with enemy contact, the formation could be "doubled" so that there would be eight ranks. This practice of "doubling" was also an existing tactic that had been occasionally used throughout the latter part of the seventeenth and early eighteenth century.

He was adamantly against deploying a battalion in less than four ranks, even in the name of increasing the battalion's fire effectiveness. His experience during the War of the Spanish Succession and later in the Turkish wars suggested that thinner formations were easily overthrown:

> "I have even known some to draw up their battalions in three deep, but misfortune has been the fate of those who have done it. Otherwise, I really believe (God forgive me) they would soon have formed them two deep, and not improbably in a single rank. For all my life I have heard it said that one should extend his order to outflank the enemy. What absurdity!"[11]

How the men in the ranks were to conduct themselves during combat, however, was quite original. Not only did De Saxe want to reintroduce the use of the pike, but he wanted to eliminate the need for any of the infantry to kneel, a practice that started to make its way into the French army during the War of the Spanish Succession. The men in the first two ranks would use their muskets from a standing position; those in the rear two ranks would be armed with a lightweight 13-foot pike. They would also each have a musket slung over their shoulders. De Saxe argued that this formation and the use of weapons offered two distinct advantages over existing ones. There being only two rows of men firing their muskets, there was no need to have a rank kneel. De Saxe's experience had been that once men were ordered to kneel, it was often very difficult to have them stand up again, since they felt safer while lower to the ground.[12]

When the battalion was close to the enemy the pikemen in the rear two ranks were to lower their pikes. These would protrude six or seven feet in front of the first rank and would allow the musketeers to aim their fire with greater confidence. The pikemen in turn, behind two ranks in the process of firing repeatedly, would be able to concentrate more of their attention on warding off any blows aimed at the front ranks. Presumably, this tactic would be used only in the final moments before the opposing groups of infantry closed, either when the French infantry fired their firearms just before charging the enemy close at hand, or before they themselves received the assault.

Once again De Saxe's ideas were taken from the pages of history. These arguments are identical to those provided by Puységur about those who had advocated "fraising the battalion" in the seventeenth century. In fact,

De Saxe's formation was nothing more than a "fraised battalion," with 50 per cent of the infantrymen carrying pikes![13]

At this point in his career, De Saxe also railed against existing grand tactics and disputed the usefulness of the extreme version of linear warfare that had come into use. He felt that these large continuous lines had a number of drawbacks. Marching was made more difficult since each battalion had to maintain its alignment with the rest of the line. This was always a difficult task, but in the days before cadence this was nearly impossible without frequent stoppages to reorder the troops. At the same time, the reliance upon these long lines made it difficult to maneuver the troops, since the emphasis was on maintaining this single large formation at all times.

At the beginning of a battle, the infantry were to be placed in the two traditional continuous lines, with the bulk of the cavalry on either flank. He accepted the ten-pace interval between battalions that had become common practice by the end of the War of the Spanish Succession. However, De Saxe proposed having the battalions in each line "double" (doubling the number of ranks, thus halving the number of files) before they began their attack. This would create a "checkerboard" formation, much like that which was often seen in the mid-seventeenth century. He argued that it was much easier to advance the battle line when the battalions were not crowded together, and it was also easier to maneuver the formations.[14]

De Saxe believed the use of a checkerboard pattern of battalions conferred another advantage: it more readily allowed individual battalions to be brought up from the second line or to withdraw battalions from the first.

He reasoned that the traditional method of using two continuous lines with an extensive *corps de reserve* was, in essence, placing a number of battalions in a row (from back to front). Experience had shown that a battalion in the first line, if repulsed and driven in complete disorder, would often plow into those in the second line when there were insufficient intervals along this latter line.

De Saxe, in agreement with Folard, argued that it was difficult and time-consuming to move a battalion from the second line into the first, if the one it was to replace was still in its original position. The problem was moving the two battalions around each other; the forward battalion first had to be moved clear of its initial position before the second could be moved in. Rarely would an enemy stand still long enough to permit this; all it had to do was to advance at a brisk pace to disrupt these attempts at maneuvering. The checkerboard pattern was seen as obviating both of these problems. The large intervals between the battalions in each line allowed the battalions to be easily maneuvered around another battalion, or in the case of defeat, to have the mass of fugitives run around the ordered formations.

De Saxe believed that this inability to maneuver individual battalions was an important deficiency in existing warfare, very often reducing an entire battle to the struggle of the two opposing first lines. An army which could replace played out formations could initiate localized counterattacks, and retaliate blow for blow. This army would not only enjoy an advantage in being able to reinforce critical areas, it would also have tremendous grand tactical flexibility.[15]

Not content with simply revitalizing an older system that had fallen into disuse, De Saxe added a number of new elements. Another weakness sometimes attributed to linear systems, as Folard had pointed out, was that it was extremely difficult for cavalry to support infantry, or for infantry to support cavalry. Placing the infantry in the center of each line meant the closest cavalry was often 400 to 500 paces away, and in the confusion of the battle unable to provide any assistance to all but the closest infantry units. According to the analysis provided in *Mes Reveries,* this undermined the confidence of the infantry. De Saxe felt that any infantryman who has "nothing behind him on which to retire or depend is (already) half beaten." This was based on his observation that often the second line would give ground while the first was still in the midst of a balanced struggle.[16]

This consideration had not been completely overlooked by commanders in previous times, and two ploys had been developed to attempt to address this potential problem. Some commanders had parcelled out cavalry along the front line, while others intermixed platoons of infantry among the cavalry on the flanks. Folard also advocated this system of intermixing cavalry and infantry along a line. As a result of experiences during the War of the Spanish Succession, both of these tactics came under scrutiny.

De Saxe argued that both of these ploys, which had been used by French and British alike during the late war, were errors. Placing infantry between the cavalry regiments on the flank created a number of problems. The presence of the infantry meant that there was necessarily less cavalry between two points than if there had only been cavalry. This meant that the cavalry now became dependent upon the support offered by the infantry beside them. If the cavalry charged ahead in front of the slower-moving infantry, they would be left with wide intervals between regiments and easily overthrown by the enemy cavalry. On the other hand, if the cavalry did advance they left the infantry behind, producing a similar situation for the infantry: each platoon was now separated from its next infantry neighbor by very wide intervals, formerly occupied by the cavalry. This tended to intimidate the infantry and their morale suffered as a result. In any case, if the friendly cavalry was defeated they were lost.

Mixing cavalry along the main body of infantry in the front line was just as bad, if not worse. This cavalry, like the infantry beside it, would be attacked by the enemy infantry. However, cavalry is much less capable of enduring an infantry attack standing still. Horses would be killed and much confusion would arise. If the cavalry stood still it would accomplish little, while if it retired, it would discourage the surrounding infantry.

Having the cavalry attack in this situation was most likely to prove even more problematic. If they charged and were repulsed, which was the most likely outcome of relatively small amounts of cavalry facing off against relatively fresh infantry, they had no where to retire without disordering their own infantry. It was completely unreasonable to expect when being pushed back that they would be able to return to their original positions in the line.[17]

The proposed solution provided in *Mes Reveries* was twofold. In addition to the large bodies of cavalry placed at the flank, there were to be "small bodies" of 70 cavalrymen 25 to 30 paces to the rear of the infantry. These could operate through the wide intervals between the infantry battalions when they were doubled. If the battalions were on a depth of four ranks, they would wait for either the opportunity to pursue the defeated enemy or attack the enemy infantry if the friendly infantry battalion in front of it started to recoil.

In order to protect the flanks of the infantry, several battalions were to be placed in squares between the first and second lines near the cavalry on each flank.[18] In addition to preventing enemy cavalry from entering between the lines, they were to bolster the morale of the infantry in the second line who De Saxe claimed:

> "will never fly so long as they see the square battalions in their front, and their appearance will also reassure that of the first line. The battalions will maintain their ground because they cannot do anything else, and because they hope for the prompt assistance from the cavalry, which, under the cover of their [the square battalion's] fire,

will reappear in an instant, wishing to retrieve the disgrace of their defeat."[19]

As far the dynamics of the actual attack were concerned, de Saxe combined the traditional French method of the *à prest* assault (the "go through" attack), where the infantry was to advance on the enemy without firing, with the theory about the use of light troops on the battlefield being experimented with at various French training camps in the late 1720's.

Prior to the beginning of an advance against the enemy, light infantry, which he called "light-armed foot," were to be dispersed along the entire front. Each battalion provided 70 light troops for this purpose. Once again, this was not a novel idea, for at least five years a number of officers in the French army had been arguing that the men in the "piquet" be used for exactly this purpose.

These light troops were to position themselves about 100, 150 or 200 paces in front of their battalion, and were to be accompanied by the *amusette* (a breech-loading light cannon) assigned to each battalion. They were to start firing when they were within 300 paces of the enemy infantry. This fire was to be aimed fire, where the individual fired at will without being directed by commands. This fire was to continue until the enemy was 50 paces distant, at which point the captain leading each group would order a retreat. The light troops would continue firing "from time to time" as they withdrew until they reached their battalion, whereupon they would pass it, in groups of ten, using the intervals separating each battalion from its neighbor.

The line of friendly infantry was to have started to move forward before the light troops withdrew behind it. Each battalion was now to double its ranks on the move, and was followed by two troops of cavalry assigned to it.[20] The author of *Mes Reveries* felt that the fire provided by the "voluntary fire" of the light troops would be more effective than anything that could be dished out by the line troops using "volley fire." Unconstrained by orders or cramped formations, they should be able to fire at least four times a minute, and each shot would be equal to "ten from any other." The light troops which started firing at 300 paces had at least eight minutes to soften the enemy.[21]

Although line troops were to be discouraged from firing while attacking in the open plain, De Saxe, like most other French officers (Puységur, De Quincy, etc.) felt firefights were necessary when the two combatants could not come to grips because of broken terrain, such as hedges, ditches, and rivers, as well as when defending against cavalry.[22] Here, once again De Saxe was against the use of volley fire, which he felt was ineffective under any conditions. As in the case of light infantry, he advocated the use of aimed fire.

The fire procedure to be used was as follows. An officer or subaltern was to be in charge of every two files. The first file under each was to advance one pace, and the officer directed the file leader where to aim his fire. He then calmly aimed at that target and fired at will. As soon as he fired, the second soldier in that file handed him his musket and he aimed and fired again. He was to continue this procedure until he had fired all four muskets belonging to the men in that file. The officer supervised his shots, exhorting him to quicken his pace if he delayed. De Saxe felt this type of firing was far more accurate than unaimed volley fire, and claimed, "it would be unusual if the second or third shot does not reach its mark."[23]

At this point, the officer or subaltern ordered the next file to step forward and the same process was repeated. The men in the first file returned to their original position and started to reload.

When it came to the cavalry arm, De Saxe believed that it should be organized into two types: light cavalry and dragoons. The term "light cavalry" is very misleading here. It has to be remembered that at this time the cuirassiers were still being classed as *cavalerie légère,* that is, light cavalry. This was because the true cavalry, the Gendarmerie and the Maison du Roi, had been equipped with three-quarter armor until late in the previous century, so the cuirassiers protected by only breastplates were "light cavalry" by comparison. De Saxe felt that the discontinuance of personal armor had been a mistake and his light cavalry should be completely covered with light armor. They were to have carbines and swords four feet long with triangular-shaped blades. Obviously, cavalrymen were to use these to stab, rather than slash, their opponents. They were not to be provided with pistols.[24]

Like Gustavus Adolphus, Maurice De Saxe had witnessed the capabilities of the Polish cavalry and was also duly impressed. The Poles, unlike the Western Europeans, never discarded the lance. This weapon can be compared to the English longbow in that it fell out of disfavor, not because it was made obsolete by more effective weapons, but because of social changes which militated against the continual use necessary for its mastery. The cavalry was to deploy in the existing French fashion, that is in three ranks. In the best of all possible worlds, De Saxe would have armed the front rank of his regular cavalry with lances. These would have stuck ten feet in front of the horsemen and if handled by competent lancers, would have proven very difficult for enemy cavalry to resist.[25]

Regarding tactics cavalry were to use on the charge, De Saxe's ideas appear to have been loosely inspired by those used by the English and Swedes during the last war. They were not to fire at the enemy cavalry being charged, instead they were to drive home the charge relying on cold steel. The school of cavalry tactics calling for the use of firearms was flatly rejected.[26] The advance was to begin at the "gentle trot" which was to continue for 100 paces; after this they were to increase their speed in proportion to the distance being advanced. The men were not to ride boot to boot, that is, in an extremely tight formation until the final moments of the charge, when they were 20 to 30 paces away from the enemy. At this point they would close, the commanding officer would yell, "Follow me!" and they would charge *a la sauvage*.[27]

De Saxe emphasized the need for the cavalrymen to stay together during the final moments, and not disperse, even if they succeeded in breaking the enemy. If victorious, the officers and standard bearers were to quickly rally the troops to be ready to accomplish their next goal.[28]

The dragoons, armed with musket and sword, were to fight in a similar fashion on the battlefield, though they were still to be trained in infantry duty in case they had to serve in that capacity in the *petite guerre,* i.e., the petty operations during the campaign.[29] One interesting difference between light cavalry and dragoons was that De Saxe envisioned the latter as being able to skirmish while mounted. The tactics he suggested were much like those that would be used much later by French *chasseurs à cheval* during the Napoleonic period. The rear rank was to disperse in front of the formation and skirmish, while the first two ranks remained ordered with their muskets slung.[30]

As far as artillery was concerned, de Saxe advocated the use of relatively lighter pieces than was currently the custom. He argued that 16-pounders were as effective as 24-pounders, and much less difficult to transport or maneuver. An army of ten legions, eight regiments of cavalry and 16 regiments of dragoons was to have fifty 16-pounders and ten mortars.[31]

Although he admitted he was initially "seduced" by Folard's proposed use of massive columns to attack the enemy, De Saxe soon rejected these heavy formations: "This idea seduced me at first; it looks dangerous to the enemy, *but the execution of it* reversed my opinion." Obviously, he or one of his fellow colonels had bothered to test Folard's formations on the parade ground!

He went on to observe that Folard's columns were the heaviest he knew of, and were invariably disordered, either by an unevenness of the ground, or simply through the act of marching. De Saxe attested that once one of these columns was disordered "no man alive can restore order," and the bulky formation was reduced to a mass of soldiers without ranks and without files and totally in confusion.[32]

CADENCE

Maurice de Saxe believed he had discovered the secret of a more efficacious use of tactics and maneuvers: "The foundation of training depends upon the legs and not the arms. All the mystery of maneuvers and combats is in the legs, and it is to the legs that we should apply ourselves." He was referring to the practice of cadenced marching, where each soldier stuck out the same foot at the same time. De Saxe observed that the Roman army used cadenced marching, and that this was the primary purpose of their military music. This capability, like many other accomplishments, was lost to posterity with the fall of the Roman Empire. At the time *Mes Reveries* was written in 1732, cadenced marching was not to be found in any major European army.

The ancient practice of providing military music was maintained, but it was only to keep the troops amused and boost their morale. Compared to the potential use of this music, De Saxe referred to its then current use as a "military ornament." However, this military music was absolutely essential for troops to march in cadence:

> "I have often noticed, while the drums were beating for the colors, that all the soldiers marched in cadence without intention and without realizing it. Nature and instinct did it for them."[33]

History has proven De Saxe's observations on the importance of cadenced marching to be absolutely correct. As he was writing these observations, Leopold of Anhalt-Dessau, was coming to a very similar conclusion. However, given Leopold's position within the hierarchy of the Prussian army, he was in a much better position to implement these ideas. As a result, the Prussians, apparently sometime during the 1730's, were the first major power to introduce the universal use of cadence marching on parade ground and battlefield. It was this advance that first allowed the Prussian infantry to be maintained at all times in close ranks, which, in turn, permitted a plethora of developments in maneuvers and tactics.

Folard, and later as he rose to preeminence, De Saxe, were to have a profound impact on French military thought. Folard's basic contribution was to question the total and unthinking acceptance of linear tactics in its purest form. He also reintroduced, albeit in a very primitive form, the notion that a lengthy line could be ruptured by a concentrated and powerful impulse. True, the form of impulse then suggested, very clumsy and massive columns of attack, was not feasible, and for a very long time tacticians focusing on the specifics of Folard's system missed the overall conceptual contribution. De Saxe also criticized linear tactics in its purest form and like Folard thought that battles could still be ultimately won with the threat of cold steel applied at the critical moment. However, unlike Folard, he truly valued firepower, when aimed and delivered by light troops dispersed in front of their battalion. Emphasis was placed on the need for reciprocal infantry/cavalry support with local cavalry reserves placed along the first and second lines.

The full impact of Folard's and De Saxe's ideas only manifested itself, at least officially, after the Peace of Aix-la-Chapelle in 1748. Then, in the short respite between wars, the notions of columns of attack, light troops fighting in skirmish order, and aimed fire were experimented with in the annual training camps. Though of these ideas only the column of attack was officially sanctioned in the regulations, events on the battlefields during the Seven Years' War demonstrated that all of these ideas had found their adherents among the officer class.

Notes

1. Folard, *Nouvelles decouvertes,* pp. 46–47; cited in Quimby, Robert S., *The Background of Napoleonic Warfare: The Theory Of Military Tactics in Eighteenth-Century France*. New York, 1957, p. 33.

2. "Traité de la colonne, la manner de la former . . .", vol. 1, p. lii–liii; cited in Quimby, Ibid., p. 28.

3. "Traité", *op. cit.,* vol. 1, p. liv.; cited Quimby, Ibid., p. 28.

4. "Traité", vol. 1, p. lxxvi–lxxxvii; cited in Quimby, Ibid., p. 30.

5. Quimby, Ibid., pp. 30–31.

6. "Dissertation où l'on examine, si l'usuage est mettre la Cavalerie sur les ailes, & l'Infanterie au centre, dans un bataille rangée est aussi bein fondé, qu'il est ancien & universal". Found on p. 42–74 of vol. 7 of 1774 edition, cited in Quimby, *op. cit.,* p. 34.

7. (p. 65 of vol. VII of 1774 edition of Dissertation . . .), Quimby, Ibid., p. 35.

8. "Dissertation où l'on examine, si l'usuage est mettre la Cavalerie sur les ailes, & l'Infanterie au centre, dans un bataille rangée est aussi bein fondé, qu'il est ancien & universal". P. 65 of vol. VII of 1774 edition; Quimby, Ibid., p. 35.

9. Quimby, Ibid., pp. 35–36.

10. "Traité," vol. 1, p. lvi; cited in Quimby, Ibid., p. 30.

11. de Saxe, *op. cit.*, p. 35.
12. Ibid., pp. 45–47.
13. Ibid., p. 47.
14. Ibid., p. 102.
15. Ibid., pp. 102–3.
16. Ibid., p. 66.
17. Ibid., p. 70.
18. Ibid., pp. 68–70.
19. Ibid., pp. 68–70.
20. Ibid., pp. 47–48.
21. Ibid., p. 50.
22. Ibid., pp. 45–47.
23. Ibid., p. 72.
24. Ibid., pp. 55–56.
25. Ibid., p. 62.
26. Ibid., p. 59.
27. Ibid., p. 63.
28. Ibid., p. 63.
29. Ibid., pp. 55–56.
30. Ibid., pp. 58–66.
31. Ibid., p. 77.
32. Ibid., p. 71.
33. Ibid., p. 31.

CHAPTER 9

Prussian Cavalry During Frederick's Reign

ALTHOUGH FREDERICK THE GREAT IS OFTEN VIEWED AS BEING THE CREATOR of the Prussian army as a highly efficient fighting machine, this honor more rightly belongs to Leopold, Prince of Anhalt-Dessau. A contemporary of Frederick's father, Frederick William, Leopold was responsible for instilling the degree of discipline and precision which became so characteristic of the Prussian army. Frederick can be rightly considered the founder of the Prussian cavalry as a first-class fighting force; Leopold had devoted all of his energies to the infantry.

During Frederick's reign, the Prussian cavalry was transformed from an ineffective arm using outdated tactical systems to Europe's foremost cavalry, a cavalry which by the time of the Revolutionary and Napoleonic Wars would serve as the model for all European cavalry arms. The most basic advances were made in the area of training, where effective and systematic methods where employed to instruct the trooper on various required drills, exercises and maneuvers. Frederick was also directly and personally responsible for the introduction of revolutionary new cavalry tactics: the adoption of the charge at the gallop, the charge in echelon, the charge in column, maneuvering while moving, as well as the use of light cavalry in closed-order fighting on the battlefield.

Writing in 1760, Frederick referred to the original mounted arm he inherited from his father, Frederick William, as "bad cavalry, in which there was hardly an officer that knew his profession."[1] This cavalry suffered from two notable deficiencies: both the men and horses were excessively large and only capable of slow movement, and the troopers did not receive any practical training, that would prepare them for any of the contingencies of the battlefield. Whatever training they did receive was applicable only to the parade ground.

As far as the size of the individual horse and man were concerned, they were on the average the biggest of any in Europe. Frederick William's passion for large soldiers hadn't been confined to his 3000-strong regiment of giant grenadiers, but found its way into the cavalry arm as well. Many of the troopers were, in fact, giants; so large, that when mounted they did not dare to walk on bad pavement or move on uneven ground. The horses, burdened by this oppressive load, were sometimes unable to reach even a trot, and could only charge at a fast walk. To make matters worse, the Prussians also experienced difficulty acquiring suitable horses for their cavalry. There was little horse-breeding in Prussia and nearly all of the mounts had to be purchased outside of Prussia: either in Poland, along the Hungarian frontier, or eastward in the Crimea.[2]

Frederick's rather harsh assessment of the cavalry that he inherited from his father is appropriate when we compare it to the cavalry he was to later create. These acerbic remarks notwithstanding, his early cavalry was probably not much worse than some of the cavalry in other armies during the same period. This was true not only of the materiel (i.e., horses and men) out of which it was formed, but also the doctrine it employed when fighting on the battlefield. In the case of the latter, it certainly wasn't distinctive, apparently being an imitation of the most popular cavalry tactics then current in Europe.

By placing very large men on large horses, Frederick William appears to have been taking an existing trend to its logical conclusion, and this policy, given existing tactical practices, was probably less of a liability than Frederick allowed in his later writings. Traditional cavalry tactics up until the 1740's placed emphasis on a unit's "weight" and its ability to retain cohesiveness, rather than on its maneuverability or its speed. Given that the most rapid pace was the trot at this time, larger horses provided an intrinsic advantage over smaller ones.

During the War of the Spanish Succession, the cavalry in all armies except the English, Dutch, and Swedish fired at enemy cavalry with their carbines or pistols just before the moment of contact. It appears that Prussian cavalry employed this tactic more enthusiastically than most others.

By the time of Frederick William, the Prussian cavalry had, in theory, shifted to the shock tactics of the Gustavus Adolphus/Marlborough tradition. How consistently this practice was applied throughout the entire corps is somewhat in doubt, though the regulations of 1727 proscribe the use of firearms during the charge, which had to be performed with a drawn saber. In 1734 Frederick William even went further by banning the use of firearms during the charge under the pain of death, but the Prussian cavalry continued to practice firing while mounted and deployed in line.

These proscriptions did not apply to Prussian hussars, who continued to use their firearms to harass the enemy from a slight distance. One of their tactics, when two hussar squadrons were together in line, was to detach a few files from each. These would advance in front of the squadrons and fire, after which they returned to their ranks and were replaced by the next several files. These tactics, which were essentially based on the caracole tactics of the early 1600's, continued in use to approximately 1745.[3]

Returning to the regular Prussian cavalry, following the conventional wisdom of the day, their doctrine called for them to attack the enemy by charging in close order. During the entirety of the charge, the men in each file within a squadron rode knee to knee with their neighbor, and were issued strong stiff boots to withstand the pressure applied by the neighboring horses. The cavalry began its advance on the enemy at the walk before ultimately proceeding to a trot. Each cavalryman had his saber outstretched while his horse moved in unison with the others in the regiment at the controlled pace offered by the trot. The use of the gallop with its increased speed was rejected because emphasis was placed on having the squadron or regiment meet the enemy as a compact unit with proper alignment, and given the level of training then current among almost any cavalry, the use of a gallop would have meant automatically losing the cohesiveness and alignment permitted by the trot.

In practice, the Prussian charge did not live up to this ideal. Prussian cavalry during Frederick William's reign had consisted of overly large men on large horses, and it was rarely possible for them to achieve anything faster than a creeping trot under battle conditions. The cumbersomeness of horses and riders, coupled with their lack of horsemanship meant that correct alignment during the critical moments was also rarely achieved.[4]

Though Frederick appears to have formed his opinion prior to his ascension to the throne, events during the Battle of Mollwitz, where his cavalry was completely and ignominiously routed even before engaging the enemy cavalry, demonstrated that the reorganization of his cavalry would have to be one of his main priorities, if his armies were to have any consistent success in the future. Ultimately, the single greatest contribution Frederick made to the development of his cavalry was to shift the emphasis underlying his cavalry's training. Though the Prussian cavalry in his father's time spent considerable effort drilling, the exercises had little practical effect for the cavalry on the battlefield. The Prussian cavalry trooper was adept at varnishing his boots, bridles, and saddles as well as plaiting ribbons in his horse's mane, but spent little time improving his horsemanship or his ability to handle a sword in combat. The few exercises intended for battlefield application that were practiced were of questionable value (for example, the cavalry learning to fire in line both on foot and horseback), and were performed mechanically without any real sense of practicality. As a result, during review they were pleasing to look at, but had little or no practical application, and did not contribute to the cavalryman's riding ability.

With this regimen, it is not surprising that the standard of horsemanship within the Prussian cavalry was abysmally low, the worst for a major army in Europe. One contemporary observed:

> " . . . in those times [1740–1742] the Prussians could neither ride nor fight, and their ignorance of the cavalryman's trade drove them to despair. They did not even know how to tighten their girths properly, so that their saddles were liable to slide and deposit them under their horses."[5]

Frederick eliminated both the large mounts and the enormous men in his cavalry arm. Now, Prussian horses were to be no larger than 15 3/4 hands for the regular cavalry and 15 1/2 for the dragoons. He forbade the use of Frisian horses, which he described as too heavy, and mounts from Holstein, Newmark and East Prussia were to be used instead. The height of the troopers was also reduced, a dragoon was to be from 5′5″ to 5′7″ and a hussar 5′5″ to 5′2″.[6]

After the fiasco at Mollwitz, Frederick realized that his cavalry could not be transformed without first learning to ride. Frederick had the drill instruction changed and his cavalry trained in the use of the sword. Frederick also had the stirrups shortened, such that when the rider stood up he now cleared the horse's back by the width of a hand. This allowed the rider to put more force behind each swing of his sword. Part of the training was to have each man practice cutting at straw dummies while at the gallop.

For the first time, a very systematic approach was taken to cultivate the trooper's riding capabilities. All recruits were thoroughly trained on foot before they were even allowed to ride. Then all except those destined for the hussars, who were presumably already expert riders, were first made to ride without saddles to teach them balance, one of the most important ingredients in "active" riding, where the rider controls the horse's movements by his own body movements and not simply by tugging on the reins. This training was applied rigorously. There was riding drill every day, and the horses had to be exercised even on Sundays to maintain their top physical condition. The troops were taught to jump ditches and other obstacles, singly and in groups. Special attention was paid to training the troopers to ride in a straight line without having the horses start to crowd together or oscillate, either of which would have disordered the line.

The ability of the Prussian cavalry increased so much as a result of these efforts that by the 1750's it was possible during peacetime maneuvers to have 30 or 40 squadrons charge in a single line without intervals between the squadrons and maintain the strictest order throughout the charge.

These were extremely important reforms, because without them none of the tactical developments that occurred over the next several years would have been possible.[7] The first area to benefit from the improvement in Prussian horsemanship was the manner in which Prussian cavalry attacked its enemy counterpart. At Mollwitz, Frederick realized that his cavalry in its present state had a proclivity toward cowardliness, and that unless corrected, this would consistently embarrass the battlefield performance of his entire army in the future. What did it matter if he and his generals cleverly outmaneuvered the enemy during the battle, if his cavalry would throw away these advantages as soon as it was threatened by enemy cavalry?

Frederick also realized there was a causal relationship between his troops' morale and their method of attack. This relationship was probably best described later by Colonel Dundas, a prominent officer in the British army late in the eighteenth century: "the spur tends as much to overset the opposite enemy, as does the sword which should complete the defeat."[8]

Frederick knew his cavalry's advance to the enemy at the slow trot did nothing for his men's morale, and reduced the cavalry encounter to a chance affair whose outcome was entirely dependant upon the corps' *elan* and the skill of the individual troopers in the action, rather than the ability of their leaders or the superiority of their doctrine. Frederick observed that the slowness of the charge at the trot had two undesirable effects. It gave the trooper too much time to think, thus providing an opportunity for cowardice. At the same time, there was a greater chance that both sides would come to blows. This prospect displeased Frederick since this meant the melee would be a series of individual fencing matches, and he was always loathe to have any outcome depend upon the individual skills of his soldiery.[9]

Consequently, when altering his cavalry's charge doctrine, Frederick sought to give his troopers a tool that would bolster their morale at this critical moment, while simultaneously serving to crush that of their opponents. Drawing upon the experiences and example of Gustavus Adolphus and Charles XII of Sweden, he concluded that this could only be achieved by increasing the speed at which his cavalry was advancing in those critical moments when both groups of hostile horseman were separated by less than 50 paces. It was at this point that one side or the other would almost invariably swerve, break, or check their motion, handing the contest to the other side.

A comment made to the Comte de Gisors by Frederick in 1745 not only provides the rationale for the entire succession of changes to the charge doctrine, but reveals some other significant attitudes as well:

> "I make the squadrons charge at a fast gallop because then fear carries the cowards along with the rest—they know that if they so much as hesitate in the middle of the onrush they will be crushed by the remainder of the squadron. My intention is to break the enemy by the speed of our charges before it ever comes to hand-to-hand fighting: officers become no more valuable than simple troopers in a melee, and order and cohesion are lost."[10]

Here, it is obvious Frederick clearly realized that his cavalrymen lacked the French troopers' zeal for the *arme blanche,* and that it was important, whenever possible, to avoid hand-to-hand combat by defeating the enemy prior to the moment of contact. It also shows Frederick's consistent abhorrence of having any part of the combat slip from under his officers' control. Frederick realized that the surest way of avoiding individual combat was to maintain order within the squadron during the final moments of the charge, regardless of how fast the horses were moving.

> "So long as the line is contiguous and the squadrons well closed, it is impossible to come to hand-to-hand combat. These squadrons are unable to become mixed, since the enemy being more open than we are and having more intervals, is unable to resist our shock."[11]

However, it must not be thought that the Prussians went instantly from the stolid trot-type charges of Frederick William's time to the lively and spirited charges we associate with the Prussian cavalry of the Seven Years' War. The process of going from the charge at the trot to the charge at the gallop was a gradual one, passing through several intermediate stages, and requiring at least three years to complete.

On June 3rd, 1741, less than two months after the Battle of Mollwitz, Leopold of Anhalt-Dessau made the first reference to Prussian cavalry moving at a gallop. The charge was still mostly conducted at the trot with the cavalrymen breaking into the gallop only during the last 30 paces. The troopers were reminded not to use their firearms, and to rely solely on their swords. This was a cautious first step, and did not yet produce an effect dramatically different from the charges made by enemy cavalry. The Austrian cavalry, for example, charged approximately 50 paces after firing their pistols.

Soon, however, the distance charged while at the gallop was increased beyond the existing standards of the age. On March 17th, 1742, in the "Selowitz" instruction, the distance to be advanced at the gallop was increased to 100 paces. Though a 1743 regulation prescribed that the charge begin at a fast trot and end at a full gallop "while keeping a compact order," still no mention was made of an all-out attack at full speed. It was only after July 25th, 1744, that the gallop was to start 200 paces from the enemy, and "towards the end of their course the horses were to be given their head."[12]

One of the most detailed descriptions of how the Prussian cavalry was to conduct this new type of charge is provided by General Warnery in his *Remarks On Cavalry,* originally an unpublished manuscript intended solely for the education of the higher nobility who were destined for service in the cavalry.

> "At the first sound of the trumpet the whole begin to move forward, first and second line, and the reserve: the attacking wing perfectly dressed in line, marches on at a walk; at the second sound, which ought to be doubled, the whole begins to trot (which the second line, and the reserve, continue to do till the charge is finished) at the third sound, which is tripled, at about 150 or 200 paces from the enemy, the first line begins to gallop, and when they approach within 70 or at most 80 paces from the enemy, the trumpets sound gay and lively fanfare or flourishes of the trumpet, then the troopers prick with both spurs, and push forward at full speed, without however entirely slackening the bridle, as all the horses cannot gallop with equal velocity; but when within about twenty paces, they must force the gallop as much as possible, to give the full impulse of the charge, or as the King of Prussia used to call it, the grand coup de collier; the rear ranks must then also press forward with all their weight and speed, as if they would force forward their front ranks or file leaders; this is called furnishing the shock."[13]

In this passage, Warnery implies that the final stage of the charge when the cavalry was advancing at the gallop actually was, in turn, subdivided into three phases. The first was initiated 150 to 200 paces from the enemy; during this phase, the cavalry though advancing at a gallop retained perfect order. The second phase of the gallop was adopted between 70 and 80 paces from the enemy and resulted in a much more spirited gallop; however, even during this phase the troopers were still to make certain they didn't advance out of alignment with the other troopers in their rank. The charge *à la sauvage* was only to take place twenty paces from the enemy when the trooper gave full rein to his horse and no attention was paid to anyone else in the squadron.

The reason for these gradual changes is not that there was a constant reevaluation of the philosophy underlying how the charge was to be conducted, but rather that these changes reflect the recognition of the increasing horsemanship of the average Prussian trooper. And, by the early 1750's, the standard of horsemanship among the Prussians had surpassed anything previously known in Western Europe. In 1748, Frederick demanded that they charge 700 yards (trot: 300; gallop: 400). In 1750 this was increased to a total of 1200 yards (trot: 300; gallop: 400; and full speed: 500). This was increased to an incredible 1800 yards in 1755, with the last 600 yards at full speed.

The protracted charge developed by the Prussians during the 1741–1756 period was totally dependent upon a very high standard of horsemanship, especially in regard to moving and maneuvering in large bodies. The Austrians, for example, though they attempted to emulate the Prussians' extended charges, because they did not address the much more fundamental issue of military horsemanship until much, much later were never able to execute these charges, becoming disordered after only fifty yards at the gallop.[14]

The adoption of the approach at the gallop proved to be a revolutionary innovation, and had at least one effect that could not have been originally foreseen by its inventors. Up until that point, horseman on smaller-sized horses, though vital to the pursuance of the *petite guerre* ("small war"), that is, the series of skirmish actions that always occurred as the opposing armies felt their way around the countryside, could not be used with any effect on the battlefield against regular cavalry such as cuirassiers, carabiniers, and dragoons. The reason for this was as much due to the limitations imposed by the horses' size as it was due to their riders' training and tactics.

Given the existing tactic of having the opposing cavalry approach one another at the trot, the advantage invariably went to the men on the larger horses. With the advent of the charge at the gallop, the larger classes of cavalry continued to possess a decided advantage over light forms, though it ceased to be the forgone conclusion it had been previously. This explains the tendency during the mid-eighteenth century to start using the light cavalry, that is, hussars, *chevaux-légères,* and *chasseurs à cheval,* not just as mounted skirmishers but also as troops capable of fighting in closed-order formation. This would not have been as feasible prior to the adoption of the charge at the gallop. In the Prussian army under the leadership of General von Winterfeld, for example, efforts were made to turn the hussars into an effective force on the battlefield. It was the hussars, for example, who proved to be one of the decisive forces in the attack on the Austrian cavalry on the right at the Battle of Prague (May 6th, 1757).

The Prussian cavalry was made more effective by a second tactical development, one rarely discussed in modern literature. This was the use of cavalry columns to attack enemy infantry in formation not previously softened up by either infantry or artillery. The reason for this continuing silence lies with the original secrecy Frederick and his top-ranking generals applied to this matter. The Prussians had developed a number of tactical and grand tactical "secrets," which they considered to be too innovative and effective to be put into print, or be discussed openly with the lower officer ranks. These included the "march by lines" maneuver which was the basis of the "oblique attack," the use of attack columns by both infantry and cavalry, and the use of horse artillery.

Most of these "secret" tactics can be discovered by an examination of various memoirs of distinguished Prussian generals, as well as a very close reading of Frederick's own writings. He often relied upon cryptic remarks to communicate to his staff, who had already been instructed on a particular matter by word of mouth.

One of Frederick's most important tactical secrets was the use of the cavalry column of attack. Like the attack in echelon its discovery appears to lie with the fortuitous events of the battle, in this case the famous charge of the Bayreuth dragoons at the Battle of Hohenfriedeberg (1745). Led by Lieutenant General Gessler, who noticed the wavering Austrian battalions, this regiment, formed in two columns, managed opportunely to ride through a gap in the first line that had appeared earlier when the Prussian army after defeating the Saxons had to change its axis of deployment 90 degrees to meet the newly arriving Austrian force. Taking these already demoralized Austrians by surprise, the single dragoon regiment in about twenty minutes overthrew as many as twenty battalions.[15]

Frederick was quick to see the theoretical basis for this remarkable success, and writing his *Instructions For His Generals* in 1753, he laid out the principles to be applied by both his infantry and his cavalry so that this technique could be used again at will:

> "As soon as the enemy commences to rally around their colors, (the Prussian infantry) have openings made in the first line to make way for the dragoons that I have placed between the battalions of the second line, as can be seen in the second order of battle. Then all the opposing infantry will be lost. Whoever attempts to flee before these dragoons will fall in the hands of your victorious second lines of cavalry, who await them and cut them off from the defiles. . . ."[16]

Though in Frederick's writings no detail is given as to how the column was formed, fortunately the details are provided in Warnery's wonderful work, *Remarks on Cavalry.*

The example Warnery gives describes an attack of fifteen squadrons, presumably taken from the *corps de reserve* behind the second line. Five of these squadrons were to be dragoons, the remainder were hussars. The squadrons of dragoons were placed in a closed column, the hussars were in line half to the right, and half to the left of the column, and even with the rear squadron of dragoons. The column was to be made as compact as possible without having the individual ranks or the squadrons become mixed up.

The dragoons and the hussars in this formation passed through the infantry, the latter forming spaces periodically along the line by doubling the line in order to allow the cavalry to pass. Initially, both the dragoons and the hussars would move forward together, allowing this hybrid formation to be maintained. However, as they neared the enemy, the dragoons would conduct a regular charge, advancing with great vivacity, throwing themselves upon the enemy sword in hand yelling and screaming. In order to maximize the "weight of charge" and simultaneously minimize the size of the target exposed to artillery fire, it was important to have the dragoons in the column retain their column order throughout their charge. The officers within the five-dragoon squadrons were placed on the column's flanks and rear. Their primary task during the advance was to prevent panicking troopers from leaving the column, and they were authorized to shoot or saber a soldier to prevent his desertion.

The ten-hussar squadrons in line did not break into a gallop but continued to advance at the trot, in order to retain perfect order and distance themselves from the dragoons as the latter contacted the enemy infantry, to support these dragoons with a charge if it became necessary. The hussar's function at this point was to provide an additional target for any enemy artillery in the area (the dragoons being in closed column were extremely vulnerable to artillery using solid shot) and to prevent the enemy infantry from easily forming flanks to the dragoons.

If the dragoons' charge was successful, the first three squadrons of dragoons, after passing through the enemy's first line, would continue to advance and then deploy some distance in front of the enemy's second line or its reserve, depending upon the situation. The fourth and fifth squadrons wheeled to the right and the left, respectively. This was to attack the enemy's newly exposed flanks, thus rolling up the infantry.

The hussars' action at this point depended upon the overall situation; their duty now was to prevent the enemy from making any movement to interrupt the attack by the column of dragoons. If the enemy's second line showed no indication of counterattacking and there were no enemy cavalry in the area, all of the hussar and dragoon squadrons would be free to continue the attack on the infantry, by now mostly in flight. If there was a threat posed by a second infantry line, or the reserve, or a body of cavalry, seven squadrons of hussars moved into line beside the forward dragoon squadrons, the remaining three hanging back to protect the flanks of the friendly cavalry line.

The cavalry commander using this maneuver had to follow the same precautions as his infantry counterpart who chose to attack the enemy with battalions in closed columns. That is, it was not to be used in situations where the enemy deployed cavalry directly behind the infantry to be attacked. If this precaution wasn't heeded, there was a good likelihood that the dragoons would be themselves crushed by the enemy cavalry as they sabered the enemy infantry.[17] Warnery informs us that this cavalry column of attack was used with success a number of times; for example, by Seydlitz at Zorndorf, Marshal Gessler at Strigau, General Leideritz at Kesselsdorf, as well as on several other occasions with success by Warnery himself.

Up until 1757, the Prussian cavalry deployed in three ranks, although deployment in two was tolerated in an emergency. It had been long recognized that only the first two ranks were necessary for any melee that might occur. The third rank acted as a reserve, supplying men to fill up any gaps that might occur as the squadron charged, or to help increase the squadron's frontage if attacking a larger force without having to open the files (the men could still ride knee to knee).[18] A lack of horses near the end of the 1757 campaign led to the adoption of a two-rank line by those regiments suffering from the shortage of horses. This modification continued over the next several campaigns, and proved so successful that it was universally adopted by the entire Prussian cavalry arm in 1760, even though the cavalry regulations of 1764, 1774, and 1779 continued to prescribe the three-rank line.

Some nineteenth-century military writers such as Denison believe that the shift from the three-rank to the two-rank line was largely made feasible by the previous adoption of the vigorous charge at the gallop. According to this view, when the charge at the gallop was conducted from a three-rank line, the second rank tended to be very constrained, and its horses were very much more vulnerable to being disordered. Any significant disorder in the second rank could disrupt the entire charge since the confusion would spread to the third rank. The utilization of a two-rank line almost eliminated this problem.[19]

Interestingly enough, this view wasn't echoed by all the officers in Prussian cavalry of Frederick's time, and as distinguished and skilled a cavalryman as General Warnery continued to extol the virtues of the three-rank system as late as 1781. According to Warnery, a two-rank line of cavalry had insufficient "weight" or strength and did not furnish the necessary shock in charging. At the same time, it was more inclined to waiver. Warnery argued that in the three-rank lines the rear two ranks drove the first onward, and a horse in the first rank even if he should lose his rider or be disabled could not go anywhere but forward, being surrounded and pressed on all other sides. The passage where Warnery argues this point, though appearing to drift from the point, offers an insight into the behavior of the horses during the fighting.

> "A squadron formed in two ranks is very subject to wavering, and much easier broken than one of three, which must naturally have a greater weight in the shock, and be much more difficult for an enemy to penetrate, even should several of the front rank be fallen or disabled: for as it causes no opening in the line, the horse will not fail to advance even without his rider, feeling pressed on each side and behind, as it always happens: for a horse must be very much wounded to make him fall on the spot. One without his rider, at Strigau, which had one of his hind feet carried away by a cannon ball, joined the left of the squadron, where he ran with the others during all of the battle, although we were several times dispersed; at the sound of the call he always fell into the same place, which was, without doubt, the same that he had before belonged to in the squadron."[20]

One can reconcile the two opposing views of expert opinion by evoking the following mathematical model. Let's assume Warnery is correct, and that when opposing cavalry forces meet, if one is deployed in two ranks and the other in three ranks, and both occupy the same frontage, the advantage lies with the three-rank unit. However, to achieve this advantage, given these preconditions, the three-rank unit would have to contain 50 percent more men.

Now, consider the next situation. A three-rank cavalry regiment engages a two-rank counterpart, and both units consist of the same number of men. In this case, the frontage of the two-rank regiment would be 50 percent greater than the three-rank regiment. Despite the fact that the three-rank regiment would enjoy an advantage for having greater "weight," the two-rank regiment would enjoy a different advantage of being able to envelop its enemy counterpart.

If we assume that the advantage of being more readily able to envelop or outflank the enemy was a greater advantage than that provided by having the greater "weight," this would explain why, on one hand, the three-rank system was abandoned after the Seven Years' War never really to return, but why on the other hand, despite its apparent advantages, many experienced and successful cavalrymen continued to argue against the adoption of the two-rank system.

Another controversy that raged throughout this period was which was more effective, the use of the edge or the point of the sword at the final moment of contact? At least one modern writer has stated that it was the Prussian practice to hold the sword over the head while standing in the stirrups in order to bring the sword down on the enemy's head in a sweeping arc. Warnery gives a different account:

> "The troopers of the front rank raise their swords to the height of their faces, the arm extended in tierce, the point against the eyes of his enemy, and the hand a little turned (clockwise) that the branch or the guard of the sword may cover his own; they must raise themselves a little in the stirrups, the body forward, and aim to place a thrust with the point against the man or the horse opposed to him; in a word, he must do his best, either by thrusting or cutting, to disable his enemy; thus the shock or charge is soon finished."[21]

General Warnery himself preferred the thrust, arguing that with it the trooper was able to reach an opponent at a greater distance than a cut motion; and cause a more dangerous wound with less effort. However, he acknowledged that opinion appeared to be equally divided in the Prussian service: half the officers preferred their men to thrust at the enemy using the points of their swords, the remainder wanted the men to use the cutting edge. Presumably, these latter argued that the thrust could only be used against an opponent directly to his front, while a cutting motion could be used to strike an opponent within the front 270 degrees and allowed him to hit the enemy as he passed. Frederick himself seemed to remain aloof or indifferent to this debate, on one occasion remarking to Warnery, "Kill your enemy with one or the other, I will never bring you to an account with which you did it."[22]

Incidentally, regardless of the way they were to use their swords, the troopers in the second and third ranks had to be careful to keep their swords pointed upward so that they would not accidentally impale the file leaders in the first rank.[23]

As of the outbreak of the Seven Years' War, most of the officers were to position themselves to the squadron's flank or rear during the course of the charge. Only three officers were to be stationed slightly to the front to lead the squadron's advance. The officer commanding the squadron was positioned directly in the center while the other two officers were in front but on either flank. The attention of these three officers was to the front. The remainder of the squadron's officers as well as the non-commissioned officers were placed on the flanks and to the rear. It was important to monitor the cavalrymen in the flank files and those in the rear rank because, during the charge, only these troopers could readily break off. At least one officer and several of the reliable non-commissioned officers were placed in the rear. Their duty also consisted of preventing stragglers from quitting the squadron, using their swords and pistols in earnest if it was necessary. These officers and NCO's in the rear also had the added responsibility of instantly throwing themselves into any part of the squadron where their presence was necessary, either because an interval between the men had opened up, or the files had thinned due to casualties, or to form a small reserve behind part of a squadron that was being hard pressed by enemy troops.

This disposition was another one of Frederick's innovations. Prior to these instructions, as was the case in all other armies, many of the officers tended to position themselves in front of the squadron during the charge. This was undesirable for a variety of different reasons. The very presence of officers impeded the charge being carried home in its final moments. Their horses tended to startle at the swords and blows and would throw themselves across the line of the charge, thus presenting an obstacle to their own troops who were trying to come to grips with the enemy. The ordinary trooper's horse being part of a high-speed boot-to-boot formation, did not have the same opportunity to bolt, and had to continue to gallop forward.

Another disadvantage of placing officers to the front of the squadron was that this led to the officers becoming involved in the melee, should one occur. This was undesirable for two reasons. It reduced the officer to a simple soldier, whereas, in the Prussian army at least, his proper role was not to partake in the fight but insure that his troops were properly led, and prevent any of his men from fleeing. The other disadvantage of having officers partaking in the fighting was that it invariably led to a higher mortality rate among the officer class. This resulted in situations where the squadron was ineffectively led for the remainder of the battle, or where there were fewer and fewer officers to rally disordered formations.

These arguments were especially true when general officers and their staff placed themselves at the head of the cavalry which was to charge. It was a complete waste to have these high-ranking officers reduced to ordinary troopers during the affair when their proper role was to attend to their supervisory and command duties. Besides, the youthful and robust troopers of the line were better suited to a fight than an old and sometimes infirm general, whose loss would nevertheless discourage the troops, and possibly demoralize them for the remainder of the combat. Frederick corrected this problem by ordering that most of his officers be stationed on the flanks. This policy resulted in fewer officers being wounded or killed, as well as the Prussians being able to maintain a consistently higher level of troop control.[24]

At least one of Frederick's tactical policies failed to generate much enthusiasm among his generals, this was his practice of having his cavalry deploy *en muraille,* that is, where the squadrons in a line were deployed immediately beside each other, without any interval between each squadron. Frederick supplied this rationale for this tactic:

> "I do not let any interval between my squadrons, because the squadrons separated from one another present as many flanks to the enemy."[25]

This was not a new invention, being used intermittently since the beginning of the eighteenth century, and appears to have been first devised by Prince Louis of Baden, who during the wars against the Turks, had been forced to close the intervals between both his infantry battalions and his cavalry squadrons. This was in order to prevent the Turkish horsemen from working their way into friendly lines by exploiting the spaces between each corps. This was not as great a problem when facing European cavalry which tended to stand or fight as a mass. Turkish horsemen, however, always strove to break the engagement down into a series of individual contests. They thrived on individual combat, being both more daring and better horsemen than their European counterparts. As soon as the Turks succeeded in penetrating a line, there would be immediate carnage, their razor-sharp weapons cutting off heads and limbs. And, if the friendly troops gave way, the Turks would instantly spread out, some continuing to attack in front, while the remainder turned the flank and attacked the rear.[26] Louis' adoption of what became known as *en muraille* simply reduced the chances for these horsemen to enter the ranks of the friendly troops, by creating a continuous front.

Puységur adopted this as an all-purpose tactic usable by infantry and cavalry for all types of situations and it continued to be used by the French army until the end of the Seven Years' War. He had his infantry and cavalry attack the enemy together, marching at the same pace. Puységur's rationale for employing this tactic was that his cavalry encountering enemy cavalry with intervals between their squadrons would be able to penetrate their lines and overthrow the enemy cavalry. It must be pointed out, however, that Puységur's tactic presupposed a slow movement of cavalry.

Although during the War of the Spanish Succession most cavalry squadrons were drawn up with relatively large intervals between them, *en muraille* gained further respectability when the Dutch and Danish squadrons appear to have been deployed *en muraille* by accident at Ramillies when they overthrew Bavarian cuirassiers and the much-esteemed French Maison du Roi. It is likely that the intervals between each of the Dutch squadrons in the first line disappeared as the Dutch cavalrymen crowded toward the center of the line in order to avoid artillery and musketry fire from the towns of Taviers and Ramillies, on their right and left, respectively.[27]

Roemer, in his classic work on cavalry tactics, suggested that Frederick adopted the *en muraille* tactic as a purely parade-ground exercise designed to test his cavalry's horsemanship in large formations.[28] However, sufficient references to his generals' continued resistance to its use on the battlefield, as well as their frequently attributing some of their defeats to its use, indicate it was applied to the battlefield as well. It is said, for example, Sedlitz attacked with 70 squadrons *en muraille* at Zorndorf in 1758.[29]

> " . . . but what, in my opinion, contributed most to this want of success, whenever this was the case, was its charging in *en muraille,* or without intervals, or at least they were too small: the King would have it so: but whenever the Generals were at liberty to leave reasonable intervals, it was always successful."[30]

Many, if not most, experienced cavalrymen considered the maintenance of intervals to be indispensable when a line of horses was brought to a gallop or even a fast trot. As the horse speeded up it required slightly more room, which meant during the trot, and still more at the gallop, the intervals between squadrons would automatically close by themselves.

These officers argued that *en muraille* could only be performed on perfectly level terrain devoid of any natural obstacles. It was impossible to employ this formation on broken or rough terrain and have the cavalry move at any speed and still preserve order.

Roemer, a cavalry officer writing in the late nineteenth century, gave this graphic description of what would happen when cavalry attempted to move *en muraille* through rough terrain while moving at speed:

> "When pressure takes place, it rolls on and on swelling like a wave, it runs out at the first interval, but if the intervals are closed, the waves meet, break the line, impede its advance and throw it into confusion. The vicious horses contribute not a little to this result. The pressure infects them, they throw themselves against each other, . . . for the ranks, or press out the weak ones from the line, and may be so exhausted as to be unable to keep up."[31]

The following account provided by Mottin de la Balme, a distinguished French cavalry officer who took part in the unsuccessful French charge at Minden, provides another vivid description of the practical dangers implicit in the use of a massive *en muraille* formation, this time in a battlefield situation:

> "A corps of English infantry, by its steady fire, dispersed the cavalry in front, the corps of gendarmerie and carabiniers received orders to charge. They advanced at the gallop, in line, without intervals. Even at the start, the center was heavily pressed upon the wings, the pressure then rolled back to the flanks, particularly to the right. The infantry opened fire from the center towards the flanks. The horses made desperate efforts to break away outward and avoid the fire. The pressure now became so great that men and horses overturned each other and rolled about in helpless confusion. Few were killed by gunshot wounds, but, with the exception of about 10 in every squadron, they were all torn from their horses, trampled to death, or had their limbs broken. The few that remained mounted were carried, some right through the enemy's ranks, others to the rear of the field. Had we advanced with only half intervals, the issue would have been very different. The attack would have been made with speed and impetuosity, the horses could not have broken away to the left or to the right, and the English would have been ridden over as at Fontenoy."[32]

An additional argument against the use of *en muraille* was that a large formation was difficult to rally when disordered. Warnery pointed out, for example, that if a squadron was as large as a battalion of infantry, which was in effect what happened when a cavalry regiment was deployed without intervals between the individual squadrons, the time required to rally it would make it impossible to regain order in the face of the enemy.

Those who opposed use of *en muraille* on a universal basis believed this formation was only to be properly employed when Prussian cavalry had the occasion to fight against irregular cavalry such as Turks or Cossacks.

In these cases, it was important that both infantry and cavalry be formed together as tight as possible. The whole would then maneuver together "close, compact and slow."[33]

We should also mention in passing that this was the only situation where Prussian troopers were officially permitted to fire at enemy cavalry while in battle order.[34] Obviously, the cavalrymen couldn't be led to charge at speed without being separated from the infantry and/or being thrown in disorder. Should this latter occur in the presence of expert horsemen such as the Turks, the Prussian cavalry would be quickly cut to ribbons. The other reason for having the cavalry retained near the infantry was that the Turks, though exceedingly brave in individual combat, were surprisingly easy to intimidate by ordered volleys of fire.

NOTES

1. *Testament Politique,* cited in Duffy, Christopher, *The Army of Frederick the Great.* New York, 1974, page 231.

2. Maude, *op. cit.,* p. 92.

3. Warnery, *op. cit.,* p. 13.

4. Roemer, *op. cit.,* p. 331.

5. KA Schreiben eines Officers des Cavallerie an seinen Freund, Koniggratz, Dec 28th 1756, Kriegswissenschaftliche Memoires, Krieg gegen Preussen, II, 24; cited in Duffy, *The Army of Maria Theresa, op. cit.,* p. 101.

6. Rogers, Colonel H. C. B., *The British Army of the Eighteenth Century.* London, 1977, p. 77; citing Sir George Arthur, *The Story of the Household Cavalry.* London 1909, p. 453.

7. Maude, *op. cit.,* p. 98.

8. Dundas, *op. cit.,* p. 5.

9. Frederick II, "Instructions For His Generals." Translated by Thomas R. Phillips. Harrisburg, PA, 1944, p. 99.

10. Maude, *op. cit.,* p. 98.

11. Frederick, "Instructions," *op. cit.,* p. 99.

12. Maude, *op. cit.,* p. 97.

13. Warnery, *op. cit.,* p. 46.

14. Maude, *op. cit.,* p. 124.

15. Carlyle, vol. 4, *op. cit.,* p. 119.

16. Frederick, "Instructions," *op. cit.,* p. 91.

17. Warnery, *op. cit.,* pp. 75–78.

18. Prussia, Kreigsministerium, *Regulations For the Prussian Infantry (1743).* New York, 1968, pp. 435–436.

19. Denison, George T., *A History of Cavalry From the Earliest Times.* London, 1873, p. 313.
20. Warnery, *op. cit.,* p. 19.
21. Ibid., pp. 46–47.
22. Ibid., p. 17.
23. Ibid., p. 48.
24. Ibid., pp. 10–11.
25. Maude, *op. cit.,* p. 98.
26. Roemer, *op. cit.,* p. 328.
27. Taylor, *op. cit.,* vol. 1, p. 381; vol. 2, pp. 383–387.
28. Roemer, *op. cit.,* p. 335.
29. Denison, *op. cit.,* p. 323.
30. Warnery, *op. cit.,* p. xvii.
31. Roemer, *op. cit.,* p. 157.
32. Cited in Roemer, *op. cit.,* p. 157.
33. Warnery, *op. cit.,* pp. 11–12.
34. Ibid., pp. 10–11.

CHAPTER 10

Prussian Advances in Infantry Tactics

BEFORE ATTEMPTING TO DESCRIBE THE VARIOUS REFORMS FREDERICK effected, it is necessary to examine the infantry as it existed during the reign of his father, Frederick William. Probably the infantry's most salient characteristic was its rigid discipline; though, by the end of Frederick William's reign, we would also have to comment on the large size of the average Prussian soldier.

Around the turn of the eighteenth century, the infantry had fallen under the tutelage of Leopold I, Prince of Anhalt-Dessau (the "Old Dessauer") who had devoted considerable time and effort to the study of the art of warfare as it then existed. The Prince was deeply convinced that discipline and obedience were the greatest sources of strength for any army. He acted on these beliefs, setting about to insure that all of the infantry were properly trained and exercised.

Years of toiling under this taskmaster had its effect, and a strong sense of discipline permeated the entire infantry arm. The soldiers in all regiments were well-drilled. The recruit was taught to assume a soldierly deportment, how to march, how to perform the manual of arms; and his relatively high level of expertise was maintained by constant exercise. A great amount of attention was paid to detail, and the number of activities defined and governed by a specific drill were greatly increased over what was standard for other armies. Nothing was too trivial to be overlooked. Each soldier regularly polished his boots and cleaned his fusil, which for the time represented an innovation.

One criticism that historians would later direct against Frederick William's infantry was that much of his and his staff's efforts were spent on creating an impressive facade. Though all of the soldier's paraphernalia was shiny and spotless, and his every movement precise; little attention was paid to the requirements of the battlefield. This, of course, would soon be corrected by Frederick who was to be embroiled in a pan-European conflict almost as soon as he ascended his throne.

One of Frederick William's peculiarities was his passion for the large soldier. His efforts to gather giant men for a grenadier battalion are well known, having been commented upon in most works dealing with the Prussian army of this period. This fixation wasn't confined to this battalion, but found its way into the selection process for all corps throughout the infantry arm and into the cavalry as well. Frederick William's mania for large men appears to have peeked in 1730 when more than 1000 crowns were paid for men six feet or larger.

The "Old Dessauer" succeeded in making a number of changes in the drill, deployment, and method of firing to be used by the Prussian infantry. A fervent disciple of the use of firepower, Leopold believed in extending the infantry battalion over as wide a front as possible, in order to bring the greatest number of muskets to bear. By the time Frederick the Great ascended the throne, Leopold even advocated deploying the battalion in only two ranks, and in this regard he anticipated British infantry practice by about fifty years. Frederick, however, never accepted this proposition, arguing that it was preferable to throw the greatest number of musket balls on the smallest possible space.[1]

To allow the Prussian infantryman to load more quickly and reduce the rate of misfires, Leopold introduced the iron ramrod in 1718.[2] The traditional wooden ramrod had to be used more carefully, and thus often more slowly. Obviously, it was also much more likely to break.

The system devised by Leopold was officially sanctioned and codified by the first official infantry regulations, appearing in print in 1726. As was the case with all other Western European armies of this period, only a limited number of infantry formations were available. These were the line, the column at full interval, the square for use against cavalry, and the column by files for crossing very narrow passages. Of these, only the line was considered to be a battlefield formation of any widespread usage; the square was to be formed only when the infantry was on the verge of being attacked by enemy cavalry, and then only in those situations where the maintenance of a regular line was no longer feasible. All columns, regardless of their type, were considered to be formations of maneuver, and unfit for use on the battlefield.

At this time, there were no "maneuvers," as we now understand that term. The concept of "maneuver" in its present form only started to emerge during the late 1740's and early 1750's as Frederick and his generals sought to find faster and less vulnerable methods to going between the column of maneuver and line and vice versa for the individual battalion. Prior to this, all movement, including formation changes, was achieved by using the same two drills in a number of different combinations: a unit would advance straight forward, then quarter-wheel up to 90 degrees, then advance again, and so on.

The platoon was the tactical unit within the battalion. A Prussian infantry battalion was divided into four divisions, each division, in turn, being made up of two platoons. The battalion deployed in line was the only formation officially sanctioned for widespread use on the battlefield. As was the case in the Austrian armies, its men were deployed in four ranks, although only the first three ever fired. The senior company was placed on the right and, moving along the line towards the left, each company was progressively less senior. Usually, the grenadier company was detached from the battalion and grouped with three other grenadier companies to form a combined grenadier battalion whose usual purpose was to guard villages, castles, and any other important places to the front or the sides of the army. However, in those cases where, for whatever reason, the grenadier company remained with its parent battalion, it was considered to be the most senior company and as such placed at the right of the line.

The column was not considered to be a fighting formation and was to be used exclusively for movement, and almost always when the enemy was still some distance away. A column was formed on either a "section" (half of a platoon) or a divisional frontage (a division contained two platoons). A third type of column, the "column by files," was only used to pass through narrow passages, and was never used to traverse lengthy distances.

The column of maneuver most often used was the "open order" column by section. This referred to the fact that the frontage of the column was a section wide, and that the distance between each section was equivalent to the width of a section. All columns of maneuver marched with the ranks open, that is, there was a perceptible distance between each rank of men in the section or division. This meant that the distance between each rank within the section or platoon was about ten feet. When the battalion was deployed in line and ready either to engage in fire combat or advance toward the enemy, the men were always to be in closed ranks, where the distance between each rank was reduced to about a third of what it was for open ranks.

Open ranks were a feature of all columns in the days before the complete mastery of cadenced marching. The relatively large distance between each rank was necessary not only to allow the troops a better opportunity of keeping the lines dressed while marching, but facilitated the dressing process once they inevitably became disordered. On the other hand, open ranks complicated the transition from column to line, since all ranks had to close in order to be able to quarter-wheel, a fundamental prerequisite for the formation of a line. It appears that the quarter-wheel was performed with a fixed pivot; that is, each rank within a section or platoon quarter-wheeled upon exactly the same spot and had to wait until the previous rank had completed its turn and vacated that position before it could advance and then itself start to turn.

The cross-country paths of those times, though much rougher than those with which we are familiar, were also wider, so the column by sections could be maintained for most of the battalion's march across the countryside. Whenever the path narrowed, as would occur at a bridge, at certain points in a forest, or along streets in a town, the battalion adopted column by files instead. This was a very clumsy formation and was never adopted for long periods, since it completely disrupted the internal organization of the platoon and section. To reduce the frontage, a number of files from the left side of each rank were placed behind the same number of files on the right side of the section, thus halving the front of the column. This could be performed a second time to reduce the total frontage to four or five files.

The Prussians continued to use the two "processional" methods of deploying into line. If line was to be formed to the left of the battalion's position, each section quarter-wheeled to the left at the same time, thereby immediately forming line, provided that the distance between sections had been exactly one "interval."

When a battalion was to form column to the front of its current position in line, the first section on the right of the line marched directly forward. The next section quarter-wheeled to the right, then immediately performed a second quarter-wheel, this time to the left. While performing this second quarter-wheel, the section's left flank, though changing direction, remained in the same position. This spot, called a *point d'appui* in French, was known as a "hook" in the Prussian army. All of the remaining sections now advanced until they each marched level to the "hook" and then quarter-wheeled to the left and followed the first two sections. Once formed, the distance between each section in the column was equal to the width of the column, i.e., full interval.

These remained the only methods that had been devised for deploying into line from column or "ploying" into column from line until around 1745. In the late 1740's, at least on the parade ground, Frederick experimented with a number of new methods of going from line to column and vice versa.

At the start of Frederick's reign, each infantry battalion was to be drawn up in four ranks; Frederick ordered all regiments marching to Silesia to form on three ranks as of November 29th, 1740, and on June 20th, 1742, this arrangement was applied to all infantry regiments throughout the entire army. The battalion was in closed order, not only referring to the spaces between each of the files, but also to those between the ranks and it occupied 160 German paces. The regulations of 1743 called for the soldiers in a rank to be close enough together so that one soldier's right arm was behind the left arm of his neighbor to the right. This extremely dense packing of the files was abolished in 1748 when soldiers were stationed elbow to elbow, giving each man about one foot, ten inches. The distance between the ranks varied from one foot to two paces, the narrow distance of one foot having become popular by the end of Frederick's reign. The open order system popular at the turn of the eighteenth century had required four paces between each rank.

Leopold's most important innovation was the introduction of cadenced marching. Now, every infantryman advanced his left then his right foot in unison, following the beat of the drums. This was later to have the greatest impact on Prussian infantry capabilities when Frederick invented a series of maneuvers to allow the infantry to change formations much more quickly than had ever been possible in the past. Cadence marching not only allowed men deployed in lines to advance further before they had to stop and dress themselves, but it also allowed men to be formed in much more compact columns. Now instead of the men marching in open ranks, where each rank was separated by a wide distance, they could march in closed ranks where this distance was reduced to one or two paces. This was significant not only because it reduced the overall length of columns, making them less unwieldy, but because later it would allow the Prussians to devise new methods of forming line.

The evidence suggests that cadenced marching was introduced into the Prussian army sometime during the 1730's. The infantry regulations of 1726 still called for open ranks while in column, a necessity before the days of cadence. Moreover, De Saxe writing in *Mes Reveries* in 1732 specifically mentions that no army in Europe was then practicing cadenced marching, which he refers to as the "secret of tactics."[3] Until the adoption of cadence, the Prussian infantry had to march with open ranks. Closed ranks were only adopted when the battalion was about to deploy, then the distance between ranks was reduced to a little over a single pace. Sometime after the adoption of cadence, the Prussians realized that it was no longer necessary to march with open ranks, closed ranks could be used for all occasions. This would have a tremendous impact on a battalion's ability to maneuver, and it was this development that allowed Frederick to devise new methods of deployment.

The efforts of the Prince of Anhalt-Dessau and Frederick William were not without their rewards. The infantry Frederick inherited, unlike its cavalry counterpart, was essentially a fine fighting force, whose practical value in battle would soon be demonstrated at the Battle of Mollwitz (April 10th, 1741), where an Austrian officer would later recount that "It did not appear to be infantry moving towards them, but moving walls."[4]

When the regulations of 1726 were first applied, many of the officers encountered difficulties when attempting to teach the troops the new systems. Much of the problem appears to have been their teaching methods which over relied on the cudgel to beat proficiency into the inept who failed the exercises. Frederick continued weeding out those officers who consistently demonstrated a substandard performance during the training activity.[5]

During his father's time, there had been no administrative staff to supervise the instructional needs of the army. Realizing that it was beyond his ability to supervise all the details of training, Frederick appointed inspectors to guarantee standardization of instruction among all regiments, and proper discipline among the troops. These inspectors were to inspect the various regiments frequently; have them perform the drill, and, if necessary, take steps to eradicate any shortcomings that might appear.[6]

Frederick realized that generals, and for that matter any class of officers, couldn't be trained by lectures and map sessions alone. The only alternative was to have officers of all grades lead troops in all types of terrain and situations. The curriculum of instruction was to include how to load and fire the musket, the methods of advancing, and the various "evolutions."

FIREARMS AND COLD STEEL IN THE ASSAULT

It is ironic that Frederick, whose personal beliefs placed him squarely in the French/Swedish school of thought regarding how an infantry attack was to be conducted, inherited the highly proficient infantry that had been molded by Leopold of Anhalt-Dessau. The "Old Dessauer," drawing on his experience during the War of the Spanish Succession and his association with Marlborough, developed the Anglo-Dutch platoon firing system to its logical extremity. Like the British and Dutch, the Prussian infantry had been trained in systematically using the firefight to overthrow their enemies. On the parade grounds, Prussian infantry were trained to fire by platoons while on the advance.

At Mollwitz, the first battle under Frederick's leadership, the remarkable effectiveness of the infantry trained under the strict tutelage of Leopold of Anhalt-Dessau was clearly demonstrated. The Prussian cavalry on the right side of the battlefield, disadvantaged by lack of numbers and faulty positioning, were quickly and thoroughly defeated by the Austrian cavalry led by General Römer. The Prussian infantry, assailed on all sides, repelled repeated attacks before being able to engage the Austrian infantry. These latter were noticeably intimidated by the superior firepower, and when confronted with a Prussian infantry advance after a lengthy firefight, retired from the battlefield. Although some of the Prussian infantry broke out in voluntary fire, not controlled by their officers, sufficient order was maintained to hold off the Austrian cavalry.

Despite this efficiency, Frederick quickly rejected the staid offensive tactics developed by Leopold which relied upon the use of slow-moving troops using platoon fire during the advance. There appear to be two different sets of reasons for this decision. The first lay in the Prussian version of platoon firing itself. It was even more demanding than that used by the Anglo-Dutch troops, and it required an extremely high level of training to be performed adequately. Even though this, given Prussian propensity for minute detail and constant training, was easily accomplished during peacetime, it could not be maintained for more than several months during an actual campaign as a stream of new recruits had to be brought in to replace casualties. The other reason for downplaying the use of the platoon firing system with its series of firefights at ever-decreasing ranges lay in the personal beliefs of Frederick himself. For the first two decades of his reign, Frederick was in favor of his infantry advancing straight to the enemy, withholding its fire, and closing to settle the affair with cold steel. What he advocated was essentially the *à prest* attack used throughout the period by the French and Swedish armies.

In his early career, Frederick had been greatly influenced by the exploits and dashing character of Charles XII of Sweden, who, for a number of years, managed to successfully frustrate several powerful opponents with his numerically smaller army. Probably unconsciously Frederick identified with Charles' dilemma of ruling a small but capable nation surrounded by much larger political entities. The French and Swedish methods of attack during the 1720's and 1730's had gained a new measure of credibility with the entrance of the Chevalier de Folard into the military intellectual arena and the controversy between the *ordre profond* and the *ordre mince* that immediately arose. The advocates of the quick advance and cold steel had adherents in almost every army, and even in Austria General Thüngen and Field Marshal Khevenhüller championed this cause.

In Frederick's first battles, the Prussian infantry reflexively fought, or more accurately, attempted to fight, the way it had been trained on the parade ground. At Mollwitz, for example, the Prussian infantry advanced mechanically, firing like automatons. In the next two years, a number of signs suggest Frederick was applying his own beliefs to offensive infantry tactics. Though the first rank had loaded with fixed bayonets since 1733, as of April 1741 all of the infantry was ordered to have their bayonets permanently fixed when they were on duty. The "Selowitz" infantry disposition (March 25th, 1742) and the regulations of 1743 also further hint at the use of the bayonet in the attack. Evidence on the battlefield of this change of tactics is vividly provided by the Battle of Hohenfriedeberg (June 4th, 1745), where the Anhalt regiment was ordered by Leopold to attack the Saxons without firing.[7]

In a number of Frederick's writings in this period (circa 1743–1760) we find his admonition against firing during the attack. In his *Commandeur de bataillon,* for example, the following is found:

> "If you attack the enemy on the plain and find yourself with the wing and the units which attack, you must march them in good order

against the enemy, begin the charge at three hundred paces, and at the slightest sign of confusion in the enemy ranks, march with lowered bayonets to bring about their defeat."[8]

In favoring the quick infantry attack, Frederick appears to have adopted a rationale similar to the one used to develop his cavalry tactics. The battle was to be won by offensive action, and the actual defeat of the enemy brought about by undermining their morale to fight, rather than physically destroying their lines. The enemy was to be intimidated by the same two elements that formed the basis of his cavalry doctrine, that is, a quick assault accompanied by strict maintenance of cohesion and formation. As was also the case with cavalry, Frederick sought to provide a systematic basis that would discourage small-unit combat, in this case, individual battalions engaging in lengthy firefights. Once again, we see his desire to maintain control over all of his forces on the battlefield, rather than relying on the initiative or ability of individual officers and units.[9]

Frederick continued to advocate these tactics after the outbreak of the Seven Years' War in 1756. At the Battle of Prague (May 6th, 1757) the Prussians were ordered to advance by "push of bayonet." If it couldn't be completely avoided, fire was only to be conducted when they could see the proverbial whites of their enemies' eyes. Judging by events during the Battle of Rossbach (November 5th, 1757), this distance was around 40 paces.[10]

There is a tendency to think that Frederick's advocacy of the advance to cold steel was an error in judgment and the length of his persistence in this matter, irrational. This view overlooks the fact that in an earlier age of wooden ramrods, when even the best-trained troops were only able to fire about twice per minute, this tactic was much more feasible. However, by the outbreak of hostilities in 1756, both the Austrian and French infantry had adopted Prussian-style iron ramrods, and the French were often employing a form of platoon fire. Though the infantry in neither army ever matched the Prussians for fire effectiveness, the volume of fire was greater than it had been in earlier wars. This, in turn, meant the feasibility of overthrowing the enemy simply by marching on them with shouldered muskets was greatly reduced from what it had been in previous wars, and the likelihood of troops stopping to return fire increased in the same proportion.

By the end of 1757, Frederick was willing to admit that it was often necessary to fire at the enemy during the assault, and from the Battle of Leuthen (December 5th, 1757) onward, Prussian infantry fire was systematically part of the attack.[11] Frederick estimated that Austrian infantry could only endure about fifteen minutes of a lively fire at close range:

> "I have observed if you step sharply up to an Austrian battalion" (within 50 paces or so), "and pour-in your fire well, in about a quarter of an hour you see the ranks beginning to shake, and jumble towards indistinctness."[12]

To what extent either platoon fire or quick assault tactics were used on the battlefield is debatable. As was the case in other armies, including the British, it was difficult to maintain platoon fire for any length of time. The first fire was universally the most effective, the pieces being properly charged prior to the start of the combat. However, during the heat of the struggle the muskets were loaded in haste.

> "You began by firing by platoons, and perhaps two or three would get off orderly volleys. But then would follow a general blazing away—the usual rolling fire when everybody blasted off as soon as he had loaded, when the ranks and files became intermingled, when the first rank was incapable of kneeling, even if it wanted to. The commanders, from subalterns to generals, would be incapable of getting the mass to perform anything else: they just had to wait until it finally set itself into motion forwards or backwards."[13]

Several contemporary French officers and an American tactician at the turn of the nineteenth century have commented that Prussian fire was a lot less effective than generally believed. Though the Prussian "quick fire" policy produced the greatest number of shots per minute possible, little attention was placed on the proper leveling of the pieces. The occasional officer or subaltern only demanded that the men "take aim at the middle of your men (the enemy)," regardless of the distance between them and their targets.[14] The result was a low percentage of hits.

GRAND TACTICAL DEVELOPMENT

Though many of Frederick's contributions to the development of the art of war were tactical in nature, he was nevertheless responsible for a new grand tactical concept: the "oblique attack." The oblique attack, in fact, consisted of two different grand tactical maneuvers that could be performed separately, or in combination, as at Leuthen. These were the "march by lines" and the "attack in echelon." Both of these shared a commonality of purpose, which was to allow the Prussian army, initially deployed in front of the enemy, to attack its flank. Unfortunately with time, the distinction between these two methods has blurred, and it has become customary to refer to either or both as the "oblique attack" without distinguishing between the two maneuvers.

Though Frederick may have developed two new ways of attacking his enemy's flank, the basic idea itself was very old; the advantages of delivering an attack to the enemy's flank or rear had been known since ancient times. The enemy attacked from the side would have to quickly redeploy or be rolled up. And, even if the enemy managed to successfully redeploy, this series of forced movements had a pronounced negative impact on the morale of the troops forced to move. However, prior to Frederick, all such flank attacks involved the piecemeal use of troops to attack a flank or rear, rather than the shifting of the entire army's line of approach, or "axis of attack." These attacks invariably had arisen out of the overall strategic situation prior to the start of the battle (e.g., the Battle of Steenkirk, August 3rd, 1692), or as a result of some favorable circumstances arising during the battle; for example, if a commander because of favorable terrain was able to surprise the enemy by stealth. There was no comprehensive grand tactic that systematically increased the commander's odds of successfully attacking a flank with a major portion of his army, regardless of the specific situation.

The attack in echelon evolved during the peace separating the end of the Second Silesian War and the outbreak of the Seven Years' War. In 1747, Frederick experimented with holding back, or "refusing" one wing while the remainder of the army assaulted the enemy. The advancing infantry whose own flank was further outward than the enemy's counterpart, partially wheeled inward as it neared the enemy's position. However, the task of rotating a lengthy infantry line proved to be impractical, and Frederick was forced to search for another way of bringing his forces to bear on the enemy's flank.

The longer the line to be wheeled, the more difficult it was to execute the rotation. After several experiments, Frederick came to this realization, and developed the following solution to avoid this problem. The infantry front was to be divided into a number of smaller units. Each of these infantry units was placed in echelon, that is, it was deployed slightly in front of its neighbor on one side and slightly behind its neighbor on the other. At Leuthen, for example, each echelon consisted of a battalion fifty paces in front of the preceding battalion.[15]

The echelon formation offered two main advantages over the simple line. Each individual echelon would encounter much less difficulty when rotating its axis of deployment; and, if the vertical distance between echelons had been properly calculated, a single line would be formed after all echelons had wheeled. The other advantage was not as obvious, though it contributed equally to the formation's potential power. Looking at the Prussian infantry from a distance, the enemy was unable to discern the formation being employed, and, in fact, thought that the Prussian infantry was advancing in total chaos. The enemy was able to see that the infantry line was fragmented; but was not able to perceive any ordered relationship between each division of the line.

Despite the appearances to the contrary, Frederick claimed that order was almost immediately restored:

> "But it needs only that the commander lift his finger; instantly this living coil of knotted intricacies develops itself in perfect order, and with a speed like that of mountain rivers when the ice breaks."[16]

The other maneuver often used in an oblique attack was the "march by lines." De Jomini felt that Frederick first came up with the principles of this maneuver during the early 1740's at the battles of Soor and Hohenfriedeberg, but it was never fully articulated in any of his military writings at this point. However, at this point he does not provide the details on how this maneuver is to be performed, and during the remainder of the War of the Austrian Succession it is not encountered on the battlefield. Frederick almost certainly realized that it could only be employed after all of his ranking officers were familiar with the technique, something that would only occur after peacetime training.

For this maneuver, the Prussian army deployed in the standard two lines in front of and parallel to the enemy's position, at about 1500–2000 paces distance; this was the initial axis of deployment. Instead of advancing toward the enemy, as would be expected, the Prussian army before the attack began quickly forming back into column, simply by quarter-wheeling by section or division, depending upon the desired width of the column. A column the length of the battlefield was immediately formed. Because all of the units could be quarter-wheeling more or less at the same time, this entire process could take as little as two minutes.

The two infantry columns would now march at a slight angle, leading them both to the flank and closer to the enemy. Because each column consisted of all the battalions which had made up the original lines, Frederick called this maneuver "marching by lines." When the two columns had gained the desired position, they quickly redeployed into line. Once again, this was a speedy process only requiring a single quarter-wheel on the part of each section or division. Once completed, the army was formed back into line facing the enemy's side or flank, and the Prussian army was now deployed along a second axis rotated 30 to 45 degrees from the original axis of deployment.

Presumably, the enemy would be taken by surprise and that, coupled with its slower methods of maneuver once it did start to respond, would make it difficult to adequately compensate for the change in the Prussian position. This being the case, the enemy's morale would be shaken, and its defeat greatly assisted.

On the surface, the oblique attack appears to be such an obvious ploy, one asks why did this grand tactic remained undiscovered until the 1750's, when all of the apparent prerequisites, i.e., the adoption of the flintlock, the use of linear tactics, etc., became available at the turn of the century? It's tempting to argue that it appeared when it did, because no one thought of it prior to that time. However, this assumes that earlier armies were just as capable of performing this maneuver; that, in fact, there were no hidden tactical prerequisites or levels of training required before being able to perform it.

A detailed look at the various steps involved in the oblique attack shows quite the opposite. An army was only able to use the oblique tactic once it was able to fulfill several basic requirements: its officers had to possess a comparatively (for the period) high level of training; the rank and file had to be expert in the art of the cadenced march, and the men had to march exclusively in closed ranks.

The first prerequisite of the oblique attack was in the collective capabilities of the officers. The success of the maneuver demanded that a large number of officers act in unison in order to have the large mechanism in the form of the Prussian army perform like clockwork. The oblique attack was a predefined and rehearsed tactic; it simply didn't pop into Frederick's mind as his troops were deploying prior to the Battle of Leuthen.

This becomes obvious when we examine the officers' roles needed to make this tactic work. Each officer had to be completely familiar with his duties and responsibilities in advance, that is, once deployed and the signal given, each was to have his battalion form back into column, roughly at the same time. They had to insure that the battalion retained exactly the required position once in column, there was no room for the type of error that could be allowed in a column of maneuver before it had entered the battlefield. Once the column had reached the new position, they had to guarantee that the battalion would promptly redeploy into line, without the delays that had been characteristic of the traditional deployment into line.

For the oblique attack to be successful it had to be performed quickly. The individual regimental commander couldn't wait for orders to arrive from his superiors to guide his every motion in the same manner as would occur in the traditional deployment process, where aides-de-camp would scurry to and fro providing orders about the smallest of details. The delays caused by waiting for orders more than any other reason accounted for the several hours usually needed to deploy. To avoid these types of delays during the oblique attack, the officer had to issue orders on his own initiatve according to a prearranged plan or model.

Although by modern standards the ability to act according to a single overall plan appears a modest enough achievement, it was beyond the collective capabilities of all officers except those in the Prussian army after the conclusion of the War of the Austrian Succession. The reason for this is simple: the Prussian army by this time had become the first truly "professional" army since the decline of the Roman Empire. Here, the term "professional" is used not only to refer to a paid standing army, but to a paid standing army with regular, effective and uniform training allowing it to perform to a minimum expected standard. Though most armies were regularly paid and on a permanent establishment, no other army could meet this added requirement. The French army, for example, though it would periodically train in large groups or camps, could not boast that its officer corps was thoroughly trained in all the details of warfare and that all officers were conversant with several detailed battle plans. In the French army this was as much caused by an ideological conflict between the proponents of *ordre profound* and *ordre mince,* as it was to deficiency in training.

The other reason for the Prussian army's then-unique ability to perform the oblique attack lay in a series of tactical developments dating from about 1742 onwards. The Prussian army, experienced in cadenced marching even prior to the outbreak of war in 1740, brought to it a then-unknown level of expertise. The introduction of a number of sophisticated drumbeats to signal various commands as well as to govern the pace of the march and the manual of arms greatly facilitated the cadenced march as well as the issuance of orders. This new level of marching competence, in turn, meant that the Prussian army was able to do away with marching in open ranks (about four paces per rank) which had complicated the marching process in general and slowed down the quarter-wheel in particular.

NOTES

1. Renard, General, *Considérations sur la tactique de l'infanterie en europe*. Paris, 1857, p. 50.

2. Duffy, Christopher, *The Military Life of Frederick the Great*. New York, 1986, p. 3.

3. De Saxe, *op. cit.*, pp. 28–31.

4. Duffy, *The Army of Frederick the Great, op. cit.*, p. 31, citing Geuder, 1902, p. 115.

5. Frederick, "Du militaire depuis son institution jusqu'à la fin du règne de Frédéric-Guillaume" Oeuvres de Frédéric le grand, Berlin 1846–56, vol. 1, pp. 176–95; cited in Luvaas, Jay, Frederick the Great on the Art of War. New York, 1966, p. 66.

6. Frederick, *The History of My Own Times*, cited in Luvaas, *op. cit.*, p. 79.

7. Duffy, *The Army Of Frederick*, p. 90.

8. *Commandeur de bataillon*, pp. 58–59, cited in Luvaas p. 148.

9. Frederick, "Instructions," *op. cit.*, p. 99.

10. Carlyle, *op. cit.*, vol. 5, p. 165.

11. Duffy, *The Army of Frederick, op. cit.*, p. 91.

12. "Frederick's Military Instructions," Carlyle, *op. cit.*, vol. 5, p. 125.

13. Berenhorst, Betrachtungen vol. 1, p. 255; cited in Duffy, *The Army of Frederick, op. cit.*, p. 89.

14. Duane, *op. cit.*, vol. 1, p. 175.

15. Duffy, *The Army of Frederick*, pp. 154–155.

16. Carlyle, *op. cit.*, vol. 5, p. 195.

CHAPTER 11

French Tactical Developments: 1713–1756

1713 TO 1748

ALTHOUGH THE YEARS BETWEEN THE WAR OF THE SPANISH SUCCESSION and the War of the Austrian Succession saw the proliferation of theoretical works about the need for new drills, exercises, maneuvers and even tactics in the French army, very few changes were actually officially approved between 1713 and 1749.

Whatever changes were made can be summed up in a paragraph. By the outbreak of hostilities in 1740, the French infantry battalion now consistently deployed in four ranks. Previously, when a portion of each battalion had been armed with pikes, the company was nothing more than an administrative unit, without any tactical meaning at all. However, once all of the men within a battalion started to be armed identically, the company began to be treated as a tactical subdivision of the battalion. The training camp of 1733 officially recognized this development, henceforth a company was referred to as a "section" in this capacity.[1]

However, the battalions continued to be arranged in the same fashion; the officers and subalterns were positioned according to the regulations of 1703, while the distances between the ranks and the files remained unchanged. Unfortunately, the highly cumbersome and time-consuming methods of deploying from column into line from line into column also remained virtually the same, although there was no lack of unofficial experimentation by the more enterprising regimental commanders.

In terms of fire systems, the only progress that could be pointed to was that French troops no longer performed the caracole version of fire by ranks. Prior to 1749–1750 there was never any official mention of either cadenced marching or a cadenced manual of arms (loading and presenting the weapons). The troops were still forced to march with open ranks (six paces between ranks), and had to close ranks before they either changed the direction of march or deployed.

The conservatism within the French army ran so deep, that despite Puységur's constant lobbying for the use of continuous lines of infantry, *en muraille,* the battalions along each line officially were still to be deployed with a full interval separating them and their neighbor as late as 1750, despite the fact that, practically speaking, this method of deployment was abandoned during the War of the Spanish Succession! Fortunately for the French, this last regulation appears to have been rarely, if ever, carried out during this era, there usually being too many battalions to deploy across the battlefield to permit such wide intervals.

A number of factors contributed to this continuing military conservatism. First, there was tradition itself, the memories of the glorious days of Turenne and Luxembourg, and there were those who sought to preserve the same time-honored ways, so successful for their forefathers. Another aspect of the problem was created by dissension among those military thinkers who sought change. The rift between those advocating the *ordre profond* and those favoring the *ordre mince* was most often as deep as it was vociferous. Prior to the start of the Seven Years' War, these two military world views appeared to be opposites, not susceptible to much compromise.

Compounding these factious tendencies was an attitude all-too-common among the nobility making up the officer class. This was the belief that what was most important in an officer was valor and honor; if the troops were brave enough and led by a daring fellow, any situation could be won. Among the higher echelon of officers, this was not so much a conscious belief, after all here the study of the "art of war" was recognized as a necessity for better performance, as it was an unconscious attitude that affected the way French officers approached the training of the men in their regiments.

These attitudes translated into neglect. Where, in the Prussian army, emphasis was placed on continual training, on developing the soldier's ability to perform what was expected of him under any conditions, in France all was taken for granted. In a circular issued to regimental commanders, dated November 14th, 1743, D'Argenson complained of the lack of training exercises. Rather pointedly, he mentioned that this deficiency was all too apparent in the various situations where they had lately been employed. He enjoined the colonels to take advantage of each available occasion to exercise their men.

An officer wrote, around 1740:

> "One does not attach enough [importance], in France, to making the evolutions of the troops; one is ordinarily content practicing the manual of arms and having the soldiers march well. That is good, but that is not sufficient . . . ."[2]

Another officer complained that in French service, recruits were sent to mount guard duty before being fully trained and were abandoned to the instruction of a corporal or a sergeant without coming into contact with any officers. Even worse, they were immediately required to drill with the other soldiers, even though they could only handle their weapons with difficulty and only succeeded in hindering everyone else during the exercise. This same officer then praised the advantages of the Prussian system of continual practice, both for recruits and veterans alike.[3]

The problem of inadquate training and incompetent officers was nothing new to the French army. The seeds of this malaise were, in fact, sown by Louis XIV himself. During Turenne's time, officers were forced to learn their duties, being promoted by display of talent and accumulated experience. According to Saint-Simon, Louvois, always attempting to extend his influence, changed this:

> "Promotion was granted according to length of service, thus rendering all application and diligence unnecessary. . . . He

> [Louvois] persuaded the King that it was [the King] who ought to direct the armies from his cabinet. The King flattered by this, swallowed the bait, and Louvois himself was thus enabled to govern in the name of the King, to keep the generals in leading-strings, and to fetter their every movement. In consequence of the way in which promotions were made, the greatest ignorance prevailed among all grades of officers. None knew scarcely anything more than mere routine duties, and sometimes not as much as that."[4]

By the time of the Peace of Aix-la-Chapelle (October 18th, 1748), it had become clear to even the most conservative French officers that the existing drill, training, and even tactical practices were now obsolete, and that the most thorough reforms were necessary. Whatever dissension existed was about what measures should be taken to revamp the French army, that strong measures were required was no longer questioned.

Historians have divided French military thinkers of this period into two major schools, those espousing the *ordre profond,* and those favoring the *ordre mince*. Those advocating the *order profond* were essentially disciples of Folard who did not want to rely exclusively on linear tactics. Their main tenet was the use of massive columns of attack to batter the enemy line, this attack wherever possible being made with cold steel without preliminary firefights. The *ordre mince* school were the traditionalists who advocated deploying a battalion on four or even five ranks along two lengthy lines across the battlefield. Some within this school advocated the use of firefights as part of the offense, although others felt the traditional advance to cold steel was the best method.

THE POST-1748 PERIOD

The period between the restoration of peace in October 1748, and the outbreak of hostilities in 1756 was marked by fervent efforts to lay a solid foundation for the training of the infantry, and to implement an effective body of tactical doctrine. The ultimate failure of these efforts, based on the conduct of the French during the Seven Years' War, was not because of lack of effort, or analysis, but partly because of the very ambitiousness of the agenda set forth by the French military authorities during this period. In a sense, they expected the French infantry to be able to run before being able to crawl.

During 1749, the Minister of War studied the need to adopt a number of elements of "Prussian drill," and a detachment formed from several regiments was used to test the various drills being considered at the Hôtel des Invalides in Paris in the presence of Marshal de Saxe. The most notable new elements were the use of cadence marching, a new manual of arms (the method of loading, presenting and firing the musket) using cadenced movements, and platoon fire. A further trial was conducted by the Gardes Françaises (French Guards) and the Gardes Suisses (Swiss Guards) the next year on May 3rd, this time in the king's presence on the plain of Sablons. Pleased with the results, the King ordered that the new maneuvers become mandatory the following week, on May 7th, 1750. Despite this official decree, these practices were anything but universally applied, or even adequately described, in any regulations or decree.[5]

One of the most important aspects of the May 3rd, 1750, regulations, one with an enduring legacy, was that for the first time a systematic regimen for training infantry was devised and at least theoretically imposed throughout all the corps making up the infantry arm. The major and aide major were responsible for demonstrating and instructing the subalterns (sergeants, corporals, and *anspessades*) in each regiment in the various drills and exercises. These subalterns then were to instruct each soldier, initially on a one-to-one basis. Next, the men were grouped together into five- or six-man squads which were instructed by a corporal or *anspessade* (lance corporal) but still under the watchful eye of a sergeant.

Initially, the soldiers were exercised without their weapons, and were literally put through the paces, which were also introduced as a result of this same regulation. The same methodical approach was used with respect to marching: first, two or three soldiers marched together, then a squad. They marched in a single rank, then in two ranks, and once they mastered this they graduated to marching in three and four ranks. Throughout the marches, the drummers used a tempo appropriate for the pace being used.

A regular timetable was set up for the various levels of training: each morning was devoted to individual training, with squad practice on Sunday mornings, while the guard went through its required motions every day after the inspection. Every second day, four companies were put through the paces and the new manual of arms in the afternoon, and unlike the lower level exercises this was practiced in front of the officers. From May 1st to September 1st each year, the entire battalion had to be exercised together every eight days: the battalions from the same regiment had to exercised together every 15 days. During the remainder of the year, the battalion was exercised every 15 days and the entire regiment together only once a month.

Unfortunately, it appears the French in their new-found devotion to the parade ground, repeated some of the same errors committed by Frederick William of Prussia twenty-five years earlier. Emphasis was placed on what appeared smart on the reviewing field, rather than what would truly be best in time of war. Most of the attention was focused on the manual of arms, instead of essential maneuvers that would have prepared the men for necessary operations encountered before and during an actual battle. Many regimental commanders dramatically reduced the size of the cuffs and the tails at the back of the *habit* (great coat) in order to eliminate anything that could catch the musket when it was being manipulated around the soldier's body.

The 1750 regulations did not significantly alter the layout of an infantry battalion, which continued to be deployed in four ranks. Each rank was one pace from the one in front, except while practicing the manual of arms, when the ranks were opened to the length of the halberd. Sergeants were now once again armed with halberds, instead of muskets, while the officers carried spontoons. There were twelve fusilier companies, the grenadiers on the right and a 45-man piquet on the left. The practice of separating each battalion along a line by a full interval continued to be official policy.

This regulation experimented with a different subbattalion set of tactical units. Now, a company, the administrative unit, equaled a section, which in turn was a platoon, the tactical unit. When in column, for the first time, it became possible to have each tier in the column separated from the one in front by a full interval, just as was being done in the Prussian army for the previous twenty to thirty years. In other words, in a column of platoons, each platoon was separated from the next platoon in the column by a distance equivalent to the width of a platoon, in a column of half battalions, each tier was separated by the width of a half-battalion, and so on.[6] This was a significant development, since now if only in theory, line could be formed when marching from the left simply by simultaneous quarter-wheels.

For the first time, all maneuvers and marches were to be conducted with cadenced steps. There were two possible steps that could be used when marching: the small pace, eight inches long, and the ordinary pace of 24 inches. Additionally, there was also an oblique step and a side pace to move a formation to the left or the right. The ordinary pace could be performed normally, at one step per second or at the double, i.e., two steps per second.[7]

The next regulations appeared on June 29th, 1753. Tactically, the company still functioned as a section, but now once again two adjoining companies formed a platoon. The most veteran soldiers were placed in the first rank, then the fourth, then the second and finally the novice troops in the third.[8]

The 1st platoon, placed on the right of the battalion was formed by the 1st and 7th companies, the 2nd on the left by the 2nd and 8th; the 3rd on the left of the 1st, 3rd and 9th; the 4th to the right of the 2nd by the 4th and 10th; the 5th to the left of the 3rd, by the 5th and 11th; the 6th platoon to the right of the 4th by the 6th and the 12th. The 1st and 3rd platoons formed the 1st *manche* (or "sleeve"); the 2nd and 4th the 2nd; the 5th and 6th platoons formed the 3rd *manche*.

The two flags were placed one between the two files of the center of the 5th platoon and the other between the two files at the center of the 6th; the file of the flag was thus composed: one sergeant at the first rank, the flag in the second, a corporal in the third, and a fusilier in the fourth. In the Swiss regiments, each company formed two platoons.[9]

The ranks were now further closed to only two feet, though when marching, the ranks continued to be in open ranks. However, the distance used for open ranks (formerly about 12 feet) was no longer a constant, but varied according to the type of column being used. When marchng by battalion there were to be 12 feet between ranks; eight feet when marching by half-column, and only four feet marching by *manche* (one-third of a battalion) or platoons. Whenever the column had to change directions, as in previous systems, it had to stop and close its ranks, conduct a series of quarter-wheels on a fixed pivot and then set off again. This invariably meant that the length of the column was elongated, which resulted in a series of lengthy delays. Clearly, though the French had officially adopted cadenced marching, they still had not come to realize its potential benefits or they would have maintained closed ranks throughout all maneuvers.

A number of different types of columns were permitted, each being defined by their width: a column by company, by platoons (two companies wide), by *manches* (two platoons), and by half-battalion (three platoons). In a column by company, platoon or *manche* the grenadier company marched in front of the main body and the piquet to the rear. However, in a column by half-battalion the grenadiers were on the right of the first half-battalion while the piquet was on the left of the second.

The 1753 regulation started to address the issue of signaling orders using drums, though the details were left to the following year. If the battalion was broken or disordered, the men were to rally to the battalion flags.

The third new infantry regulation appeared on May 14th, 1754. The two major innovations in this regulation were the adoption of the three-rank battalion, employed in some other armies for over fifty years and the standardization of drum signals throughout the entire infantry arm. The company from that time onward had 11 files and the formation of the platoons was as follows:

Until this regulation, each regiment or corps had been free to create its own set of drum signals and this was confusing, especially in camps containing many different regiments. The establishment of a universal cadence, at either 60 or 120 steps per minute meant that for the first time the drum beatings could also be standardized.

The new standardized drum airs were the *appel,* the assembly, the charge, the flag, the internment (drum only); the dismissal; the general; the ordinary march, the march at the double, to order (drum only); the proclamation (drum only), the prayer, the retreat, and the particular march for each corps. The music specific to each was recorded using the same musical notation used today. Each battalion had four hautboys (oboes) or fifes, though most of the musical airs were played by the drummers. Each regiment was allowed to retain one distinctive drum beating to be used whenever it had to rally its men. Here, the distinctive beat allowed a mass of fugitives to each recognize his own regiment, avoiding the confusion that would have occurred if all the regiments were beating the same airs to rally their men.

In order to disseminate these new standardized drumbeats, the drum majors from each regiment were assembled at Versailles on December 1st, 1754, under the command of the drum major of the Gardes Françaises. To practice, they beat the various drumming airs under the King's windows.[10]

CHANGES IN FIRING SYSTEMS

After 1713 the more primitive methods of delivering fire were abandoned, and when in open terrain the French infantry exclusively relied upon fire by ranks (the non-caracole version, where the last rank fired first). This fire system, although simple to use and capable of powerful initial volleys, was not at all conducive to continuous evenly flowing fire. The problem was that, though the third and fourth ranks standing upright could easily start to reload after they fired, the first and second ranks either had to attempt to reload while in a stooping or kneeling position, a very difficult task, or stand up to make their task easier. However, if they stood up, by definition, the ranks behind them couldn't fire.[11]

Many French officers still believed that firepower was only important in those situations where the French infantry could not close to the enemy, such as when their movement was interdicted by ditches, hedges, etc. This view had little or nothing to do with the *ordre profond* and *ordre mince* controversy; most officers in both schools believed that the proper way for the French infantry to attack was endure the defender's fire and advance *à prest*.

The possibility of allowing infantry to fire voluntarily, without being regulated by officers' commands, was also discussed among the military intelligentsia. This was often used by French troops stationed behind entrenchments and other types of fortified positions. According to Monsieur La Botte, writing around 1750, the Prussians and the Austrians only feared French voluntary fire, French volley fire being "defective,"[12] and Bombelles declared: "Our *chasseur* fire (voluntary fire), well aimed, is the most deadly; that made by commands produces a mediocre effect and *chasseur* fire is the most suitable to the genius of the French nation."[13]

De Saxe had considered using voluntary fire as early as 1732 when writing his famous *Reveries*. Although De Saxe was very much an advocate of the *à prest* method of attack, he agreed that firepower was necessary in rough terrain where it was difficult, if not impossible, to close with the enemy, or where the infantry was attacked by cavalry.

> "But the method should be simple and natural. The present practice is worthless because it is impossible for the soldier to aim while his attention is distracted awaiting the command. How can all these soldiers who have been commanded to get ready to fire continue to aim until they receive the word to fire? A trifle will derange them and, having once lost the critical instant, their fire is no longer of much use. Let no one think it does not make a great difference; it will amount to several yards. Nothing is so easy to derange as musket fire. And besides this, and according to our method, they are kept in a constrained position."[14]

De Saxe's remarks not withstanding, the majority view was to continue with some form of volley fire, even when behind entrenchments. "Voluntary fire," as the practice of allowing the men to fire on their own was called, was looked down upon for two reasons. French military authorities felt that unless the battalion's fire was strictly controlled, the battalion could be denuded of fire at a critical moment, such as when approached by enemy cavalry. Volley fire, at least in theory, allowed the officers to choose when and where it was to be delivered.

At the same time, voluntary fire was considered to be disorderly and leading to the irreversible confusion of the entire battalion. The act of commanding the men was viewed as maintaining discipline over the men and helping to take their minds off of dangers around them. It was believed where troops were left without commands they would soon start to break if seriously threatened.[15]

Although some officers, such as Monsieur de Rostaing, in his memoir manuscript, the *essai of the Legion,* continued to look down on the use of firepower offensively, there was a growing number of officers sufficiently impressed by the British and Prussian methods to have them imitated by French infantry. Apparently, the point had been driven home on the battlefields of Dettingen (June 27th, 1743), Fontenoy (May 11th, 1745), and Rocoux (1746). Marshal Noailles wrote to Louis XV after Dettingen describing the enemy's performance:

> "Their infantry was closed and held themselves brazenly, they conducted a fire so lively and so sustained that the old officers never had seen anything like it, and so superior to ours one could not make any comparison, this resulting from our troops being neither exercised nor disciplined as to be suitable."[16]

Around 1750, the official view was that the French infantry, if properly disciplined, could be made to deliver orderly volleys, and that the effect was preferable to "confused and irregular fire." However, to achieve this a simple system with "little formality" was needed.

Santa-Cruz, a famous Spanish general of the period, experimented with a "rolling fire" that was a cross between the fire by ranks and platoon firing system, and this seems to have influenced some French military thinkers. The first rank in the right half of the first company fired, and then was followed by the first rank in the right half of each of the other companies, in succession. These were followed by the second ranks in the right half of each command, and then the third.

When all the ranks in the right half of each company had fired, then the left half of each company would follow suit. The other suggestion Santa-Cruz made, was to place the best men in the first rank, to provide an example for the rest of the men.

This proposed system was obviously cumbersome, and the French authorities leaned toward platoon firing. A few general principles started to be adopted. During the War of the Spanish Succession, the higher officers remained several paces in front of the battalion even in the middle of fire combat. Now, officers were to "incorporate themselves into line" when fire was being delivered. This meant that they entered the first rank and placed one of their knees on the ground. Otherwise, in a few moments there would be no officers left: they would either have been shot by their own troops or, standing up and attracting a lot of attention, they would be picked off by aimed fire specifically directed at them. The notion that the infantry should level their weapons according to the range of the general target also started to gain acceptance: at "half musket range" the soldiers were to aim at the enemy's "bellies," if infantry, and at the horse's breast, if cavalry.

The value of interlocking the ranks, not having each man standing directly behind the one in front, but staggered a few inches over, started to be appreciated. The men in the first two ranks placed one of their knees on the ground, while the rear two ranks stood upright. However, the four interlocked ranks were drawn much closer together than previously (30 inches in 1750, two feet in 1753), and care had to be taken that each soldier positioned his feet properly, so as not to interfere with those to his front or rear.

The reason for bringing the four ranks so close together was to allow the barrels of the muskets in the fourth rank to protrude beyond the shoulders of the men in the first rank. This was imperative if the number of men shot by friendly troops in the rear ranks was to be minimized. However, despite these precautions even during exercises, those in the first rank continued to have their wigs burnt, and musket balls often passed through the officers' clothing. One of the reasons why the French finally adopted the three-rank line in May 1754 was to avoid this problem.[17]

The May 3rd, 1750, regulation introduced several major innovations to the French army. The wooden ramrod was abandoned and replaced by an iron ramrod, which allowed the infantryman to reload his weapon more quickly. In fact, he was now expected to be able to fire three volleys per minute. The musket was to be loaded in only 14 movements and for the first time the cadence used during this process was standardized: there was to be one movement per second. The charge in a cartridge was fixed at 1/42nd of a pound of powder, and the cartridge-pouch was to contain 19 cartridges.

The 1750 regulation permitted three different methods of delivering fire: fire by ranks, platoon fire, and *billebaude* (voluntary fire). In all varieties of fire the men in each rank were "interlocked," that is staggered slightly over from the man in front so as to have a clear line of sight. In the case of fire by ranks, both the third and fourth ranks fired together, then the second stood up and fired, and finally the first. The four ranks then all loaded together. During platoon fire, the first and second ranks placed one of their knees on the ground. In the case of voluntary fire, each man fired successively, then the fire continued by the men in the first and second ranks only.[18]

Fire by ranks, which had survived long past its time, finally disappeared with the regulations of 1753. Emphasis was placed on the platoon firing type of systems in which the battalion's fire was divided into portions along its front. Each volley could be conducted by section (company), platoon, *manche,* half-rank, or the entire battalion.[19]

The 1754 regulations for the first time introduced a standard model of musket for universal service in the infantry. These regulations also show exactly how divided opinion was in the top French military circles, and how tenaciously some adhered to the older methods. Platoon fire, described in the previous two regulations, was maintained but two other fire systems were added: fire by file, and *chasseur* fire. In platoon fire, which now had only the first rank placing one of its knees on the ground, could be delivered directly in front or obliquely to either side. The "fire by file" method could be delivered by *manche* (one-third battalion), half-rank, or the entire battalion. The men in each file fired in turn and then moved to the right and started to fire again once they reloaded. *Chasseur* fire was essentially caracole fire, but was now reserved for use in the massive Folard-style columns of attack prescribed by the regulations. Each subdivision along the front of the column fired, and then proceeded to the rear of the column to reload. The men in the next rank fired as soon as they were uncovered by those in the preceding rank.[20]

During the Seven Years' War, the French infantry occasionally succeeded in employing platoon fire; however, there is no record of their ever producing an effect comparable to the Prussians at Mollwitz or the English at Dettingen or Fontenoy. Most often when firing had to be resorted to, voluntary fire, where the soldier fired without waiting for orders, was used.

ORIGINS OF LIGHT TROOPS IN THE FRENCH ARMY

During the period under consideration, traditional military philosophy had most of the infantry and cavalry in Western Europe fighting in closed order, that is, they were drawn up into tight formations, using very controlled techniques to move and attack. By the advent of the Seven Years' War (1756–1763), however, the use of light infantry that fought in an irregular fashion had been firmly established for a number years in both the Austrian and French armies. In this type of fighting, men were not packed together in dense formations, but were spread out and allowed to take advantage of whatever cover was offered by surrounding terrain.

This development appears to have at least two separate origins: in the southeastern Hapsburg domains, and in France. In areas such as Hungary, Croatia, etc., given the nature of their Turkish enemies and the rough terrain on which they fought, the inhabitants were forced to develop looser, more flexible tactics. For many years, this type of fighting remained little heard of in Western Europe; however, this changed during the War of the Austrian Succession. In 1740, Maria Theresa, the heir to the Hapsburg domains found herself hard-pressed by her enemies who, finding the Hapsburg hereditary territories having no male heir, wanted to strip it of some of its more attractive provinces. Faced simultaneously with several powerful opponents, Maria Theresa was forced to draw upon her southern subjects to provide a larger number of independent infantry and cavalry units. These, though now faced with an enemy who used closed order methods of fighting, continued to utilize their traditional methods, which proved extremely effective, not only in the rigors of the "small wars" that constituted each campaign, but also in any broken terrain that might be found on a battlefield.

Both the Prussians and the French suffered considerable embarrassment due to the effectiveness of these troops, but each responded to this new type of threat quite differently. The Prussians reemphasized the need for order. In other words, they took a number of systematic precautions to counter this threat. The methods of the irregular troops appealed to the French, whose own tactics were offensively oriented and left the soldier to his own initiative much more than in either the British or German military traditions. They were quick to realize the advantages of these "open order" fighting tactics for the "small war" (reconnaissance expeditions, etc.), as well as on broken terrain on the battlefield.

This willingness to adapt to this irregular warfare as practiced by the Croatian, Rascians, and Bants they encountered was also due to the fact that the French had already experimented with the use of light troops *(troupes légères)* during the previous fifty years. Individual free companies *(compagnies franches)* were first introduced in 1684, during the siege of the city of Luxembourg. These company-sized units were not permanent, but were formed on an ad hoc basis from a miscellanea of men taken from various regular corps within the army. They were used exclusively in a *petite guerre* (small war) capacity, that is, to observe the enemy, to reconnoiter his positions, and harass him with a series of false attacks.

However, it was only in 1689 in Catalonia and France's north and eastern frontiers that the notion of *troupes légères* evolved to something similar to that found in the second quarter of the eighteenth century. One Monsieur de la Croix was the first in the French army to fully understand the role of light infantry. Previously in the service of the Landgrave of Furstenbourg, he was very familiar with the broken terrain in the area between the Meuse and the Rhine, and was very sensitive to the shortcomings of the line infantry when operating in this type of environment. As a result of his intelligent, energetic use of these ephemeral company-sized units on September 18th of that year, Louis XIV rewarded him with the first two permanent free companies: a fusilier company and a dragoon company, both of 100 men.

De la Croix's success did not go unrecognized, and on March 2nd, 1693, he was made lieutenant colonel. When six *regiments de fusiliers des frontiers* (frontier fusiliers) were formed in 1695, they were trained and exercised according to his teachings.[21]

Though in the beginning, light troops were simply regular line infantry made to perform a new set of tasks and duties, quickly new recruiting and training practices were developed. Men were chosen on the basis of their strength and agility and not simply by height. According to General Grandmaison, a lieutenant colonel in the *volontaires des Flandres* during the Wars of the Austrian Succession:

> " . . . a man of five feet with good legs is preferable to one of five and a half, who is not equally strong and vigorous."[22]

When the French first started to raise large numbers of light troops during the 1744 and 1745 campaigns, they initially utilized large numbers of young men, whom one would quite naturally assume to be perfect for this type of duty. However, it was very quickly discovered that these younger men for the most part lacked the long-term stamina needed for this very demanding type of work, and veterans in their thirties were much preferred.

Light troops, though also equipped with swords, depended upon their flintlocks and bayonets. Unlike the regular infantry, which at that time were garbed in long white greatcoats, light troops were dressed in short blue and sometimes brown uniforms, which at the time were considered to be the colors least easily seen at a distance in the countryside. Most often, they were given exotic looking caps, which were found to facilitate recruiting. Their light and short uniforms were not without their own disadvantages, however. It was soon discoverd that these provided insufficient protection against the inclement weather during the late Autumn, and resulted in large numbers of men becoming ill in each unit.

The horsemen in the light troops were selected from slightly taller men, from between 5′2″ to 5′4″ (5′4½″ to 5′ 7″ English measurements), in proportion to the size of their horses. Once again, they had to be strong and active. They were equipped with light muskets, pistols and sabers.[23]

Unfortunately, the lackluster performance of the great majority of line regiments during the War of the Spanish Succession, brought discredit to all units within the French army. With the reduction of forces that invariably accompanied the reestablishment of peace, the light troop units were among the first to be forgotten. Most of the *compagnies franches* were eliminated in 1715, and those that survived were assigned to garrison duty. For example, the *Compagnie Franche* of Monsieur Saumery (later Montbossier) as of July 16th, 1725, was to guard the Ile de Provence.[24]

During the War of the Polish Succession, new light companies were raised and these were relatively successful, carrying out the various tasks and operations making up the *petite guerre*. Leaders of the independent companies, such as Jacob-Pasteur, Lacroix, Dumoulin, and Klienholds received the recognition due their efforts. Monsieur Jacob, for example, with 80 dragoons managed simply by his reputation and sudden appearance to intimidate 300 Austrian grenadiers, already formed in square, into surrendering without a fight.[25]

However, the multitudes of Austrian light troops the French faced during the War of the Austrian Succession, forced the French to increase the number of light troops in their army by several orders of magnitude. Relentlessly pursuing their irregular warfare during the Bohemian and Bavarian campaigns, the Hungarian, Croatian, Liconian, Slavonian, Warasdin, Bant, Rascian and Pandour units managed to continually keep off balance the French regular forces. They frequently captured or destroyed French convoys, hospitals and baggage and systematically defeated French foragers, marauders and detachments whenever they met.

Initially, the French were only able to oppose this threat with two under-strengthed hussar regiments and the small independent light companies established in the 1720's and 1730's. The French found their armies being seriously threatened before they even came to grips with any organized groups of the enemy.

Because of their relatively small size, about 120–150 men in wartime, the free companies were of limited value when used separately. To rectify this, starting in 1744, the French started to raise a number of larger units; and, in the same year, all of the existing miscellaneous company-sized units were amalgamated to form the *Volontaires Royal,* which was about the size of an infantry regiment.

The initial organization of the *Volontaires Royal,* consisting of two infantry battalions, six squadrons of dragoons, a company of carpenters, another of *pontonneirs,* and a third of fusilier guides, as well as two regimental cannons, evinces an entirely new philosophy behind the use of light troops. The *Volontaires Royal* was a substantial force, capable of acting on its own, and sustaining itself without reinforcements for quite a while. Also, the principle of combined arms is clearly apparent in the form of the dragoons and the two cannons. The other corps of light troops, such as the Arquebusiers de Grassin, formed at Metz on January 1st, 1744, were of similar size and organization (900 *fantassins* and 300 cavalrymen).

Now, the French in their Flanders campaigns started to find they could do to the Dutch and the English what the Austrian light troops had been able to do to them, in the previous several campaigns in Bavaria and Bohemia.

Although these large light troop units tended to be used primarily for the vital rigors of the "small war" they occasionally found themselves forced to fight on the battlefield. The action of the Arquebusiers de Grassin in the Wood of Barry at Fontenoy, where they faced and held off a much larger Anglo-Hanoverian force, is probably the most famous case. In these situations, the light troops fought completely in open order, where each soldier was separated by about a pace or more, taking cover behind whatever natural protection was available. All fire was voluntary, aimed, and not coordinated by orders. This tactic was referred to as *débandade,* literally meaning "helter-skelter," and referred to the frenetic quality of the fighting, which was totally left to the capabilities and initiative of the individual soldier.

During the 1720's, many French military authorities started to consider much more controlled light infantry tactics to be used in conjuction with traditional closed order tactics on the battlefield. The idea of forming a platoon-sized *piquet* (50 men) in each battalion to serve as a type of second grenadier company had already gained popularity by the War of the Spanish Succession. Now, the idea of scattering the grenadiers and the piquet in front of the battalion to occupy advantageous terrain such as a hedge, mill or the border of woods gained some acceptance. This was in part due to the fact that skilled infantrymen now could fire one to two shots per minute and individual fire (as opposed to volley fire) could have a more significant effect.

For the first time in many years, the French military found itself faced with a lengthy period of peace, and it relied upon "camps of instructions" to train its troops. One of the interesting aspects of the camp of instruction of 1727 was the experimentation with light infantry tactics on the battlefield. In one of the exercises, the battalion's grenadiers were spread out in front of the battalion to fire at the enemy. After firing, they retired around the left and right flanks of the battalion to start reloading at its rear.

In another exercise, as the battalion advanced toward the enemy it was preceded by the grenadiers who maintained a fire. Behind the grenadiers were the men in the piquet who started to fire after the grenadiers retired. In a third exercise, a battalion detached its piquet and grenadiers after being repelled. These covered the battalion's retreat allowing it to rally more readily.[26]

These experiences served as a basis for Marshal de Saxe's views on deployment and use of light infantry, as found in his famous *Reveries* written in 1732 while recovering from an illness. De Saxe advocated placing light infantry, presumably supplied by the grenadiers and the piquet, along the front 100, 150 or even 200 paces in front of each battalion. These were to begin firing when about 300 paces from the enemy and continue until they advance to within 50 paces. The firing was completely on an individual basis, without any words of command.

The captain commanding the battalion's light troops would then order that they retire in an orderly fashion behind the regiment taking care that they would continue to fire occasionally as they withdrew. The grenadiers were to pass through the battalion slipping through the intervals between the battalions in groups of ten. As soon as the grenadiers passed the battalion, it would start to advance toward the enemy and double its ranks from four to eight while doing this. De Saxe also advocated the use of local cavalry support for the infantry. He believed two troops of cavalry (about 70 men) should be placed behind each regiment.[27]

Very similar tactics were experimented with at the Camp of Gray in 1754. In some of these exercises, the piquet, grenadiers and the entire battalions on the two wings deployed in three ranks 20 paces in front of the rest of the infantry. The army advanced until 120 paces from the "enemy." As the detached infantry advanced, the remaining infantry redeployed in six ranks. As soon as it succeeded in doing this, the battalions continued their advance and rejoined the detached infantry in front. Then the entire line attacked the "enemy" infantry in the middle of its line. During these exercises, the detached troops appear sometimes to have been in regular order, and sometimes in open or "skirmish" order. The report concluded that the fire produced by the detached grenadier and piquet companies, was greater than that which could be produced by an entire battalion deployed in three ranks and firing along its entire front.[28]

As we will see in a later chapter, these tactics would often be used in the Seven Years' War. During the winter of 1758–1759, the Champagne, Navarre, Belzaunce, and Auvergne, Le Roi (King's) regiments were among the first to systematically train 50 men per battalion to serve as *chasseurs*. These men fought in open order, using aimed fire. After the French defeat at Minden (August 1st, 1759), the practice of detaching the piquet to hold off or harass the enemy proved to be very useful, especially at the skirmish near Hamlen.

Seeing the utility of these tactics, De Broglie, commander of the French army in the field, ordered that the regiments under his control universally adopt these practices. A number of colonels expressed concern over the adoption of this tactic, apparently fearing that their battalions would be weakened by the loss of these men, should they be permanently detached from their parent unit. However, De Broglie assured these officers, and the Minister of War later, that these 50-man piquets would only be used locally, in conjunction with the battalion from which they were formed.

De Broglie later noted that one additional benefit, apart from an immediate tactical advantage, was that this practice served as the best sort of training for the men, more than marches and even participating in set piece battles, themselves. The troops developed flexibility and initiative, something that could never be taught when they were confined to standing in tight closed order formations.[29]

FRENCH CAVALRY

The gradual development of military thought was not limited to the infantry arm. French cavalry doctrine was undergoing a similar type of transformation. During the War of the Spanish Succession, French cavalry was to enter enemy cavalry ranks through the use of the sword, according to Puységur, meaning that once the two opposing lines of cavalry met, the individual cavalrymen were to make headway through swordplay. Obviously, this tactic presupposed that each line stopped once the enemy was contacted, and also that the enemy was not advancing knee to knee.

By the 1730's and 1740's the French had become more aware of the value of shock and the role of speed in winning close order combats. In his *Reveries* De Saxe stated, "Such that cannot go at speed over a couple of thousand yards to pounce upon the foe, is for nothing in the field."[30] However, Colonel Mack's comments that Austrian cavalry could not gallop 50 yards without 25 per cent of the horses becoming disordered, were probably as applicable to French cavalry.

At the Battle of Fontenoy (1745), Marshal de Saxe ordered his cavalry to break the British infantry column that had advanced behind the French lines, using the "breast of their horses." Of course, given the sharp rows of enemy bayonets, cavalrymen never found this an easy task.

The debate over whether firearms should be used by cavalry started to slacken, with most cavalry officers believing they should never be used during a battle when meeting their enemy counterpart. According to Grandmaison:

> "A horseman should never use his pistols but on the most pressing occasions, either to save his life, or disengage himself from some disagreeable situation."[31]

Another debate was not so easily resolved. This was the question of which was more effective, the sword when used to thrust (stab) or when used to cut (slash). The French were not alone in trying to answer this question. Nearly the same debate raged throughout most other armies during this period. However, it appears many experienced officers preferred the straight sword to thrust at an opponent. They argued that one wound caused by a stab is often deadly while this wasn't the case for "twenty cuts."[32]

However, these remarks notwithstanding, the French cavalry generally relied on the edge of the sword, not its point. Light cavalry, for example, were invariably armed with curved sabers, and it is not with surprise that we find most cavalry casualites suffered cuts, rather than stab wounds.

The French continued to believe that cavalry capability against infantry and other cavalry was largely the result of "weight of horse." When attacking enemy infantry, French cavalry used a different set of tactics. Previously, French cavalry had used pistol or carbine fire when attacking formed infantry. However, the success of this method declined with the adoption of the socket bayonet. Also, any attempt to have an entire line of cavalry close with a line of infantry necessarily resulted in extensive casualites, because of the number of men exposed to musket fire. These considerations, as well as exposure to new methods used by Austrian light cavalry during the first two campaigns of the War of the Austrian Succession led the French to develop new cavalry tactics during the mid-1740's.

These newer tactics were based on the principle that a few brave and experienced men would create the necessary gaps in the enemy infantry's line, and then the remainder of the squadron would exploit these. The fewer number of men initially exposed to enemy fire would mean correspondingly fewer casualties. Each squadron leader commanding experienced troopers would have 15 to 20 of his bravest men, presumably his "commanded" men positioned on each flank of the squadron, attack the infantry in line while the remainder of the squadron advanced in an orderly fashion behind them. This first wave advanced at the trot until 20 paces or so away from the line then moved in at the gallop.

The concentration of muskets directed against this handful of horsemen was such that most, if not all, would be hit by resulting fusilades. However, it was an accepted cavalry maxim that only 50 per cent of the horses and men hit by musket fire would be disabled, and, in fact, if the attacking cavalry was sufficiently close when fired upon, the remainder generally redoubled their efforts upon being hit. This interesting observation was made by General Grandmaison of the *Volontaires des Flandres:*

> "The other half [of those hit by gunfire] animated by the fire and the blood, falls with fury and impetuosity on the infantry, whose brestworks of bayonets is not able to sustain the weight of the horses in fury. The riders cannot any longer command them, they rush headlong, and make an opening for the rest of the squadron, to penetrate and break the battalion, which it cannot oppose this shock, a maneuver sufficiently quick and exact."[33]

It had long been known that horses would not voluntarily impale themselves upon the hedge of bayonets offered by an ordered line or square. The above strategy was to position the attacking cavalry close to the line or square being attacked at the moment of fire, so that the horses infuriated by the pain of their injuries, especially those in the chest, would forget the danger of the bayonets and in their agony involuntarily move onto the infantry they were attacking. Grandmaison cites a case during the Bavarian campaign of the War of the Austrian Succession where a hussar's horse after being shot overturned a *chevaux de frise* upon which it had impaled itself and exposed the infantry taking refuge behind it.

If any gaps were created in the line of infantry, the remainder of the squadron still in good order would attack the line. It should be pointed out, however, that this attack could be delivered at the trot at the quickest, since the squadron would have been 20 to 30 paces behind the leading element. It was hoped that the first group of attackers would, contrary to the wishes of the enemy officers, succeed in drawing the fire of all the enemy ranks. Then when the main body of horsemen closed, the infantry would be caught without fire. The cavalry, under these circumstances, could advance to contact much more easily, and the infantry were much more inclined to break.

The French believed that this type of tactic, the use of a "small party" to attack prior to the main body, was especially useful when attacking infantry squares. Previously, a cavalry regiment meeting with a square would circle the square, with individual groups attacking each side as they saw fit. This usually proved both ineffective and costly. The cavalry attacks were piecemeal and lacked any form of coordination. On the other hand, the entire regiment in the meantime was exposed to musket fire at extremely close range, while the full force of the infantry square, i.e., its four sides, could be brought to bear. This quickly resulted in significant losses among the cavalry with little result on the infantry square.

The alternative was to attack a single face of the square, so that the cavalry were only exposed to one-quarter the number of muskets. This could be performed by one or more squadrons in line, but some French cavalry commanders felt that sending in an initial small party would still lower the number of casualties to be taken.

These considerations were important because cavalrymen and horses were much less expendable than infantry, which were relatively speaking, replaceable. Each trooper and each horse represented a considerable investment of time and training. This type of resource once lost would not be available again for the remainder of the campaign. For this reason, cavalry officers were enjoined against making expensive attacks unless specifically ordered to do so by higher officers, or there were obvious grand tactical reasons making it necessary. Expensive attacks were particularly to be avoided in the "small war" making up most of the campaign.[34]

Unfortunately for the French, there was a down side to these tactics. Although they fulfilled their purpose of reducing the number of casualties incurred in any localized attack, by their very nature they tended to work against massive attacks, conducted in unison, against large enemy formations.

The ineffectiveness of piecemeal charges conducted with limited forces was demonstrated clearly at Fontenoy, where a number of French cavalry regiments were thrown one at a time against the British column that had succeeded in penetrating the French line between the redoubt in the Wood of Barry and that of Fontenoy. Only the assault led by De Vignecourt had any success. This officer and 14 men managed to momentarily break through the enemy formation but were immediately killed or wounded. All these attacks, made without any initial preparation or agreement and made with limited forces, were defeated by the compactness of the British formation and the steadiness and discipline of British platoon fire.[35]

NOTES

1. Colin, *op. cit.*, p. 34.
2. *Archives de la guerre,* carton no. 7, cited in Colin, *op. cit.*, p. 33.
3. *Archives de la guerre,* carton no. 7, cited in Colin Ibid., p. 33.
4. Saint-Simon, *op. cit.*, vol. 1, p. 354.
5. Belhomme, *op, cit.*, vol. 3, p. 186.
6. The commander of the battalion placed himself four paces in front of the center. The captain of the grenadiers was two paces in front of his company, his *sous lieutenant* to his left and one pace in the rear, the lieutenant in *serre file,* the two serjeants to the right of the first and fourth rank. The captain of the piquet was two paces in front, the lieutenants in *serres files,* and the two sergeants to the left of the first and fourth ranks. In the half-battalion of the right, the captains were two paces in front of the right of their company; the lieutenant at one pace behind the left. one sergeant on the right of the 1st rank and one at the left of the fourth rank. In the half-battalion of the left this order was reversed. The ensigns carrying the flags were one pace in front of the united battalion. The drummers formed two groups on the two ranks at the right and the left of the battalion, Belhomme, *op. cit.*, vol. 3, pp. 186–187.
7. Ibid., vol. 3, p. 188.
8. The two center files of each platoon had to be formed for corporals and *anspessades* (lance corporals). The company of 40 men gave eight files on four ranks deducting the sergeants, drummers and men of the piquet or on service. Figure 1 hereafter shows a platoon formed and the placed occupied by the grades. Figure 2 shows the grenadier company which had nine files, and figure 3 the piquet also of nine files. Belhomme, Ibid., vol. 3, p. 195.
9. Ibid, vol. 3, pp. 196–197.
10. Ibid., vol. 3, p. 198–199.
11. Le Blond, *op. cit.*, p. 409.

12. Ibid., p. 411.

13. Bombelles cited in Colin, *op. cit.,* p. 51.

14. de Saxe, *op. cit.,* pp. 45–47.

15. Le Blond, *op. cit.,* p. 410; 417–418.

16. Bère, F., *L'armee française*. Paris, n.d. p. 42.

17. Le Blond, *op. cit.,* pp. 411; 417–419.

18. Belhomme, *op. cit.,* vol. 3, 187.

19. When fire was conducted by sections the following order was followed: the 1st, 6th, 3rd, 5th, 4th, and 2nd (right section of each platoons), the left sections the grenadiers, the right section of the piquet, the 1st, 6th, 3rd, 5th, 4th, and 2nd (left section of each platoons), the right section of the grenadiers and the left section of the piquet. Once all of these sections had fired, fire recommenced by the first section on the right of the first platoon, and followed the same order.
In platoon firing, the platoons fired in the following order: 1st, 6th, 3rd, 5th, 4th, 2nd, grenadiers, and piquet. In fire by *manche,* the fire took place: 1st *manche* (1st and 3rd platoons); 2nd (2nd and 4th platoons); 3rd (5th and 6th platoons); grenadiers and piquet. The fire by half-rank started by the right. The fire by section and platoon firing could be executed while the battalion was marching in battle: the platoon stopped to fire and then retook its place at the double pace (Belhomme, op. cit., vol. 3, p. 198.

20. Belhomme, Ibid., vol. 3, p. 199.

21. Grémillet, Paul, *Un regiment pendant deux siècles (1684–1899): histoire du 81e de ligne*. Paris 1899, pp. 33–34.

22. Grandmaison, *op. cit.,* p. 10. The five feet referred to here is actually 5′ 2″, since 12 French inches equals 12½ English inches.

23. Ibid., pp. 10; 14–16.

24. Grémillet, *op. cit.,* pp. 33–34.

25. Grandmaison, *op. cit.,* pp. 107–108.

26. Colin, *op. cit.,* p. 47.

27. de Saxe, *op. cit.,* pp. 47–48.

28. Colin, *op. cit.,* pp. 47–48.

29. Colin, *op. cit.,* p. 79.

30. de Saxe, *op. cit.,* p. 64.

31. Grandmaison, *op. cit.,* p. 17.

32. Ibid., pp. 16–17.

33. Ibid., p. 108.

34. Ibid., pp. 109–112.

35. Voltaire, F.M., *History of the War of 1741*. New York, 1901, p. 243.

CHAPTER 12

Tactical Developments in Other Armies

AUSTRIAN CAVALRY TACTICS: 1740–1748

As already pointed out, the Austrian cavalry began the War of the Austrian Succession using tactics that were virtually identical to those commonly employed during the War of the Spanish Succession, about a quarter of a century earlier. The British and Dutch cavalry successes against their highly vaunted French counterparts, and the exploits of Charles XII's cavalry, had made virtually no impact on Austrian thinking, and the use of firearms during the charge continued unabated even when this practice had fallen from favor in the Prussian army.

Because of Austria's geographic location and her proximity to south-eastern European powers, the Austrian cavalry had to develop two different sets of tactical doctrine: one for when fighting against the irregular horseman encountered during any Turkish war, and the other for when engaging any of the disciplined armies of Western Europe. When fighting against the Turks, the cavalry was deployed up in closed order in three ranks. The Austrians had learned to avoid playing into the Turkish game of reducing the cavalry action to a series of individual combats that would necessarily occur during a protracted melee. So, approaching the enemy at a slow and determined pace, they would halt, taking considerable caution to remain in good order, and then start to deliver ordered volleys. This had proven to be very effective against Turkish forces who, although very skilled swordsmen and highly dangerous at close quarters, were usually discomfited by the small-arms fire delivered in a continuous and orderly fashion and the tight formation retained throughout the firing.[1] We can assume that the Austrians delivered this attack *en muraille* (a curtain), that is, with the squadrons side by side without any spaces between.

If they succeeded in defeating the Turks, in theory only a portion of the regiment was to pursue the fleeing enemy. The remainder was to rally. However, this was little practiced, and the whole regiment usually slipped from their officers' control, and pursued the temporarily defeated enemy until pushed back, in turn, by other masses of Turkish cavalry.

The Austrian cavalry used the same basic tactic when attacking Turkish infantry, though they often met with failure, since the charge was conducted at the trot or a moderate canter. The Turks who charged the Austrian infantry charging recklessly at a full gallop were more often successful, and once they managed to enter the ranks quickly cut the enemy infantry to pieces. As a result the Austrian infantry continued to carry *chevaux de frise* connected by chains, and whenever they stopped they would erect these obstacles in front of them for protection.

The Austrian cavalry used a different approach when fighting the cavalry from Western European armies, one that dated back to at least the 1680's or 90's. The regiment was again formed in line, but in this case was deployed along in two ranks. Advancing, each cavalryman had his saber hanging from his wrist while holding his pistol. The line advanced and as they neared the enemy the gallop was ordered; 20 paces from the enemy line the cavalrymen fired their pistols and then continued their attack at the fastest possible speed. The men were enjoined to then hit the enemy horses on the top of their heads with their swords, since "this always has good effect."[2] Firing from horseback was never very effective, but firing while at the gallop had to be even less effective.

These were essentially the same type of tactics used by Germanic armies as early as the 1680's, and they often met with the same results. At the battle of Hohenfriedeberg (June 4th, 1745) several Austrian cavalry regiments assigned to the Saxon army refused to charge the Prussian horse, and when threatened, in turn, ran off.[3] Later the same year at the Battle of Soor (September 30th, 1745), fifty squadrons of Austrian cavalry met a similar fate when General Buddenbrock led the cuirassiers on the Prussian right "furiously" up a steep incline and met with only a sputtering of carbine fire. The Austrian cavalry were "tumbled over" and pushed back on the second and third lines of horse which were similarly disordered and driven back.[4]

When fighting Western opponents, the Austrian hussars used a variant of the traditional Austrian firearms tactic. They would advance toward the enemy cavalry and then the leading sections of hussars would start to engage in fire combat, while the remainder of the hussars would try to work their way around the enemy's flank.

In practice, a third type of charge, charging by troops, was usually employed when engaging enemy infantry. The "New Regulations" of 1757 for Prussian infantry described the Austrian charge as follows:

> "The Austrian cavalry have frequently charged a battalion of Prussian infantry in full gallop, at the distance of 150 paces, and have stood its first general discharge [of the Prussian infantry], in order to [attempt to] break through it afterwards by troops."[5]

It continued to say that the Prussian infantry responded with platoon fire, and the Austrian cavalry was regularly repulsed.

An interesting question to ask is why the Austrians, familiar with the technique of the prolonged gallop (approximately 200 paces), which they used when charging infantry did not make any serious attempts to apply this tactic to cavalry versus cavalry situations. The answer is that given the Austrian attitudes on the subject, they probably would have preferred to attack both infantry and cavalry using their carbines. However, as we have already seen, for the sake of accuracy this demanded a relatively slow approach to the enemy with the gallop being postponed until the carbines were discharged during the final 20 paces of the advance. To use this technique against infantry, who now loaded their muskets using iron ramrods and prepared cartridges, would be suicidal. Approaching infantry at a trot would take approximately twice as long as when at the gallop, and consequently they would be exposed to increased fire and hence greater casualties.

AUSTRIAN CAVALRY TACTICS: POST-1748

Although the Austrian cavalry fared well during the first campaigns of the War of the Austrian Succession, during the later years of the war, as Prussian cavalry enhanced its training methods and battlefield doctrine, the shortcomings of the Austrian cavalry started to become evident. Nowhere was the impotence of the Austrian cavalry more clearly demonstrated than at Soor (September 30th, 1745).

The Austrians under Prince Karl executed a night march and caught Frederick off guard. Deployed along three lines on some heights overlooking the right of the Prussian camp, the Austrians made the fatal mistake of not immediately attacking. Despite being exposed to *grénades royales,* as case shot was often called, the Prussian infantry changed its front toward the right and formed a single line facing the Austrians above them. Frederick ordered General Buddenbrock and his cuirassiers on the right flank to attack the Austrian cavalry. Despite having the incline against them, the cuirassiers advanced quickly. The Austrians failed to countercharge, despite their positional advantage and superior numbers, and delivered a "mere sputter of carbines" as Carlyle described it. The first rank of Austrian cavalry ridden over by the Prussian cuirassiers were too tightly packed together and the rear lines were also completely disordered. Within moments all fifty squadrons headed for the woods behind them and were permanently out of the battle.

In 1748, under the presidency of Prince Charles of Lorraine, a military commission was created to reorganize the Austrian army and redress the various problems that came to light during the last war. As a result, two regulations pertinent to the cavalry were published during this period: in field service regulations of 1749 and the cavalry regulations of 1751. The cavalry regulations of 1751 banned the use of the carbines during a charge and required cavalry regiments when not supporting infantry to begin their charge at 200 paces, by moving at the trot. When they came within 20 to 30 paces of the enemy cavalry they were to then attack at the gallop.[6]

The subalterns (NCO's) in the Austrian cavalry were armed with carbines. This was an unfortunate choice, since it reduced the subalterns to simple soldiers, instead of allowing them to perform their real duty which was supervising and controlling the men around them. In 1760, some of the cuirassiers in the front rank were given *tramblon* or blunderbusses with wide muzzles. They were loaded with 10 to 12 small pistol balls which would presumably have a "shotgun" effect when fired.

General Warnery has commented that the Prussians who faced the Austrians armed in this manner "never perceived any effect from them."[7]

It is very interesting and somewhat ironic that the Austrian cavalry when finally forced by the late Prussian cavalry success to abandon the use of firearms in the charge began to overhaul their charge doctrine with the same timid steps taken by the Prussians after Mollwitz. The type of charge advocated by the 1751 regulations was very similar to that developed by the Prussians in 1741 when Frederick exhorted his men to begin the gallop when 30 paces from the enemy. The Austrian military authorities apparently completely missed further development in Prussian theory of the charge, which saw the gallop initiated at an ever-increasing distance from the enemy. On March 17th, 1742, the Prussians required that the charge begin 100 paces away from the enemy, and on July 25, 1744, this was increased to 200 paces where it remained until the end of the Seven Years' War.

This was the theory. In practice, there appears to have been little change in the Austrian cavalry's performance. Colonel Mack, writing in 1780, said of the post-Seven Years' War Austrian cavalry: "Even in 1769 the cavalry could not ride, could not manage to control their horses. Not a single squadron could keep its dressing, and before they had gone fifty yards, at least ten out of forty horses in the first rank would break out to the front. Of quick and orderly changes of formation there was no idea."[8]

The Austrians were slow to implement the training regimen that had produced such tremendous results in the Prussian army during the early 1750's. Indirect evidence of this was produced during the Seven Years' War when the Prussians would attempt to use captured enemy horses. Warnery comments on the general fitness of these horses: "At first those troopers who received them were dissatisfied with their want of activity, but after having felt the Prussian spur for a few weeks, they were as fleet as the others." This shows the level of the training of the cavalry in other armies. If they were better trained their horses would have been in better condition.

BRITISH CAVALRY DEVELOPMENTS

Up until the first several campaigns of the Seven Years' War, British cavalry doctrine had not significantly changed from that used during Marlborough's time. The Duke of Cumberland's instructions on how British dragoons were to conduct themselves during combat is illustrative of all British cavalry during this period.

When attacking, the dragoon regiment was to form a column of squadrons, each squadron deployed in two ranks. Prior to advancing, the men were ordered to draw their swords, then shorten their bridles, before bringing their swords to their thighs. Some of the officers and quartermasters in each troop did not participate in the charge but rode behind the squadron to rally anyone attempting to flee and bring them forward with the next squadron in the column.

The advance was begun at a walk or slow trot until the squadron had advanced to about sixty paces from the enemy. At this point, the squadron commander would order his men to "trot out," that is, ride forward now at a fast trot.

As in Marlborough's time, the emphasis was placed on maintaining strict order within the squadron's formation. The troopers were to remain knee to knee throughout the charge. The rear rank was to keep itself close enough to the first rank to push it toward the enemy, yet distant enough to avoid being stopped in its tracks, if the first line was defeated.

The squadron commander if possible was to attempt to have the squadron advance obliquely to the right as it advanced, to be able to take a portion of the enemy line in flank as they met. In actuality, given the level of British cavalry training at this period, this proved difficult in practice and the two forces usually met head on, if they actually closed to contact.

If the attack proved to be successful, the squadron was to halt at the position previously indicated for this purpose by the squadron commander. Here, it was to reorder itself to be able to respond to an enemy countercharge or wait to be supported by the squadrons following in column behind it. Should the first squadron's charge be checked, instead, its men were to ride to the left and to the right to clear the front so that the squadrons behind could continue the attack.[9]

The success of the Prussian cavalry reforms (1741–1747) did not escape the attention of the military authorities elsewhere. And, by the Seven Years' War, the salient features of the new Prussian cavalry doctrine were being experimented with in most other armies. By the Battle of Warburg (July 31, 1760), there is clear evidence that offensive doctrine in the British cavalry service had undergone a profound change. In the well-known charge led by the Marquess of Granby, the British approached the French horse at a "sharp" trot, and then received successive orders to gallop and then charge. This was clearly based upon the Prussian cavalry model of attack.[10]

British cavalry lacked the thorough training and appear to never have mastered the multiphased aspect of the Prussian charge at the gallop. British cavalry tended to charge enthusiasticlly without being able to maintain the same tightness of formation. To rectify this problem, in 1779 Lord Amherst ordered that the cavalry cease "the continued vehemence of the charge which served only to break up the squadrons." From this point on, British cavalry was to advance at the trot, only breaking into a gallop when within fifty yards of the enemy.[11]

This switch to Prussian-based cavalry techniques was not limited to the British army. The same type of transformation started to occur within the cavalry arm of many of the German states, especially during the Seven Years' War. New Saxon cavalry regulations in 1751–52, for example, prescribed that the cavalry walk twenty paces, then trot for another 50 to 60 paces before setting off at the gallop. Interestingly enough, unlike the Austrian cavalry regulations of 1751, the use of firearms during the charge was still not forbidden. These tactics appear to be a compromise between Austrian and Prussian doctrines, a phenomenon that was apparent in Saxon infantry tactics as well.[12]

The Hanoverian cavalry appears to have been even more conservative, relying on the traditional advance at the trot and, the discharge of firearms prior to closing with the sword. One interesting feature of the Hanoverian cavalry charge was that the troopers in the third line would "double," that is, they would close into any spaces provided by the intervals between squadrons or the files within the squadron to tighten up the formation. From 1758 onward, on the orders of Prince Ferdinand, the Hanoverian cavalry deployed in two ranks rather than in three as formerly.[13]

BRITISH INFANTRY

When Britain entered the War of the Austrian Succession her military machine, like her French counterpart, remained for the most part what it had been twenty-five years earlier.

In 1745 Richard Kane published *A New System of Military Discipline for a Battalion of Foot* which described much of the tactical systems then current in the British army. Interestingly enough, this is the same Richard Kane who was the acting commander of the Royal Irish regiment at the Battle of Malplaquet 36 years earlier. This regiment's use of the platoon firing system on this earlier occasion was immortalized in Robert Parker's memoirs and has been examined in an earlier chapter.

The firing technique and the method of advancing to the attack in the "new system" was probably very similar to that used during the War of the Spanish Succession, as described by Captain Parker. The only notable change was the consistent use of the drum to supplement the colonel's voice while issuing orders.

The men in a battalion were deployed just as thirty years earlier. A battalion of between 800 and 1000 men was deployed in three ranks, the men having fixed bayonets onto the ends of their muskets. The grenadiers were placed on both flanks, while the officers were ranged in front of the battalion. The colonel in front, or the colonel (in his absence, the lieutenant colonel), sword in hand, was on foot eight to ten paces in front of the men, in the center of the battalion. He was accompanied by an "expert drummer" who stood beside him. The battalion continued to be divided into four "grand divisions," each of four platoons. Counting the two grenadier platoons this gave a total of 18 platoons which were tolled off into three "firings," each of six platoons.

The major difference between platoon firing as conducted near the turn of the eighteenth century and that 36 years later is the use of drums to transmit orders. Richard Kane, who provides a very detailed account of platoon firing as it existed around 1745 advocated that the drum be used in addition to verbal commands. He argued that not every commander had a sufficiently loud and clear voice, and it detracted from the regiment's self-image if the orders had to be given by the major or an adjutant during the actual battle. Also, it avoided the confusion that could arise during the heat of the battle, if the commander was killed or otherwise incapacitated and a new voice was heard issuing orders.

When the battalion was in line, and the general action was about to begin, the colonel would order that the drummer make a ruffle. Then, positioned a distance in front of the battalion he would deliver a short "cheerful" speech to encourage the men. Having finished speaking, the colonel would order the march and the drummers would beat to the march. He stood still until the battalion closed to four or five paces of him, then he turned around and slowly marched with the battalion toward the enemy.

The grand tactical theory behind the dynamics of the assault remained unchanged: the battalions were to engage the enemy in a series of firefights, at an ever-decreasing range, and break the enemy's will to fight by a succession of ordered volleys. The advance was to continue until the enemy opposite the battalion began to fire, at which point the colonel ordered the drummers to stop. Turning to face his men once more, the colonel ordered the men to halt and the drummers to beat a "preparative." As soon as this order was given, the men in the six platoons of the first firing, and all the men in the first rank (except those in the two center platoons) were to prepare themselves to fire. The front rank knelt, and placed the butts of their muskets in the ground under their left feet and angled their weapons upward. This posture was assumed to defend themselves from cavalry. The men in the rear two ranks closed in on the front rank, and kept their thumbs on the cocks of their muskets taking care to keep their arms "well recovered."

Kane mentions that there was a tendency to practice firings by individual platoons. This had to be avoided on the battlefield, as it had little weight compared to when the fire from six platoons "rained" in on the enemy at a single moment. To achieve this, it was imperative that the colonel command the firings, not the captains commanding each company. These latter, along with their subordinate officers and subalterns were to see that their men did their duty, that is, withheld their fire until so ordered by the colonel, and then to fire quickly with their muskets leveled properly.

When the first firing was to fire the colonel ordered the drummers to beat a "flam." The men in the front rank dropped the muzzles of their muskets to the ground, while the two rear ranks presented their arms. The officers and subalterns in these platoons made certain that the muskets were leveled according to the range of the enemy so that the volley would have the best possible effect. At the same time, they had to caution their men to withhold their fire until the next orders on the drum.

As soon as the first firing was properly presented, the colonel ordered a second "flam" to be beaten, and the men fired their weapons. Immediately, these men recovered their weapons, fell back and started to load as fast as they could. The sergeants' task at this point was to see that this reloading was done without hurry and disorder. The men in the first ranks did not fire and were part of the battalion's reserve fire. These men kept their muzzles on the ground and their thumbs on the cocks. The colonel then immediately ordered the drummers to beat a second "preparative," and the platoons in the second firing prepared themselves to fire. The same set of orders and drumming was used to command this firing to fire.

When the second firing had fired, the same procedure was followed for the third firing. In theory, this routine was followed to produce a near-continuous fire, without significant hesitation between firings. If the need arose for the reserve to fire, the colonel ordered the first rank of all but the two center platoons to present arms, and then the same set of commands was used as for the other firings.

If at any point during the firings the enemy started to retreat, the men were ordered to cease fire. The next firing were to "half-cock" their weapons so as to be ready to fire later. The battalion was to march after the retreating enemy, rather than waste ammunition and time firing upon them. This was yet another reason why it was important for the colonel, as opposed to the captains, to control the firing. The firing would tend to continue for a much longer time when the captains controlled the firings of their individual platoons.

On the other hand, should the enemy infantry maintain their ground, the British battalion was to recommence its advance. Another "preparative" was beaten to order the next firing to make ready. Ordering the battalion to march, the colonel waited until the first rank was two paces from him before turning around and starting to march himself. The nearer the battalion approached the enemy, the closer he was to position himself near the first rank. This was important, otherwise, he would stand out as an easy mark for enemy fire. When the battalion arrived at the appropriate distance away from the enemy holding its ground, the colonel was to order the battalion to halt. Immediately, the front rank knelt as before and the rear ranks closed forward. On the next "flam," the next firing fired its muskets. The colonel now went through the same orders as before, making the various firings deliver their fire as quickly as possible until the enemy started to give ground.

Official doctrine purposely avoided prescribing what was to occur in the final moments of an encounter, where the threat of actual contact was imminent. This was left to the discretion of the battalion's commanding officer. The one enjoinder was that should the enemy retreat faster than could be followed while still maintaining order, the infantry was to stop and continue firing until the enemy was out of range. The task of pursuit was left to the cavalry.[14]

BRITISH FIRING METHODS IN PRACTICE

Despite the relatively high level of training of the British foot soldier and the theoretical virtues of the platoon firing system, on the battlefield British infantry did not always fight by the book. In a series of letters to his wife, Lieutenant Colonel Charles Russell, described how the British infantry actually conducted themselves at the Battle of Dettingen (June 27th, 1743) where they defeated the French:

"Our men and their regimental offices won the day, not in the manner of Hyde Park discipline, but our foot almost kneeled down by whole ranks, and so fired on 'em a running fire, making almost every ball take place; but for ten or twelve minutes 'twas doubtful which would succeed, as they overpowered us so much, and the bravery of their *Mason du Roy* coming upon us eight or nine ranks deep; yet our troops were not seen to retreat, but to bend back only—I mean our foot—and that only while they fresh loaded; then, of their own accord, marched boldly up to 'em, gave them such a smash with loud huzzas every time they saw them retire, that then they were at once put to flight. The English infantry behaved like heroes, and as they won the major part of the action, to them the honours of the day were due. They were under no command by way of Hyde Park firing, but the whole three ranks made a running fire of their own accord, and the same time with great judgment and skill, stooping all as low as they could, making almost every ball take place . . . . The enemy, when expecting our fire, dropped down, which our men perceiving waited till they got up before they would fire. . . . The French fired in the same manner, I mean like a running fire, without waiting for words of command, and Lord Stair did often say he had seen many a battle, and never saw the infantry engage in any other manner."[15]

Russell went on to point out that Lord Stair, the commander of the British contingent in 1743, often remarked that in his experience fire combat always devolved into individual fire, as opposed to the orderly volley fire called for by the regulations. The term "running fire" usually referred to ordered fire that rippled along the front of a battalion from one side to the other, as would occur in some forms of platoon fire. However, in the above passage Russell uses it to refer to an irregular fire, where the men fire without commands.

There appears to be an increasing incidence of uncontrolled fire after 1740 over the preceding period. One frequently finds references to volley fire quickly turning into individual fire during various Seven Years' War battles. However, there had been fewer references to the same phenomenon during the Nine Years' War and the War of the Spanish Succession. The literature of the period does not directly deal with this issue, and we can only conjecture at the answer. It is known for a certainty that fire combat was conducted at a slower rate of fire prior to the introduction of the iron ramrod and the methodical training methods introduced in Prussia during Frederick William's time. This higher rate of fire meant that a more deadly fire could be poured out for a greater length of time.

This, in turn, meant that the attacker would be more frequently stopped in his tracks and forced into a desultory type of fire, unplanned and uncontrolled by any of his higher officers.

In earlier times, when an attacker could march up to the enemy before more than three or four volleys were fired, it was much more likely that he could come much closer to the enemy before he decided to fire. In these types of situations one or two quick volleys often proved sufficient to settle the affair, and most firefights, because of the closeness of opposing parties, were settled in a few minutes. By 1740, when, for example, the Prussians at times were able to fire up to five rounds per minute, even if only for a few minutes, the attacker lost the ability to simply advance to 20 or 30 paces before delivering one or two salvos, something that had been much more common at the turn of the eighteenth century. Now, the attacker was forced into prolonged firefights at longer ranges, and the breaking down of volley fire became noticeable after several minutes.

Another reason why irregular fire started to occur much more frequently appears to have been connected with a change in the way various fire systems were conducted. In platoon fire as described by both Captain Parker and Richard Kane there was little opportunity for ordered fire to break down into individual irregular fire. In this system, each time the battalion stopped to fire only one or two firings got off a volley before the battalion moved off to continue the advance. Moreover, the colonel waited for each firing to be ready before the next salvo was ordered.

By Napoleonic times, we find quite a different state of affairs in the British army. Müller, writing in 1811, criticized the use of platoon firing, arguing that platoon firing as it now existed invariably led to irregular fire. He proposed that the fire by division system be used. He argued that in this system, where fire was delivered rank by rank in order, the officers could control the fire and make certain that "voluntary" or irregular fire would not break out.

As Müller describes how platoon fire of this period should be performed, the problem becomes obvious. Influenced by the Frederick's "fire as fast as you can" philosophy, the British had adopted the practice of compressing the greatest number of firings in the shortest possible time.

Common muskets took 11 seconds to reload; those equipped with cylindrical iron ramrods, only eight or nine seconds. According to Müller, there had to be one to one and a half seconds allowed between firings. This meant the latter could be fired, at least initially, at five to six times per minute. By dividing each company into four divisions, with a new firing every three seconds, it was now possible for a company to deliver fire 20 firings per minute. The enemy on the receiving end, provided this rapid fire continued, would feel devastated by the continuous fire.[16]

The problem was that this rapid succession of firings was impossible to maintain for any extended period of time. Initially, the battalion would deliver a number of ordered firings in quick succession, but these would very quickly become disorganized as individuals would lose their place and start to fire on their own.

It isn't possible to date exactly when this newer form of platoon fire, with its emphasis on rapid succession of fire, replaced the older system in which the officer's control of the firing was paramount. Possibly, some British officers, quite independently of the Prussians began to place importance on rapidity of ordered fire made possible by constant training. In any case, the advent of Prussian influence on the British army after 1748 is indisputable.

NOTES

1. Mollo, John, *Uniforms of the Seven Years War 1756–63*. Poole, Dorset, 1977, p. 44.

2. Maude, *op. cit.,* p. 81.

3. Carlyle, *op. cit.,* vol. 4, p. 117–119.

4. Ibid., vol. 5, p. 153.

5. *New Regulations For the Prussian Infantry.* London, 1756, pp. 33–34.

6. Duffy, *The Army Of Maria Theresa; op. cit.,* p. 100.

7. Warnery, *op. cit.,* p. 16.

8. Maude, *op. cit.,* p. 124.

9. Rev. P. Sumner, "Standing Orders for Dragoons", *Journal of the Society of Historical Research,* vol. XXIII, 1945; cited in Rogers, *op. cit.,* p. 77.

10. Arthur, Sir George, *The Story of the Household Cavalry.* London 1909, p. 453; cited in Rogers, Ibid., p. 77.

11. Fortescue, vol. 3, *op. cit.,* p. 538.

12. Mollo, op. cit., p. 59.

13. Niemeyer, Joachim and Georg Ortenburg, *The Hanoverian Army During the Seven Years' War.* Copenhagen, 1977, p. 44.

14. Kane, *op. cit.,* pp. 111–120.

15. Lieutenant-Colonel Charles Russell, letters to his wife June 29 & August 6 & 7th, 1743: cited in Skrine, *op. cit.,* p. 80.

16. Müller, William, *The Elements of the Science War.* London, 1811, vol. 2, pp. 185–187.

PART III

Doctrine and Training in the Seven Years' War Period

Introduction

THE FIRST TWO PARTS OF THIS BOOK HAVE DEALT WITH THE EVOLUTION OF tactics and grand tactics from 1690 to the outbreak of the Seven Years' War. A slightly different approach is used in the next portion of the book. This last section attempts to reconstruct the full body of doctrine as it would have been understood by capable officers of the period. Because of the wide difference that then existed between the tactics in the French and Prussian armies, both systems are presented independently.

A significant portion of any doctrine was provided by various official "regulations" and ordinances. However, this was only a fraction of any doctrinal system, and was usually limited to those areas of the troops' activity where each motion could be clearly defined and prescribed. The earliest regulations dealt with the exercises of arms, and then gradually came to include marching procedures, deploying into line and reverting back to column. By the early 1750's, some had started to enumerate the new "maneuvers" as well.

However, the regulations almost always did not attempt to dictate how the troops were to respond to even the most basic situations on the battlefield. It gave the most basic tools, such as the type of formations they were to use, but it didn't describe how to use these tools. Though a few authors, such as La Vallière, attempted to meet this deficiency in the seventeenth century, it was only in the 1720's that a sizeable number of military thinkers (Folard, De Saxe, Quincy, Khevenhüller, etc.) turned their literary attention to this problem. These authors expounded on how troops were to act on the battlefield, both in terms of tactics and the various grand tactics available.

A thorough examination of the various major theories that had evolved by this time is absolutely essential to our understanding of what actually occurred on the battlefield. Not only does it offer us an insight into the training of the combatant forces during this period, but it also allows us to reconstruct their expectations as they entered the battlefield. Some might argue that the doctrine of this period shows us little about how warfare was actually resolved, there always being a very large gap between theory and practice.

This would be a much stronger argument if it were possible to rely solely on firsthand accounts of what actually transpired during a battle. However, these firsthand accounts consistently provide certain types of information, while systematically overlooking other vital types of information. The diarist focuses on what makes a particular battle distinctive: the types and strengths of the forces involved, the terrain the battle was fought on, the particular stratagems of the two commanders, etc. Only occasionally do we find momentary glimpses of what the soldiers in the ranks were actually doing. Even then, these descriptions often describe something that was memorable, that is, something that departed from the norm. It is rare that we find good firsthand accounts of what was the normal practice.

It goes without saying that not all the various tactics, maneuvers, etc., contained in the various training manuals of the day equally reflected the reality of the battleground. The reality quotient not only varied between manuals and from army to army, but from one formation or maneuver to another within the same document. Some maneuvers were very useful and were frequently employed, for example, the "deploy"; others, such as a multibattalion change of face, were rarely actually used on the battlefield.

One issue here is to what extent a doctrinal theory was officially accepted by the military authorities. This is a real issue when we look at systems proffered by the Chevalier de Folard and his disciples. If a system had neither a sizeable number of advocates in the officer class nor was officially accepted, it then had little or no bearing on what would happen on the battlefield, since it would never be applied. This is not the case when we examine the systems described by the likes of De Broglie (commander of the French army during part of the Seven Years' War) or

Frederick the Great. When we examine Frederick's tactical and grand tactical prescriptions we understandably have a higher expectation as to their actual use, than if we were looking at a document having a similar purpose for some other army.

There are two distinctly different reasons for this. First, all of Frederick's writings were intended for a practical application, and mostly for an application on the battlefield. Frederick had a lot to lose by issuing faulty or inefficient instructions. What was written was based on his experience and that of his general staff; he was not a theoretical writer such as Folard, experimenting with new systems. The second reason was that, again unlike someone like Folard, Frederick did not have to endlessly debate his prescriptions and lobby for years in order for them to receive some fleeting and half-hearted trial. Frederick, in addition to being Prussia's master military analyst, was also the king. What he said went; his decrees immediately became official policy. His generals might not always agree with all of their contents, but they could only deviate from these prescriptions when opportunity arose, where they would not appear to be disobeying orders.

Frederick's power and influence regarding military matters was greater than even the average sovereign during this age. Unlike George II and Louis XV, he was also the permanent commander-in-chief of Prussia's main army in the field. In the French army, for example, when De Broglie, the commander-in-chief of the main French army, disagreed with the views of the King and his ministers in Paris about the role of skirmishers on the battlefield, he was able to employ them in actual situations because ultimately he was commander-in-chief of a specific army in a specific situation. A lieutenant or major general in the Prussian army usually didn't have this advantage of distance. During a battle, he often had to do things according to the accepted fashion, because the King was personally observing his motions.

The other and most serious criticism of looking at doctrine as a clue as to what occurred on the battlefield, is that doctrine by definition represents what troops would attempt to do, if they were perfectly free to perform what they had been trained to do. However, in reality, their actions were always affected by those of the enemy, with the result that what did occur very frequently was different from that which was intended. Nevertheless, in telling us how troops were trained, and what they attempted to do, we have a much better chance of piecing together what happened even after their actions started to be modified by those of the enemy.

An analogy might be useful here. The effect of the enemy's actions on the friendly troops is very similar to that of one team on another in modern-day sport competitions with a vast number of events happening quickly, many at the same time, and many affecting someone else's actions. Knowing the complete lexicon of the formal "techniques" that were available to each of the combatants allows us to reassess various descriptions and identify many tactics and practices that otherwise would go unrecognized. It also provides a standard to measure to what extent the practices on the battlefield departed from those that were practiced on parade grounds and in training camps. When we go back to the various firsthand accounts that have survived, we find that what happened on the battlefield was not simply actions and practices that were unique to the battlefield. Rather, what occurred tended to be a complicated mixture of what the troops were trained to do coupled with a number of practices that arose out of necessity. Moreover, where the doctrine of an army was based on realistic expectations of what average soldiers could do under the worst of conditions, it tended to be of practical importance in action. Doctrine based on unrealistic expectations went by the wayside very quickly.

CHAPTER 13

Prussian Maneuvers: 1747–1756

NEW METHODS OF FORMING LINE

PRIOR TO THE 1750'S, THE TERM "EVOLUTION" WAS USED TO REFER TO THE process of changing formations, because there were only a few possible ways of forming line from column and column from line. One could say a line "evolved" from a column. However, from this point onward because of the proliferation of formations, as well as the methods of forming these, the term "maneuver" came into vogue and has remained in use.

Although the Prussian army continued to use the traditional processional methods of forming line when it came to deploying into battle line prior to the start of battle, the Prussian infantry started to experiment with other methods of forming line for the individual battalion around

1745. Emphasis was now placed on methods allowing perpendicular deployment where a battalion deployed in front of its line of march and did not have to traverse from left to right or right to left across the area where it was to deploy. Over the next ten years, a number of different maneuvers evolved, eliminating the need for a battalion to turn and march laterally, thus exposing its flank to the enemy.

There were several reasons why a perpendicular method of deployment was useful. Because, on the average, battalion would march less than in a parallel deployment, the deployment could be performed in less time. This, in turn, meant an army could deploy more closely to the enemy than was possible previously. Two other reasons were more tactical in nature. As long as an infantry battalion or cavalry regiment was limited to deploying to its left or right, it was extremely vulnerable during the entire time of deployment. A column marching parallel to the enemy presented "so many flanks," referring to the fact that each row in the column offered its flank to the enemy.[1] A battalion which deployed perpendicularly, that is, to the front, avoided this particular problem, since the enemy was located toward its front and its flank was never exposed. The ability to deploy into line while moving forward was also important in that it allowed individual battalions confronting difficult terrain in their path to pull out of line, form into column, march past the obstructing terrain and then reform line, when convenient.

The first method to be developed for deploying towards the front relied exclusively on the *traversierschritt,* a curious type of oblique march that was then used by the Prussian infantry. The column opened to a full interval, or even to a slightly larger distance, and positioned itself immediately behind where the final line was to be formed. The front-most platoon in the column, in fact, was stationed in exactly the same position it was to occupy after the line was formed. The men in the rear platoons inclined, that is, oblique-marched directly to their final position in line. If the platoons in the column were in their normal sequence with the senior platoon at the front, the oblique march would be performed to the left; on the other hand, if the column was in an inverted sequence with the senior platoon at the rear, the men would incline toward the right. This was so that regardless of the arrangement of the platoons in the column, line was always formed with the senior company on the right and the least senior on the left.

The Prussians must have found this a particularly awkward maneuver. The *traversierschritt* version of the oblique march then practiced by the

Prussians was quite a bit more complicated than the simple lockstep form of the oblique march found in later times. If the incline was being performed to the right, each man first stuck out his right foot, and then crossed over his left foot, thus moving the man slightly forward and slightly to the right. Each man would then move his right foot forward again, and so on. This process was repeated until the line advanced to the desired location, and all the while the mens' shoulders were kept rigidly in line.[2]

There were two deficiencies in this maneuver: this version of the oblique march demanded a great degree of concentration on the part of the men, and was barely practicable on the parade ground, let alone the battlefield. The other problem was that it maximized the distance each platoon had to traverse in order to reach its place in line, and the oblique march had to be performed along a relatively shallow angle, somewhere between 20 and 35 degrees.

This first method of deployment was soon discarded, and in a 1748 appendix to the regulations a slightly different maneuver is described. The closed column would position itself in the same relative position to the intended line as in the previous maneuver. However, each of the rear platoons, instead of immediately oblique marching to their final positions, would first wheel to face the direction they were about to march. After completing this 1⁄16 wheel, they would now oblique march until the front-most flank of the platoon reached its place in line. At this point, the men in the platoon would stop their oblique march and then 1⁄16 wheel into line. As was the case with the previous maneuver, the men could oblique march either to the left or the right depending upon whether the platoons in the column were in ordinary or inverted order, but now the oblique march was almost straight ahead.

The advantage of this maneuver was that it allowed the men to oblique march along a much less acute angle, and in a more straight-forward direction (30 to 45 degrees). This apparently represented a great improvement, and even though this maneuver was replaced by a third maneuver in 1752 it was never totally forgotten. In fact, even in the 1830's, a version of this maneuver is found in the drill booklets of practically every European power.

The *en tiroir* maneuver, or deployment by "square movements" was adopted in 1752. Its purpose was to obviate the need to rely on any type of oblique march, and to allow a battalion to deploy from a closed order, rather than first having to open up to full interval. As with the other methods of deploying into line, it could be performed either to the left or right depending upon whether the platoons in the column were in ordinary or inverted sequence.

To describe this maneuver let's treat the example where a column of platoons was in normal sequence, that is, the senior company was at its front and the least senior at its rear. In this case, to achieve the required sequencing while in line the maneuver would have to be performed to the left. The front platoon would remain in place or advance a little forward. The men in each of the remaining seven platoons would turn to their left and march forward (moving away from the column's position, toward the left). As the lead men in the second platoon moved to a position perpendicular to their position in the final line, they and the rest of the platoon stopped and all simultaneously faced toward the intended line, after which they advanced into line and then halted. The men in the third platoon performed exactly the same sequence, but, of course marched exactly one interval (the width of a platoon) further to the left. This was also true of all the other platoons, but each successive platoon marched to the left an ever-greater distance.

This maneuver could also be performed to the right, if the column was in an inverted order with the least senior company at its front. As we will see later, at this period the Prussians also started to experiment with a divisional column two platoons wide. In this column the platoons on the right were in inverted sequence while those in the left were in normal sequence. When this type of column was to deploy using the *en tiroir* method the platoons on the right performed this maneuver to the right; those on the left maneuvered to the left.

The Prussians also experimented with another method of deploying into line that has come to be called Rosch's method, after the Prussian captain who was presumably its author. It was, in fact, the opposite of the *en tiroir* method. It also relied on "square movements," but in this case the men marched along the other two sides of the "square." The men in the first platoon, if the column was in normal order, turned to the right and marched straight ahead. As soon as the lead men reached what would be the right edge of the intended line, they stopped and all the men in that platoon turned toward the left, that is, the front. The men in the second line advanced to the original position of the first platoon and then performed the same sequence of movements. Of course, they didn't have to march quite as far, stopping when they reached the left of the first platoon, now in line. Each of the remaining platoons did the same, advancing to the first platoon's original position in the column and then flank marching to the right until they assumed their final position in the line.[3]

This maneuver was a minor version and was quickly abandoned. The reason for this probably lies with the fact that unlike the other methods, at least a portion of the battalion was exposing its flank until the very completion of the maneuver. This wasn't the case with the other maneuvers where either the men in each platoon were facing the front throughout the maneuver (as in the *traversierschritt*) or were protected by troops already deployed in line (as *en tiroir*).

Another major discovery, called the "adjutant's walk," was made during this period. Its origins can be traced to when the order of battle was formed using the traditional parallel methods of deployment. During the deployment process, it was customary to have at least one officer, from each battalion ride ahead to the final place of deployment. The officer selected for this role was invariably an adjutant officer. This was a convenient practice for two reasons: the officer served as one more guidepost by which the battalion could maneuver to its intended position; and the adjutant made certain that there was enough room for the entire battalion to deploy, that is, that there was one interval of space between him and the next adjutant.

As the column approached the battlefield either from the left or the right, the adjutant left the column and rode directly to the position where the battalion was to form line. The adjutant's path was a much shorter one than was taken by his regiment: the regiment had to march along two sides of a right-angled triangle. The first side being when it marched up to the intended line; the second side being when it marched parallel to the intended line until it reached its proper place along this line. The adjutant, on the other hand, rode along the hypotenuse of this triangle.

As long as the parallel methods of deployment were available, the fact that the adjutant was able to ride directly to the final position in line really couldn't be exploited as far as the rest of the battalion was concerned. This was because it was absolutely necessary that the battalion in a column at full interval march along the intended line prior to deploying. As soon as methods of forming line perpendicular to the column's position became available, this precondition disappeared and it became possible to conceive of the battalion taking the shortest route to its final destination, that is along the same path taken by its adjutant officer.[4]

These experiments with new deployment procedures have often been regarded as purely training exercises to heighten the soldier's familiarity with drills and military routine, as well as to instill discipline, and as not intended to be employed on the battlefield. The usual argument used to support this view is that during the Seven Years' War, which commenced after the Prussians had developed a multitude of these new methods, the Prussians in all but three battles deployed their armies using the traditional processional (i.e., parallel) methods of forming line. This view is an unfortunate oversimplification that ignores not only the contemporary rationale underlying the maneuvers developed in the 1745–55 period, but also many of the events occurring during the battles of the Seven Years' War.

It is clear that Frederick and his generals, although they had succeeded in putting together a completely new repertoire of tactical tools that they could utilize on the battlefield if they so chose, were unwilling to make a radical departure from the linear grand tactical systems they had inherited, which had been common currency throughout Western Europe since the 1690's. They were willing to use the new tactical systems only to the extent that they fit in with the existing linear grand tactics.

When the Prussians set about designing maneuvers such as the *traversierschritt* or *en tiroir* methods of forming line, they primarily envisioned these to be used by individual battalions or regiments in isolated situations to reform line, both on the battlefield and when crossing the countryside, whenever, for various reasons, they had been forced back into column.

For example, we are able to establish that, by 1756 at the latest, the Prussian infantry battalion was under standing orders to form temporarily back into column whenever it encountered a sizeable obstruction as it advanced in line, even if on the battlefield. An official Prussian regulation translated into English just prior to the outbreak of the Seven Years' War lists these obstacles forcing units into column: ponds, morasses, hollow ways (formed by roadways), and clearings though woods.[5]

And, of course, once back in column it was imperative that the battalion possess an easy and expeditious means of reforming line even if in proximity to the enemy. Just picture a battalion after having been forced back into column attempting to reform line using the traditional parallel method during the course of the battle! Not only would this require more time, but the battalion's flank would often be exposed to the enemy within striking distance.

Some of these new maneuvers were also used to gain a positional advantage over the enemy. For example, at least twice during the Battle of Freiberg (1762), a Prussian infantry battalion was able to overthrow enemy infantry by working towards the latter's flank and then quickly wheeling the line to roll up the enemy's flank.

By the outbreak of the Seven Years' War, Frederick, at least, was determined to use the new maneuvers to deploy his entire army prior to battle. One Seven Years' War veteran later commented how during the opening campaigns Frederick pressured his senior officers to use the new perpendicular methods of deployment, rather than the traditional parallel methods.

As a result, the Prussians attempted to use the new maneuvers to deploy during three battles or actions during 1757: at the Battle of Lobositz, at Reichenberg, and at Gross-Jägersdorf. At Lobositz, the hilly terrain greatly interfered with the maneuvers being carried out and the artillery was initially forced to remain behind the infantry until it managed to wend its way to its proper position in front by circumnavigating various obstacles. At Reichenberg, the army under the Duke of Bevern managed to deploy, but critics later pointed out that had the army deployed from the right using the processional method, the right wing would have automatically been anchored on the woods on this flank. The unevenness of the terrain made this very difficult after the army deployed from the center using the newer methods.

The newer methods of deployment were never used to deploy an entire army after Gross-Jägersdorf. There appear to be two reasons for this: the greater amount of artillery present on the battlefield and practical command control considerations.

The perpendicular method of deployment required that the battalions to be deployed initially be positioned one behind the other in column near the center of the battlefield. Unfortunately, the increased presence of artillery during the Seven Years' War made these great columns increasingly vulnerable to round shot. This, in turn, meant that deployment could only be made outside artillery range, thus greatly limiting its use to surprise the enemy.[6]

The maneuvers permitted a number of battalions also to deploy much more quickly, but, when used for a large number, required a much greater amount of coordination. The proper position of each battalion, regiment, or brigade was not intuitively obvious at all times, and the officers had to pay the closest attention to their final destination as well as the movement of the other battalions. This required far more initiative than was possible in the Prussian army of that time, so the traditional methods continued to be relied upon. In a processional method of forming line, a battalion's position was always indicated by the battalion to the front, so if the column was led to the proper position the individual battalions pretty much had to be in the right place.

MISCELLANEOUS MANEUVERS

Though between 1748 and 1756 the Prussian infantry experimented with a number of different methods of deploying individual infantry battalions into line from column, the threat of war forced the Prussians to evaluate these various maneuvers and choose the one they felt offered the most advantages.

The new method, known as the "deploy," was a highly effective way of deploying troops; the Comte de Gisors witnessed 14 battalions and five squadrons using this method to form battle order in nine to ten minutes.[7] It was to be performed as follows. Each of the regiment's two battalions marched toward the intended line of battle side by side in "columns by platoons" (each eight platoons one behind the other) until the first platoons in each of the two columns reached where the line was to be formed. At this point, a signal in the form of a cannon shot was delivered and the frontage of each battalion column had to be doubled to form "column by divisions" (each column consisting of four divisions, one behind the other). This was done having the odd-numbered platoons (1st, 3rd, 5th, and 7th) oblique-march a little toward the right; the even-numbered platoons did the same toward the left. These even platoons marched a little further to the front to align themselves with the platoon that had been to their front to form a single division. When the columns were at closed order, there was to be only one pace between each division.

If this maneuver was being used to form a large number of battalions into line, the battalion commanders would await the signal, a second cannon shot, to complete the deployment. The men in the first battalion column would be ordered to face the right; those in the second, to face the left. With the command to march, the men in each division would "passage" to their approximate place in line, if the men in each rank oblique-marched in the appropriate direction. The oblique march used by this time was a simpler march than the *traversierschritt* used several years earlier. Now, if the men were oblique-marching to the right, they would stick out their right feet with the point facing the right, but when the left foot was advanced it was facing directly in front. Special attention had to be paid so that during the oblique march the men retained proper order and the files remained closed.

As soon as each platoon occupied its position in line, the captain advanced six paces in front of the line and ordered the men to face the right so that they could properly dress themselves (i.e., form one straight line). A third cannon shot was the signal that the entire multibattalion line had been formed. If the line was to advance this was indicated by a fourth cannon shot. This maneuver had been designed to do more than deploy the two battalions making up a single regiment, and could be used to deploy lengthy multibattalion columns. In this case, only the first division of each column remained in place, while all the divisions of each of the battalions behind the first in the column would oblique-march to the flank, following close to the division to its front so that each battalion would eventually reach its position in line.[8]

In his short but instructive work, *The Tactick or Grand Manoeuvre of the Prussians,* the Comte de Gisors recounts that, to speed up the process of deployment, each division in the column would march by files instead of using the oblique march. In this version the men in each division would form three lengthy files as they marched in a diagonal direction toward the flank and front. This change was especially important if a number of battalions were deploying, since some of the rear battalions would have to "defile" up to several hundred paces to the flank.

During the Seven Years' War this maneuver was never used to deploy a number of battalions in a lengthy column into line prior to the start of a battle. Some believe this is proof that the utility of the various maneuvers the Prussians experimented with between the wars was strictly limited to the parade ground and used solely as a means to inculcate the needed discipline into the Prussian infantrymen. The reason why the "deploy" did not replace the traditional processional deployment was that the latter was essentially "follow the leader." The "deploy" required a greater degree of *coup d'oeuil,* each commander of the rear battalions having to guesstimate the approximate position along the intended line of his battalion before it actually occupied that location. Though the "deploy" could be performed much more quickly than the processional method, it was very much more susceptible to human error. This was a critical concern before any battle.

The real value of the "deploy" during the Seven Years' War lay in its utility to the individual battalion or regiment. A battalion encountering rough terrain could form into column, move past the obstructing terrain and redeploy into line. This now could be done more quickly and much closer to the enemy than ever before.

Whenever a regiment encountered "hollow ways," i.e., sunken roads, morasses, ponds, etc., in its path while advancing, its battalions were to form columns until they had bypassed the problematic terrain. The maneuver that was used was essentially the reverse of the "deploy." To form two columns the regiment was halted. It was normal in this type of situation for the regiment's two battalions to march in line side by side, with the 1st battalion on the right. The two battalions were also to form column side by side, and this meant that the 1st battalion would form column behind its left-most platoon while the 2nd formed behind its right platoon. These two platoons remained stationary as the men in all the others first turned to the left or right, as appropriate, and then marched diagonally and to the rear until they reached their proper place in the column, when they were ordered to face the front.

The various platoons were to remain as close as possible to their neighbors as the men marched to the rear and center. This was to reduce the distance that had to be marched, speed up the process, and reduce the potential for confusion. The two battalion guns remained with each battalion's 8th platoon, so as to be to the left of the front of the 1st battalion column, and to the left of the rear of the 2nd. These guns were not to advance from these positions until line had been reestablished, so that they were not needlessly exposed. Platoons in the first column remained in the normal sequence, with the 1st platoon in the front, while those in the second column were in "inverted order."

If an individual battalion encountered obstructing terrain that did not affect the regiment's other battalion, it was to form "column by the center." The process was very similar to when the entire regiment formed columns, but now two smaller columns were formed behind the center of the battalion. The first column was formed to the rear of the 4th platoon and was made up of four platoons in normal order. The second column, also of four platoons, was behind the 5th platoon and was in inverted order.

WHEELING THE BATTALION

Prussian drills also dealt with the contingency where a battalion would be forced to change its front "with expedition," such as would occur if the enemy suddenly approached from the flank. In this case, the entire battalion would pivot on one of its ends, like a quarter-wheel performed by a solitary platoon. To insure that the battalion would be deployed in the required direction, the major and the adjutant would ride to the flank of the battalion on which the pivot was to be made. Here, they would march out, six, eight or ten files, or even an entire platoon and have them dress along the new alignment. This being done, the commanding officer would order, "Dress!" and the remainder of the battalion would march in a circular course until it was aligned with the files on the pivot which had been positioned by the major.

CENTRAL CONVERSION

A similar type of maneuver could be used to pivot the battalion on its center, though even the drill booklet cautioned that this was more appropriate for the parade ground. It went on to advise that short turns of this type, 90 degrees or less, could be useful and practical to perform. This maneuver was identical to that entitled "central conversion" in the French regulations of 1755.[9]

COUNTERMARCH

Much more useful was the type of maneuver known as a "countermarch." The purpose of a countermarch was to have a battalion that was deployed in line and facing one direction quickly face the opposite direction, without causing confusion and without changing the order of platoons along the line. The modern reader might think this was merely having all the men make an "about face." This was rarely done, and then only in the most dire of circumstances. Simply having the individual men turn around meant that the original first rank was now the rear rank and so on. This was anathema because the "greatest force," i.e., the largest men, were placed in the first rank, and having these men suddenly occupy the rear rank was perceived as ceding a slight but significant advantage to the enemy opposed to them.

There was a second reason why the men were turned to face the opposite direction. Doing so meant the order of platoons in the line would be reversed, and though Prussian tactics tolerated inverted order when in column, it was to be avoided when the battalion deployed in line. This was because firing systems such as platoon fire required that the fire be delivered by a prearranged sequence of platoons. Needless to say, there would have been great confusion when the platoons' order was reversed.

The Prussians used two versions of the countermarch. The first was the more rigid of the two and relied on a series of quarter-wheels, advances, and about faces. The second was simpler, relying on a lengthy march by files. The following is how the Prussians performed the first version of the countermarch. As complicated as it appears to us, commanders were occasionally forced to resort to its use under fire.

The first step was to have all eight platoons simultaneously quarter-wheel 90 degrees to the left. The left-most platoon would now "file" about one and one-half intervals to its rear (i.e., it would march a distance approximately one and a half times its width). Having done this, the men turned to their left (they were now facing the right of the battalion) and marched behind the width of the battalion until that platoon was behind the original position of the 1st platoon where it halted. As this was occurring, the 7th platoon advanced to the original position of the 8th platoon, and duplicated the motions of the 8th platoon. The remaining platoons successively did the same. When each platoon was directly behind the one in front and separated by an interval (i.e., the space between each platoon equaled the width of the platoon), all the men were ordered to turn around. Finally, all eight platoons simultaneously quarter-wheeled, and if the distance between each was indeed one interval, a line, facing 180 degrees to the original, was immediately formed.[10]

The second version of the countermarch was much simpler to perform. The soldiers in the line were ordered to face to their right, and then to take one large step to the right. The first files (the first three men on the right of the battalion) quarter-wheeled to the right and started to march behind the battalion. They were followed by the rest of the men who marched by files, i.e., each of the three original ranks now became a long file. This was continued until the three file leaders reached a point even with but a few paces behind the original left of the battalion. At this point, all the men halted and then faced to their left, i.e., they now were in line again, but now facing the original rear.

CROSSING A BRIDGE

The following maneuver was used if a battalion had to cross a bridge in the presence of the enemy, especially when under fire, if the bridge was wide enough. The battalion was to be deployed in a line facing the bridge, with the 5th platoon directly in front of the roadway across the bridge. This allowed the battalion to deliver roughly an equal amount of fire on both sides of the bridge as the 5th platoon crossed. The 5th platoon marched directly forward onto the bridge, while the 4th and 6th platoons "wheeled by files" and then marched by files behind the cover provided by the 5th platoon. The 4th platoon followed the three right-hand files of the 5th platoon, while the 6th followed the three left-hand files.

As soon as the bridge was crossed, the 5th platoon halted 20 to 30 paces in front, while the men in the two platoons ran by files to form line on either side of it. If the enemy was near, the 5th platoon would fire, followed by the 4th, then the 6th. In the meantime the remaining platoons would have crossed, marching by files and quickly resuming their proper place in line to the right and left of the three already in position. If the officers had the correct timing, the platoon crossing the bridge would just reach its position in line when it was to present arms, before firing several moments later. In this way a regular platoon fire was established as the battalion crossed the bridge. If, after all eight platoons had fired, additional fire was necessary, the commander would order the battalion forward a few paces, and then order that the platoon fire be delivered while advancing, first from the right, then the left and finally the center.

Of course, part of the repertoire of Prussian drills dealt with the contingency where friendly infantry was attacked by enemy cavalry. A special formation, the "hollow square," had been occasionally used in many armies at least since the early seventeenth century. During Frederick's reign, the Prussians experimented with a number of different versions of the hollow square.

The 1726 infantry regulations allowed three types of squares: a battalion square, a "quick" regimental square and a "slow" regimental square. The "slow" regimental square called for most of the platoons to move a shorter distance; however, the first and second platoons of the left battalion had to march a greater distance, and hence its name. The battalion square was officially discarded in 1733, while the quick regimental square fell into disfavor in 1743. The slow method, although its rear face took longer to form, had proven to be preferable since it was conceptually much simpler.

The Prussians also discovered that a solid square could be performed on the two center platoons of a battalion by forming closed column. The battalion square was recognized once again in 1752.[11]

THREE-SIDED SQUARE

Among the more obscure maneuvers devised was one which allowed a battalion threatened by enemy cavalry to use nearby obstructing terrain as one of the sides of the normal infantry square. The battalion would deploy with its back about 100 paces away from the morass, river or pond in question. All men, except the grenadiers and those carrying the battalion's colors, were ordered to face the rear. The grenadiers turned to their left and then marched to the center of the battalion. The color reserve continued to face the front and dressed behind the grenadiers when they arrived at the center of the battalion.

While this was being done, the remainder of the battalion wheeled to form the second and third sides of the square. The first four platoons (the right "wing" of the battalion) wheeled inward to the right, the last four (the left "wing") wheeled inward to the left. They each wheeled 90 degrees until the two halves of the battalion came face to face. The commanding officer now ordered all the men other than the grenadiers to about-face. The first four platoons would be ordered to advance so that they would form a right angle with the grenadier company; then the other four platoons would similarly advance to be flush with the grenadiers' left. The battalion's two guns were positioned between the two sides of the square and the obstructing terrain.

The drill called for the right wing (the first four platoons) to advance 10 or 20 paces, while performing platoon fire: the 1st platoon fired first, then the 4th, then the 2nd, and finally the 3rd platoon. After the 3rd finished firing the four platoons in this wing returned to position behind the right of the grenadiers using a backwards oblique step. Now, the other wing would be ordered to advance and fire, after which it would return to its position in the square. After both wings had performed their platoon fire it was the turn of the grenadiers making up the other side. They were to advance the same distance, but to perform their fire differently. The rear rank was to fire first, reload quickly, and then by the backwards oblique march return to their position in the square. Next, the center rank fired, reloaded and moved backwards, followed by the first rank.

As soon as the enemy was repulsed, and if there was no further danger to the battalion's flanks, it was to reform line. To do this, the right and left wing each wheeled towards the original position of the line. Upon completion of the two wheels, the men in the eight platoons would dress toward the center, i.e., the center platoons would form the basis for the battalion's alignment. At the same time, the grenadiers faced to the right, and then marched to their original position, where they would next be ordered to face the front. Finally, the color bearers would reoccupy their original position.[12]

THE OBLONG SQUARE

The formation of larger regimental squares were also practiced in case individual regiments traveling independently across the countryside were attacked by hostile cavalry. Apparently, the square used by Field Marshal Lehwald during his retreat out of Moravia served as a model during the mid-1750's. In this case the Field Marshal was able to defend himself for three days against a combined force of 3000 light infantry and cavalry. Lehwald's regimental square, or "oblong square" as it was called, was formed in the following fashion. The regiment's two battalions were each first divided into ten platoons, rather than the normal eight. Next, the two battalions were formed in column at full interval, side by side. The first of these special platoons in the two battalions remained stationary. All of the others, except the two 10th platoons, quarter-wheeled. Those of the first battalion wheeled to the right, those of the second, to the left, thereby forming the two long sides of the square. The men in the two 10th platoons were ordered to turn around.

The "back" and the "front" of the square were to be protected by the grenadiers. The drill conveniently assumes that the regiment forming square has the use of four grenadier companies, rather than the two one would expect from the official organization. Two of these grenadier companies were positioned in front of the two battalions to form the "vanguard"; the other two were positioned in the rear, to form the "rearguard." Each company was deployed in column of four tiers. Each tier, in turn, was divided into two subsections. By a series of quarter-wheels the two groups of grenadier companies formed at either end of the oblong square, and one gun was placed in the space between the grenadiers and the main body of the regiment.

If the regiment was to march while in this formation, all men were ordered to face the direction of the march, which would be either the front or the back. If the square was being attacked by enemy cavalry, the regiment would stop marching, all the men face outward, and conduct platoon firing standing in position. If, on the other hand, they were attacked only by infantry, the square could continue to march and conduct platoon firing while moving. This rather ambitious system was performed as follows: each platoon would march out 10 or 20 paces, in succession in the normal order required by platoon fire. After delivering its fire when commanded, its men would be commanded to turn to the left (assuming the regiment was marching to the front) and march keeping up with the moving regiment and gradually march into its original position within the square.

THIRD RANKING FACING REARWARD

This, strictly speaking, wasn't a formalized drill, but rather an informally transmitted technique, "common knowledge" among experienced officers. Its usefulness was recognized in those situations where one or more battalions in line were attacked from the rear and there was not enough time to form square. It was a very simple technique. The battalions remained in position with the men in the last rank ordered to turn around and face the rear. The order of the platoons was no longer important, firstly because of the gravity of the situation and also because, if the men were attacked by cavalry, firing by successive ranks would be used instead of platoon firing, and here the order of platoons within the battalion was unimportant.

It has been remarked that during the eighteenth century, commanders were more apt to rely on this technique than to form battalion or regimental squares. It is usually argued that commanders, appreciating the limitations of their men, recognized that the square was a cumbersome formation to get in and out of, and was unnecessary. The same argument goes on to hypothesize that squares were more commonly used during the Napoleonic Wars because of the decline in troop quality, thus forcing the officers to now rely on this otherwise undesirable formation. Though the reliance on squares, as a protective mechanism against enemy cavalry, did increase during the Napoleonic Wars, the argument ignores the basic transformation that had occurred on both tactical and grand tactical levels which elevated a formation that had been only marginally useful to one that would now become essential. The lowering of the average level of training, if this indeed did occur during the Napoleonic Wars, did not enter the equation as far as the necessity of forming square. It was purely a case, where one simple procedure (having the third rank facing the rear) became untenable once an army adopted the formations, tactics, and grand tactics that we subsume under the term "Napoleonic."

Up to the beginning of the French Revolutionary Wars, as we have already seen, the armies invariably deployed their infantry in lengthy lines, with little or no intervals between the individual battalions in the line. Cavalry, for the most part, was positioned on the flanks, and usually was to combat the enemy cavalry directly opposite it. These two facts had a profound impact on the type of formations that would be used to ward off cavalry, because they dictated the type of cavalry attacks the infantry would tend to face. Because the cavalry was on the flanks, the infantry in the center was less likely to encounter enemy cavalry until the middle or even end stages of a battle, and then, only if its own mounted arm had been sufficiently defeated for the enemy cavalry to be able to attack the infantry's flank. If this flank was secured against a river, stream, or village, the flank wasn't that vulnerable and the enemy cavalry would ride between the two friendly lines of infantry and/or behind the second line so as to attack one or more of these lines from the rear. Under these circumstances, it was not only unnecessary to form square, it was actually undesirable to do so, since it was a difficult operation, considering the number of battalions involved. It put the entire infantry on the defensive and opened gaps between the squares which the enemy cavalry could try to penetrate to return to their own infantry forces.

Enemy cavalry beating the friendly cavalry and then riding between the ranks occurred to an extent at Mollwitz, and was carefully provided for by the Prussians, as we will see in the next chapter, when they made it *de rigeur* to post grenadier battalions at each flank of the infantry running between the first and second line, thus forming one permanent army square that would last throughout the entire battle.

This certainly wasn't the case with the French army in Napoleonic times, where linear warfare was only occasionally used. Brigades and divisions formed separate grand tactical "impulses" that were often separated from their neighbor by sizable distances. This coupled with the tendency of armies to apportion some cavalry intermittently along the battleline meant that friendly infantry was much more likely to be attacked by enemy cavalry at an earlier stage of the battle. Also, the brigade or division wasn't offering one continuous line, but a much shorter line and a number of battalion columns on either side, and especially to its rear. The battalions in line, if they did not have their flanks protected by closed-order columns on either flank, by necessity would have to form hollow square, or be cut down. The battalion columns, already in a compact formation, would only have to have some of their men face the sides to form a "closed square," which was a sturdy formation usually capable of fending off cavalry.

NOTES

1. Warnery, *op. cit.*, p. 83.
2. Duffy, *The Army of Frederick, op. cit.*, p. 88.
3. *Essays on the art of war,* 3 vols. London, 1809, vol. 1, p. 232.
4. Ibid., vol 1, p. 232.
5. New Regulations, *op. cit.*, p. 39.
6. *The British Military Library. op. cit.*, vol. 1, pp. 268–269.
7. Prussia, *"Infantry Regulations," op. cit.*, pp. 426–427.
8. *New Regulations, op. cit.*, pp. 36–39.
9. Ibid., p. 42.
10. Ibid., pp. 43–44.
11. Grosser Generalstab, *op. cit.*, vol. 1, p. 135; Duffy, *The Army of Frederick. op. cit.*, p. 85.
12. Ibid., pp. 48–50.

CHAPTER 14

Lexicon of French Maneuvers: The Infantry Regulations of 1755

THE INNOVATIONS INTRODUCED INTO THE FRENCH ARMY BETWEEN THE Peace of Aix-la-Chapelle (1748) and 1754 have already been discussed in an earlier chapter. This chapter is self-consciously theoretical, its purpose being to present the May 6th, 1755, regulations essentially in their entirety. A later chapter will cover the tactics actually used by the French infantry during the Seven Years' War.

The importance of the 1755 regulations lay in the fact that they served as the theoretical basis for French infantry doctrine throughout the Seven Years' War, and did, in fact, contribute to the foundation of an entirely new grand tactical system, the "impulse" system, which would flourish during the French Revolutionary and Napoleonic era.

VARIETY OF MARCHES

Like their immediate predecessors, the regulations of 1755 detailed the exact manner the French infantryman was to march in various circumstances. As in the previous regulations (1754), all marches were cadenced, and began with the men advancing their left feet in unison. Three different types of marches were used: straight ahead, oblique, and circular. When marching straight ahead, the men could be ordered to use the small pace, the ordinary pace, and the redoubled pace (i.e., "at the double"). The small pace measured one foot from heel to heel; the ordinary and redoubled paces were both two feet long. Whenever the men had to use either the small pace or the ordinary pace, they marched 60 steps per minute, and 120 steps for the redoubled pace. The oblique pace, also 60 per minute, was 18 inches long and was made in the direction of the oblique march. It also could be made both at the ordinary or redoubled tempo. The circular march was used whenever a quarter-wheel was to be performed to change the direction of march.[1]

DISTANCE BETWEEN RANKS

Despite the fact that cadenced marching had been introduced, the 1755 regulations continued the old system of having the ranks either at an "open" or "closed" order. When a battalion marched with open ranks, a distance of six ordinary paces was to be maintained between each rank. Closed ranks were to be adopted either before performing a maneuver or before advancing toward the enemy in combat. Then, there was only to be 12 inches between the point of the soldier's leading foot and the heel of the soldier to his front in the same file. In both cases, each rank was considered to occupy a depth of 18 inches. As far as the distance separating the files, the closed-ranks formation was tighter than it had been in previous regulations, and was very similar to that used by the Prussians between 1743 and 1748. Each soldier was to be as close as possible to his neighbor with their arms touching, without however making it too confined.[2]

THE BATTALION'S STRUCTURE

Each battalion was to be made up of 12 ordinary companies and a company of grenadiers. Essentially, these were administrative units. A fourteenth company-sized unit, the "piquet," was formed by taking a number of men from each of the 12 ordinary companies and grouping them together to form a special force, consisting of a captain, a lieutenant, two sergeants, 48 fusiliers and a drummer. In an effort to accommodate the adherents of the *ordre profond* approach to tactics, the regulations of 1755 allowed the infantry to be deployed in either three or six ranks, except for the piquet and grenadiers which were always to be in three ranks. The other platoons were always to conduct their exercises in six ranks, but were to conduct fire when in three. The 12 ordinary companies were coupled together to form platoons. These were to be deployed in line, column, and in camp.

In theory, this order could be reversed, and was called "inverted order." In practice, given the level of training found among French troops the normal order was invariably used.

Though the 1755 regulation, apparently influenced by Puységur's *Art de la Guerre,* clearly stipulated that there were to be no "intervals" between each of the battalions, it is improbable that this was carried out exactly as stipulated in the regulations. In practice, there would have been a small interval of at least several paces between battalions. This represented a marked theoretical improvement, since the 1751 regulation had continued to mandate the use of full intervals between each battalion in line.[3]

When in line, battalions from the same regiment were placed side by side, and in the following order from right to left: 1st, 2nd (when two battalions); 1st, 3rd, 2nd (when three); 1st, 3rd, 4th, 2nd (when four).[4] These battalions would follow the same order, from front to back, when in column. The regulation allowed the battalions to be placed in reverse or "inverse" order, but as with inverted order of platoons within the individual battalion this was rarely used.

Whenever the regiments were deployed "in battle" (i.e., in line) in three ranks, the officers were positioned as follows: the colonel was five paces in front of the center of the 5th platoon of the 1st battalion, the lieutenant colonel one pace in the rear to his left; the battalion commanders were four paces in front of the 5th platoon of their battalions; the captains and lieutenants in front of their companies, the captains two paces from first rank, the lieutenant one pace in the rear at their left in the companies forming the right of the platoon and one pace in the rear at their right in the left company in each platoon. The sergeants were stationed on the right or the left of the first and third ranks, according to the formation of their company in the platoon. In the absence of the colonel and lieutenant colonel, their place was to be taken by the most senior captain. This same method was used to fill in for a vacant battalion commander.[5]

The captain of the grenadiers was in the center of his company, two paces in front; the lieutenant one pace in the rear of the captain on his right and a second lieutenant on his left. The two sergeants on the right of the first and third ranks. The captain of the piquet was at the head of his troops two paces in front; the lieutenant on his left one pace to the rear; the two sergeants formed the left of the first and third ranks.[6]

When the battalion started to fire, the senior officers several paces in front of the formation each stepped two paces closer to the first rank in order to be less conspicuous. For example, the colonel now was three paces in front, instead of five. On the other hand the rear of the formation was also strengthened. Many of the captains, lieutenants and sergeants previously at the front or the side of the companies entered into the ranks or passed behind the formation to the rear of the third rank, except for the captains of the grenadiers and the piquet who remained in front of their companies.[7]

THE BATTALION IN COLUMN

The regulations provided for a number of different types of columns, each characterized by a different width. Column could be formed "by platoon" (it had the width of one platoon), "by third of a rank" (⅓ the width of the entire battalion, i.e. two platoons), or by "half ranks" (three platoons). Provision was also made for a column by companies or sections, but only in those situations where the battalion had to march a fair distance through a very narrow space.[8] Regardless of the width of the column, the grenadiers were to march at the head of the battalion; the piquet at its tail.[9]

The men in all columns could be deployed in either three or six ranks, except for the column by sections (one company wide) where they could only deploy in three ranks.[10]

When the battalion was in column, the officers were placed at the head of their troops in the positions described for the line whenever the ranks were closed. However, when it was necessary to open distances between the ranks, the lieutenants of the fusilier or "ordinary" companies and the second lieutenant of the grenadier company marched two paces in front of their companies, the same distance as the captains. In either case, the lieutenants of the grenadier company and those of the piquet position were themselves two paces behind the last rank.[11]

When the establishment of the battalion was increased to one grenadier and sixteen "ordinary" fusilier companies on August 1st, 1755, the structure of the column was affected. A column by half-rank now had four platoons (eight companies) in each of its two tiers. The former "third rank" column fell into disuse and was replaced by a "quarter-rank" column, which in actuality had the same frontage, i.e., two platoons.

When a battalion was to march in column by divisions with closed ranks, it was to be deployed at "full interval." This meant that each division in the column was separated by a distance equaling the frontage of the column. This distance was measured from the first rank of one division to the first rank of the preceding one.[12] However, unlike the Prussians, the French infantry had not yet acquired the ability to march in close ranks at all times. When a battalion had to march for any considerable distance, as it would when crossing the countryside in columns of route, it had to march with open ranks, i.e., six paces between each rank.

There were a number of situations where the battalions had to adopt either a two- or four-pace distance between the ranks. The four-pace distance between battalions was used when a column had to "defile," i.e., it had to march by either flank to change positions laterally. To do this, the row of officers along the front of the division and the first rank of men would start to march forward as soon as the last rank of the division in front of it. However, if the distance between the divisions in the columns was less than ten paces, they would wait until the mandatory ten-pace distance was reestablished before starting to advance. The two-pace distance was used whenever the battalion was to deploy from column into line. This was true regardless of whether the battalion was in three or six ranks. This same two-pace distance was maintained by the officers in front of each division as well as the row of *serrefiles* in the rear.[13]

MANEUVERS

Forming Line

When the regiment or battalion arrived where it was to form line, the major had the drum beat to indicate that the ranks were to close.[14] The men in the first rank of each division would march at the ordinary tempo (one step per second). The men in the rear ranks of every division would march on the double, still using the small step, until the distance between ranks had been reduced to the required one foot. The drummers would now begin to beat the "general salute" and all the divisions other than the first continued to march using the ordinary pace until the necessary distance between divisions was established.[15]

If the battalion in column arrived on the terrain from the left side, the traditional method of line was used. The battalion stopped, the drummers beat the "flag," and each division of the column quarter-wheeled to the left, and line was immediately formed. If the battalion moved onto its intended position from the right, the grenadier company would quarter-wheel to the right and march four paces to the front with its ranks closed. The first division would continue until it had reached the left of the grenadiers and then it would quarter-wheel to the right and then advance four paces bringing it into line with the grenadiers. Each of the succeeding divisions would do the same until the entire battalion was in line, including the piquet.

The drummers signaled the progress of the battalion's development. The drummers would initially be drumming the "general salute." Essentially, as each division moved into line its drummers would switch to the "flag." When all the drummers were beating the "flag" the officers knew that line had been formed. The drums would continue until the major ordered them to stop. All the drummers of the right placed themselves in two ranks on the right of the first rank and those of the left on the left of the first rank.[16]

Forming Column

The French army continued to use a variation of the traditional method of forming column. The grenadier company would start to march first, advancing straight ahead. When it had advanced a distance equaling twice the width of each division (i.e., the width of the column to be formed), the first division would also start to march.

This first company would also advance two "intervals." Then it would quarter-wheel first to the right and then to the left to bring itself behind the grenadier company. Each succeeding division would wait until the one to its right had advanced this same distance, then it would start to march, ultimately performing the same two quarter-wheels to bring itself into column.[17]

However, the 1755 regulations also allowed the use of another, faster method of forming column. When a column was to be formed from a battalion in line, the commander first notified the men on which side the column was to formed, and the intended width of the column (i.e., by platoon, third of a rank, or half of a rank). The men would then march by files directly into their proper place in the column. Once in position, they would halt and then be ordered to face the front. The column was thereby formed.[18]

The term "marching by files" requires some explanation. Normally, when marching in an already formed line or column formation, the men marched by ranks. Though they followed the man to the front of them, they paid special attention to remain in a straight line with the men in their rank. Sometimes when it was necessary to move a platoon, for example, a short distance to the left or right, the men were ordered to turn 90 degrees to face the direction to be marched. They would then march straight ahead forming a unit that now had only three files and a large number of ranks. This was "marching by files," and was only used for short distances, especially when changing from one formation to another. It was an essentially unstable formation that would soon become disordered because it was impossible to retain the proper distances between the men for more than very short distances.

While the column was being formed, as the major gave the commands, the most senior officer of each division advanced one pace in front of the center of his first rank or that formed by his officers. The officers were cautioned to make sure when forming to maintain the various distances required by the type of march being used. The colonels, lieutenant colonels, or commanders of the battalion always marched at the head of the 5th platoon of their battalion in column.

The normal order for a column was to have the platoons from the right of the line in front. However, the regulation also allowed "inverted order." When forming column in this case, the grenadier or piquet on the left of the battalion would march in front and then quarter-wheel in the direction the battalion was to march. If this was to the right, it would advance across the entire length of the battalion. The remainder of the companies or platoons, depending upon the width of the column, would follow, each stepping out of the line, one at a time.

If the formation was to march with open ranks, only the first rank of the grenadier company would initially leave. Each successive rank in the column would set off on the third or fifth step of the preceding rank depending upon whether there were to be two or four paces between each rank. Additionally, the first rank in each division of the column would wait an additional number of steps so that the proper interval would be established between the divisions of the column.[19]

Doubling the Divisions While Marching

Occasionally, the battalion commander would find it desirable to increase the frontage of a column. This was performed by either "doubling" or "tripling" the column's front.

When doubling the column's front, the battalion would first be brought to a halt. Then the odd divisions in the column (the first, third, etc.) would remain stationary, while all other divisions (the even numbered ones) using the oblique march would advance obliquely toward the front and left. This would continue until the right sides of the even divisions were to the left of the preceding division. At this point, the even divisions still behind their odd-numbered counterparts would march at the double, using the small pace until they caught up. Once this happened, both divisions would now be in one straight line and would resume the ordinary pace.

The commander could also reverse the process and halve the width of his columns, assuming the column had a front of two divisions. In this case, the odd-numbered divisions, each to the right of an even-numbered division would continue marching. While they did this, the even-numbered divisions would march toward the front and right using the oblique march, thus each one placing itself behind the division which had been on its right. In cases, where the divisions had been in "inverted order," where the odd-numbered divisions had originally been on the left and the even on the right, the even divisions would oblique-march towards their left, instead.

If the battalion was marching in column with a front of either a platoon or one-third battalion, the regulations allowed the commander to triple the front of the column. In the case of the column by one-third battalion, tripling the width of the column put the battalion into line. The first division (the 1st and 3rd platoons) marched obliquely to its right; the second division (the 5th and 6th platoons) continued to march in front at the small pace, until the left of the first division was no longer in front of it, at which point it started to march at the ordinary pace to catch up. When these two divisions were aligned, both then marched at the small pace, until the third division caught up and aligned itself with them.

This third division (2nd and 4th platoons) at the beginning of the maneuver marched obliquely to the left, until it cleared the left of the preceding division. Then it marched at the double pace to catch up to the other two divisions. As soon as all three divisions were in the same line, they adopted the ordinary pace. During this maneuver the grenadier company, at the head of the first division, marched obliquely to the right while the piquet behind the third division did the same to the left. When each reached the appropriate lateral position they marched forward, the piquet on the double.

A very similar process was used to triple the width of a column by platoons. The first division (1st platoon) marched obliquely to the right; the second division (the 3rd platoon) marched in front until it was aligned with the first. The third division (5th platoon) oblique-marched to the left so that its right file was next to the left of the second division. These three divisions now formed a "half rank." The remaining three divisions would do the same to form the second "half rank" in the column. The fourth division (6th platoon) marched obliquely to the right; the fifth division (4th platoon) marched straight ahead; the sixth division (4th platoon) marched obliquely to the left. The grenadier company had to march even more obliquely. The grenadiers positioned themselves on the right of the first half-rank, the piquet on the left of the second half-rank.

The regulations also allowed, at least in theory, a column that had had its front tripled to readopt its original frontage. If the battalion was completely in line, the grenadier company would step three ordinary paces in front and then start to march obliquely to the left. The next two platoons (the two to the left of the grenadiers) would step three or six paces, depending upon whether they were deployed in three or six ranks, where they would also start to march obliquely to the left. The two platoons in the center would simply march straight forward using the small step. Soon after, the two platoons on the left of the battalion would oblique-march to the right.

If the battalion was in column by two "half-ranks," the grenadier company and the 1st and the 6th platoon were to march obliquely to the left; the 3rd and 4th platoons marched in front of them by the small step; the 5th and the 2nd, as well as the piquet, marched obliquely to the right. To perform this maneuver, it was necessary that each division wait for those in front to gain the required distance separating the divisions.[20]

Changing Direction

By 1755, a certain amount of progress had been made when it came to performing a "quarter-wheel." This was no longer performed a single rank at a time. Usually a battalion would march with open order between its ranks (i.e. six paces apart). Prior to making the quarter-wheel, each division in the battalion would have to bring its ranks to closed order, one foot apart. This was to occur whether the battalion was deployed in three or six ranks in each division.

As the commander of each division issued the orders to close ranks, the last ranks would immediately close toward the first on the double, while these first ranks continued to march at the ordinary pace. The officer giving the command had to pay attention that the last rank closed at the exact moment the first rank reached the place where the division would turn. Then all the ranks would perform the quarter-wheel together quickly, either at the ordinary pace or at the double. Each man followed his file leaders, but kept his eyes on the officers positioned on the exterior flank.

As soon as the quarter-wheel was made, the ranks continued in closed order until the last rank passed the point where the turn occurred. At this point, they were commanded to open their ranks; the first rank continued to march, while the other ranks stopped to successively regain the original distances they had before making the quarter-wheel. While one division was performing the quarter-wheel the next division continued its march at its normal rate, and was not to slacken its pace.[21]

The regulation of 1755 also provided for turning a complete battalion or even an entire multibattalion regiment. The procedure to be followed was very similar to the quarter-wheel by platoon or division, only on a much grander scale. The regiment or battalion to be turned was deployed in line in closed ranks. When ordered to march, all men in the units to be turned started to march, bringing their left foot forward first. The men turned using the circular step and followed their file leaders while keeping their eyes on the outside flank. Needless to say, this was a textbook exercise and had little practical application on the battlefield, being far too cumbersome to employ in the presence of the enemy.

An entire battalion was able, at least in theory, to change the direction it faced by turning on its center. This was known as a "central conversion." For example, if the battalion was to face to the right of the original position, the following procedure was used. The men in the right half of the battalion would about-face (turn around). Both halves of the battalions would now quarter-wheel clockwise. The two center men along each rank, each facing a different direction, moved slowly side by side touching one another. At the end of this movement the men in the right half of the battalion faced about once again, and now the entire battalion faced to the right of the original line. A similar process was used to face the battalion to the left.[22]

Passage of a Defile

Occasionally, a battalion marching across the countryside would have to pass through a narrow clearing in a woods or a passageway between hills, etc. These corridors were called "defiles" in military parlance. If a battalion already in column encountered a defile narrower than its front, it had to temporarily reduce its front until it cleared the obstruction. If the passageway was to the front but also slightly to the right side of the column, the men on the left of each rank who were not able to march directly in front, would file behind the men on the right side of that rank. Similarly, if the defile was a little to the left, then the men on the right side of each rank in a division would move behind the men on the left and follow them through the defile. When the narrow passageway was directly in front of the column, then the men in the center who could march ahead without being blocked would pass the obstacle to be followed by the men on the left and right file behind the center. Once the division had successfully passed through the corridor or defile, the men who had broken ranks and fallen behind some other files would march on the double to regain their proper place along the rank. It was important that this be done quickly so as not to slow down any subsequent divisions that would still have to pass through the defile.[23]

Column of Attack

The regulations of 1755 differentiated between two types of massed columns: the column of attack and the column of retreat. Both were formed from two battalions, each deployed in six ranks, and positioned side by side. As their respective names imply, one column was used to march toward the enemy to attempt to crush the enemy line using cold steel, the other, when it was necessary to retreat from a victorious enemy who was threatening on all sides. The column of attack was designed so that the men, though in a compact formation boosting their own morale and menacing the enemy, were still able to move quickly toward the front. In the column of retreat the priority was on being able to defend in all directions, and much less emphasis was placed on being able to move quickly.

The first step in forming a column of attack was to insure that each platoon contained an equal number of files. The piquet was disbanded and its men returned to their original company. The men from the larger-sized platoons were placed in those platoons with an inadequate number of men. During this operation, the major might be required to open up the battalion to be able to introduce these men into their new platoons. Any supernumerary troops were not included in this evening-off process, but were grouped together in the center between the two battalions. They were deployed in three ranks and if they were less than 30 men they were commanded by a lieutenant; otherwise, they were commanded by the captain and lieutenant previously leading the piquet.

At this point, the 1st platoons in each of the two battalions marched eight paces in front at the double and then turned and marched by files to the center of the two battalions. When the two platoons met, the men turned once again to the front and marched up to form the head of the column. In theory, if the battalion was forming column of attack when threatened by the enemy, the platoons could march behind the line rather than in front of it. Next the 3rd platoons did the same, as soon as the two 1st platoons had passed in front of them. This placed them in column immediately behind the first two platoons. The same maneuver was then made successively by the 5th, 6th, and 4th platoons of each battalion. The 2nd platoon, as soon as the 4th platoon had passed in front of them, turned to the left or the right (depending on whether they were in the front or second battalion) and simply marched towards the center.

The column thus formed had a front of two platoons and a depth of six. These twelve platoons were divided into three sections (four platoons apiece); the first composed of the 1st and 3rd platoons of the two battalions; the second section of the 5th and 6th platoons; and the third of the 4th and 2nd platoons. Each section was separated by four paces from the one in front or back. The rear two platoons within a section were only separated from those in front by the normal distance between ranks.

The grenadier company of the battalion on the right flank marched to the right, occupying the space created by each platoon as it successively marched ahead to place itself in column. It continued to slowly flank-march until it arrived two paces to the right of the last platoon in the column and then stopped. The grenadier company from the battalion on the left did the same, of course flank-marching slowly to the left.

The platoon composed of supernumerary soldiers positioned itself behind the column, four paces in the rear of the last rank. The drummers, except two who were placed on either side of the column, were positioned to the right and the left of the supernumerary platoon. While the column was being formed, they beat the "assembly." The officers and sergeants occupied slightly different positions while in a column of attack. The two battalion commanders were placed at the head of the column. Those officers and sergeants who were *serre-files* in the 1st platoons repositioned themselves with the officers in front of that platoon. The *serre-files* in the 2nd platoons retained their ordinary place, however, those in the remaining platoons exited the column and placed themselves on the flanks.

The attack column was to advance at the ordinary pace as soon as the major ordered them to march or the drummers beat "to the field." It could also be ordered to advance on the double, with the soldiers marching with their flintlocks raised. This was to be executed as soon as the drums beat the "charge" or the major or commandant signaled them by carrying his spontoon in front of him. In either case, the two rear sections of the column took wider steps to close the four-pace gap down to the "point of the sword."

If at any point, the column was ordered to halt, the drums were to stop beating; and the soldiers immediately shoulder their arms. The last section would halt, the second advance four additional paces, while the first continued eight paces. This was to insure that the required four paces between sections were maintained.

The regulation also provided for the situation where the column—closed together while advancing at the charge—could reassume the ordinary pace with its normal distancing without the column of attack having to halt and reorder itself. To do this, the drummers would beat "to the fields" and the soldiers shouldered their arms. The first section would again move ahead from the second four paces at the double pace, the second section then would adopt the ordinary pace as soon as the drummers had changed the beatings. The third marched at the small pace until it was four paces behind the second section.

In theory, the column of attack could be made to march to either side or even the rear. To make the column march toward the right or the left, the major announced "to the right" or "to the left" and the soldiers faced to the appropriate side. The drummer on this side (only) would start to drum. The other drummers would only pick up the beat after the soldiers completed their turn. To march to the rear, the major commanded the men to about-face and then the drummers would beat the "retreat." As soon as the soldiers were ordered to halt, all the men had to immediately turn around and face the front with shouldered arms, unless they were ordered to do otherwise.

Following the Chevalier de Folard's theory, the French battalion was trained to divide up after having penetrated the enemy battalion. The major would order the column of attack to halt and have the drummers on the right flank of the second section and the left flank of the third section roll the drums. The first section was to remain facing the front, while the second turned to the right and the third to the left. Then the major would order them to march, the drummers were to beat the "field," and the three sections would advance in the direction they were then facing. If they were to advance at the double, the drummers would beat the "charge," the officers would advance with their spontoons leveled in front, and the men would advance with their weapons raised.

In theory, a single section could be detached. In this case, the drums would only beat on that side. During this process of dividing up the column to exploit a successful charge of the enemy's line, both the grenadiers and the supernumerary platoon were to remain in their original positions next to the column. Here, they could be used to fire on the defeated enemy, or perform other tasks. The French obviously had no idea how difficult this last proposition would be in actual combat, and the officers were enjoined to have these sections practice all types of marches, the oblique march, on the double, etc.

Once the enemy was overthrown, the column was to be reformed. To this end the drummers were to beat the "assembly." The sections were to either form behind the first section, or behind the supernumerary platoon, if desired.

If the column of attack was to march along roads, it was permissable to divide into six sections, each of two platoons. A distance of only two paces was to be maintained between ranks, rather than the usual four. On the command to reform line, the two first platoons in the column turned 90 degrees and marched toward the flank to the spot which they would occupy in line. As soon as they arrived at these positions, they faced once again to the front. At the same command, all the other platoons to the rear marched forward. As soon as each platoon arrived where the 1st platoon was in the column, its men turned to the left or the right (depending on whether they were in the left or right battalion) and then marched toward the flank until they arrived where they should be in line, and then they, in turn, faced toward the front.

The supernumerary platoon marched alongside the two 2nd platoons, and upon arriving where the 1st platoon originally stood in column divided itself in two. The men in these parts then went into their battalion's piquet, if this is where they had come from in the first place. As soon as the 1st platoons had started to march, the grenadiers marched on the double to place themselves on the outside flank of the 1st platoons. The drummers meanwhile took the shortest path to place themselves on the flank of the grenadiers.[24]

Column of Retreat

The column of retreat was formed from two battalions in line positioned side by side. When ordered to form the column of retreat, all of the men in the two battalions, except for the two 1st platoons, the piquets and the grenadiers, shouldered their arms and turned around. The two grenadier companies advanced six paces in front, the two piquets three paces. The grenadier company of the right battalion turned to the left and then marched by the flank till it was beside the piquet. The piquet of the left battalion marched on the double, and positioned itself beside the piquet of its battalion by performing two quarter-wheels. The two piquets were separated by a distance equaling two platoons. This would be the width of the front of the column of retreat.

The column's two sides were formed as follows: all of the troops in the right battalion, except for the 1st platoon, quarter-wheeled to their right, while those of the left, except for the 1st platoon, quarter-wheeled to the left. After quarter-wheeling, the men in each of these lines marched toward each other. Those of the right battalion aligned their last rank on the right file of the 1st platoon of that battalion. The platoons in the left battalion aligned their last rank on the left file of their 1st platoon. Once in position, the men on each of these two sides of the column turned facing outward, thus forming the two sides of the column.

The two first platoons which remained stationary turned toward the flank and marched toward the center and placed themselves behind the piquets and the grenadiers of the right battalion. Once in position, they faced the front forming the front of the column of retreat.

During this operation, the drummers of both battalions marched on the double, to position themselves in one file at the center of the column, between the officers and the sergeants of the *serre-files*. However, two drummers remained on the outside of each of the column's four corners.

When the column of retreat was finally formed, all of the men in the front of the column, that is, the two 1st platoons and the piquet and grenadiers of the right battalion, remained facing the original front. The two flank files of these two 1st platoons would turn to face the flanks. All of the other men in the two battalions turned to their right, so that they now faced the rear (the direction in which they would now be retreating). Whenever the column halted, all the men along its two sides would face outward and raise their weapons. This was to protect themselves from any possible enemy attack.

The direction of the march was indicated by which of the outside drummers started to beat their drums. If they were to march toward the rear, the four in this direction would start, and so on. The other drummers only picked up the beat once all the soldiers faced the intended direction of march. If the column was to march by the ordinary pace, they were to beat the "fields"; if they were to march at the double, the "charge" was played instead. The soldiers marched on the double with their weapons raised, and the officers with their spontoons in front.

The column was to form line basically by reversing the maneuver used to form column originally. The drummers beat the "flag" and reoccupied the positions that they had when in line. The 1st platoon of the right battalion turned to the right and marched back to its original position; the 1st platoon of the left battalion did the same by turning to the left. At the same time, the grenadiers of the right battalion flank marched on the double to the right. The five platoons on the right side of the column advanced five paces in front, and then quarter-wheeled to the left. The five platoons on the left flank of the column advanced 15 paces in front and then along with the left grenadiers, who by this time had rejoined them, quarter-wheeled towards its right.

During this procedure the piquet of the right battalion marched back to its original position, while that of the left did the same by two quarter-wheels and marching on the double. Finally, when all were roughly in position, line was formed by dressing toward the center of the two battalions.[25]

Platoon Firing

Platoon firing was usually performed when the battalion was deployed in three ranks, each of these "closed to the point of the sword," i.e., in closed ranks. The 12-company battalion was divided into six platoons. Each platoon in turn consisted of two companies, also called two sections. Firing began from the center of the battalion, and then spread to the wings, alternating between platoons on the left and right. The 5th platoon fired first. The men in its first two ranks each placed one of their knees on the ground and all three ranks fired together.

Immediately after this discharge, the 6th platoon fired. Two seconds later, the 3rd and then the 4th platoons were to fire in succession, followed by the 1st and then the 2nd platoons, two seconds after that.

Finally, the men in the piquet and the grenadier company fired two seconds later.

Like the British system of platoon firing, this method had about 25 per cent of the men in a battalion firing at the same time. However, in the French version emphasis appears to have been placed on having the platoons maintain a continual fire, two seconds between salvos. The British instead stressed the need to wait for the colonel's command to fire. The reason for this difference was that the French saw platoon firing as a defense tactic, where continual fire was appropriate. The British, also using platoon firing on the offense, had to use a system that could be easily interrupted so that the advance could resume.

Firing by sections was similar to platoon firing, except individual salvos were conducted by half-companies rather than platoons. The 11th company fired first, then the 12th, then the 3rd, 4th, etc.

Indicative of just how resistant some circles were to reform, even these latest regulations continued to tolerate the "fire by ranks" system whereby the first and second rank placed their knees on the ground, and the third rank fired. The second then stood up and fired, and then the first.[26] However, given the interruption in fire when all the ranks began to reload at the same time, this system was made completely obsolete by the use of platoon firing.

These were the regulations of 1755. Although usually judged by the performance of the French troops during the Seven Years' War, it certainly represented a tremendous improvement over the state of affairs just five years previously. The French infantry was now deployed in three ranks, marched in cadence, used platoon firing on the defense, and benefited from a systematized use of drums to signal the various orders. Some of the most basic drills serving as the basis of the more complex maneuvers were simplified: quarter-wheeling was now performed with closed ranks. This meant that the width of a part of a battalion was greater than its depth, thus avoiding many of the problems encountered by earlier French armies during deployment or maneuvering.

Despite these advances, the 1755 regulations contained a number of drawbacks, which helped limit the effectiveness of the French infantry during the next round of campaigns. Although these regulations theoretically offered tremendous flexibility, they were overly optimistic about the marching capabilities of the average French soldier. The Prussians who were considerably better trained, nevertheless used a much simpler maneuvering system.

The French were very slow to realize that the use of cadenced marching, once mastered, meant that open ranks were now no longer necessary, and closed ranks could be maintained even while maneuvering. It was this realization that gave the Prussians such an edge, and why they were able to use effective maneuvers such as march by lines to outflank an enemy. The French continued to march with open and half-open ranks while in column, which meant needless delays before the troops could maneuver and also created lengthy columns.

Another serious defect, that was to become painfully obvious during the Seven Years' War, was the belief that the heavy column of attack could be used effectively on the offense. By the end of the war both the Prussians and the French realized that columns could occasionally be used with great effect offensively, if reserved for a critical moment. However, these columns had to be organized so that it was easy and quick for the divisions to form and then as simple to redeploy into line, when necessary.

NOTES

1. de Briquet, Pierre, *Code militaire au compilation des ordonnances des rois de France concernant les gens de querre,* 8 vols. Paris 1761, vol. 4, p. 422.
2. Ibid., vol. 4, pp. 425–426.
3. Ibid., vol. 4, p. 398.
4. Ibid., vol. 4, pp. 383–384.
5. Ibid., vol. 4, p. 387.
6. Ibid., vol. 4, p. 384–385.
7. Ibid., vol. 4, p. 385–387.
8. Ibid., vol. 4, p. 440–441.
9. Ibid., vol. 4, p. 429–430.
10. Ibid., vol. 4, p. 442.
11. Ibid., vol. 4, p. 385.
12. Ibid., vol. 4, p. 426.
13. Ibid., vol. 4, p. 426–427.
14. Ibid., vol. 4, p. 397.
15. Ibid., vol. 4, Ibid., p. 430.
16. Ibid., vol. 4, Ibid., p. 397–398.
17. Ibid., vol. 4, p. 443–44.
18. Ibid., vol. 4, p. 441.
19. Ibid., vol. 4, p. 442–444.

20. Ibid., vol. 4, p. 444–448.
21. Ibid., vol. 4, p. 423; 428–429.
22. Ibid., vol. 4, p. 448–449.
23. Ibid., vol. 4, p. 427–428.
24. Ibid., vol. 4, p. 450–458.
25. Ibid., vol. 4, p. 458–464.
26. Le Blond, *op. cit.*, pp. 408–409.

CHAPTER 15

Prussian Battlefield Tactics (Part I)

THE PRUSSIAN ARMY, WITHOUT DOUBT, WAS THE MOST EFFECTIVE FIGHTing machine of its age, outdistancing its adversaries by a considerable margin. Though it wasn't always successful on the battlefield, its overall performance is truly remarkable when we consider the number of enemies it fought and their combined superiority in numbers and resources. This preeminence is usually attributed to the machine-like discipline of the Prussian infantry, the newly acquired tactical capabilities of the Prussian cavalry, and the development and use of such grand tactical ploys as the "oblique attack."

The Prussian soldiers' capabilities were also enhanced by the existence of a fourth factor; one which unfortunately has been generally overlooked. This was the nascent idea shared by Frederick and his top advisors that officers could be systematically trained to use a large set of principles to govern their actions on the battlefield or during the campaign.

Today, we would call a collection of these principles an army's "doctrine." However, it would not be appropriate to apply this term to any of the military thinking of the period. No such self-conscious awareness of the relationship of military thought and military action existed during the mid-eighteenth century. Although the typical officer of Frederick's time believed in the idea that there was an "art of war" which could be learned by a combination of study and practice, this art was generally viewed in a way similar to the manner in which many would view the fine arts today. The notion that its most important secrets could be reduced to a number of tenets, and hence be transposed onto paper and disseminated throughout the officer corps was only slowly emerging.

Most armies by Frederick's time had already begun to systemize and codify their required drills and exercises into published regulations and instructions. Nevertheless, these armies were very far from enjoying a comprehensive and standardized doctrine that would cover most of the contingencies encountered on the battlefield. The most important part of the modern concept of military doctrine is that it is intended to serve as a basis on which to conduct oneself during combat when encountering a series of specific predefined situations. The existing drill manuals, instructions, and regulations did provide detailed procedures on how to load and fire a musket, how to march, and so on; but nowhere in any of these works was there any mention of the tactics and/or grand tactics to be used on the battlefield or in a skirmish. In this regard, the novice officer was left on his own to ferret out what advice he could obtain from more experienced officers.

Throughout his lengthy reign, Frederick devoted a tremendous effort to redress this deficiency. He was the author of a large number of instructional works. Though these varied widely in form, some being instructions, others regulations, and still others histories, they all shared the primary purpose of instructing the next generation of officers and leaders about the expected realities of the military campaign and the battlefield.

One of the indirect results of Frederick's writings was to change the very way officers would look upon military knowledge. The sort of expertise suggested by the phrase "art of war" gradually started to be viewed in a way that would later be denoted by the modern term "doctrine." Although this transformation was just beginning, only to be fully developed after the Napoleonic Wars, Frederick's writings significantly contributed to this process.

Unfortunately (from our perspective) neither Frederick nor his contemporaries followed the modern practice of dealing with all the issues germane to a given issue or topic in a single document. We find his opinions and analyses about a given subject dispersed throughout his writings. In this sense, anyone wanting to reconstruct the entirety of Frederick's thoughts about the "art of war" and present them as a whole is faced with an enormous jig-saw puzzle.

The purpose of this and the following chapter is to figure out this jig-saw puzzle, and present all of those military principles relating to battlefield tactics that were either handed down to or practiced by the Prussian officer class. Our main sources will either be Frederick's works themselves, or autobiographical-type works, such as Warnery's *Remarks on Cavalry.*

THE APPROACH

Before the army set out, the commander-in-chief informed the quartermaster general of the intended route of march. The quartermaster-general then turned to the colonel of the pioneers and the captains of the guides, instructing them on the number of columns that would be used, their individual routes of march, as well as the rout of the artillery, provisions, and baggage.

Whenever the army moved across the countryside, it was divided into the vanguard and the main body. The vanguard was usually the army's *corps de reserve,* or reserve corps, and contained both infantry and cavalry elements, usually a mixture of hussars, dragoons, and heavy cavalry. It was made up of grenadiers and other specially chosen and resolute troops who were prepared for every type of enterprise.[1] Its duty was to reconnoiter the enemy and prevent its advance while the main body of the friendly forces deployed into battle formation ("order of battle").[2] In order to accomplish this, its men had to be proficient in occupying advantageous terrain such as defiles, wooded areas, and villages and fighting off all the attacks of the enemy until the main body of troops had arrived and deployed. Frederick insisted that the vanguard was never to operate more than two miles in front of the main body. This was to insure that the vanguard was never so isolated that it could not be easily supported by sufficient numbers of reinforcements.[3]

As the vanguard advanced, its constituent forces formed a single column. A body of hussars, in an ordered formation, rode a slight distance in front of the column. A thin shield of "flankers," horsemen armed with carbines, were dispersed to the front and the sides of the hussars and served as a type of early warning system. The main body of the vanguard was headed by some dragoons followed by the grenadiers, then more dragoons, followed by more grenadiers. The rear of the column consisted of the heavy cavalry followed by ordinary infantry.

Relative to other armies, who were not as adept at deploying into battle order, the main body of the Prussian army marched across the countryside divided into a small number of columns. The infantry was divided into two columns, as was the cavalry. The infantry usually marched in columns of platoons at "full interval"; although closed columns with a minimum distance between platoons were also used. Prior to 1760, the field and heavy artillery were strung together to form a separate column.

When the army marched through a wide plain, if the enemy was still distant, the cavalry and artillery columns would march in the center with an infantry column on each flank. This was for the defense of the cavalry against a sudden surprise attack, for the mounted arm could not defend itself in such position. The infantry, on the other hand, could defend themselves without dispersing, and the sudden appearance of an enemy detachment wouldn't disorder the army during its march. If, on the other hand, the army was marching through a wide plain as it approached the enemy, the cavalry were to retain their current position. As a precaution, however, Frederick recommended that several grenadier battalions be placed at the head of each cavalry column, so that, if attacked, the cavalry would be able to preserve its order of battle.[4]

All of the high-level officers rode at the head of a column: first came the generals' aides-de-camp at the very front, followed by the general commanding that column. Next, came the colonels and any other regimental commanders. These were followed by the infantry battalions or cavalry squadrons, depending upon the types of column. The King rode with his regiment at the front of one of the infantry columns and was accompanied by his personal aides-de-camp and all of the brigade majors with the army.[5] The captain of the guides rode with the army's commander-in-chief, the King, if he were present, while an officer of the guides accompanied each of the other columns.[6]

Also near the head of each column, presumably between the general officers in front and the first battalion, rode a detachment of carpenters on wagons. Their purpose was to facilitate the column's march. These wagons carried beams, planks, and whatever else was necessary to throw across small rivers or other miscellaneous obstacles.[7]

Each regiment was accompanied by its "regimental" guns. These and the regimental strongbox were positioned in the space between the regiment's first and second battalions; while any prisoners being guarded by the regiment marched between the first and second rank of the 8th platoon. Starting in the 1730's, each company had two pack horses to carry the soldiers' tents and blankets. Previously, these had been carried by the men themselves.[8] Starting after the Battle of Mollwitz, there were also regimental transports carrying the additional rounds for the infantrymen.[9] All of the officers would be mounted during the march, except for a subaltern officer who would march on foot at the head of each platoon. This officer would be relieved by a new officer each hour.[10]

If a column passed a nearby spring or well, the men would be allowed to go to this source of water, a few at a time, as long as they were accompanied by an NCO who was responsible for seeing that the men did not drink too much water or attempt to desert. Nevertheless, whenever the column's progress was temporarily stopped because it had to pass through a narrow clearing in a woods or between hills or because it had to bypass a swamp, etc., the sergeants in each company would perform a roll call to determine if any men were missing.[11]

The two cavalry columns were to be preceded by hussars in the front. The cavalry columns were in either open column of quarter squadrons, half-squadrons, or squadrons (the Comte de Gisors says that he usually witnessed the column by quarter-squadron). If, however, the cavalry had to pass through a defile, i.e., a narrow passage, or if it had to march along a narrow lane, the column was thinned down to five and sometimes only two files, depending upon the girth of the defile.[12] Regardless of the cavalry column's width, it was usually flanked by a number of troopers riding singly, one behind the other, about 150 paces distant. Their task was to protect the column from any sudden attack, and these men rode with their carbines poised in their hands.[13]

If the infantry and cavalry columns were separated by any considerable distance, several cavalry squadrons were to ride between each of the columns, in order to guarantee easy communication between the columns. Wherever possible, these squadrons were not to ride near the head of the columns, but to be positioned about a quarter of the way back towards the rear. The reason for this rearward position was that their flanks were protected by the columns on the right and the left, and at the same time, they were able to charge the enemy if the latter approached the head of the columns.[14]

Up until 1760, the Prussian army followed the then-universal practice of placing the heavy cannons (at that time usually referred to as "positional artillery") in a single column while the army was on the march. This column could be located on the left, right, or middle of the other columns depending upon the circumstances, and was commanded by the quartermaster of the artillery and the wagonmaster. Frederick suggested that several infantry battalions be assigned to the artillery column, especially during a forced march. Their presence was as much to provide a local pool of manpower, which could be used to extricate the guns from ruts or aright a cannon that had fallen over, as it was to protect the artillery from the sudden appearance of the enemy. This allowed the artillery column to effectively move at a faster rate and reduced the number of times the infantry and cavalry columns had to stop and wait until the artillery was ready to begin moving again.[15]

While in column of route, the heavy artillery pieces were placed at the column's front and the powder wagons and miscellaneous carriages in the rear.[16] The artillery was only divided into batteries by the commander-in-chief and given to its assigned brigade once it had neared the enemy or entered the prospective battlefield. However, the use of a separate artillery column was abandoned in 1760, when each artillery battery was assigned to a different infantry brigade which it accompanied while in column of route.

The officers' private baggage rode separately from any of the five columns, as also did the camp followers or women accompanying the army. Women usually had the choice of marching with the baggage or with a separate group of followers. The army's provost general had the responsibility of making certain that the general group of followers were always one hour march ahead of any column following the same path, so as to never impede its progress.[17]

Men not specifically assigned to the baggage did not have this choice, and were immediately arrested if they followed the baggage. The baggage train was commanded by the wagonmaster general, and was accompanied by an escort of twenty hussars and the provost general and a quartermaster who were to insure that there were no stragglers, no thievery from the baggage, or plundering from the villages and gardens being passed. The wagonmaster general assumed the rank of the most junior lieutenant colonel in the army and had complete authority over the baggage train. He was only responsible to the quartermaster general who provided him with the exact route he was to follow during that march. The wagonmaster general had standing orders to immediately shoot anyone who disobeyed his commands. If the baggage train was ever attacked by an enemy detachment, the wagonmaster was responsible for its defense and would order the use of a *wagenburg,* if necessary.[18]

As the army marched along, in spite of the efforts of its vanguard, often its main body met with detachments of enemy troops along its line of march. These would usually attempt to enter between the columns in an effort to throw these into confusion. As mentioned earlier, each Prussian cavalry column was led by hussars. It was their duty to stop the harassment of these enemy detachments. A small number of hussars rode on either side of the column as "flankers." These maintained their position protecting the column at all times whether the enemy was known to be in the area or not. The remainder of the hussars rode in an orderly formation at the front of the column. These hussars were accompanied by a number of marksmen called *"chasseurs"* who carried rifled carbines and *amusettes.*

When enemy detachments made their appearance, the *chasseurs* and hussars in the column fanned out, to interdict the enemy's movement. The *chasseurs* were positioned in the front, but were always protected by hussars, still in formation, never more than 150 paces to the their rear. If the hussars in the formation at the head of the column were attacked, in turn, by a large number of irregular enemy troops, they were to remain in their tight formation, and await relief provided by the squadrons stationed between the columns.[19]

Writing in 1745, Frederick advised his generals to form order of battle when five miles distant from the enemy, while in another disposition of this era he recommended three miles.[20] The time required by the enemy to traverse this distance guaranteed the Prussian army, using even the slowest of processional methods, enough time to fully deploy into line.[21] Reflecting the growth of the Prussian general staff's experience and confidence, as well as the troops' increased ability to form line quickly because of the maneuvering advancements made in the late 1740's and early 1750's, Frederick in his later writings reduced this distance to 2000–1500 paces.[22] Although he felt his army could approach even closer to the enemy and still under any circumstances have enough time to deploy, Frederick adhered to this new recommended distance because it placed friendly forces out of effective range of the enemy's artillery while still in a dense column of route. This was very important because the army's dense closed columns were especially vulnerable to artillery firing round shot while in a column of route.

DEPLOYING THE ARMY INTO LINE

During the 1748–1755 period, Frederick experimented with a number of methods of deploying a battalion or regiment into line on the parade ground. Nevertheless, during the Seven Years' War, when it came to deploying an entire army prior to a battle, the same two processional methods were used: forming line from the left of the battalion and from the right.

This method of forming line, although it could be performed only when the enemy was sufficiently distant (between 1500 paces and one mile), was conceptually very simple. The entire order of battle could be formed in the first attempt, since the order of battalions in each column was the same as the order they would occupy in line. The ineptitude of individual officers could not jeopardize the operation: each battalion simply followed the one in front of it, and since there was no occasion for individual initiative, there was absolutely no room for individual errors.

The infantry would be formed into columns by platoons "at full distance" (i.e., at full interval). In Frederick's father's time, the lengthy columns used to form line were either a section (½ platoon) or two platoons wide. Frederick appears to have favored columns with a single platoon width.

The regimental guns were positioned beside the 1st and 8th platoons of each battalion as the battalions moved across the battlefield in column.[23] At the sound of the first signal (in the form of a cannon shot) the army would halt, and each regiment's officers would make certain that the distance between each platoon was exactly equal to its frontage. Upon hearing the second signal, each platoon quarter-wheeled to the left, immediately forming one continuous straight line. Prior to 1760, when the artillery entered the battlefield in a single column, it could enter the battlefield either on the left or the right. After this date, it would march into line along with the infantry in the brigade to which it was assigned.

Regardless of whether the perpendicular or the parallel approach was being performed, each wing was given specific bearings by which to judge its movements. These were called points of view, and consisted of a steeple, an isolated tree, etc. These points of view were located to the side of where the line was to deploy. For example, if a church steeple was to serve as a "point of view," then all of the troops in that line would align themselves on the church steeple. If any enemy troops were near while line was being formed, the regimental artillery was positioned in front of where line was being formed. It was to fire while the infantry deployed behind it. Once the infantry was in position, its artillery ceased firing and was retired to the intervals between the battalions.[24]

ORDER OF BATTLE (THE BATTLE FORMATION)

If the enemy that was to be attacked was deployed along mostly clear terrain, the main body of the infantry was to be deployed along two lengthy lines. The cavalry, also deployed on two lines, was positioned on either side of the infantry. It was important that the cavalry not be interspersed among the infantry line. To do this was to court disaster, since as soon as the cavalry moved forward, which it would have to do to serve to any useful purpose, large gaps would be left along the infantry line.[25]

The grenadiers often were divided into two or three groups, and placed on both flanks of the infantry between the first and second lines. If the army was to encamp on the intended battlefield the night prior to the battle, each battalion would camp near where it was to deploy the next day. However, several battalions of grenadiers would be posted on each flank. These would be transferred to their proper position with the infantry the next day before the start of the hostilities.[26]

Returning to the infantry, its two lines were to be parallel. For a period during the Silesian Wars, doctrine required this second line to be placed 800 paces behind the first. In this layout, to make up for the relative remoteness of the second line, whatever forces were available for a reserve were placed immediately behind the first line near its center. This 800-pace distance was a departure from the standard 300-pace distance traditionally used. Undoubtedly, Frederick chose this distance so that the second line would be less exposed to enemy artillery fire.

By the advent of the Seven Years' War the distance between the two lines was reduced to the traditional 300 paces. Experience had shown that if the second line was to be of any use it had to be able to quickly support the first line. Infantry stationed 800 paces distant was not only unable to reach a critical position along the first line in time, but was also too far away to support it with its musket fire. The proximity of the supporting second line meant that the *corps de reserve* could be returned to its traditional place behind the second line.

At the start of Frederick's reign, each infantry battalion was to be drawn up in four ranks; Frederick ordered all regiments marching to

Silesia to form in three ranks as of November 29th, 1740, and on June 20th, 1742, this arrangement was applied to all infantry regiments throughout the entire army. The battalion was in "closed order," not only referring to the spaces between each of the files, but also to those between the ranks, and occupied 160 German paces (two Rhineland feet to a German pace). The regulations of 1743 called for the soldiers in a rank to be close enough together so that one soldier's right arm was behind the left arm of his neighbor to the right. This extremely dense packing of the files was abolished in 1748 when soldiers were stationed "elbow-to-elbow," giving each man about one foot, ten inches. The distance between the ranks varied between one foot to two paces, the narrow distance of one foot having become popular by the end of Frederick's reign (the "open order" system popular at the turn of the eighteenth century required four paces between each rank).[27]

The generals and the regimental commanders were charged with insuring that the battalions were properly aligned, i.e., that they formed one straight line. The brigade's officers were also responsible for insuring that reserve ammunition was available to their brigade. This was in order to prevent a loss occasioned solely because of lack of powder and ball, which could occur in a prolonged engagement. After the Battle of Mollwitz, where many of the Prussian infantrymen almost ran out of ammunition, an additional 30 rounds were handed out to each foot soldier immediately prior to the start of an engagement.[28]

The colonel and his various subordinate officers, once they had their men in line, were to continue to exhort the men to do their duty and do everything that was possible to make the upcoming task appear easy.[29] The officers commanding each platoon were now to inspect the soldiers' weapons, making certain that there was sufficient priming in each musket's pan, and that any shortcomings were immediately corrected.[30] The majors and adjutants were to ride continuously up and down the battalion's front in order to prevent these battalions falling into confusion.[31]

Each regiment was allowed to send a number of men back to help guard its baggage. However, at Mollwitz, Frederick noticed that the regiment's best men were always used in this capacity. After the battle, he declared that henceforth only three captains-at-arms accompanied by the "worst" soldiers, i.e., the sick, infirm, or otherwise incapable, were to be used for this task.[32]

Although the infantry officers were told to have the various battalions drawn up in a single continuous line there was always, in fact, a space of seven or eight paces between each battalion. These were mostly for the benefit of "regimental" guns allocated to each regiment. During the first and second Silesian Wars an average of two cannons were assigned to each regiment. However, in practice, fewer guns were distributed to the battalions positioned in the second line than those in the first. Initially, these regimental guns were 6-pounders drawn by five horses, but, these proved to be too heavy and unwieldy for this infantry support role. Consequently, in the spring of 1742 a light 3-pounder was introduced despite Leopold of Anhalt-Dessau's criticism of its lack of range and power.[33] Each gun was serviced by six gunners and three carpenters ("hatchet-men") from the regiment and drawn by three horses.[34]

A number of new chambered 6-pounders were produced in 1755, so at the beginning of the Seven Years' War Frederick asked that these be distributed among the battalions of the first line; and two "long" 3-pounders (also made in 1755) were allocated to each battalion in the second line. The *New Regulations* of 1756 called for four pieces of artillery per regiment (i.e., two per battalion).[35] A 7-pounder howitzer started to be manufactured in 1758 and was distributed one per battalion along the first line, and by 1762 all battalions were equipped with this piece.[36] Each free battalion was equipped with two 3-pounders.

At the beginning of the Silesian Wars, the regimental guns were to be positioned approximately 200 paces in front of the regiment when deployed in line, provided that the enemy was still distant. However, a number of regimental guns were lost at Mollwitz, so thereafter the regimental guns were to be positioned only 50 paces in front of the line.[37] During the Seven Years' War, when there were four guns per regiment (at least for those battalions in the front line), two of the guns were positioned in front of the 1st and the 8th platoons of the second battalion, while the remaining two guns were placed in front of the intervals between the battalions.

Prior to the start of the battle, all the regimental guns were loaded with round shot.[38] In a 1754 manual for the regimental guns, Frederick required the regimental guns of the first line to commence firing at 1200 paces. When 400 paces from the enemy, the gunners were to switch to canister (case shot). Throughout this time, the pieces advanced by being physically manhandled by the crew. The artillery in the second line was to be loaded only with grapeshot, so that if it became necessary to fire on enemy hussars (which could circle around the heavier cavalry) the artillery fire could not injure friendly troops in the first line or damage equipment parked behind the lines in a *wagenburg*.

The grenadier battalions were divided into three groups and positioned behind the first line on the left flank, the right flank, and presuming there were enough grenadiers, directly behind the middle of the first line. The grenadiers on either extremity were normally three battalions in strength with any remaining grenadiers being placed in the center. During the course of the battle, the grenadiers on the flanks were to be placed *en potence,* that is, they quarter-wheeled (backwards) toward the flank, forming a continuous line facing outward, and with the regular infantry in the two lines, formed one very large oblong square. If possible, a local grenadier reserve of two companies was to be maintained on either flank.

There were several reasons for placing the grenadiers in these flank positions. The most obvious was that the large oblong square made the Prussians relatively "independent of cavalry." The grenadiers positioned on the flanks between the first and second lines were not only able to stop a victorious enemy cavalry from rolling up the infantry flanks, but were able to inflict punishment in the form of a brisk and ordered volley fire if the enemy cavalry ventured too close. This also had the advantage of usually facilitating the rallying of the Prussian cavalry who were able to regroup under the protection of the still undefeated infantry.

The other advantage of positioning the grenadiers on the flanks was that it prevented the defeated Prussian cavalry from fleeing into the area between the first and second infantry lines, as would have invariably happened if the friendly cavalry was defeated and the grenadiers were not there to stop them. It was very important to prevent the friendly cavalry from entering this area, since not only did it hinder the activity of the second line, but also tended to confuse and disorder the friendly infantry, which threatened to cause the defeat of the entire army.[39]

This placement of grenadiers was invented by the Prussians at Mollwitz. When the army first deployed, there was not enough room for two or three grenadier battalions along the first line, so these were placed "interline" (i.e., between the first and second lines). After the battle, Frederick and his advisors concluded that this rather accidental placement of these grenadier battalions "interline" contributed greatly to preventing the destruction of the Prussian infantry by the initially victorious Austrian cavalry on the right flank.[40]

If an entrenchment, enemy battery, or a village was to be attacked and the wind was blowing in a favorable direction, it was to be bombarded by howitzers.[41] If this wasn't possible, a portion of the line immediately in front of the obstacle would adopt a checkerboard pattern. This was to allow additional troops to eventually be brought to bear on the defeated troops in the front line, to be advanced in an orderly fashion through the 50- to 80-pace intervals that separated each battalion.[42] Another method of attacking these types of strongpoints was to have a battalion, regiment, or brigade lead the assault. This would be followed by a lengthy "battle line," no more than 100 paces behind the leading element. This was to quickly provide any necessary support that might be needed during the attack.

When the battle was to be fought on clear and level terrain, the cavalry was to be stationed in two lines on either side of the infantry. Because the cavalry action most often would be resolved by the first series of engagements, the first line was made as strong as possible. This meant that as much true battlefield cavalry, i.e., cuirassiers, were placed in the first line as room would allow. The dragoons had sufficient weight to be effective in shock, but were faster than the cuirassiers. They were therefore placed in the second line, where they would be required to perform the most maneuvering. Because their lighter horses could do little against closed bodies of enemy horse until these were disordered, the hussars were placed in reserve.[43]

Early in the first Silesian War (part of the War of the Austrian Succession), Frederick had ordered that three brigades of dragoons (400 dragoons apiece) be placed in the second line on the right of the infantry; while the hussars were to be placed in a similar position on the left wing; any remaining dragoons were to be placed in the reserve immediately behind the first line.[44]

However, as was the case with the 800-pace distance between infantry lines, this disposition appears to have been short-lived and by July 25th, 1744, a more symmetrical deployment was adopted: the dragoons were now to be placed in the second line on both wings, while the hussars were to be stationed on the cavalry's outer flank as well as behind the dragoons in the second line. The hussars on the extreme flank were positioned two squadrons abreast, five rows deep. It is interesting to note that as of this date (July 25th, 1744) the hussars were now expected to function as true battle cavalry (like cuirassiers and dragoons), should the occasion arise. This was the reason for their deployment on the flank where they could be used both offensively and defensively. By covering the regular cavalry's flank and rear, they allowed the cavalry to direct all of its attention to the front. At the same time, they were also in position to outflank and fall upon the enemy should the opportunity arise. Frederick also insisted that a portion of the hussars be kept as reserves and were to be stationed 300 paces behind the second line.[45] These were to be used solely to pursue the enemy if he left the battlefield in a disorganized fashion.

On unbroken terrain, the squadrons in the first line were to be deployed *en muraille,* i.e., tightly packed so that if they did not, in fact, form one continuous line they were no more than ten paces apart, and in 1753 Frederick asked for as little as four paces between squadrons.[46] Those squadrons in the second line, and the third, if there was one, were separated by intervals of 40 to 60 paces.[47] Some officers recommended larger intervals for the second and third lines; the intervals being up to the full width of the cavalry regiments or infantry battalions in the second line, and even greater intervals for the third line, should one exist.[48]

The second line was to be deployed 300 paces behind the first line of cavalry, except for those squadrons immediately next to the infantry, which were to be no more than 150 paces behind the front. This was in order to be able to support the cavalry in the first line if the latter was attacked on its outer flank, or to fill in any gaps that may occur in the first line in the event of an enemy breakthrough. These squadrons were thus in an ideal position to, in turn, attack the enemy cavalry's flank should the first line be defeated. The cavalry regiment immediately beside the infantry was to remain 30 paces from the neighboring infantry line.

According to the regulations, as in all other cavalry arms, the Prussian cavalry in each line was to be formed in three ranks. The hussars were traditionally drawn up in two ranks. Because of a shortage of horses late in the 1757 campaign, necessity forced many units in service to adopt a two-rank line. This proved to be very successful, demonstrating the original third rank to be superfluous, and by 1760 this practice was universally adopted throughout the Prussian cavalry arm. These innovations did not make their way into subsequent cavalry regulations and as late as 1779 the regulations officially called for a three-ranked line.[49]

Each brigadier general was to be positioned in front of his brigade; the lieutenant generals, on the other hand, were prohibited from being in front, and were to focus their attention on redressing any disorder that might occur between regiments and to guarantee that the second line was always ready to support the first.[50] From the time the cavalry was deployed on the battlefield until it was directed to charge, the officer commanding each squadron was to move back and forth along the length of his squadron. He was to focus his attention almost exclusively on the opposing cavalry and the movement of his squadron in relation to his line or wing and not be distracted by any of his subordinate officers or men.

The responsibility of dressing the lines and making certain that the troopers were in readiness was left to the remaining officers and subalterns.[51]

Usually, when we conjure up images of how the Prussian cavalry of this period deployed, we visualize each wing consisting of two perfectly parallel lines, both of exactly the same length. However, by the outbreak of the Seven Years' War, the Prussians had admitted a number of minor variations designed to accommodate both the differences in the topology and the situation they found themselves in at the start of the battle. If the general commanding a wing found his position cramped, he was allowed to deploy his cuirassier and dragoon regiments in three lines instead of the normal two. However, the cavalry regiments were to maintain the same intervals as they would have when forming two lines. If, on the other hand, the cavalry on a wing found itself on a wide expanse, squadrons from the second line were to be transferred to the first so that the cavalry would not be outflanked by the enemy.[52]

Also, the general commanding a cavalry wing could protect the flank of his first line by having the second line extend a greater distance outward. Whenever possible, the cavalry in the second line was to extend beyond the first flank by two or three squadrons. The hussars of the third line were to similarly extend beyond the second line. This was to insure that if the enemy attacked the flank of the cavalry in front, the next line of cavalry would, in turn, take it in flank.[53]

Another way of achieving the same result was not to deploy the second line, but use this cavalry to form a number of echelons instead. In this case, a number of squadrons were placed on the flanks behind the first line. These squadrons were divided into groups, each with an equal number of squadrons; each group was deployed in line 100 to 150 paces behind the group to its front. Each successive group was also positioned further to the flank. This not only allowed each row of squadrons to protect the flank of the row immediately in front of it, but also by wheeling outward, each row was also able to maneuver separately or by advancing straight forward to reunite into a single straight line.

If hussars were used to form these echelons, a slightly different echelon formation was adopted: each successive row in echelon outflanked the previous row by only half an interval (i.e., half of its width). The reason for the difference between the hussar-type echelon and the regular cavalry echelon was that a single echelon of hussars would never be expected to act independently of the others. If an enemy appeared on the flank all of the echelons would quarter-wheel 45 degrees toward the flank forming an oblique line, and if a wider echelon had been used, that is, if each successive echelon was further to the flank, intervals would appear between the squadrons as soon as the oblique line was formed. The second reason for the hussar version of the echelon was that the hussars were expected to be able to quickly form column then move off and attempt to outflank the enemy prior to or during the actual combat.[54]

By the time of the outbreak of the Seven Years' War, the artillery in the typical army had been greatly increased over the size it had enjoyed during earlier wars of the century. As a result, several of the more discerning military leaders, such as the Count Saint Germain, General Warnery, and Frederick the Great started to wonder if the cavalry would not be better placed at the start of the battle behind the infantry in low ground where it would not be vulnerable to artillery fire. Essentially, the rationale for this change in grand tactics was that the cavalry, when positioned on the flanks, no longer posed a serious threat to the infantry which had now learned to cover its flanks. Also, the cavalry was vulnerable to artillery fire from the moment it deployed. At the same time, the enemy was easily able to deploy counter measures to neutralize the friendly cavalry in the form of their own cavalry, also deployed on the flanks.[55] However, though this question of reevaluating the role of cavalry and especially its initial position on the battlefield was raised ever more increasingly, typically the cavalry still remained deployed on the flanks.

The layout of the land could affect the deployment of the army in a number of other ways. If there was a hill immediately in front of a cavalry wing's position, it was to advance and occupy the hill. This was done so that the cavalry would not have its ability to observe blocked by the hill. At the same time, it gave the friendly cavalry the advantage of attacking downhill, if threatened by the enemy.[56] Whenever there was a hill or crest, or a cluster of trees in the area between the two infantry lines, the officer commanding the cavalry was to exploit this. Several squadrons were to be placed behind the covering terrain. This cavalry was not exposed to enemy artillery fire, and was in an ideal position to surprise the enemy should the latter manage to break through the Prussian infantry's first line, thus providing the infantry's second line time to move forward and restore the position. On the other hand, should the Prussian infantry in the first line manage to throw the enemy infantry into disorder, these squadrons were ready to quickly advance upon them and complete their defeat.[57] The cavalry commander was also instructed never to position his cavalry too close to a forest, lest he be attacked by enemy infantry that had managed to traverse the woods.

Frederick always insisted that his officers take the greatest care to allocate sufficient artillery on either flank. In order to decrease the flank's vulnerability, the heavier and greater number of guns were placed on the flanks.[58] Writing in a disposition of August 10th, 1744, Frederick ordered the 24-pounders, organized into batteries, and some of the howitzers to be allocated to the flanks; the 12-pounders were to be scattered individually among the regiments to supplement infantry fire.[59] By the time of the Seven Years' War, all of the heavier guns (the 12- and 24-pounders) were organized into batteries, each of ten cannons. The army's mortars, however, were usually divided into five-gun batteries. These were initially placed in a reserve and were at the commander-in-chief's disposal to use as he saw fit. Unlike the Austrians, the Prussians never mixed guns and howitzers in the same battery. Though the 12-pounders now grouped into batteries were no longer scattered among the regiments, they were still allocated to the central portions of the line. One 12-pounder battery was assigned to each infantry brigade in both lines.[60]

Whether the battery was placed in the center of the line or on a flank, it was always to utilize advantageous terrain. This was not to be too elevated, since fire from high positions produced "plunging fire" whose trajectory allowed no secondary ricochet. Each battery regardless of type was accompanied by a platoon of infantry which was positioned to its immediate rear. In addition to positioning their guns and making certain that the guns were loaded with the appropriate ammunition, the artillery officers also had to insure that sufficient reserve ammunition was placed near each battery.

A new type of artillery, horse artillery, was introduced during the Seven Years' War. These were mobile batteries made up of ten light 6-pounders drawn by picked horses. However, the chief distinction between horse and foot artillery was the way the artillerymen moved from position to position. In the case of horse artillery, the artillerymen were either mounted on horses or rode on wagons or caissons. This allowed them to quickly move to whatever part of the battlefield the commander-in-chief desired.

It is usually thought that horse artillery was invented by the Prussians and introduced by Frederick in 1759. Actually, during the campaigns of 1757 and 1758 the Prussian cavalry encountered enemy artillery in several engagements that otherwise involved only cavalry. The Prussians concluded that the Russian artillerymen were either riding on horseback or mounted on wagons, thus allowing them to keep up with the cavalry.

The Prussian authorities thought this was a very good idea and decided to follow suit, introducing a light 6-pounder battery of horse artillery at their camp at Landeshut in May 1759. Frederick realized that the other Western powers were as yet unacquainted with this development and so he declared this new type of artillery a "state secret." As a result, we can be certain that after their creation these were initially placed in the second line, if not within the *corps de reserve* at the start of the battle.[61]

Whenever possible, the Prussians believed in having a *corps de reserve,* or reserve corps. There were a number of reasons why a reserve was considered to be invaluable. If while deploying the army had used "false" points of view, a number of intervals would appear between some of the battalions or cavalry regiments in the lines, and as the troops continued to move, these gaps would only be enlarged. This could be quickly remedied by having some battalions or squadrons march into the intervals, whichever was appropriate. The other reasons were more grand tactical in nature. The reserve corps' cavalry could be used to support any portion of the line that was being hard pressed, or due to casualties had its ranks thinned out. It was especially important to reinforce a position where the enemy had succeeded in breaking through, but had not as yet had the time or opportunity to fully exploit. However, if after all efforts the day was lost, the *corps de reserve's* role was then to secure the retreat of the army.

The cavalry in the *corps de reserve* could also be used offensively. It was to advance upon the enemy infantry as soon as the latter appeared to waver, as was the case of the Bayreuth dragoon regiment at Strigau. It was also to charge enemy troops who covered the retreat of their own troops when, for whatever reasons, this was beyond the capability of the Prussian infantry.[62]

The *corps de reserve's* infantry was to play a much more limited role. Because the infantry in the reserve corps could not be moved nearly as quickly as the cavalry, it could not realistically be expected to move to the critical point in the first line in time to repel the enemy or conversely administer the *coup de grace*. The only service that could be expected from the infantry within the reserve was to cover the army's retreat should it become necessary.

Ideally, the *corps de reserve* was to consist of both infantry and cavalry and was to be proportional in strength to the size of the army. Light cavalry was the most appropriate type of cavalry for this type of service.

Because of its speed, light cavalry could be most easily brought to bear at any point in the line that was heavily pressed by the enemy and needed reinforcements. Experience had shown that the timely arrival of fresh troops at a critical point was more important than the actual form of these reinforcements.[63]

At the beginning of his reign, Frederick had the reserve placed closely behind the first line of infantry. However, he quickly had this disposition modified to behind the second line, where it was to remain for the remainder of his reign. The *corps de reserve* was to be divided into three groups: one behind each cavalry wing, and the third behind the infantry. The troops in the reserve were usually deployed as a third line, as close as possible to the second line. The intervals between these troops was even greater than the full intervals found between the elements making up the second line. However, occasionally, some of its cavalry squadrons could be placed in the intervals between the infantry battalions as the battle progressed. This was to allow some local cavalry support for the infantry in the first line should they be hard pressed, or to attack the enemy infantry should they start to break. Whether the cavalry of the reserve was placed in a third line or in the intervals between the infantry of the second line, great care had to be taken that it was not unnecessarily exposed to enemy artillery fire.[64]

Unfortunately for the Prussians, they were rarely in a position during the Seven Years' War where they could afford a large reserve. As a result, whatever reserve they could muster consisted only of a few hussar regiments and one or two free battalions which were usually stationed in a central position behind the infantry.[65]

As soon as the army was deployed in its order of battle, the officers began their task of encouraging the men. The NCO's positioned behind the lines were cautioned not to "bring the soldiers into confusion by useless words." They were instead to keep a watchful eye on the men in their platoon, and should a soldier step as much as a foot out of his line with the intention of breaking rank the NCO's were instructed to kill him on the spot. Failure to comply with this standing order meant a dishonorable discharge.[66]

Major generals and adjutants in both lines were to be positioned at the head of their brigade; their responsibility was to make certain that their regiment did not fall into confusion. To insure this end they were to ride up and down the length of their battalion or brigade.[67] This was not the case for lieutenant generals who were prohibited from a frontal position, and relocated to the space between the two lines. This was to insure that they were in a position to redress any disorder in either line, and also insure that the second line supported the first line whenever the occasion demanded their services.

Lieutenant generals were also to have several orderly officers, that is to say, aides-de-camp, who being active, intelligent, and well mounted, were to carry their orders either to the various subaltern officers under their authority or, when the need arose, to the commander-in-chief, which was usually the King himself. The lieutenant general was also to be accompanied by a trumpeter whose duty was to sound the signals. The various trumpeters belonging to the subordinate units within his command would respond to these signals by either initiating their own signal or repeating the lieutenant general's signal.[68]

NOTES

1. Warnery, *op. cit.*, p. 59.

2. Frederick, "Disposition, wie es bei vorgehender bataille bei seiner Königlichen Majestät in Preussen armee unveränderlich soll gehalten werden . . ." (June 1745), *Oeuvres de Frédéric le grand.* Berlin 1846–56, vol. 30, pp. 145–50; cited in Luvaas, pp. 163–164.

3. *Essays on the art of war,* vol. 3; *op. cit.*, art. 1, p. 375.

4. "Das militärische Testement von 1768", Die Werke Friedrichs des Grossen, Berlin, 1913, 10 vols. Vol. 6, p. 229; cited in Luvaas, *op. cit.*, p. 108.

5. New Regulations, *op. cit.*, p. 9.

6. Ibid., p. 23.

7. "Testement von 1768" Werke, *op. cit.*, vol. 6, p. 229; cited in Luvaas, *op. cit.*, p. 108.

8. Frederick, "Du militaire depuis son institution jusqu' á la fin du règne de Frédéric-Guillaume", *Oeuvres de Frédéric le grand.* Berlin 1846–56, vol. 1, pp. 176–95; cited in Luvaas, p. 67.

9. Lloyd, *op. cit.*, p. 153.

10. New Regulations, *op. cit.*, p. 10.

11. Ibid., p. 10.

12. Lloyd, *op. cit.*, p. 153.

13. Prussia, *Regulations For the Prussian Infantry, op. cit.*, p. 439.

14. Warnery, *op. cit.*, p. 92.

15. Frederick, "Du militaire depuis . . ." *Oeuvres, op. cit.*, vol. 1, pp. 176–95; cited in Luvaas, p. 108.

16. *New Regulations, op. cit.*, p. 55.

17. Ibid., p. 9.

18. Ibid., pp. 13–14.
19. Warnery, *op. cit.*, pp. 91–92.
20. *Essays on the art of war,* vol. 3, *op. cit.*, art. 2, p. 375.
21. Frederick, "Disposition" (1745) *Oeuvres, op. cit.*; cited in Luvaas, pp. 163–164.
22. Frederick, "Pensées et règles générales pour la guerre," *Oeuvres de Frédéric le grand,* Berlin 1846–56, 28, pp. 110–11; cited in Luvaas, p. 170.
23. *New Regulations, op. cit.*, p. 33.
24. Frederick, *Instructions, op. cit.*, p. 89.
25. Warnery, *op. cit.*, p. 85.
26. Luvaas, *op. cit.*, p. 52.
27. Duffy, *The Army of Frederick, op. cit.*, p. 83.
28. Lloyd, *op. cit.*, p. 151.
29. *Essays on the Art of War, op. cit.*, vol. 3, art 5, p. 375.
30. Ibid., vol. 3, art. 19, p. 376.
31. Ibid., vol. 3, art. 14, p. 376.
32. Ibid., vol. 3, art. 8 & 9, p. 376.
33. Duffy, *The Army of Frederick, op. cit.*, p. 112.
34. Frederick, *Instruction militaire,* pp. 160–161; cited in Luvaas, *op. cit.*, p. 157.
35. New Regulations, *op. cit.*, p. 33.
36. Duffy, *The Army of Frederick, op. cit.*, p. 113.
37. Ibid., p. 118.
38. New Regulations, *op. cit.*, p. 33.
39. Warnery, *op. cit.*, p. 53.
40. Lloyd, *op. cit.*, p. 159; Carlyle, *op. cit.*, vol. 6, p. 241.
41. Frederick, "Pensées. . ." *Oeuvres, op. cit.*, vol. 28, pp. 110–11.; cited in Luvaas, *op. cit.*, p. 172.
42. Frederick, *Instruction militaire,* pp. 32–39, 151–154; cited in Luvaas, *op. cit.*, p. 144.
43. Maude, *op. cit.*, pp. 101–102.
44. *Essays on the Art of War, op. cit.*, vol. 3, art. 12 & 16, pp. 376–77.
45. July 25th 1744.
46. Frederick, *Instructions, op. cit.*, p. 88.
47. Friedrick, *Militärische Schriften,* p. 505.
48. Warnery, *op. cit.*, p. 48.
49. Duffy, *The Army of Frederick, op. cit.*, p. 106.
50. July 25th 1744.
51. Warnery, *op. cit.*, p. 19.

52. July 25th 1744.

53. Frederick, *Instructions, op. cit.*, p. 89.

54. Warnery, *op. cit.*, pp. 53–54.

55. Warnery, *op. cit.*, p. 50.

56. July 25th 1744.

57. Warnery, *op. cit.*, p. 96.

58. Frederick, "Testement von 1768" Werke, vol. 6, pp. 230–231; cited in Luvaas, *op. cit.*, pp. 158–159.

59. Duffy, *The Army of Frederick, op. cit.*, p. 118.

60. Frederick, "Eléments de castramétrie et de tactique" *Oeuvres,* vol. 29, pp. 38–39; cited in Luvaas, *op. cit.*, p. 156.

61. *The British Military Library. op. cit.,* vol. 1, pp. 19–20.

62. Warnery, *op. cit.*, p. 75.

63. *op. cit.*, p. 73.

64. Ibid., p. 79.

65. Ibid., p. 74.

66. *Essays of the Art of War, op. cit.* vol. 3, pp. 375–376.

67. Ibid., *op. cit.*, vol. 3, art 14, p. 375.

68. Warnery, *op. cit.*, p. 45.

CHAPTER 16

Prussian Battlefield Tactics (Part II)

ALTHOUGH THE EXACT NATURE OF THE PRUSSIAN BATTLE PLAN VARIED according to the nature of the terrain and the position of the enemy, the Prussian commanders were instructed to always take the offensive. When the totality of Frederick's instructions are examined, very little detail is provided about defensive operations; for example, Frederick gives a lot of advice on how to attack an enemy on good terrain, but surprisingly little on how to take advantage of terrain defensively.

Following the conventional wisdom of the day, the infantry and cavalry were divided into separate bodies which during the course of the battle would act relatively independently from one another. As with other armies from that and the preceding period, the cavalry was usually placed on the wings with the infantry in a continuous body in the center.

The deployment of the cavalry was subject to the following considerations. Unlike infantry, which could fight in any type of terrain, European cavalry (Asiatic horsemen could fight over the most rugged terrain) could only effectively fight in the open countryside. As a result, Prussian cavalry commanders were instructed not to position their cavalry in a large forest or marshy ground where it would get bogged down and be unable to advance. For the same reason, commanders were admonished against leading their cavalry into low ground intersected by deep sunken roads. The cavalry commanders were also to take precautions so that their cavalry was not needlessly exposed to enemy musket or artillery fire. For this reason, it was not to approach woods where enemy infantry could fire upon it.[1]

In most cases, the battle was to open with an effective artillery bombardment or the launching of an impetuous cavalry charge. The former was used especially when the enemy was discovered to be already deployed and occupying a favorable position; the latter in those cases where the enemy was found to be still deploying, and time was of critical importance in exploiting the existing weakness in the enemy position.

If while moving onto the battlefield the Prussian commander-in-chief found the enemy in an unprepared state, he was to begin his attack immediately, without any hesitation, before the enemy was able to maneuver into a more advantageous position to receive the Prussian assault. Although a majority of the army was to be deployed, the commander was not obliged to wait for all of his troops to have maneuvered into their battle position before beginning the advance. The theory was that the advantageous occasion had to be immediately exploited or the opportunity would be wasted. If regiments in the first line were needed, battalions and squadrons from the second line were to be moved into their position from the second line.[2]

The commanding general of each cavalry wing was under standing orders to advance immediately and then attack (by a vigorous charge) should he find the enemy either vulnerable or making the "slightest movement." This was especially important when the Prussian cavalry was already in line and the enemy cavalry was caught in the process of deploying. Only if the enemy cavalry was in good order and completely stationary was he compelled to send some aides-de-camps to the army's commander-in-chief and await further instructions.[3]

If the commander-in-chief was confronted with an enemy already ensconced in a strong natural position, he was warned against making any rash or premature attack, and was to first thoroughly reconnoiter the enemy's position.[4] The commander-in-chief was also to take whatever steps were required to insure that the enemy would be subjected to a brisk fire from the artillery prior to the assault.

He was in all cases advised against making a "general assault" along the entirety of the enemy's front. These tended to be very bloody, and too hazardous, being an all-or-nothing proposition. Instead, he was instructed first to discover, and then attack only where the enemy was the weakest. A majority of the artillery would be positioned so as to support this assault, and, if possible, a crossfire would be directed against that portion of the enemy's line about to be attacked.

If the enemy was deployed over an area which included a number of hills or knolls, Frederick advised his generals to direct their first assault against the highest position. The rationale behind this was that if the Prussian attack succeeded, the adjoining areas would then inevitably fall into the Prussian hands; whereas if a general succeeded in taking one of the lesser hills, his position would not be defensible, and his forces easily driven back.[5]

That portion of the Prussian line furthest away from the attack would be "refused," i.e., deliberately withheld from engaging the enemy. They would demonstrate against the enemy, i.e., appear to be preparing an assault, and thus force a majority of the enemy to their front to remain in position rather than being relocated to where the fighting was actually occurring.[6]

This method of "limited attack," even though it was less costly than a general assault, if it proved to be successful would destroy the enemy just as effectively. On the other hand, if it met with failure, it also had the advantage that the army's main force remained available to cover the retreat, and thus the army was never really vulnerable to a crushing defeat.[7]

Though a commander was to consider using a portion of his light cavalry to conduct a circuitous attack or demonstration on the enemy's flank or rear, if his army had a sufficient amount of light cavalry, he was also cautioned against the potential dangers of this tactic. The goal was to attack the enemy cavalry on its flank or rear the moment the latter was readying itself for the charge. The appearance of friendly cavalry at such a critical moment could not fail to have an important effect on the enemy horse. Unfortunately, military history was replete with examples of unsuccessful efforts, including those directed by the most talented generals. Charles XII of Sweden unsuccessfully attempted to attack the Russian flank the night before the disastrous battle of Poltava (July 9th,

1709), while Prince Eugene failed in his effort to surprise the French at Cremona (February 1st, 1702).[8]

Light cavalry when used in this role had to be careful to choose a roundabout way to their goal and avoid taking too direct a route in order to best avoid the enemy's posts or detachments. This type of enterprise was not very risky when conducted by experienced light cavalry, provided it was well led. If it was intercepted by a superior enemy force, it was able to easily extricate itself by any of a hundred different methods, and according to Warnery, who himself led light cavalry in just that type of mission on numerous occasions, was never able to be cut off.[9]

When the battle started, both infantry and cavalry elements were to start the assault at the same time. The cavalry assault on each side was to be conducted by the entire wing, insuring that the cavalry action did not degenerate into either a number of different engagements or an action where the regiments were fed in piecemeal one after the other. The initial goal of the Prussian cavalry was to defeat its enemy counterpart; afterwards, if successful, it would then be turned on the enemy infantry forces. However, special circumstances could force the Prussian cavalry to first attack the enemy infantry.

As Frederick gained experienced, his views of how a battle should be fought were gradually modified, and by the time of the Seven Years' War a number of significant modifications had been made to his grand tactical overview. No longer able to count on surprising the enemy simply by the Prussians' marching skills, as in 1740, Frederick had to resort to artifices to shake the enemy out of a strong position. Between wars, Frederick contemplated using the "attack in echelon," a system where his infantry approached the enemy in a series of staggered steps or echelons. This proved easier in theory than in practice, and Frederick resorted to an idea he originally had had in 1742, which became known as the "march by lines." Its purpose was identical to the "attack in echelon," only the means of implementation was different. The Prussian army was to deploy into line in front of the enemy army in the usual fashion. However, before the commencement of hostilities, the Prussians would quickly redeploy into column and then march around the enemy's flank, where they would quickly redeploy into line. Frederick attempted this at the battles of Leuthen, Prague, Kolin, and Zorndorf, but was most successful at Leuthen.

There were a number of other significant grand tactical changes during the Seven Years' War: the increased use of artillery, positioning cavalry behind the infantry lines instead of on the flanks, and the use of both infantry and cavalry columns of attack at the critical moment to break still-fresh enemy infantry at an important part of the battlefield.

THE ATTACK

The beginning of the action was signaled by the firing of three centrally located cannons. The remainder of the artillery was to immediately join in and deliver a brisk fire until the order to cease fire was sent from the commander-in-chief by adjutant generals.[10] Because the positional artillery would often continue firing at the initially selected targets for a significant period of time, if not for the entire battle, it was important that the initial selection of targets and aiming be performed by the captains and lieutenants of artillery rather than the gunners.[11] When the preliminary bombardment had ceased, the signal for the attack was given by another three cannon shots.[12] The positional artillery would soon start to recommence firing, but new targets would be selected if the previous line of fire traversed the paths of the attacking Prussian forces.

Usually the attack was delivered by only a portion of the army, the remainder adopting a "refused" position. When the assault began, it was important that both the infantry and the cavalry begin their advance together. This offered several advantages. The enemy cavalry on the side being attacked was no longer free to respond to the Prussian infantry's advance, since it was, itself, threatened by the advancing Prussian cavalry. The second reason had to do with reducing the amount of artillery fire to which the Prussian cavalry would be subjected. By advancing both the infantry and the cavalry at the same time, the number of potential targets for the enemy artillery was greatly increased, reducing the amount of cannon fire aimed at the Prussian cavalry compared to what would have been the case if the Prussian cavalry had started to move by itself. Once the cannonade became general for the artillery of both armies, the cavalry no longer had to regulate its movement according to the progress of its infantry, and was free to advance at its own pace.[13]

Almost always, the initial goal of the Prussian cavalry was to defeat its enemy counterpart. If it was successful in this, it was then to help defeat the remainder of the enemy's forces. With the elimination of the enemy cavalry, the defeat of the enemy infantry would be easily accomplished, being attacked in the front by the Prussian infantry and on both the flanks and the rear by the cavalry. However, the exigencies of the battle might require the cavalry to first attack enemy infantry, if the latter were already weakened by either artillery or small arms fire and could be quickly overthrown. In this case, Frederick preferred that the cuirassiers conduct the assault since they, having confidence in their breastplates, charged more vigorously and could be expected to have a higher rate of success.[14]

Frederick believed it was of primary importance that the cavalry assault be conducted by the entire wing. To avoid a general assault breaking down into separate engagements, it was imperative that all the squadron commanders begin the trot and then the gallop simultaneously, so that the enemy was hit with the entire line at the same instant.[15] Before the cavalry was unleashed against the enemy, it was very important to first warn the gunners in order to prevent the artillery from accidentally firing upon their own troops.[16]

Although Frederick called for massive charges, where all the regiments in the front line moved together in unison, he also realized that various circumstances could force a regiment into individual action. Frederick was keenly aware of the demoralizing effect of being caught standing still or moving at a walk when confronted with a faster-moving enemy. As a result, the colonel of each cavalry regiment was under strict orders to aggressively attack his adversary and was under no circumstances to be attacked by the enemy first. Any colonel who allowed himself to be attacked by the enemy was subject to *infamer cassation,* i.e., dishonorable discharge. A special rider rode with the army in order specifically to enforce this regulation.[17] Whenever a regiment left the line to preempt enemy cavalry from attacking it, it was to be accompanied by flank columns, if there were any behind it. If not, that portion of the second line immediately behind it was to follow, instead. Both these measures were intended to provide support for the attacking element in the first line. A flank column was preferable to a second line because it could more readily be used to outflank the enemy.[18]

When the final assault began, the cuirassiers in the front line, who as we already have seen, if Frederick had his way, were deployed *en muraille* (one continuous line without any "intervals" between each squadron), were to maintain this continuous order during the actual assault. Frederick once commented that to tolerate intervals between the squadrons as they advanced was to "multiply the flanks without any advantage gained thereby."[19] However, Frederick's generals never appeared to have used *en muraille* when they could avoid doing so without incurring Frederick's displeasure.

Before describing how the Prussian cavalry charged its enemy cavalry, it must be mentioned that the officer commanding that cavalry wing was to observe the old maxim never to leave an infantry flank completely devoid of cavalry support. Even in those situations where the entire wing was to advance to attack the enemy cavalry, several squadrons were to remain behind to help guard the infantry's flank. This was to be done regardless of what precautions the infantry and artillery had already taken to secure this flank. Warnery remarked that even the formation of the army-sized oblong infantry square, where the two flanks of grenadier battalions were facing sideways, was defective without some cavalry.[20]

When the infantry had formed an oblong square (the grenadiers were *à potence*), the squadrons that remained behind were placed so as to be a continuation of the second line of infantry. This was to allow the cavalry to charge the flank of any enemy force that made its way around the flank of the first line of infantry while the friendly infantry facing outward on the flank was charging this same enemy head on. On the other hand, if the infantry did not have its flanks closed, the cavalry squadrons left behind to guard the flank (usually dragoons), were to be placed in interline, that is in line and parallel to the infantry but midway between the two infantry lines. In this case, when more than two squadrons were being left behind with the infantry, the added squadrons were placed in echelon toward the rear of the first two squadrons.[21]

Before the actual charge began, the regimental officers had to make absolutely certain that the regiment's front was parallel to that of the enemy being charged. This was extremely important, since otherwise the regiment would drift to the left or to the right during the charge, depending upon which way it was originally slanted. This, in turn, would create a wide interval between the regiment and its neighbor, which the enemy would be certain to try to exploit.

It was also important that the all of the officers commanding the squadrons involved in the charge agree among themselves on the exact target of the charge, and the points of view each squadron was going to use to guide it toward its target. When the enemy to be charged was in plain view, the officers had to be informed that the attack was being directed toward a particular enemy standard, such as the eighth, tenth from the left, etc. In those cases, where the enemy was not yet in sight, the charge was aimed using a point of view, such as a height, steeple, bush, tree, etc. This consultation also had to include the more junior officers, in order that they could lead the charge if the more senior officers became incapacitated for any reason. If these precautions were omitted, and the officers leading the charge were killed or wounded, it was possible that the squadrons would cross each other, or attack exactly the same point in the enemy's line. Both of these events would lead to noticeable confusion, and, of course, guaranteed the failure of the charge.[22]

Traditionally, most of the officers had positioned themselves in front of the squadron as it began its charge. Unfortunately, this led to a disproportionately high number of officers being killed or wounded as well as poor control over the troopers during the charge, so this practice was abandoned by the outbreak of the Seven Years' War. From this point on, most of the officers positioned themselves on the squadron's flank or rear during the charge. Only three officers were to be stationed slightly to the front to lead the squadron's advance. The officer commanding the squadron was positioned directly in the center, while the other two officers were in front but on either flank. The attention of these three officers was directly to the front.

At the beginning of Frederick's reign, the Prussian cavalry charged at the slow trot. Unlike the Austrians, who relied upon the cavalry delivering fire just before the shock, the Prussian cavalry was strictly forbidden to use their carbines on the battlefield. It did not take long for Frederick to realize the deficiencies of the advance at the trot, and through a series of reforms he ordered his cavalry to gallop for ever-increasing distances.

Incidentally, the second line and the reserve, should one be located on that wing, began the advance at the walk at the same time as the first line. Likewise, both lines responded to the call to the trot at the same moment. However, when the third trumpet ordered the first line to the charge, the second line and the reserve continued to trot until the first concluded its charge, trying to maintain, on one hand, the 250–300-pace distance separating it and the first line but also trying to avoid trampling troopers of the first line who were dismounted or wounded during the charge. The subsequent movement of the second and third lines would then depend upon the charge's success or failure.[23]

During the advance, if a squadron in the first line was disordered because its course was to take it through a ditch or some other type of obstacle, a squadron from the second line was to move up immediately and fill in the gap temporarily created in the first line. Moreover, if the advance of the first line ran into difficulty because of determined resistance on the part of the enemy, the second line was to come to its support immediately without waiting for orders to do so.[24]

When the cavalry was to charge enemy cavalry, every effort was made to keep the troopers silent; this was so that they could all hear the words of command and the signals of the trumpet. However, it was an entirely different situation when attacking infantry. Here the cavalry was to give loud huzzahs or screams. The purpose of these were twofold: first, to frighten and confuse the enemy, and second, to prevent both friendly man and horse from hearing the whistling sound of the musket balls flying past their heads. This sound often had a more deleterious effect on their morale than any casualties they might suffer.[25]

By the Seven Years' War, the Prussian cavalry started to use sophisticated preliminary maneuvers before the assault in an effort to gain an advantage over the enemy cavalry. When attempting to engage enemy cavalry, Prussian cavalry regiments were instructed to avoid approaching the enemy in a straight line, and attempt to outflank the opposing cavalry force. In practice, the regiment would cease making large-scale lateral maneuvering when 1000 paces from the enemy, though small internal maneuvering within the regiment continued until the enemy was 500 paces distant.[26]

Two specific stratagems were usually employed to outflank the opposing cavalry. Often, when the enemy cavalry was directly in front of the enemy cavalry, the Prussian cavalry would advance obliquely towards the enemy (let's say, towards the left). The Prussian cavalry in the second line would in the meantime advance obliquely toward the other direction (the right), thus outflanking the enemy if it had roughly the same frontage as the Prussian forces in the front line. The other means the Prussian cavalry used to outflank its opponent during the charge was to have one or two squadrons at the end of the first line drift slightly farther afield in that flank. These units during the final moments of the gallop and the subsequent charge would follow a semicircular path and outflank the enemy.[27] This tactic by itself was nothing new, the French having used it in the 1720's. However, in the French version 20 or 30 "commanded" men per squadron were used; the Prussians used entire squadrons, which were far more effective.

If the Prussian cavalry's charge was successful, either they would immediately be rallied, or a portion of the cavalry would be ordered to pursue the fleeing enemy cavalry. However, before doing either, any surviving pockets of cavalry from the enemy's first line had to be completely driven off. The various regiments within the line had to support one another in order to do this quickly.[28] If they were to be rallied, a portion of the cavalrymen would spread out and then draw their pistols to fire a parting shot at the enemy.[29] At this point, the officers were expected to be very active and reform the ranks as quickly as possible, and the cavalrymen who had fired their pistols would turn, face their colleagues who were already in line, and then ride into the spaces left for them in this line. Writing in 1744, Frederick suggested 20 or 30 hussars from the flank be used to pursue the enemy cavalry after they started to break.[30]

At the beginning of Frederick's reign, the cavalry when being rallied always faced the direction from whence they came, i.e., towards their original starting position. However, this was found to not be conducive to either pursuing the beaten cavalry or attacking other enemy targets, and made the rallying cavalry highly vulnerable to an enemy cavalry charge. As of 1747, any victorious Prussian cavalry was to always rally in the direction of the enemy.[31]

If the defeated enemy cavalry was to be pursued, it was to be chased to the next defile. Here, a detachment was to be posted to guard against the enemy cavalry's return to the battlefield. The remainder of the victorious cavalry, not involved in the pursuit, was to proceed to attack the enemy's infantry in the flank and the rear. This was as much to cut the enemy infantry's retreat as it was to destroy it; this latter task was primarily the responsibility of the Prussian infantry.[32] As this was being done, it was very important for the victorious cavalry commander to inform nearby Prussian infantry so that they would not accidentally fire upon the cavalry while their attack was in progress.[33]

Whether or not the defeated enemy cavalry was to be pursued, it was important to quickly start to attack the enemy infantry in the flank. There were a number of ways of doing this. The simplest way was for the commanding officer to order the cuirassier and heavy cavalry regiments to quarter-wheel toward the enemy infantry to roll up their flank. The disadvantage was that it ignored the defeated enemy cavalry who, if left totally unmolested, would probably return to the battlefield at a later point.

Another way, permitting a significant portion of the cavalry on the victorious wing to pursue or observe the enemy cavalry, was to have only a fraction of the first and second lines turn on the enemy infantry. A few squadrons from the first line would form column and then attack the flank of the enemy's second line of infantry, while several squadrons from the second line did the same to the first enemy line of infantry. The remainder of the cavalry, those who did not form column, if not ordered to pursue the enemy cavalry, could maneuver by a series of quarter-wheels to a position in front of the first line of enemy infantry, which they would attack frontally while the columns charged the flank.[34]

As already mentioned, while the cavalry began its assault, the infantry would be set in motion and march in long strides toward the enemy. In theory, any light troops (i.e., the "free battalions") the commander had elected to use in the action were to march in the first assault, in order to draw the enemy's fire and generally cause confusion. This was to pave the way for the second assault line, consisting of regular infantry moving in compact formations and in good order. Because the light infantry in Prussian service was never of high quality, they had to be closely followed by line infantry in close formation, the fear of whose bayonets would compel the light troops to "attack briskly and with ardor."[35] In practice, however, this doctrine was rarely, if ever, applied since there were never enough free battalions available to implement these tactics.[36]

The regular infantry was to advance in good order and in tight formation. The 1743 regulation prescribed marching at a rate of 65 paces per minute, each pace being two feet; however a rate of 75–80 paces per minute was used while either performing a maneuver or charging an enemy. A 45 paces per minute rate was reserved for when the infantry was ordered to fire while either advancing or retreating. If part of the first line had "advanced upon false points," that is, had chosen the wrong landmark to align its march, and thus gaps appeared in several places, the needed number of infantry battalions were immediately to be taken from the *corps de reserve* and inserted in the gaps.

For the first two decades of his reign, Frederick attempted to make his infantry use the *à prest* attack ("go through") used by the French and Charles XII of Sweden. During the advance, the officers and NCO's were to take the greatest care that the men were not to fire until ordered to do so. The battalions were to advance side by side so that no gaps appeared. Meanwhile, the regimental commanders were charged with making sure that everyone advanced and no one fell behind. It was especially important that the officers take every precaution to prevent their men from firing without orders.[37] This was especially important when the attack was to be delivered against an elevated position. In this case, the officers were instructed to have the men march quickly and directly toward the enemy. This was to prevent the Prussian infantry from firing, since any volley fire they delivered, being aimed uphill, would have little or no effect.[38]

In those cases where the soldiers began firing without orders, the officers were to make them cease firing, shoulder their muskets and advance without any further halts.[39] This was to deprive the troops of any further opportunity to start shooting. This was fine in theory. The problem, if course, was in the first step, getting the troops to stop firing, something that wasn't always possible. All too often battalions would be pinned down in long, ineffective firefights which took place conveniently, as far as the troops were concerned, outside of the killing zone.

By the end of 1757, Frederick realized that given the increased effectiveness of his opponents, who had advanced well past their 1740 capabilities, the occurrence of firefights could not be completely avoided. As the commanding officer ordered the battalion to fire, the drummers on the flanks faced right and marched to the rear of the 1st and 8th platoons.[40] The officers were to give the orders to fire loudly and distinctly and were to place themselves one pace in front of the men in order that they could be easily heard and see how the men were progressing with reloading. Should they order the men to fire prematurely, there would be an increased chance of inflicting casualties on friendly troops within the ranks.[41]

As soon as the advance was ordered, the regimental artillery in the first line was loaded with round shot and moved from in front of its assigned battalion and into the seven- to eight-pace interval between the battalions, which had been left expressly for this purpose.[42] These pieces advanced with the battalion, being hand-drawn by men, until the line had advanced to within 500 paces of the enemy when they were to begin to fire.[43] They were to continue firing as long as the regiment was engaged. This fire was as much to terrify the enemy troops as it was to inflict physical casualties. The fire was to be continuous, without any letup during the advance. Between firings, the men were to continue to advance the guns, gradually bringing them closer to the enemy. Case shot was only to be used once the guns succeeded in advancing to within 100 paces of the enemy. It was expected that if the regimental guns were advanced to within 80 to 100 paces of the enemy their fire (now case shot) would have a devastating effect and within a few minutes decide the action.[44] The regimental artillery attached to the battalions in the second line was only to start firing if the first line was defeated and retired beyond the second line.

Although the heavy artillery was considered to play a key role assisting the infantry's advance, it was important to not have it fire prematurely. Inexperienced commanders often tended to order the artillery to fire as soon as the enemy was within maximum range. This was a critical error not only because it led to the wastage of valuable ammunition, but because it slowed the advance of the friendly troops.[45]

This same indiscretion was committed by officers on all levels if attacked, when they would clamor for artillery support. There was a natural tendency for the artillery to give in to the impassioned pleas from infantry officers from the adjoining platoons to start firing as soon as possible. Unfortunately, this practice often led to half the artillery's ammunition being wasted on ineffective volleys, and the battery's fire would dwindle just when it should have been the heaviest.[46] The only time premature fire was to be excused was when it was intended to divert attention away from the area where the attack was to come.

When it came time for the artillery to open fire, it was to fire by either half-battery or by the entire battery, rather than firing by the single gun. Individual firing was frowned on because it was largely ineffective; however, battery fire, although effective, led to longer delays between salvos.[47]

The Prussian attitude toward counterbattery fire changed as experience grew. In the 1740's, Frederick had advocated that artillery fire at opposing artillery. However, by the Seven Years' War, when it was seen just how ineffective this practice was, artillery officers were cautioned against it and the practice fell into disuse. Now, the heavy artillery's fire was to be directed against the enemy infantry, delaying their advance, preventing orderly movement, and generally throwing them into disorder. The destruction of the enemy infantry would necessarily mean the defeat of the opposing artillery since unsupported it would soon fall into friendly hands.

Artillery officers were additionally instructed to advance their pieces and keep up with the general advance instead of firing over the heads of their own troops. Firing over the heads of friendly troops had several disadvantages: it could result in "plunging fire" which had little ricochet, and even more importantly, the friendly troops tended to cower, making their advance more difficult and much slower.[48]

When the area of attack had been cleared of enemy cavalry and the advancing line of friendly infantry had closed within 200 paces of the enemy, each battalion was to begin fire by platoons (in another of his writings Frederick says the infantry would begin the charge at 300 paces).[49] Although the fire could have little effect at this range, it was intended to accustom the soldiers to the fire and thus help blind them to the danger by the noise, smoke, etc.[50] At the slightest sign of confusion in the enemy ranks, the infantry was to march forward quickly with lowered bayonets.[51]

When the enemy began to give way, the infantry was to stop and deliver a volley by battalion. In this situation, fire by battalion was preferable to the more orderly and deliberate platoon fire, since the entire battalion's fire could be delivered in the few moments available before the enemy had time to flee beyond musket range. While the infantry was firing by battalion, the heavy positional guns were to move forward and quickly deliver the last volley "by way of wishing them (the fleeing enemy) *bon voyage*."[52]

Were the enemy to remain steady, the advance continued, the troops periodically halting to deliver fire. Whenever the troops were stationary, the brigade commanders were to ride up and down the ranks exhorting the men to do their duty. The majors and the regimental adjutants, on the other hand, were to remain behind the battalions. Their responsibility was to make certain that whenever a gap appeared in the battalion because of casualties, it was filled up with the men from the third rank. Their other concern was to insure that the battalion's alignment remained straight.[53]

All the while, the officers within each platoon were to exhort the men to fire accurately, adjusting each volley according to the results of the previous.[54] The non-commissioned officers, standing two steps behind the lines were to remain silent while keeping a watchful eye on the men. If a soldier stepped as much as one foot away from his position in the line, the NCO's had standing orders to run him through with their short swords and kill him on the spot. If the fighting was heavy, reinforcements for the first line were to be provided by one regiment from the left, another from the right of the second line.[55]

One surgeon in every battalion was to remain with the men as they marched into battle; the remainder were sent back to the *wagenburg,* the large circle of supply wagons usually placed between the first and second lines. The battalion's oboists, drummers, and fifers were to double as medics, carrying or in any other way assisting men and officers back to the *wagenburg* where they would receive proper medical attention (by the standards of the times). Frederick impressed upon his men, however, that anyone wounded who could make it to the *wagenburg* on his own, was to do so.[56]

As the infantry advanced, should the distance be reduced to between 10 and 20 paces with the enemy still holding their ground, the commander was to order his men to give the enemy "a strong volley in the face" after which they would charge with the bayonet while shouting at the enemy to throw away their bayonets. However, Frederick believed that an actual melee was unlikely in this situation since the Austrians, seeing their own cavalry defeated, would be unwilling to stand, and would soon follow their cavalry.[57] If his troops were successful, the commander was cautioned against allowing a too-spirited pursuit, unless specifically ordered to do so by the brigade commander. Infantry capturing the crest of an enemy-occupied hill were to drive the opposing infantry from the base of the hill and keep the departing enemy under heavy fire while doing so. Once the enemy was driven from the hill, they were to regroup on the summit which it was now their task to hold. The task of further chasing the fleeing enemy was left to the cavalry.[58]

A full local pursuit was only advocated when 1) the position being taken did not possess any real grand tactical or operational importance, 2) most of the friendly forces had not taken part in the engagement, and 3) friendly casualties were slight. The first constraint was in recognition that a pursuit necessarily meant the victorious friendly forces would advance past the position just taken, exposing it to recapture by any fresh enemy troops that might be in the area. If the position just taken was either important to the outcome of the battle or had operational significance for the remainder of the campaign, the commander was advised against risking recapture. Similarly, a pursuit shouldn't occur where there had been a general engagement on both sides, or where there had been heavy fighting. In either of these situations, it would be difficult to send in fresh reinforcements to occupy the ground just vacated by the victorious troops.

When it became obvious the friendly forces were victorious, the general advance was to halt, and the officers were to order a cease-fire. At this point, the cavalry and the hussar reserve were to march out to pursue the enemy, and attack whatever troops were left behind to cover the retreat. This was another situation where cavalry was authorized to attack completely formed infantry. Fresh infantry, in formation and prepared to meet attacking cavalry were usually able to beat off the attack; however, infantry covering a retreat, though possibly in good order, were rarely able to put up the same resistance, being discouraged by the flight of the main body of the army.

Usually several infantry regiments were selected to join the cavalry in the pursuit. These were chosen by the King or the commanding general. During the pursuit no soldier, under pain of death, was to break ranks and plunder the dead. Those regiments that remained behind were to stay in their current positions with shouldered muskets until specifically ordered to move. Under no circumstances were these men allowed to break ranks.[59]

So far, we have described the battle as though only a single advance was necessary to decide the issue. In reality, myriad problems could arise on both sides. The advancing line would lose its alignment, individual battalions or regiments would suffer horrendous losses and be unable, or unwilling, to continue their advance, not to mention necessary changes in plan, as the enemy's actions made themselves felt. In addition, quite frequently troops unable to take the suspense of marching into the lethal zone directly in front of the enemy infantry would start to fire at a longer range before being ordered to do so.

During the general advance, should the infantry encounter enemy cavalry, it was to limit its fire against this threat. Only the platoon most endangered by the enemy cavalry was to fire, and then only at 40 to 50 paces. Adjacent artillery, meanwhile, had to withhold their fire until the enemy cavalry reached the 800- to 900-pace range. Predictably, the officers of the threatened infantry would beg the artillery to use case shot. The artillery officers were under orders to resist these pleas and continue to use round shot as long as there was enough time to switch to canister. This (the canister) broadside was to be delivered at 50 to 60 paces.[60] Meanwhile, the remainder of the infantry, not under attack, was to continue the advance without firing.[61]

By the end of the Silesian Wars, Frederick recognized the problems created by enemy artillery batteries using case shot. If these batteries were large enough, between 14 to 16 cannons, in strong positions and supported by infantry, it would be very difficult for infantry to overthrow them. Learning from his experiences at the battles of Soor (September 30th, 1745) and Kesselsdorf (December 12th, 1745), Frederick believed that the best way of taking artillery batteries, in these situations, was to initially attack these batteries with weak battalions. When these were forced to retire, which they inevitably would, the enemy infantry near the artillery would chase the fleeing men. Stronger elements behind the weaker battalions would now be thrown into the attack, and would easily be able to take the batteries, which couldn't fire because of the presence of their own men in front of them.[62]

Returning to the conflict at large, should the enemy provide stiff resistance inflicting significant casualties on the attacking Prussian infantry line, the lieutenant generals could advance a regiment from the second line to replace or support a particularly bloodied regiment in the first. Regiments were to be moved out of the second lines in pairs; one on the left side of the line, the other on the right. When this happened, the entire second line was advanced closer to the first line in the thick of the fighting.[63]

Cavalry elements could also be taken from the *corps de reserve,* and be used to check localized enemy successes, if the enemy was able to penetrate portions of the first line. Unlike the infantry in the reserve, which was limited to a narrow radius of action, the cavalry because of their speed could move quickly to where they were needed on the battlefield. This was an especially important function, since it had long been recognized that the arrival of fresh dependable troops greatly revitalized hard-pressed friendly units, and at the same time dampened the enthusiasm of the enemy troops.[64]

The *corps de reserve* could also be used offensively. Fresh reinforcements could be sent against the enemy just at the moment it was appearing to waiver, accelerating its defeat. This type of service was performed by the Bayreuth dragoons at Strigau.

Frederick also had another use for some of the elements in his *corps de reserve,* one that he rarely mentioned in writing. This was his use of infantry and cavalry attack columns. Secretly, he placed much confidence in these formations. These were to be used to attack enemy infantry that was still fresh but whose immediate destruction was, for whatever reason, necessary. The attacking column, if cavalry, was to be taken from the *corps de reserve,* and from the second line, if infantry. In the case of infantry, the column's advance was initially masked behind four squadrons of friendly cavalry. When the infantry column was six hundred paces from the enemy, it was to pass between the cavalry regiments and close toward the enemy. All the while, the regimental artillery, as well as any nearby field pieces, would fire at the enemy line about to be assaulted.[65]

Frederick claimed this tactic would be successful against an enemy line, regardless of its size, provided that the men being attacked had already been provoked into firing. This appears to be the purpose of the four squadrons initially accompanying the infantry columns: to induce the enemy to start firing. Frederick also stipulated one additional restriction for the use of infantry attack columns: this type of assault was not to be made if the enemy had posted cavalry immediately to the rear of the part of the line to be attacked. Frederick felt that attacking Prussian infantry would then become vulnerable to the inevitable cavalry attack, and he appears not to have been aware of the defensive qualities of the closed column that would be utilized so often in later wars.[66]

The cavalry column of attack appears to have been used on a number of occasions during the Seven Years' War and had two major versions. The first was a very sophisticated affair used when there was sufficient time. A dragoon regiment and a hussar regiment, both from the reserve, were teamed up to form a hybrid formation. The dragoon regiment formed closed column while the hussar regiment was deployed on either side of the column at its rear.

This formation advanced through the first and second lines and then began to assault the enemy. The dragoons were to attack quickly, charging at the gallop, all the while screaming as much as possible, if attacking infantry. The hussars initially served a reserve function and continued at the trot. Their purpose was to prevent the enemy infantry from defending themselves against the dragoons by changing to an *en crochet* formation (i.e., by refusing that part of the line from the dragoon charge).

The first three squadrons of dragoons would ride beyond the enemy infantry and deploy into line. This was to protect the remainder of the dragoons who were to continue to attack the infantry. The hussars were now to either join the dragoons in running down the enemy infantry, or move up to join the dragoons in line. Their course of action depended upon whether the enemy made any move to come to the aid of the infantry being dispersed.

This cavalry column of attack was to be used with the following precaution: it was never to be used to attack infantry that had friendly cavalry deployed behind it. If enemy infantry were attacked in this situation, the dragoons would find themselves overrun as they themselves ran down the enemy infantry.[67]

The second type of cavalry column of attack was the ordinary column of maneuver, at either full or closed interval (closed order column). This was to be used whenever the enemy exposed himself and time was of the essence in order to capitalize on a transient opportunity.

One of the best examples of this type of situation was provided at the Battle of Mollwitz. The Prussian cavalry on the right flank led by General Schulenberg was attempting to deploy into line. However, first it had to advance its leading squadrons to the right in order to anchor that flank on the town of Herrendorf. The Austrian cavalry commander, General Romer, seeing the Prussian riding to the flank in a column of squadrons, and thus offering their flank to the Austrians, decided to immediately take advantage of this Prussian error. Though his troops were still deployed in column of maneuver, he had his troops charge precipitously, something that wasn't that usual for Austrian cavalry of the period. The Prussians, further disadvantaged by being also greatly outnumbered were easily dispersed and this led to the crisis which almost resulted in the defeat of the Prussian infantry.

So far, we have examined what the Prussians were to do if successful, but their doctrine also covered the contingency of defeat. If the first line of infantry was defeated and forced to retire, the regimental artillery in the second line was quickly brought to bear against the pursuing enemy.[68] In this way, it was hoped the second line would repulse the attack and allow the retiring first line to reform.

In theory, the infantry portion of the reserve could be used as a last-ditch effort to halt a victorious enemy. However, it was considered to be a very bad crisis, indeed, if it was left to the reserve infantry to cover the retreat. The first reason for this was that they would more than likely be carried away by the masses of friendly but broken troops that would be struggling to escape the reach of the pursuing enemy. But, even if the officers managed to form the reserve into an effective line to await the enemy's approach, they couldn't take effective action, not being able to fire, or even distinguish the enemy until it was "within reach of their sabers" because of the close intermingling of friendly and enemy troops.[69]

Should it prove necessary for the entire army to retreat, the commander's first concern was to save as much artillery as possible: while a portion of the artillery was advanced to cover the retreat, the heavy artillery was withdrawn first. If the path of retreat was down a steep incline, the regimental pieces followed next; otherwise, they were to be withdrawn alongside the infantry regiments to which they were permanently attached. Finally, the infantry was to be arrayed *en echiquier* (in a checker-board pattern). This formation provided the best chance for the infantry to retreat without being disordered. The first line of infantry would withdraw through the wide intervals in the second line until they were about 300 paces behind the second line. Here, they would turn around and wait until the second had passed through their intervals and formed line once again to their rear. This process would continue until the army had withdrawn completely out of range of the enemy.[70]

In those cases where an infantry regiment was pierced by enemy cavalry, its officers were to order its men to turn about and charge the enemy cavalry.[71] In contrast, if the rear of either rank of infantry was threatened by hussars or "similar rabble" who had slunk around the army, the officers were to order the battalion to face the rear and deliver platoon fire.[72] That the well-trained Prussian infantry was able to do this was admirably demonstrated in Frederick's first battle, Mollwitz. The Austrian cavalry was able to quickly defeat their counterpart on the Prussian right, and encircle the Prussian infantry. Attacked from behind,

Leopold of Anhalt-Dessau ordered the second line to face about and deliver fire, which it did with both vigor and order, and repulsed the Austrian cavalry.[73]

Because of the close call at Mollwitz, where his cavalry fled the field before even coming to grips with their Austrian counterpart, Frederick could not tolerate cowardliness on the part of his cavalry. The Prussian grenadiers had standing orders to fire on friendly cavalry that had the misfortune to be repulsed and "shoot them down to the last man."[74] This stricture, along with new training and tactics, had a profound effect on the cavalry.

WHEN THE ENEMY OCCUPIED ADVANTAGEOUS TERRAIN

When the army was to attack an enemy entrenchment, or village, or was to attack an enemy in mountainous or otherwise broken terrain additional reconnoitering was appropriate, and an immediate attack was called for only if the enemy's line was found to be broken. In any case, the following changes were made to the detailed picture we have just put together describing the attack on an enemy in open terrain.

Where the enemy had ensconced himself in generally broken terrain, the cavalry was to form a third line behind the two infantry lines. Little or no cavalry was placed on the wings. The initial assault would have to come from the infantry, the cavalry initially remaining idle. However, if the cavalry commander noticed that the enemy cavalry was deployed close behind its own infantry, he had to insure that his cavalry followed the friendly infantry, which would be vulnerable to a counterattack by the enemy cavalry if it succeeded in completely routing the enemy infantry.

Once the infantry had succeeded in creating a gap in the enemy's line, then one or two regiments of cavalry, advancing in columns of squadrons were to exploit the infantry's initial success, by enlargening the break-through and sowing as much panic and confusion among the enemy as possible. When given the choice between attacking fleeing infantry and enemy infantry still in formation, the cavalry was to attack the latter only if they were able to assault the formation's rear; otherwise, they would pursue the already retreating troops.[75]

Frederick and his generals devised several methods of assaulting strongpoints such as villages, entrenchments, and so on. If the enemy position in question was fairly lengthy, the infantry in the first line in front of the strongpoint was to be deployed *en echiquier,* in "checkerboard" formation. This was to provide immediate support to the front line, which was presumably taking significant casualties, by allowing fresh troops from the second line to advance into the fray and take over their position in the fight.[76]

Another method was suggested for attacking a village when the enemy had deployed his army along a line running through or just behind this village. The Prussian army was to deploy as it would in completely open terrain, i.e., in two infantry lines; however, in this case, it was to remain 900 paces in front of the enemy's position until the village in question was stormed and taken by friendly forces. Depending upon the overall situation, the cavalry was either placed in its traditional position on either side of the infantry or, if the battle was fought on generally broken terrain, behind the second line of infantry and out of range of the enemy artillery.

The attacking force consisted of three or four infantry "columns," each column consisting of three lines of battalions separated by 150 paces. Though each of these columns would be marching toward the same objective, the village, initially they would be deployed some distance apart. This was not only to allow the several batteries gathered to support the attack to fire at the village until the last moments before the assault, but also to prevent the columns from intermingling with one another.

When attacking a fortified position, it was general practice for the attack to be supported with at least 10 mortars. This artillery, whose batteries usually also contained heavy howitzers, was grouped into two concentrations sufficiently separated to create a crossfire focusing on the point in the enemy line or position to be attacked while the friendly infantry advanced toward the same target.[77] The mortars were only to fire if the wind was blowing in the direction of the enemy. If the wind was blowing toward the Prussians, they were prohibited from firing, since the resulting smoke would have obscured the Prussian infantry's advance.[78]

In the case where entrenchments were to be attacked, a procedure very similar to that already described for use against villages was to be used. The only difference was that several bodies of infantry or laborers were given the task of filling up the trenches with "fascines," a bundle of brushwood used like sandbags in a later age. Once the Prussian infantry captured the entrenchment, it was not to advance further. Workers were to immediately create openings in the trenches through which the cavalry could pass and penetrate the interior of the enemy's main position.[79] If the enemy was protected by trees and the Prussian artillery did not enjoy the advantage of higher terrain, howitzers were to be trained on this enemy position before the infantry launched its assault.[80]

WHEN THE ARMY WAS DEFENDING

Frederick strongly advocated that the Prussian army always be used offensively, and consequently, a Prussian general, unless confronted by the most onerous situation, should never voluntarily place his troops defensively in an entrenchment. However, when for whatever reason this became a necessity, the following procedure was to be used. It was important that the entrenchments be strongest on the flanks, and the ditches in front of all the entrenchments very wide. They were to be strengthened using *chevaux-de-frise,* concealed pits, etc, and salients were to be pushed in front in order to take the enemy in the flanks as he approached. Lastly, redoubts were to be placed at intervals along the entrenchments, no more than 400 paces apart, so as to be mutually supported by friendly artillery.[81]

The commanding officer was to, at all costs, maintain two large groups of reserves. These were to be moved from point to point as needed. The infantry were to garrison the entrenchments, while any cavalry were placed in a third line behind the infantry and the reserves. In those cases where the army was being attacked in a strengthened position, each commander would defend his particular position by having his men perform rapid fire, which was found to be most effective in these types of situations.[82]

NOTES

1. Frederick, "Eléments de castramétrie et de tactique", *Oeuvres,* vol. 29, p. 38; cited in Luvaas, *op. cit.,* p. 149.

2. Frederick, *Instruction militaire,* pp. 32–39, 151–154; cited in Luvaas, *op. cit.,* p. 145.

3. Ibid., p. 152.

4. Frederick, "Pensées . . ." *Oeuvres, op. cit.,* vol. 28, pp. 110–11; cited in Luvaas, *op. cit.,* p. 172.

5. Frederick, "Réflexions sur la tactique et sur quelques parties de la guerre, ou, Réflexions sur quelques changements dans la façon de faire la guerre", *Oeuvres,* vol. 28, pp. 154–66.; cited in Luvaas, *op. cit.,* p. 299.

6. Frederick, "Pensées . . .:, *Oeuvres, op. cit.,* vol. 28, pp. 110–11; cited in Luvaas, *op. cit.,* p. 172.

7. Frederick, "Réflexions sur la tactique . . . sur quelques changements . . .", *Oeuvres,* vol. 28, p. 154–66; cited in Luvaas, Ibid., p. 269.

8. Frederick, "Des marches d'armée, et de ce qu'il faut observer à cet égard"; cited in Luvaas, *op. cit.,* p. 120.

9. Warnery, Ibid., p. 70.

10. *Essays on the Art of War, op. cit.,* vol. 3, art 21, p. 377.

11. Ibid., vol 3, art 22, p. 377.

12. Ibid., vol 3, art 21, p. 377.

13. Warnery, *op. cit.,* p. 45.

14. July 25, July 25, 1744.

15. July 25, 1744; Luvaas, *op. cit.,* p. 153.

16. July 25, 1744; Luvaas, *op. cit.,* p. 158.

17. July 25, 1744; Luvaas, Ibid., p. 152.

18. Denison, *op. cit.,* p. 335.

19. Prussia, *Regulations for the Prussian Infantry, op. cit.,* p. 435.

20. Warnery, *op. cit.,* pp. 94–95.

21. Ibid., p. 95.

22. Ibid., pp. 43–44.

23. Ibid., p. 46.

24. July 25th 1744—Luvaas, Ibid., p. 153.

25. Warnery, *op. cit.,* p. 76.

26. Von Schmidt, *Instructions for Training, Employment, and Leading of Cavalry.* Translated by Captain C. W. Bowdler Bells. London, 1881; reprinted New York 1968, p. 145.

27. Ibid., p. 132.

28. July 25th 1744—Luvaas, *op. cit.,* p. 153.

29. Prussia, *Regulations for the Prussian Infantry, op. cit.,* p. 443.

30. Frederick II (the Great); *Militarische Schriften;* compiled by von Taysen, Berlin, 1882, p. 506.

31. Duffy, The Army of Frederick the Great, *op. cit.,* p. 108.

32. July 25th 1744 Luvaas, *op. cit.,* p. 153.

33. July 25th 1744 Luvaas, Ibid., p. 153.

34. Warnery, *op. cit.,* p. 48.

35. Frederick, "Instruction fuzur die Frei-Regimenter oder leichten Infanterie-Regimenter," *Werke,* vol. 6, pp. 295–300; cited in Luvaas, *op. cit.,* p. 148.

36. Taylor, *op. cit.,* vol. 2, pp. 383–387.

37. Frederick, "Disposition fuzur die Sazummtlichen Regimenter Infanterie, *Oeuvres,* vol. 30, pp. 74–77, cited in Luvaas, *op. cit.,* p. 147.

38. Frederick, "Commandeur de battaillon", pp. 58–59; cited in Luvaas, Ibid., p. 148.

39. Frederick, *Instruction militaire,* p. 156; cited in Luvaas, *op. cit.,* p. 147.

40. *New Regulations, op. cit.,* p. 32.

41. *Essays on the Art of War, op. cit.*, vol. 3, art 26, p. 378.
42. New Regulations, *op. cit.*, p. 33.
43. July 25th 1744—Luvaas, *op. cit.*, p. 157.
44. Frederick, "Instruction für meine Artillerie, etc.:" (May 1782), *Werke,* vol. 6, pp. 337–40; cited in Luvaas, *op. cit.*, pp. 160–166.
45. July 25th 1744—Luvaas, Ibid., p. 160.
46. Frederick, "Instruction für meine Artillerie, etc." (May 1782), *op. cit.*, cited in Luvaas, *op. cit.*, p. 160.
47. July 25th 1744—Luvaas, Ibid., p. 161.
48. Frederick, "Instruction für meine Artillerie, etc.: (May 1782), *Werke,* vol. 6, p. 337–40; cited in Luvaas, *op. cit.*, pp. 162.
49. Frederick, "Commandeur de batallion", pp. 58–59; cited in Luvaas, *op. cit.*, p. 148.
50. *Essays on the Art of War, op. cit.*, vol. 3, art 24, p. 377.
51. Frederick, "Disposition", (1745), *Oeuvres, op. cit.;* cited in Luvaas, *op. cit.*, p. 165.
52. Frederick, *Instruction militaire,* pp. 160–161; cited in Luvaas, *op. cit.*, p. 157.
53. Frederick, "Disposition für infanterie" pp. 76–77; cited in Luvaas, *op. cit.*, p. 146.
54. *Essays on the Art of War, op. cit.*, vol. 3, art 20, p. 377.
55. Frederick, "Disposition", (1745), *Oeuvres, op. cit.;* cited in Luvaas, *op. cit.*, p. 165.
56. Frederick, "Disposition für infanterie" pp. 76–77; cited in Luvaas, *op. cit.*, p. 147.
57. Frederick, "Disposition für die Sämmtlichen . . .", *Oeuvres,* vol. 30, pp. 74–77; cited in Luvaas, p. 146.
58. Frederick, "Commandeur de bataillon", pp. 58–59; cited in Luvaas, *op. cit.*, p. 148.
59. *Essays on the Art of War, op. cit.*, vol. 3, art. 28–31, p. 378.
60. Frederick, "Instruction für meine Artillerie, etc." (May 1782); cited in Luvaas, *op. cit.*, p. 161.
61. Frederick, *Instruction militaire, op. cit.;* cited in Luvaas, *op. cit.*, p. 145.
62. Frederick, *Instructions,* p. 85.
63. *Essays on the Art of War,* vol. 3, art. 17, p. 377.
64. Warnery, *op. cit.*, p. 74.
65. "Pensé es . . .", *Oeuvres.* vol. 28, pp. 110–11; cited in Luvaas, *op. cit.*, p. 183.
66. Frederick, "Pensées . . .", *Oeuvres; op. cit.*, vol. 28, p. 110–11; cited in Luvaas, Ibid., p. 171.
67. Warnery, *op. cit.*, pp. 75–78.
68. Frederick, "Testament von 1768", pp. 230–31; cited in Luvaas, *op. cit.*, pp. 158–159.
69. Warnery, *op. cit.*, p. 80.

70. Frederick, "Eléments de castramétrie . . ." *Oeuvres*. Vol. 29, pp. 42–43; cited in Luvaas, *op. cit.*, p. 159.

71. Essays on the Art of War, *op. cit.*, vol. 3, art. 27, p. 378.

72. Frederick, "Disposition für die Sämmtlichen . . .", *Oeuvres*, vol. 30, pp. 74–77; cited in Luvaas, *op. cit.*, p. 146.

73. Carlyle, *op. cit.*, vol. 3, p. 242.

74. *Essays on the Art of War*, vol. 3, art 13, p. 378.

75. Frederick, "Instruction pour les généraux-majors de cavalerie" *Oeuvres*, vol. 28, pp. 171–172; cited Luvaas, *op. cit.*, p. 150.

76. Frederick, *Instruction militaire*, pp. 32–39, 151–154.; cited in Luvaas, Ibid., p. 144.

77. Frederick, "Pensées . . .", *Oeuvres; op. cit.*, vol. 28, pp. 110–11; cited in Luvaas, Ibid., p. 172.

78. Frederick, "Pensées . . .", *Oeuvres;* vol. 28, pp. 110–11; cited in Luvaas, *op. cit.*, p. 172.

79. Frederick, *Instructions; op. cit.*, p. 78.

80. Frederick, "Testament von 1768", pp. 230–31; cited in Luvaas, *op. cit.*, p. 157.

81. Frederick, *Instructions, op. cit.*, pp. 78–80.

82. Frederick, "Commandeur de bataillon", pp. 58–59; cited in Luvaas, *op. cit.*, p. 148.

CHAPTER 17

French Doctrine and Practice During the Seven Years' War

THE EXPERIENCES DURING THE FIRST CAMPAIGNS OF THE SEVEN YEARS' War forced the French to modify a number of elements in their existing tactical and grand tactical doctrine. In 1760, Marshal de Broglie issued a set of instructions that changed not only the way a French army was to deploy into battle but the command structure as well.

By this time, the French military authorities had become painfully aware that their troops were unable to deploy into line with the same alacrity as the Prussians. The latter were able to deploy quickly from lengthy columns, which meant that their infantry was able to march onto the battlefield in only two columns: one containing the troops intended for the first line; the other, those for the second line.

Since Luxembourg's time, the French had also deployed from a small number of columns. However, given the French infantry's rudimentary skills in this area, their deployment was tremendously slow in relationship to the new standards set by the Prussians. In response to the Prussian developments, the French reduced the number of battalions per column by multiplying the columns used while deploying, reducing the time required by the column to form line.

Another unexpected benefit would have a lasting and profound effect on the organization of the French army. The use of a greater number of columns greatly increased the potential for confusion when it came time to form these columns. To minimize the possibility of a corps not knowing its proper position, it was imperative that a column always consist of the same corps. It became necessary to institutionalize a larger unit of organization, one that reflected the content of each column. The infantry was now divided into four equal divisions, the composition of which was to remain constant throughout the entire campaign. A division, led by a lieutenant general assisted by two *marèchaux de camp* and four brigadier generals, would have up to 16 battalions and eight cannons from the artillery park and was organized into four brigades. A *marèchal de camp* commanded two of these brigades plus half of the divisional artillery, i.e., four pieces. Each brigadier commanded his brigade, consisting of four regular battalions and a battalion of grenadiers or *chasseurs*, commanded by a lieutenant colonel or battalion commander assigned to this battalion for the entire campaign. The brigade was named after the senior regiment.[1]

This innovation, in addition to speeding up deployment, lessened the French army's dependence on deploying in strict accordance with each regiment's seniority. The French army had long been renowned for following this principle to the point of absurdity. Upon occasion, the French army had passed up momentary opportunities to attack a surprised or weakened enemy because the regiments who were supposed to deliver the attack by virtue of their designated place within the line were not present at that moment, and protocol called for the attack being delayed until their arrival. The other problem with always deploying in the same sequence was, of course, that it allowed the enemy to easily predict the army's deployment so that it could attack the least experienced regiments.[2] The adoption of the divisional systems lessened this proclivity to a degree; now, regiments only had to deployed within sequence within the division to which they had been assigned.

According to De Broglie's instructions, the army now was to normally march in six columns: the four infantry wings and the two cavalry wings, with the artillery marching with the infantry division to which it was assigned. When the army was forced to march in four columns, the first line of cavalry marched with the first division, etc. Each infantry column usually was headed by four grenadier or *chasseur* battalions. Prior to setting out on a march across the countryside, the infantry regiments were deployed into columns, each with a frontage of one platoon.[3]

An ordinance dated January 20th, 1757, had given a light 4-pounder to every infantry battalion, accompanied by two sergeants and 16 soldiers. These marched with their battalion. Being inspired by the light cannons first distributed among the Swedish infantry by Gustavus Adolphus, these were referred to as *canons à la suédoise*.

Relative to the Prussians, the French were not skilled in marching. When war broke out in 1756, the French were still familiarizing themselves with the cadenced march. Unlike the Prussians who were able to march and maneuver with the closed ranks, the French had to alternate between open and closed ranks depending upon the situation. If the direction had to be changed during a march, the officers had to immediately stop to close the ranks, followed by a quarter-wheel of the closed ranks, then reform a new set of open ranks. The quarter-wheels were always made on a fixed pivot and caused considerable lengthening in all columns.[4]

Learning from the lessons of the recent campaigns, De Broglie ordered that the battalions march closer together when in column. Now, each platoon was to be only three paces from the one in front, and only 12 paces separated each battalion. This reduced the length of a 16-battalion column to 1000 paces. Immediately prior to deploying, this column would be split in half, with the front half of each smaller column destined for the first line, the remainder for the second. This meant that the troops of each line in one of these small columns occupied a depth of 250 paces. This insured that battalions were able to deploy quickly with a minimum of delay.[5]

DEPLOYING

When the heads of all the columns had reached the battlefield, a cardboard bomb was to be exploded to warn the infantry that the deployment process was about to begin, and each battalion unfurled its colors. The cavalry waited until it heard a bugle call to start its movements. The officers would be judged by how quickly their division performed its movements and by the proper alignment of the troops once in line, as well as the precision of the intervals between the battalions.

The troops of the first and second lines, and the reserves, if any, were simultaneously to deploy into line. The second line was to deploy 300 paces behind the first. As each column deployed, it did so under the protection of the grenadier and *chasseur* battalions placed at the head of each column for this purpose (two battalions per smaller column). The first task of the general officers was to divide each column into two or more smaller columns. Whenever possible, half of the troops in each of these small columns were destined for the first line; the other half, for the second line.

The French continued to use a variant of the old processional systems of deployment. Now, however, instead of there being two columns marching the length of the battlefield from left to right (very occasionally from right to left), there were a minimum of eight columns that proceeded to the general area where each was to deploy. Up to this point, the troops continued to march toward the enemy. Upon reaching where they were to form line, each column turned and marched across to the position where it was to deploy; again, most often this was a left to right movement.

While the columns were in motion, it was extremely important that the general officers make certain that the columns under their command were separated by sufficient distance laterally at all times to allow the troops in these columns to deploy at a moment's notice. If the columns were too close together, not all the battalions in the columns would be able to deploy, without one of the column's first moving further away; a time-consuming, confusing and demoralizing process. To insure that the proper distance was maintained, a major officer "with some intelligence" rode between the two columns (presumably the two that previously made up a larger column) and issued a warning whenever the distance became too little or too great.

These procedures suggest an unconscious, but very different, set of assumptions about how the army was to act while forming line. Rather than operating a large single mass following the battalion in each of two columns, (even the method of deployment viewed by the Comte de Gisors utilized troops originally along a single axis), the army was now divided into 6 to 12 smaller units which marched separately to the general area where they were to be deployed. In this sense, the French inability to use the two-column system inadvertently promoted a grand tactical advance which was in later years to have the greatest significance. One of the results was that the "division," instead of being merely an organizational unit, started to take on a grand tactical significance; i.e., a division started to be a separate body of men that marched on its own *prior* to the start of the battle. The next step would be to see it as a separate body of men that acted on its own *during* the battle.

BATTLE ORDER

Despite the fact that prior to the war De Broglie had proclaimed himself to be an advocate of the *ordre profond,* the battle order he prescribed was based on the traditional model. The infantry continued to be in two lines in the center of the battlefield parallel to the enemy's position, flanked on either side by cavalry. Ideally, a reserve would consist of grenadiers, carabiniers, the gendarmerie from the Maison de Roi, as well as two brigades of infantry and two of cavalry. The reserve was to be 300 paces behind the second line.[6]

The infantry in each division was distributed along the first and second lines, so in a full-strength division there would be eight battalions along the first line and eight along the second. Each of these was referred to as a "section" and was commanded by a *marèchal de camp.*

Normally, when a regiment was made up of more than one battalion, these battalions were deployed along the line side by side without any sizeable gap between the battalions, though with the reintroduction of battalion guns in 1757, there had to be 10 to 15 paces between the battalions. The battalions within a regiment were positioned in a prearranged order. The colonel's battalion or that led by the most senior officer was on the right, that commanded by the next most senior officer on the left. A third battalion, if one was present, was placed in the center. When the regiment contained four battalions, they were deployed from right to left as follows: 1, 3, 2, 4 (1 being the most senior, 4 being the least senior).[7]

One important difference between De Broglie's battle order and that prescribed by tradition was that De Broglie appears to have been influenced by De Saxe's and Folard's ideas about light troops, and called for the 50-man picquets to be removed from each battalion and placed in groups along a third line. They were to position themselves behind any intervals that existed between battalions in the second line. They were to run up through these intervals and charge the enemy infantry should it be disordered, in order to prevent it from rallying. These picquets were to be "unladened," that is, all superfluous equipment was placed behind their position prior to the start of the battle, retaining only their coats, weapons and ammunition.

The battle order of French cavalry was very similar to that used by their Prussians counterparts, to which it probably owes its origin. French cavalry in the first line were to be placed *en muraille* (i.e., no spaces between squadrons), though sizeable intervals were tolerated in the second line. The dragoons and hussars were distributed equally on both wings; these were positioned in a third "line" and actually deployed in a column by squadrons. They were to attack the enemy's cavalry should the French cavalry successfully charge. If, on the other hand, the enemy's charge was successful it was quarter-wheeled into line on the flank of the retreating friendly cavalry and then charged the enemy in flank while the infantry brigade on that wing fired on the enemy cavalry at point-blank range.[8]

Each cavalry wing was to be accompanied by an infantry brigade which initially was maintained in column. This brigade was to form line (by the right or the left) and fire on the enemy cavalry only should the friendly cavalry break and then be pursued. Here is an example of the French using infantry columns as "waiting formations" which would move forward or deploy, as the situation warranted. This conception would be even more frequently employed during the Napoleonic era, especially in the form of "mixted order."

GRAND TACTICS

The various official documents are thin on "grand tactical" advice. It was assumed the battle would be fought using the same linear precepts which had governed the battlefield for the previous 60 years. Unless there were special considerations arising from the terrain or fortified positions of the enemy, the French army was to deploy parallel to the enemy then attack straight on.

The only grand tactical finesse mentioned in De Broglie's instructions, for example, is that the general officers are enjoined whenever possible to use the terrain such as wheat fields, hedges, small woods, etc., to conceal their march on the enemy's flank. This was to surprise the enemy and force an unexpected change of position thus adversely affecting the opposing troops' morale. The main body of friendly troops, in this type of situation, were not to be preceded by any advance guard, which would have necessarily warned the enemy. During the approach, the attacking force was to march shoulder to shoulder without any gaps between the units along the front. The grenadiers were to be at the front of the column and were to withhold their fire until the last possible moment when they were to devastate the enemy either with the force of their fire or with their bayonets.[9]

Once the army was deployed in line and the commander-in-chief deemed it appropriate, he would have the trumpets sound the charge. The infantry was to advance at the double, withholding its fire as long as possible; while the cavalry advanced at the "grand" trot. This represented a theoretical improvement for the French cavalry, which as late as the War of the Austrian Succession had advanced at a medium or even slow trot.[10] However, this attack at speed nowhere could be compared to that delivered by post-1744 Prussian cavalry. When French cavalry did succeed in delivering a charge at speed, it invariably was not in close formation, but loose and even scattered. Such a charge was referred to as a charge *en forageurs.*[11] The French, like the Austrians of this period, could only deliver ordered charges at a trot.

Another advance was that De Broglie now advised the infantry to shake the enemy infantry by first delivering fire before charging the enemy's first line at the double with lowered bayonets.[12] If they were successful, there were two courses of action, depending upon the scope of the success. If it was general, in other words they had succeeded in pushing back all of the enemy's first line, they would continue to pressure the retreating enemy. The victorious infantry, however, before attacking the enemy's second line at the double was to regroup first. This second line would be easier to defeat as a result of the disorder caused by the retreat of the enemy first line.

If the attack on the enemy's first line was only partially successful, the infantry that did overthrow the enemy was not to pursue the retreating enemy in front of them, but were to maintain their order or rest for a few moments as they were reordered, and then quarter-wheel and roll up the flank of the remainder of the enemy's first line.

If after several attacks the enemy still remained ordered, the commander was to order a retreat. To signal this, 20 cardboard bombs were to be set off. Each division of infantry was to form a separate column with a battalion-sized frontage. The *chasseurs* and grenadiers, however, were not to march in the main body of a column but were to be placed in the intervals between the columns, instead.

De Broglie's instructions also specified how to attack strong positions such as villages or entrenchments. The attacking force was to advance on the objective by column of battalions (one battalion behind the other, all in line) or column by half-battalions (a column with a half-battalion frontage). This force was to take as much cover as was offered by the surrounding terrain as it advanced. Any friendly cavalry in the area was to be positioned behind the attacking force. Its purpose was to attack the enemy should they be forced out of the village, etc.

EXPERIENCES DURING THE SEVEN YEARS' WAR

Jean Colin, author of the *L'infanterie au XVIIIe Siècle: la Tactique,* an extensive study of pre-Napoleonic French infantry tactics, believed that the miserable performance of the French army during the Seven Years' War, was ascribable almost completely to poor high-level leadership and the abysmal level to which the officer class, in general, had sunk. Colin went on to argue that the actual tactics used by the French not only were mediocre, but also presaged most of the more important elements associated with "Napoleonic" warfare: the use of skirmishers, mixed order, battalion guns, divisional level organization, columns of attack and columns of waiting.

Since this important work is no longer readily available to most of those interested in eighteenth-century warfare, it is probably not out of place to recap the major points in his analysis. Colin pointed out that despite the passion with which Folard's disciples advocated the use of the *ordre profond* prior to the Seven Years' War, almost every time the French fought on clear terrain, the traditional disposition of troops (the use of lengthy lines, battalions deployed in three ranks, etc.) continued to be employed, such as was the case at Crefeld. However, when the French were forced to fight on broken or mixed terrain they started to utilize a number of new methods and formations.

Rossbach, for example, provides an example of some French regiments attempting to use the *ordre profond.* The French and Imperial troops, marching in three tightly packed columns were surprised and did not have time to deploy into line. Several regiments at the head of the columns, such as Piémont, Saint Chamant, realizing the impossibility of forming line and the necessity of forming self-contained formations deployed into column of attack instead. The efficacy of Prussian infantry fire, as well as Seydlitz's well-timed cavalry charge made these efforts useless and the entire French army was shattered in about twenty minutes.

The much-vaunted column of attack was rarely used on the battlefield. However, French battalions during this war used columns of maneuver repeatedly. The first use of these columns was simply to move to another position, or to avoid an obstacle. A skirmish near Meer (August 5th, 1758) where Chevert was surprised by enemy forces furnishes a detailed example of how a regiment using the new maneuvers would deploy into line, return back into column and then redeploy latter on, when required by circumstances. The Colonel of the Perigord provides details of this combat:

> "Our infantry after having debouched into battle, according to the terrain [types of terrain it encountered], broke [into column] by quarters of rank and platoon, occupied different orchards and enclosures, where they remained for the battle. Some troops on our left retired precipitously. As soon as I perceived this, I had the entire Périgord regiment enter the field of the battle in the front most [occupied] hedge [in line], which won hedge by hedge crying "Vive le roi!" The Royal-Lorraine regiment followed before the Périgord regiment, marching with the same frontage, also occupying the most advanced hedges. The two regiments were then fired upon by the enemy at point blank range. They stood firm, bayonets on their muskets, without firing a shot, or being shaken or broken by heavy casualties. I then retreated the Périgord regiment by platoons after having kept the position for awhile. Finding the left flank free of troops, but being outflanked by several enemy formations, the regiment retreated, and was broken three times by enemy fire. Rallied each time to face the enemy we fired by both platoons and at will, and succeeded in making good our retreat."[13]

The French quickly started to appreciate the use of a new type of formation, the *ordre mixte* (mixed order). Typically, mixed order consisted of one or two battalions in line with several other battalions in columns in the rear. This is a formation that would become very popular in the French army in Napoleonic times.

At Minden (August 1st, 1759), the very self-conscious use of mixed order is evident. In his instructions issued prior to the battle, Marshal Contades, commander of the French army, ordered that the first battalion (the one on the right) remain deployed in column, while the others deploy into line. If the brigade had to advance or attack any considerable distance, all battalions were to form into column again. However, regardless of whether the brigade had to move or fight, the first battalion had to remain in column. The Duc d'Avre, responsible for holding the heights, was to use light troops grouped in outposts to fend off whatever skirmishers the enemy should throw against them.

The variety of formations was even greater in those battles fought in Hesse and Westphalia. At Hastenbeck, Chevert's division which engaged on wooded heights, advanced with its grenadiers in front, and a small number of pickets and volunteers in front of each of its four brigades. The battle reports unfortunately provide few details, however, it appears that the division, given the broken terrain, had to fight mostly in skirmish order, except, possibly, for grenadiers held in reserve.

The Picardie, Marine, and Eu brigades facing these woods were deployed each in a "column of battalions," that is, each battalion in a brigade was deployed in line, but one behind the other. When they were ordered into this thick wood they had to "break" into several columns, each with narrower platoon frontages. After defeating the enemy and advancing into the open terrain on the other side of the woods, it proved to be impossible to keep these troops in such dense formations. The three brigades retreated to the edge of the woods, the Eu brigade in a column of platoons with the other brigades in the division positioned five or six paces from one another. It must be added that these columns were ordinary columns of maneuver, and not the columns of attack described in the regulations.

Further examples of the use of ordinary columns during a battle are found at Kloster-Kamp (October 16th, 1760). Here, the Auvergne brigade attacked while still in column of maneuver. Interestingly enough, the column was in reverse order with the left battalions in front and those of the right behind. In contrast the Alsace brigade was deployed in line to attack the outskirts of Kamp, while the Tour-du-Pin brigade advanced in column but deployed its first and second battalions in line just prior to the start of the attack; the remainder waited until they closed to the last hedge in front of the village while the four battalion guns played against the enemy in front of them. The Normandie brigade, six battalions strong, positioned between those of Auvergne and Alsace, waited in column until the enemy started to beat Auvergne whereupon it deployed its first battalion into line and attacked the enemy.

The use of mixed order implied another conceptual development: the benefits of using a column of maneuver as a "column of waiting." Prior to this the column had traditionally been used as a maneuver and march formation. Folard and his disciples also advocated its use as a formation of attack. But now this fourth usage was added. The column of waiting was simply a column that waited in position until the necessity of maneuvering or deploying into line presented itself. This allowed large battalions which occupied a lot of space when deployed to be positioned in a much smaller area in column. This made it possible for battalions to be positioned in rougher terrain or more closely together than had been possible previously. These practices clearly presaged practices popular during the Napoleonic period. In this single battle we see the three uses of the column so strongly associated with the Napoleonic period: the use of the column to attack, to maneuver, and as a waiting formation which could be transformed at a moment's notice.

A second major tactical development was the frequent use of skirmishers, especially by a number of men detached in front of regular line battalions. Sundershausen (July 23rd, 1758) provides a clear example of the effective use of skirmishing. Most of the twelve French battalions were deployed into line. Two hundred meters in front of the line, seven grenadier companies were dispersed as skirmishers. Three other grenadier companies did the same in a small woods anchoring the French right flank, while a volunteer corps covered another small woods on the opposite flank. These volunteers succeeded in outflanking the enemy line during the attack and pushed back much of the enemy's forces. Roughly while this was occurring, the Rohan and Royal-Bavière regiments succeeded in changing their front, a difficult maneuver under fire, to meet a flanking move on their left.

A number of other examples of skirmishers being used are provided in the 1758–59 period. At the combat of Lutternberg (October 10th, 1758), the bulk of the French infantry was formed into line preceded by skirmishers prior to the start of combat. Both volley and voluntary fire were found on the battlefield. The French right formed into three small columns to traverse a woods. These columns were covered by skirmishers, most provided by independent light corps, to their front and their right flank.

At Lippstadt (July 2nd, 1759), Melford ordered the dragoons to dismount in order to drive off Hanoverian jaegers. Then, in order to cover his right flank, he placed an infantry "picket" behind a hedge. When his main column finally arrived to support this advance guard, each infantry battalion deployed skirmishers to its front. The skirmisher line was approximately 500 meters long and was closely supported by the regular infantry behind them.

At the Battle of Bergen (April 13th, 1759), for the first time we find general reserves in a massive formation. Instead of a second line, as usually employed, behind the village of Bergen (occupied by eight battalions), the Duc de Broglie stationed in column the five Piémont battalions and Royal-Roussillon and two Alsace battalions to support the front line. Behind these were the Castellas and the Diesbach regiments in columns as well as the Rohan and Beauvoisis regiments ready to march to the village if need be.

> "To the left were placed the Saxon corps, and behind them in reserve the Dauphin, Enghien, Royal-Bavière, Nassau, Bentheim, Berg, and Saint-Germain regiments forming three brigades . . . . This disposition was accomplished by 8 o'clock, at this time a few enemy troops appeared who attacked our volunteers in the woods, in front on the left at the beginning of the hedges of the village on the right."[14]

This battle of skirmishers in the woods lasted all day without any decisive victory on either side. Around Bergen the regular troops fought in line or as skirmishers, then in column (depending upon circumstances), and then back again.

> "The enemy appeared around 9:30 after having erected a screen to cover their movements, and attacked the village of Bergen in three columns. The attack occurred with great vivaciousness around 10 o'clock. The Duc de Broglie seeing that the enemy was attacking with large forces ordered Monsieur le Chevalier Pelletier to bring at the head of the village the majority of the park artillery where the enemy was arriving, and ordered the Piémont, Royal-Roussillon regiments, as well as the two Alsace battalions and the Castellas and the Diesbach regiments were ordered to the right flank. This stopped the enemy advance who, however, came back with reinforcements and forced us to retreat a few steps. The Duc de Broglie led the Rohan regiment along the hedges and ordered the Beauvoisis regiment to enter the village by the main street, and ordered the Dauphin and Enghien regiments to support it."[15]

In addition to these examples, we know that Marshal de Broglie, stating in 1758, started to regularly train the "piquet" of each battalion to function as *chasseur* companies, i.e., to skirmish. Colin concluded that these examples definitively demonstrated that despite peace-time enthusiasm for the *ordre profond,* the traditional line continued to be the mainstay on the battlefield, even when fighting in hedges, orchards, and gardens. However, a number of new practices were called upon to supplement the traditional methods. Columns were used when fighting small detachments or when surprise was an important element.

A new formation, mixed order, starts to be used, and with it the concept of the "column of waiting." Here a force remained in a column of maneuver so as to be able to deploy into line when the occasion demanded it. This allowed a force to be positioned in a smaller area than would have been possible if it had remained in line. Skirmishers started to be used much more frequently than during the War of the Austrian Succession. Independent light corps were deployed in forests where they would sometimes fight *à la debandade* (the entire corps fighting as skirmishers). On the other hand, the piquet started to serve as a *chasseur* company, skirmishing in front of the remainder of the battalion deployed into line.[16]

To Colin's analysis we must add one other observation. These examples of regiments changing back and forth between formations as well as the practice of supporting traditional line formations with either columns or skirmishers shows that these tactics demanded and promoted greater officer initiative than the traditional systems. To see this more clearly we just have to compare these systems with those by the Prussian army of the same period, where the lengthy tactical formations and tactics like marching by lines were used precisely to avoid relying upon officer initiative.

Notes

1. Colin, *op. cit.,* pp. 80–81.
2. Tilke, J. G., "An Account of Some of the Most Remarkable Transactions of the War Between the Prussians, Austrians and Russians." 2 vols. London 1787, vol. 2, p. 46.
3. Colin, *op. cit.,* p. 81.
4. Belhomme, *op. cit.,* vol. 3, p. 197.
5. Colin, *op. cit.,* p. 81.
6. Ibid., p. 84.
7. de Briquet, *op. cit.,* p. 384.
8. Colin, *op.cit.,* p. 84.
9. Ibid., p. 86.
10. Mollo, *op. cit.,* p. 37.
11. Denison, *op. cit.,* p. 316.
12. Colin, *op. cit.,* p. 85.
13. Ibid., p. 75.
14. Ibid., p. 77.
15. Ibid., p. 78.
16. Ibid., pp. 74–79.

CHAPTER 18

Conclusion

Tactics during the seventeenth century had revolved around the capabilities of the matchlock musket and the dependence of the musketeers on the body of pikemen in each battalion. However, the last ten years of the century saw the large-scale introduction of the flintlock musket and the bayonet. The advent of these new weapons did not instantly effect an overall transformation in methods of combat: the general repertoire of tactics and grand tactics remained similar to those used at the close of the seventeenth century. In the French, Swedish and Bavarian armies, for example, the advance with shouldered muskets to attempt to grapple with the enemy with cold steel remained in fashion. In fact, in Sweden under Charles XII the infantry charge with sword and bayonet was conducted with even greater zeal.

Several changes did manifest themselves. The effectiveness of the bayonet's defensive capabilities made the pike superfluous, and it quickly disappeared from the battlefield. Another change, not related to the new weaponry, was that larger armies started to be fielded, and battalions were usually placed closer together than thirty years previously. In addition to the larger size of the armies, the experiences of the Turkish wars and the development of new tactics to take advantage of exposed flanks all contributed to this tendency. Marlborough occasionally took advantage of the large number of battalions to place a number of short lines one after the other where he wanted the critical assault to be delivered.

The introduction of the flintlock musket and bayonet did have another important effect. Sometime in the last decades of the 1600's, the Dutch developed the platoon firing system which was adopted by the British around 1700. This resulted not only in a new, more efficient method of loading and delivering organized volleys, but under Marlborough resulted in the use of a new set of offensive tactics. British infantry, for example, were instructed to deliver a portion of their fire at medium range and then close in to resume firing at a slightly closer range. This process was to continue until the enemy lost its resolution to hold its ground.

This tactic of relying upon firepower to weaken the enemy's resolve was markedly different from the conventional tactic of having the infantry assault the enemy infantry with shouldered musket. The British did employ the advance-without-firing tactics, but only when attacking entrenchments, villages, and so on, where the defenders would have to be physically ejected from their position, and couldn't be driven out by firepower.

The flintlock musket with its slightly higher rate of fire made the straightforward attack much more difficult. It is difficult to determine exact rates of fire for either matchlocks or the early flintlocks, but it appears that the maximum rate of fire went from one round per minute to about two. This meant that the attacking infantry was subject to about twice as much fire, and was more inclined to stop and fire back. The French were impressed enough with the British/Dutch system of platoon firing that in 1707 they started to use a similar method of delivering fire. However, this was intended only for use when on the defensive, and there is little evidence it was extensively applied even in these situations.

In terms of cavalry tactics, the French temporarily took a few steps backward between 1693 and around 1704 when they copied the German fashion of firing their carbines before closing with the enemy. This trend appears to reverse itself once again after the gendarmerie's fiasco at Blenheim. The British cavalry, under Marlborough, and the Swedish cavalry under Charles XII assumed the ascendancy, renouncing the use of firearms and advancing more quickly at the charge than had been the practice previously. The British cavalry, concerned with the need to retain closed order, still advanced at the trot, while the Swedes began to charge at a full gallop.

With the return of the state of relative peace in Europe by the 1720's, most of those in the military expected any new hostilities to be conducted in the same fashion as in the last round of wars (i.e., the War of the Spanish Succession and the Great Northern War). In most armies, the infantry were deployed in four ranks. When the troops marched, they did so without the use of cadence. There were few maneuvers other than the traditional "processional" methods of forming line, and it continued to be necessary to keep wide distances between the ranks as they marched across the countryside and onto the battlefield.

There were two centers of change, where new tactics were being experimented with, that would have a great impact on how warfare would be conducted in the future. The first of these was in France, where military theoreticians such as the Chevalier de Folard began to abandon linear grand tactics, at least in its purest form. In addition to recommending the use of deep columns of attack, Folard wanted a sizeable portion of the infantry to be reequipped with the pike. The heavy columns thus formed were to be relatively independent and would minimize the reliance on lengthy, thin lines that had by now become universal.

Cavalry, instead of being allocated solely to the wings, would be placed intermittently behind the first line to provide local support. De Saxe, who later become famous during the 1740's and rose to become a Marshal of France, advocated similar grand tactics, except that he rejected the use of Folard's extremely ponderous columns, and emphasized the importance of light troops fighting in conjunction with each battalion and the effectiveness of aimed, as opposed to volley, fire.

The other source of change and reform originated in Prussia under the auspices of Frederick William and Prince Leopold of Anhalt-Dessau. Probably the most fundamental aspect of this reform was simply the importance attached to continual training, not just for the common foot soldiers, but for all levels of the officer class as well. This was to provide the basis for all the later innovations devised by Frederick and his generals, which would prove so effective.

The first fruit of this high level of training was the adoption and mastery of both cadenced marching and a cadenced manual of arms. These accomplishments proved to be of the greatest importance, and by 1740 allowed the Prussian infantry to maintain itself always in closed ranks, rather than marching in open ranks and having to change into closed ranks every time the column was to turn or maneuver into line. The introduction of cadence and with it the exclusive use of closed ranks allowed the Prussians to experiment with entirely new methods of going from column to line and vice versa. Prior to this, the only methods that were known were the processional methods, where all of the battalions in a line marched across the battlefieldprior to or while they deployed.

Now, Frederick and his generals started to devise new, faster ways of deploying both individual battalions and lengthy columns when approaching the battlefield, without ever having to march along the intended line. This not only reduced the amount of time needed to form line, but also meant these battalions no longer had to offer their flanks to the enemy as they deployed. The original methods of going from column to line or line back to column were known as "evolutions," since the formation being formed was seen as evolving out of the original formation. The newer methods of changing formations, whose use at first was usually limited to avoiding terrain obstacles, now started to be viewed as "maneuvering" from one position or formation to another, and soon became known as "maneuvers."

However, practically speaking, these new methods of forming line were rarely, if ever, used on the battlefield to deploy large numbers of battalions. The older processional methods, in the case of many battalions deploying together, were conceptually simpler and only required that the highest level of officers understand the overall situation and know where the line was to form. The rear battalions took their direction and their place from those in the front of the column. The newer methods would have meant that battalion and regimental officers would have had to have the same type of information and participate in the decision-making process. This was something Frederick was totally unwilling to tolerate.

Another reason why these new maneuvers were never used to deploy entire lines prior to the start of a conflict was that they ran counter to the entire linear system, which demanded that large groups of formations act together in unison as lengthy linear bodies. An infantry wing would not only deploy as a whole, but in action would advance together as the same grand tactical unit. As the French started to demonstrate here and there during the Seven Years' War, these new maneuvers worked best when used to deploy a small number of battalions, which were acting together as their own separate unit.

For the first half of his reign, Frederick adhered to the common wisdom as applied to offensive tactics: he extolled his infantry to advance to the enemy with shouldered muskets, withholding their fire until at very close range, ideally ten to twenty paces. This tactic, which had its share of successes in the earlier years, ceased to be feasible by the outbreak of the Seven Years' War. Part of the reason lay with the contribution to the art of war made by the Prussians infantry themselves. Their fire effectiveness had become legendary, and by this point the infantry in other armies had followed the Prussians lead and introduced the iron ramrod. Some believed this increased the average rate of fire by roughly an additional 150 per cent (up to a maximum of five shots per minute during the first few minutes).

In the late seventeenth century, it had often been possible to advance to within close range before the enemy was able to get off more than several volleys. Now, realistically the advancing infantry might have to endure five to ten volleys. It was no longer possible to advance close to an enemy delivering that volume of fire, without first firing at the enemy to undermine their will to hold their ground.

Frederick's cavalry, so deficient at the start of his reign, by the outbreak of the Seven Years' War was the standard by which all other cavalry forces were measured. Between 1741 and 1744 the Prussians cavalry introduced a series of reforms that had the effect of creating an entirely new method of attack. By this later date, the Prussians cavalry was able by the final stages of the charge to advance at the gallop, maintaining the strictest order within the formation. This proved extremely more effective than the older methods of either charging quickly with little cohesion or with order but only at the trot. This type of charge was quickly established as the model for cavalry of all other nations, and remained as such past Napoleonic times, well into the nineteenth century. The Austrian and Hanoverian cavalry by the Seven Years' War were found delivering a charge at a faster pace then they had previously, and by 1760 the British cavalry also was charging at the gallop during the last stage of the advance. However, none of these imitators ever managed to achieve the same standards of training as the Prussians cavalry, and thus were never able to deliver the charge at speed with exactly the same effect.

At the battle of Hohenfriedeberg, the Bayreuth dragoons still deployed in column, succeeded in overturning a large number of Austrian infantry. Impressed by this accomplishment, Frederick started to think of how to allow his cavalry to systematically duplicate this feat upon demand. By the start of the Seven Years' War, he advocated the sparing use of cavalry columns of attack to be delivered against already weakened enemy infantry at the critical moments of the battle.

Frederick's contribution to the art of war was not limited to tactics, and he and his generals managed to effect some changes in grand tactical thinking as well. Frederick rejected the attack along the entire front that had been accepted as axiomatic by many previous commanders-in-chief. Part of the Prussian army was to be held back, that is "refused," with the main assault being delivered elsewhere.

A related grand tactical ploy was Frederick's use of the "oblique attack" which was made up of two techniques: "march by lines" and "attack in echelons." In the march by lines, the Prussians, already deployed in battle order, would form column quickly by having each squadron or division of a battalion quarter-wheel. Minutes later, the entire army would be ready to march around the enemy's flank, where it would perform a second series of quarter-wheels to redeploy back into line. Although this tactic had been thought of by many earlier military theoreticians, the lack of cadenced marching and the ability to maneuver with closed ranks, had made it impossible to perform march lines quickly enough to surprise the enemy.

The attack in echelons consisted of the infantry battalions being deployed in a staggered formation, with those on one side further advanced than those on the other. The advantage of this tactic was twofold. First, it made the advancing Prussian line appear very ragged, and made it extremely difficult for the enemy to judge the numbers of men advancing or their final destination. It also had the advantage of making a change of face (the direction in which a line was facing) much easier to perform. At Leuthen, Frederick used both techniques one after the other to successfully outflank the Austrian left, and this remains the most classic instance of the successful use of the "oblique attack."

Though, by 1757, the Prussians had developed the most efficient fighting machine, man for man superior to anything that could be thrown against it, this very accomplishment placed them in an evolutionary dead-end street. The reason for this had nothing to do with the Prussian tactics; these remained dominant until the demise of smoothbore weapons, but were caused by strict adherence to linear grand tactics demanded by Frederick and the Prussian social system. This explains the relative wartime neglect of many of the manuevers and tactics developed by the Prussians between 1748 and 1756. During this time, the Prussians experimented with a large number of different methods of forming line, all of which were quicker and more efficient than the traditional processional methods. During the next round of hostilities, these enjoyed limited usage on the battlefield, being generally limited to allowing individual battalions to form column and then redeploy back into line in order to bypass embarrassing terrain. The real reason for the reluctance in using these new techniques is that they didn't easily mesh with the requirements of traditional grand tactics, where the movements and activities of each battalion had to conform to that of the larger formation of which it was a part.

THE ORIGIN OF NAPOLEONIC (IMPULSE) GRAND TACTICS

The common view is that the French army was completely inferior in all respects to its Prussian counterpart during the Seven Years' War, the phenomenal successes of the later French army during the Revolutionary and Napoleonic Wars being attributable to events and developments that occurred after 1762. Though this view does not lack numerous obvious arguments, and there were many aspects of the Prussian army that were substantially superior to the French, it glosses over some very positive developments within French military thought and, in fact, makes impossible any real understanding of how the "Napoleonic" system actually developed.

The traditional view tends to paint the French army of the period as being led by at best mediocre officers, commanding ill-trained men hampered by chimerical tactics, developed and sponsored by a lunatic group of reactionaries who wished to rearm the foot soldier with the pike. If we judge simply by how the French army performed in a majority of instances during the war, this view is not that unreasonable.

Up until 1748, the French, with the exception of the gradual development of light tactics, continued to practice essentially the same fighting methods as those that had been in use near the end of the War of the Spanish Succession. This quickly changed during the several years following the Treaty of Aix-la-Chapelle (1748). The new Prussian methods were examined, and a number of them introduced into the French army. The cadenced manual of arms was adopted, as was cadenced marching. A number of steps were also taken to raise the standard of French training. Despite the advent of cadenced marching, the French infantry clung to a number of obsolete practices: the infantry continued to march and maneuver with open ranks, only to close ranks when changing direction while in column or when starting to deploy into line.

By 1753, many of Folard's ideas gained official recognition. The regulations of 1753, 1754, and 1755 all prescribed the use of a column of attack, in one form or another, though all of these were much lighter than the cumbersome columns originally advocated by Folard. Also, the French authorities, obviously impressed with the efficacy of British and Prussian firepower during the last round of wars, finally suppressed fire by ranks and introduced a number of new fire systems, including platoon fire.

ELEMENTS IN THE IMPULSE SYSTEM

Although overall, the French infantry performed dismally during the Seven Years' War, here and there it is possible to notice the beginnings of an entirely new method of fighting on the battlefield. Despite the peacetime advocacy of the *ordre profond* by many ranking officers, the French army, when fighting on clear terrain, continued to use linear-style tactics. However, there was a growing willingness to exploit broken terrain, and use light infantry tactics. The various light infantry corps raised after 1744, when need be, fought completely in skirmish order, when fighting in woods and villages. As of 1759, most battalions started to train the piquet to serve as a company of *chasseurs*. Often, these would precede the battalion which was in line, and harass the enemy with fire while in skirmish order.

A second development grew out of a need to allow the French infantry to deploy more quickly than had previously been possible. The infantry was divided into a number of permanent "divisions." In this sense, the term no longer referred to a fraction of a battalion, but instead to a number of infantry battalions "permanently" grouped together for the duration of a campaign.

The third development was the use of columns in a number of new applications. Though the column of attack was used (unsuccessfully) in a few rare situations during the Seven Years' War, two other usages proved dramatically more successful: specifically, columns of maneuver and columns of waiting. Coupled with this was the use of mixed order allowing several battalions, deployed in line while the remainder were retained in column, to be deployed at a later time when circumstances permitted.

Although these developments are noticeable only in isolated incidents, and the majority of the actions were resolved in the traditional linear fashion, the beginnings of a new type of warfare, so closely associated with the Napoleonic era had its crudest beginnings.

This newer collection of diverse tactical elements is often referred to as "Napoleonic" tactics and grand tactics. However, this term is very misleading, since it implies the system so named was developed and in use only during the period for which it was named. Another term that has been occasionally used, and one that is both less misleading and more descriptive is the term "impulse" grand tactics. The term originates from one of the most distinguishing features of the new system of warfare: the abandonment of the extended front acting in concert, with the division of the fighting into a number of "impulses," varying in their strength, purpose, and timing.

In this newer system, the offense was broken up into a series of attacks, rather than a single broad-front effort, all happening together and acting along the same axis. These individual attacks represented a concentration of force that selectively attacked portions of the enemy's position. Rather than a single commander attempting to control the movement and actions of an entire army, local control was handed over to subcommanders who controlled divisions and corps.

This use of a concentration of force to break a critical portion of the enemy's position was in itself not new. Marlborough used a similar device repeatedly during the major battles in the Flanders theater in the first decade of the eighteenth century. However, to achieve the needed concentration of force, he stacked one line behind the other.

Nearly a hundred years later, during Napoleonic times, a concentration of force was achieved in an entirely different manner, through the use of mixed order and columns of maneuver and waiting. Rather than deploying short lines one after the other, most of the troops were retained in columns of waiting that were to be deployed into line as needed. This allowed a numerically large force to selectively assault a portion of the enemy's line, and feed in additional units as needed until the enemy line gave way. The attacking force, still mostly in column, was in a position to exploit the local success, either advancing to seize important posts or attacking any nearby enemy forces, whichever was required by circumstances.

Cavalry doctrine underwent a similar transition. Though in the Seven Years' War Prussians cavalry continued to provide the model for tactics, there were very profound changes on a grand tactical level. Folard's and De Saxe's ideas about cavalry support for infantry at interior points along the battlefield would be successfully employed, and cavalry no longer would be limited to action on the flanks on either side of the battlefield.

Although in broad concepts the "impulse" system was based upon grand tactical conceptions first formulated by the French during the Seven Years' War, for successful execution it was entirely dependent upon the employment of the experimental Prussian infantry tactics, that were largely neglected during the same war. In this sense, Napoleonic warfare on the battlefield was the amalgamation of the French grand tactical aspirations as displayed during the Seven Years' War with the Prussian tactical systems that had evolved between 1748 and 1756.

Bibliography

Austria, Armee, *Reglement Fur Die Kaisserlidh-Konigliche Cavellerie*. Vienna, 1806.

Austria, Armee, *Reglement Fur Die Kaisserlidh-Konigliche Infanterie*. Vienna, 1807.

Bacquet, Capt., *L'Infanterie Au XVIIIe Siecle: Organization*. Paris, 1907.

Bardin, E. T., *Dictionnaire De L'Armee De Terre*. 4 vols. Paris, 1851.

Bavaria, Kriegministerium, *Geschichte Des Bayerischen Heeres*. 11 vols. Munich, 1908–1931.

Beca, Colonel, *A Study in the Development of Infantry Tactics*. Translated by Capt. A. Custance. London, 1911.

Belhomme, Victor L., *Histoire De L'Infanterie En France*. 5 vols. Paris, 1893–1902.

Bère, Frédèric, *L'Armee Francaise*. Paris, n.d.

Bismarck, F. W., *Lectures on the Tactics of Cavalry*. London, 1827.

Bismarck, F.W., *On the Uses and Application of Cavalry in War*, (annotated by North Ludlow Beamish). London, 1855.

Botte, Captain, *Militaires Contenant L'Exercice De L'Infanterie*. Paris, 1750.

de Briquet, Pierre, *Code Militaire Au Compilation Des Ordonnances Des Rois De France Concernant Les Gens De Guerre*. 8 vols. Paris, 1767.

———. *The British Military Library*. 2 vols. London, 1801–1804.

Carlyle, Thomas, *History of Frederick the Great*. 6 vols. New York, 1872.

Chandler, David, *The Campaigns of Napoleon*. New York, 1966.

Chandler, David, *The Art of Warfare in the Age of Marlborough*. Guildford, Surrey, 1976.

Chandler, David, *Marlborough as Military Commander.* London 1973.

Chandler, David, ed., *Robert Parker and the Comte De Merode-Westerloo: The Marlborough Wars.* London, 1968.

Colin, Jean Lambert Alphonse, ed., Schauenbourg, Balthazzar, *La Tactique Et La Discipline Dans Les Armees De La Revolution.* Paris 1902.

Colin, Jean Lambert Alphonse, *L'Infanterie Au XVIIIe Siecle: La Tactique.* Paris, 1907.

Cononge, General Joseph Frederick, *Histoire Et Art Militaire.* 4 vols. Paris, 1900–1908.

Daniel (Père), *Histoire De La Malice Francoise.* 2 vols. Paris, 1724.

Decker, C. D., *Batailles Et Principaux Combats De La Guerre De Sept Ans Considerес Principalement Sous Le Rapport De L'Emploi De L'Artilleries.* Translated from German by Capt. Simonin. Paris, 1840.

De Jomini, Henri, *Histoire Critique Et Militaires De Guerres De Frederic II.* Brussels, 1842.

De la Colonie, Jean-Martin, *The Chronicles of an Old Campaigner: 1692–1717.* Translated from French by Lt. Col. Walter C. Horley. London, 1904.

Denison, George T., (Lt. Col.), *A History of Cavalry from the Earliest Times.* London, 1873.

Duane, William, *The American Military Library or Compendium of the Modern Tactics Embracing the Discipline, Manoeuvres, & Duties of Every Species of Troops.* Philadelphia, 1809. Contains translation of the *The System of Discipline and Manoeuvres of Infantry Forming the Bases of Modern Tactics* (For use by the National Guard and French Armies, 1805).

Duane, William, *The Modern Military Reader.*

Duffy, Christopher, *The Army of Frederick the Great.* New York, 1974.

Duffy, Christopher, *The Army of Maria Theresa.* New York, 1977.

Duffy, Christopher, *Austerlitz: 1805.* London, 1977.

Duffy, Christopher, *The Military Life of Frederick the Great.* New York, 1986.

Dundas, David (Colonel): *Principals of Military Movements Chiefly Applied to Infantry.* London, 1788.

———: *An Epitome of the Whole Art of War, Etc.* London, n.d. (circa 1690).

———. *Essay on the Art of War.* London, 1761.

———. *Essays on the Art of War.* 3 vols. London, 1809

———: *The Field of Mars: Being an Alphabetical Digestion of the Principal Naval and Military Engagements.* 2 vols. London, 1781.

Fortesque, Sir J. W., *A History of the British Army.* vol. 1. London, 1899.

France—Ministère De La Guerre, *Ordonnance Du Roi Sur L'Exercice De L'Infanterie,* (May 6th, 1755). Paris, 1755.

France—Ministère De La Guerre, *Ordonnance Du Roi Sur L'Exercice De La Cavalerie,* (June 22nd, 1755). Paris, 1755.

France—Ministère De La Guerre, *Reglement Concernant L'Exercice Et Les Maneouvres De L'Infanterie* (August 1st, 1791). Paris, 1821.

France—Ministère De La Guerre, *The System of Discipline and Manoeuvres of Infantry Forming the Bases of Modern Tactics* (For use by the National Guard and French Armies, 1805). See William Duane, *The Modern Military Reader.*

France—Ministère De La Guerre, *Instruction Concernant Les Maneouvres De La Cavalerie Legere*. Paris, Year VII.

France—Ministère De La Guerre, *Manual Des Sous-Officiers De Cavalerie*. Hamburg, 1812.

France—Ministère De La Guerre, *Ordonnance Provisoire Sur L'Exercice Et Les Manoeuvres De La Cavalerie,* (1st vendemaire Year XIII). Paris, 1813 (includes *Sur L'Exercice Et Les Maneouvres De La Lance,* September 24th, 1811).

Frederick II (the Great), *Instructions for His Generals.* Translated by Brigadier General Thomas R. Phillips. Harrisburg, PA, 1944.

Frederick II (the Great), *Militarische Schriften.* Compiled by von Taysen. Berlin, 1882.

Glover, Michael, *Wellington's Army in the Peninsula* 1808–1814. New York, 1977.

Grandmaison General de (formerly Lt. Col. in Volontaires des Flandres), *On the Military Service of Light Troops in the Field and in Fortified Places.* Translated from French by Major Lewis Nicola. Philadelphia, 1777. Originally published as *Petit querre; au traité du service des troupes legérè en campagne,* Paris, 1756.

Great Britain, The War Office, *Rules and Regulations for the Formations, Field-Exercise and Movements of His Majesty's Forces.* London, 1798.

Great Britain, The War Office, *An Education of Several Parts of His Majesty's Regulations for the Formations and Movements of Cavalry.* London, 1803.

Great Britain, The War Office, *The Manual and Platoon Exercises.* London, 1804.

Grémillet, Paul, *Un Regiment Pendant Deux Siecles* (1684–1899): *Histoire du 81e De Ligne*. Paris, 1899.

Grose, Francis, *Military Antiquities.* 2 vols. London, 1786–88.

Grosser Generalstab, *Die Kriege Friedrichs Des Grossen.* 20 vols. Berlin, 1890–1913.

Hamilton, Edward P., *The French Army in America.* Ottawa, 1967. Contains translation of *Manual of Arms* specified by 1755 ordinance.

Hatton, R. H., *History of Charles XII.* London, 1968.

Haythornthwaite, Philip, *Weapons & Equipment of the Napoleonic Wars.* Poole Dorset, 1979.

Held, Robert, *The Age of Firearms: A Pictorial History.* Northfield, Illinois, 1957.

Hennet, Leon, *État Militaire de France Pour L'Annee* 1793. Paris, 1903.

Hohenlohe-Ingelfingen (Kraft Prinz zu), *Conversations on Cavalry.* Translated by Lt. C. Reichmann. London, 1897.

Hughes, B. P. Major General, *Firepower: Weapons Effectiveness on the Battlefield, 1630–1850.* London, 1974.

Hughes, B. P. Major General, *Open Fire: Artillery Tactics from Marlborough to Wellington*. Chichester, Sussex, 1983.

Hughes, B. P. Major General, *British Smooth-Bore Artillery: The Muzzle Loading Artillery of the 18th and 19th Centuries.* London, 1969.

Imbotti, Bernardin, *La Milice Moderne Ou Sont Comprises Les Evolutions Tant De Cavalerie Que D'Infanterie*. 1646.

Jeffries, George, Ned Zuparlco, ed., *Tactics and Grand Tactics of the Napoleonic Wars.* 1982.

Kane, Richard (Brigadier General, Governor of Minorca), *A New System of Military Discipline for a Battalion of Foot on Actions with the Most Essential Exercise of the Cavalry.* Contained in *Campaigns of King William and Queen Anne from 1689 to 1712*. London, 1745.

Kemp, Anthony, *Weapons & Equipment of the Marlborough Wars.* Poole Dorset, 1980.

Kosciusko, General, *Manoeuvres of Horse Artillery.* Translated from French by Jonathan Williams. New York, 1808.

la Vallière (Chevalier de), Francois de la Baume le Blanc, *The Art of War Containing the Rules and Practice of the Greatest Generals in the Maneouvres.* Philadelphia, 1776.

Le Blond, M., *Elemens de Tactique*. Paris, 1758.

Lemau de la Jaisse, *Carte Generale De La Monarchie Francoise Contenant L'Histoire Militaire Depuis Clovis.* Paris, 1733.

Lemau de la Jaisse, *Septieme Abrege De La Carte Generale Du Militaire De France Sur Terre Et Sor Mer.* Paris, 1741.

Lloyd, Earnst M., *A Review of the History of Infantry.* London, 1908.

Longueville, Thomas, *Marshal Turenne*. London, 1907.

Luvaas, Jay, *Frederick the Great on the Art of War.* New York, 1966.

Malibran, H., *Guide A L'Usage Des Artistes Et Des Costumiers Contenant La Description Des Uniforms De L'Armee Francais De 1780 À 1848*. 2 vols. Paris, 1904.

Maude, F. N. Lieut. Col., *Cavalry: Its Past and Future*. London, 1903.

Mirabeau, Honore, Gabriel Riquechi (Comte de), *Monarchie Prussienne Sous Frederic Le Grand.* 4 vols. + atlas. London, 1788.

Mollo, John, *Uniforms of the Seven Years War 1756–63*. Poole, Dorset, 1977.

de Montondre, Longchamps, de Roussel, *Etat Militaire De France, Pour L'Armee 1758–1793*. 36 vols. Paris. 1759–1793.

Müller, William, *The Elements of the Science of War,* 3 vols. London, 1811.

———, *New Regulations for the Prussian Infantry.* London, 1756.

Niemeyer, Joachim, and Ortenburg, Georg *The Hanoverian Army During The Seven Years' War.* Copenhagen, 1977.

———, *The Officer's Manual in the Field, or a Series of Military Plans Representing the Principal Operations of a Campaign*. Translated from German, 2nd edition. London, 1800 (reprinted New York, 1968). Original work written in Prussia several years after Seven Years' War under auspices of General Czetteritz.

Oman, Charles, *A History of the Art of War in the Sixteenth Century.* London, 1939.

Paret, Peter, *Yorck and the Era of Prussian Reform 1807–1815.* Princeton, 1966.

Prussia, Kreigsministerium, *Regulations for the Prussian Infantry* (1743). New York, 1968.

Prussia, Kreigsministerium, *Regulations for the Prussian Cavalry* (1743). New York, 1968.

Puységur, Jacques Françoise de Chastenhat (Maréchal de France; Marquis de), *Art De La Guerre Par Principes Et Par Regles.* 2 vols. Paris, 1748.

Quimby, Robert S., *The Background of Napoleonic Warfare: The Theory of Military Tactics In Eighteenth-Century France.* New York, 1957.

Quincy, C. S. (Marquis de—Lt. Gen. d'artillerie), Maxims Et Instructions Sur L'Art Militaire. Bound in volume 7 of *Histoire de régne de Louis le grand.* 7 vols. Paris, 1726.

Reihn, Richard, "Linear Tactics and the Wargame," In: *The Courier.* vol. II, nos. 4 & 5, Jan–Apr, 1982.

Renard, Jean Baptiste (General), *Considerations Sur La Tactique De L'Infanterie En Europe.* Paris, 1857.

Roberts, Michael, *Gustavus Adolphus: A History of Sweden 1611–1632.* London, 1958.

Roemer, Jean, *Cavalry: Its History, Management, & Uses.* New York, 1863.

Rogers, Colonel H. C. B., *The British Army of the Eighteenth Century.* London, 1977.

Saint Paul, Horace, *A Journal of the First Two Campaigns of the Seven Years' War.* Cambridge, 1914.

Saint Simon (Duc de), *Memoirs of Louis XIV and the Regency.* Translated by Bayle Saint Johns. London, 1901.

de Saxe, Maurice (Compte de, Maréchal de France), *Mes Reveries.* 2 vols. Paris, 1757. *Reveries on the Art of War.* Translated by Brigadier General Thomas R. Phillips. Harrisburg, Pa., 1944.

Sicard, François., *Histoire Des Institutions Militaires.* 5 vols. Paris, 1834.

Simon, Edith, *The Making of Frederick the Great.* Boston, 1963.

Skrine, Francis Henry, *Fontenoy and the War of the Austrian Succession.* London, 1906.

Smirke, Robert, *Smirke's Review of a Battalion of Infantry.* New York, 1811.

von Steuben, Frederick William, Baron, *Regulations for the Order and Discipline of the Troops of the United States (May 1792).* Boston, 1794; Reprinted New York, 1985.

Susane, Louis A. V. V., *Histoire De L'Ancienne Infanterie Françoise.* 8 vols. Paris, 1849.

Sweden: *Reglemente for Akande Artilleriets Tjenstgoring Och Exercise.* Stockholm, 1808.

Sweden; *Forordning Och Reglemente For Regementerne Til Fot*. Stockholm, 1794.

Sweden: *Forordning Och Reglemente For Regementerne Til Fot;* Stockholm, 1813.

Taylor, Frank, *The Wars of Marlborough 1702–1709*. 2 vols. Oxford, 1921.

Tilke, J. S., *An Account of Some of the Most Remarkable Transactions of the War Between the Prussians, Austrians and Russians*. 2 vols., London, 1787.

Trevelyan, George Macaulay, *England Under Queen Anne*. 3 vols. London, 1932–34.

Turner, James, *Pallas Armata: Military Essays of the Grecian, Roman, and Modern Art of War.* London, 1683 (reprinted New York, 1968).

Vernery, Peter, *The Battle of Blenheim*. New York, 1976.

Voltaire, François Marie, *History of the War of 1741*. New York, 1901.

Von Schmidt, Major General Carl, *Instructions for Training, Employment, and Leading of Cavalry.* Translated by Captain C. W. Bowdler Bell. London, 1881 (reprinted New York, 1968).

Wagner, Eduard, *European Weapons and Warfare 1616–1648*. Translated by Simon Pellar. London, 1979.

Warnery, Major General, *Remarks on Cavalry.* Translated by Lt. Col. G. F Koehler. Whitehall, 1805.

White, Jon Manchip, *Marshal of France: The Life and Times of Maurice De Saxe 1696–1750*. London, 1962.

Appendix: Formation Diagrams

PART I

Chapter 1

#1 Ranks and Files

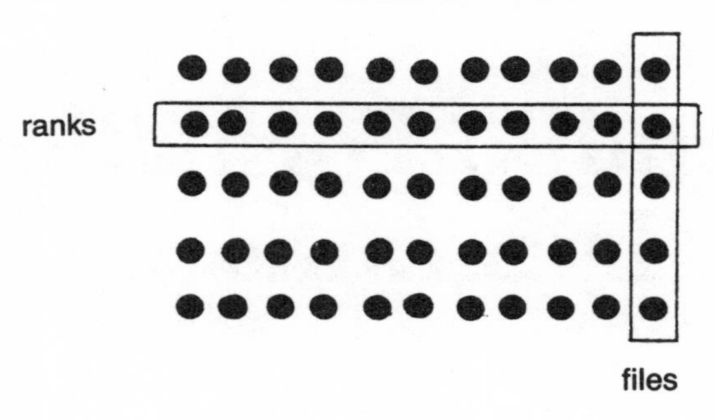

#2 Battalion Divided into 3 *Manches*

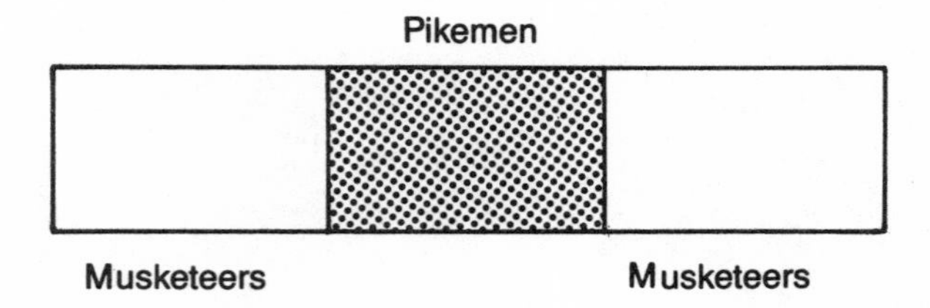

Chapter 2

#3 Pikemen Stationed Near Flanks of Battalion (French Army 1693)

Initial Layout of Battalion

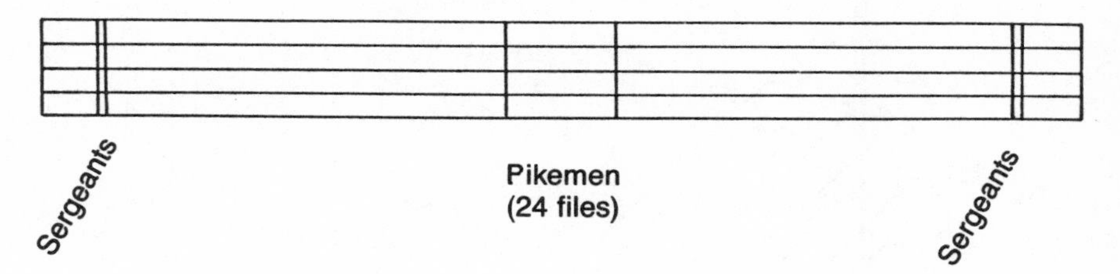

After one-half of Pikemen Are Ordered to Flanks

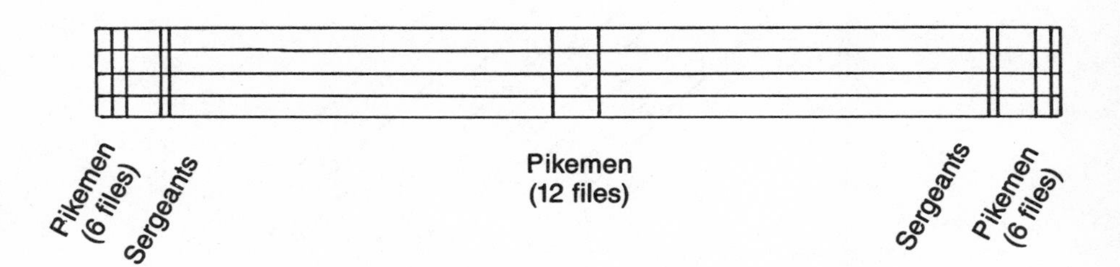

Chapter 4

#4 Quarter-wheeling along Wide Front (all ranks turning at the same time)

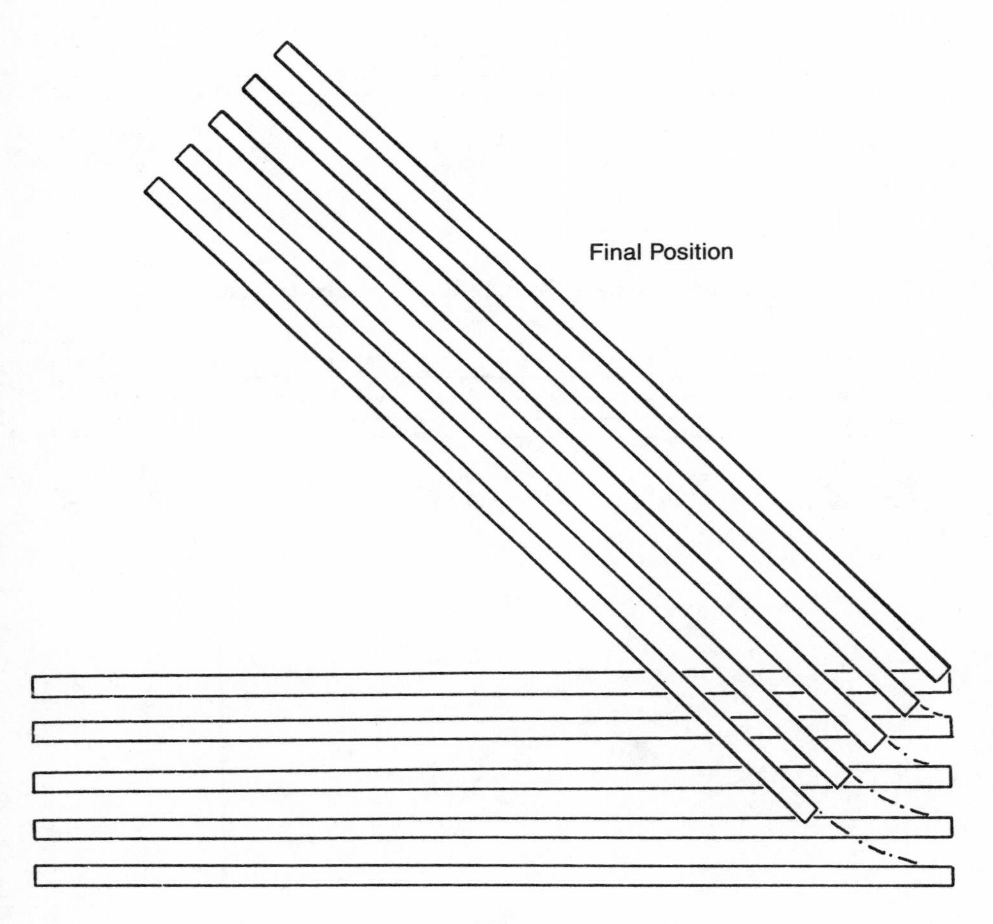

#5 Quarter-wheeling along Narrow Front (one rank turns at a time)

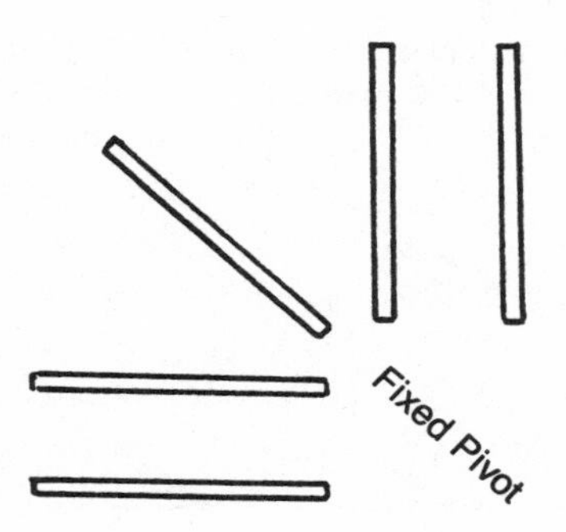

#6 Difficulty of Quarter-wheeling Wide Divisions in French Infantry Battalion

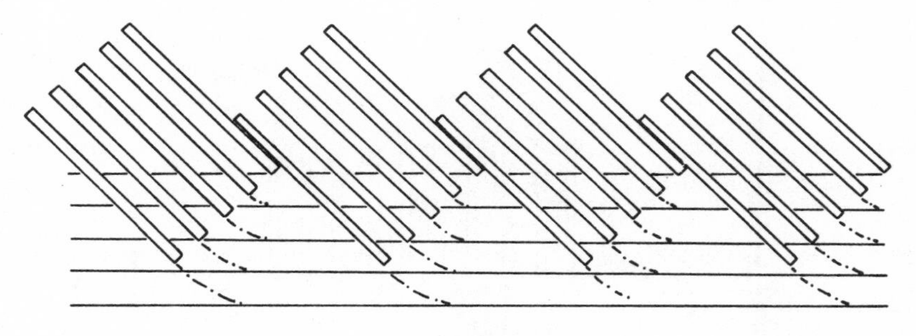

#7 French Battalion Forming Column by Simultaneously Quarter-wheeling Four Wide Divisions

In this case each division is sufficiently wide so that the men in the front ranks do not bump into those in the rear of the previous division.

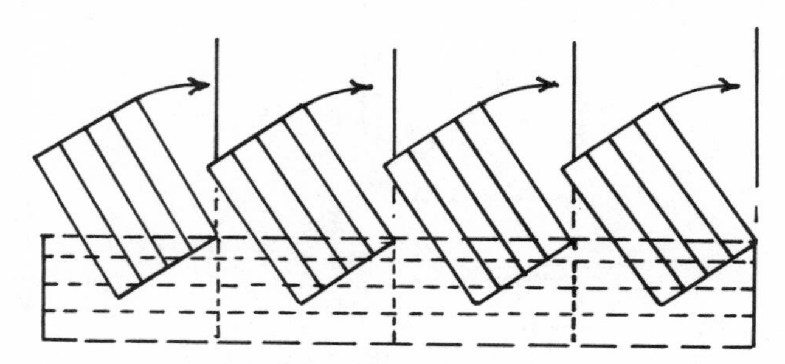

Here, the column's length is approximately equal to the width of the battalion in line.

#8 French Battalion Forming Column of 5 Divisions (plus grenadiers)

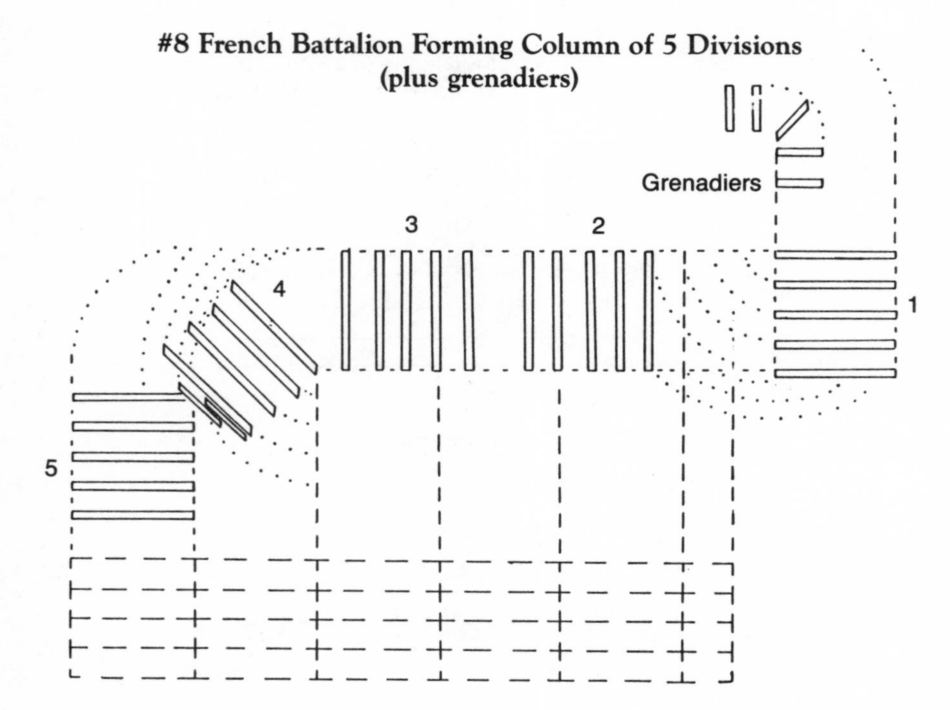

#9 French Battalion Forming Column of 10 Divisions (plus grenadiers and picquet)

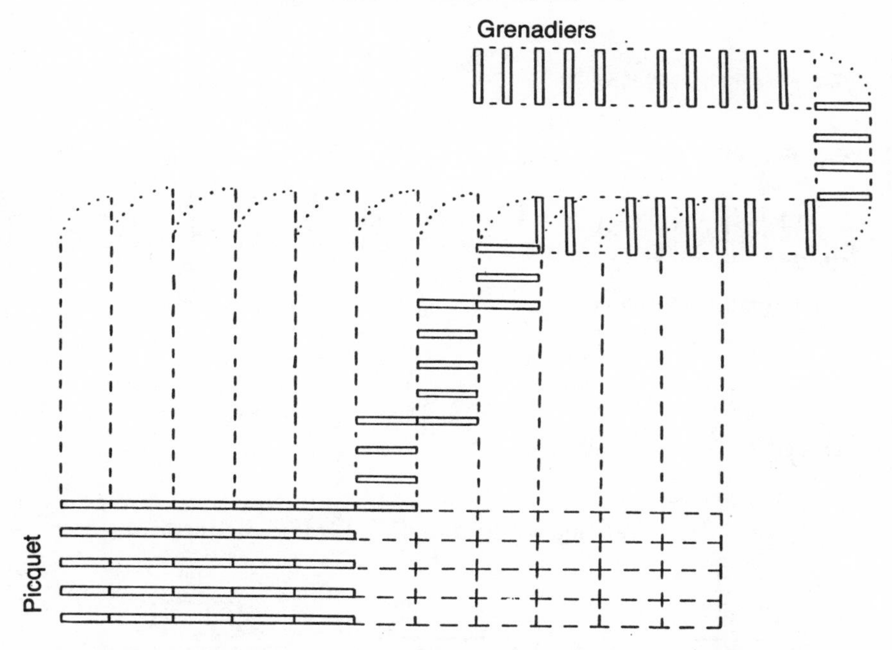

Length of the column will be several times the width of the battalion in line.

#10 Battalion Deploying to the Left of Column

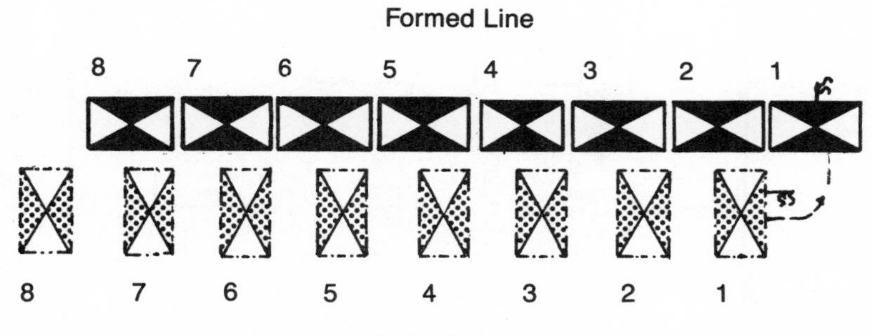

#11 Battalion Deploying to the Right of Column

Chapter 5

#12 Various Multi-battalion Orders of Battle

Battalions Forming a *Cinquin*

#13 Typical Battle Order, Circa 1700

First Line

Infantry

Cavalry

Cavalry

Second Line

Corps de Reserve

#14 French Battalion, March 2, 1703

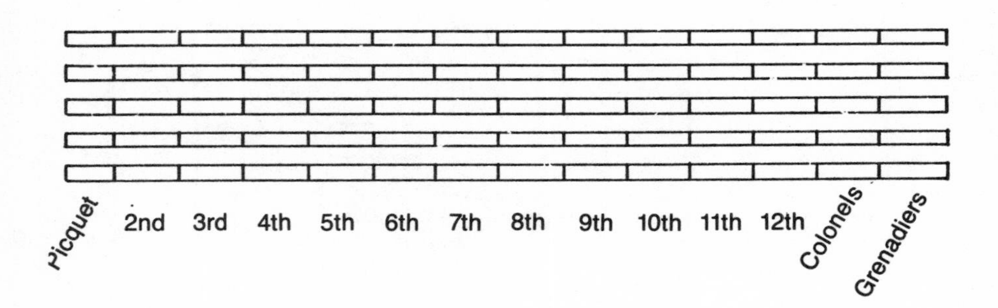

#15 British Battalion Circa 1709

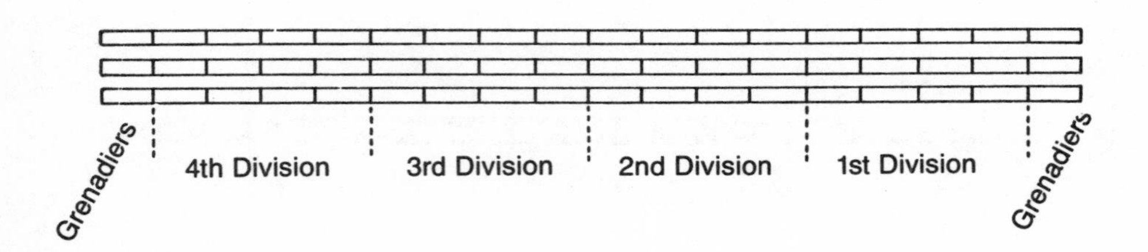

PART II

Chapter 8

#1 Folard's Proposed "Mixed Order"

Infantry and cavalry brigades alternate along the first and second lines

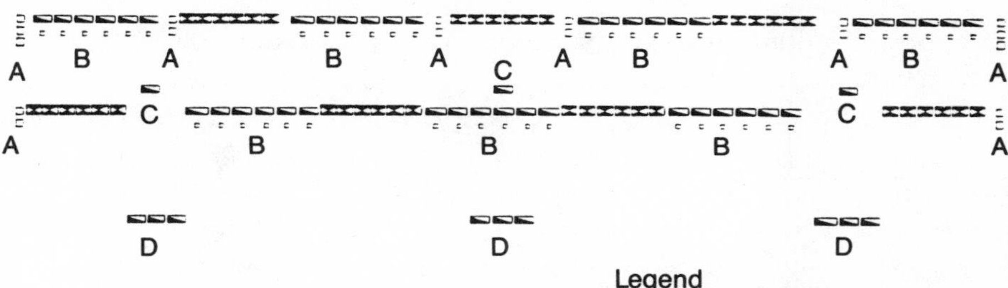

Legend
A Columns of battalions
B Grenadier platoons
C Interline Hussars
D Dragoon reserves

#2 Converging Fire from Folard's Columns

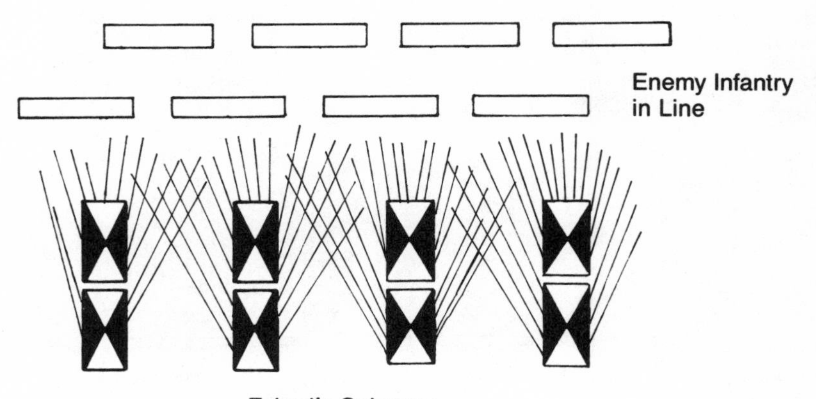

Chapter 9

#3 Prussian Cavalry Column of Attack in Action

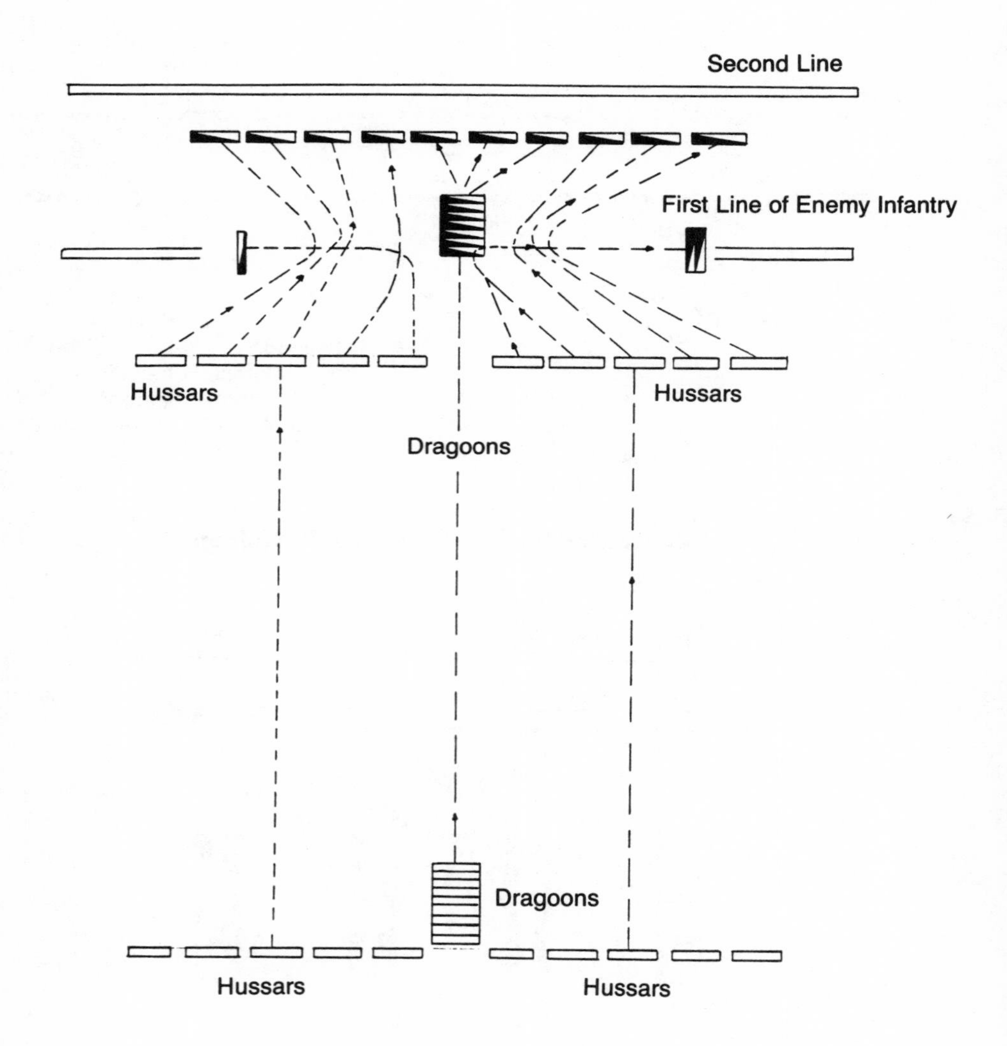

Chapter 10

#4 "March by Lines" to Effect Oblique Attack

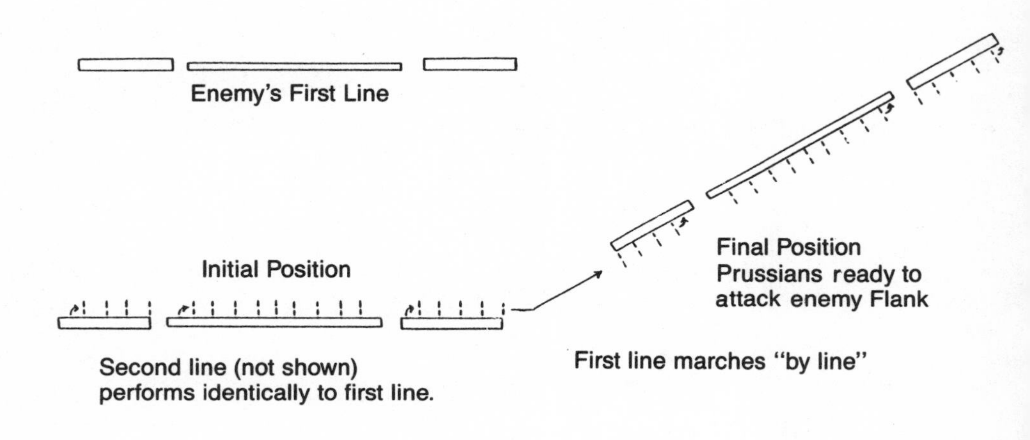

Chapter 11

#5 Layout of French Battalion, June 29, 1753

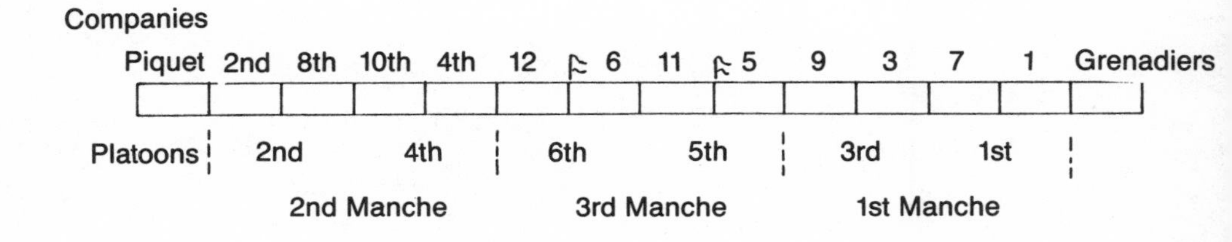

#6 Layout of French Companies, June 29, 1753

Fusilier Company

Grenadier Company

Piquet

captain or 2nd captain
lieutenant
sergeant
corporal
anspessade

#7 Layout of French Company, May 14, 1754

PART III

Chapter 13

#1 Forming Line with Series of Quarter-wheels

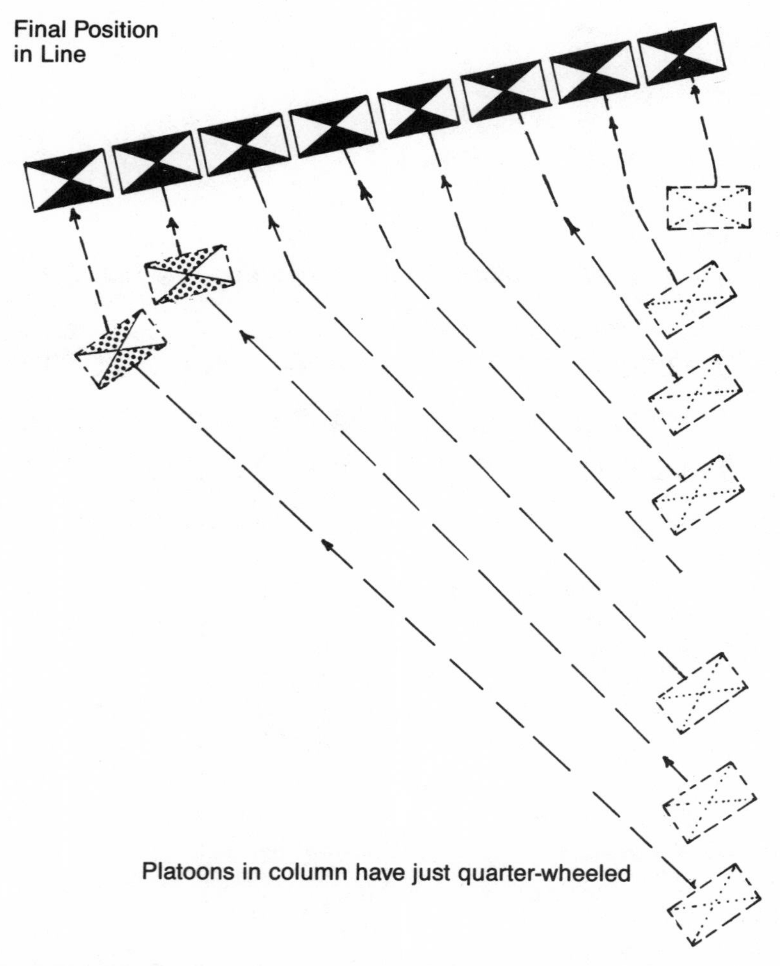

Note: in this instance the line formed is not quite perpendicular to the original column.

#2 Regiment Deploying into Line

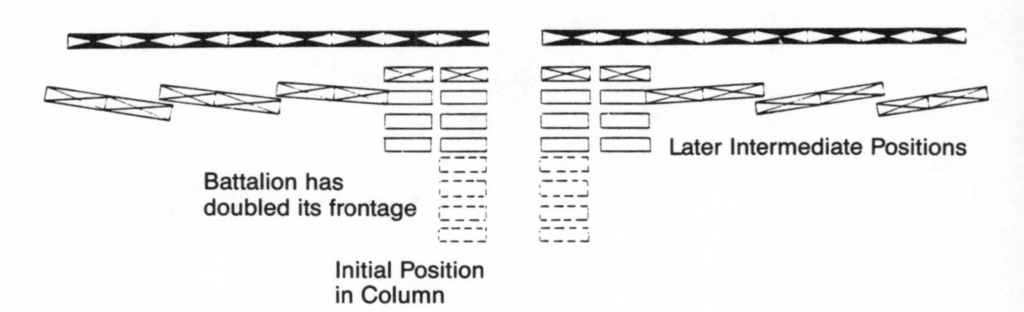

#3 Regiment (2 battalions) Ploying into Column

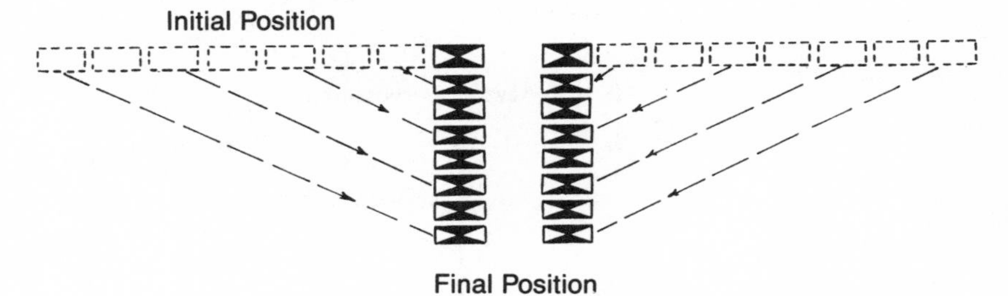

#4 Battalion Ploying into Column

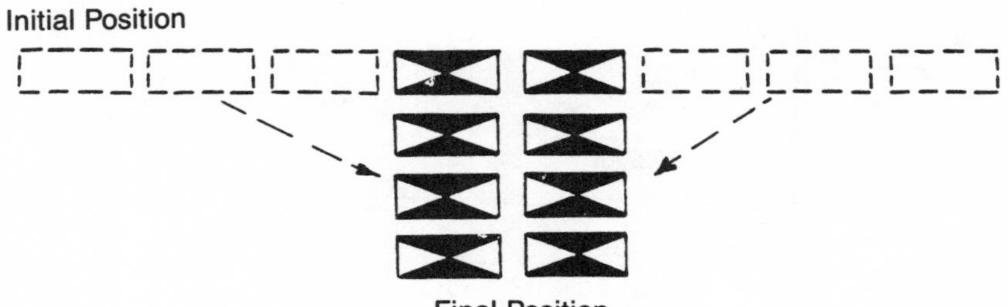

This double column was used as a temporary formation to maneuver around terrain obstacles

#5 Wheeling a Battalion

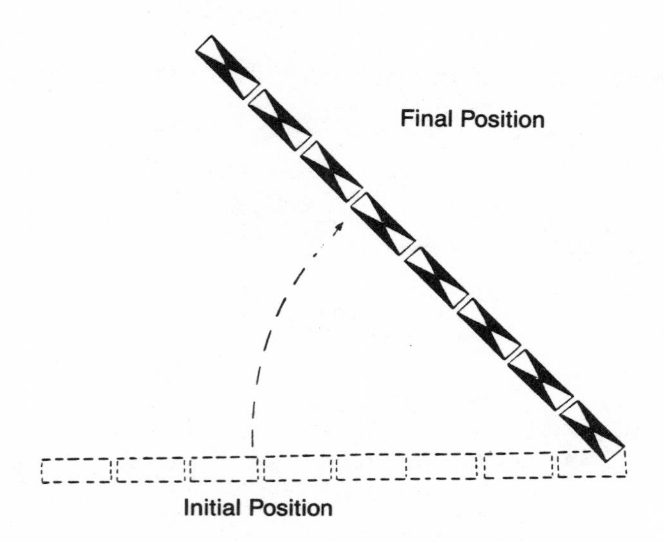

#6 Central Conversion

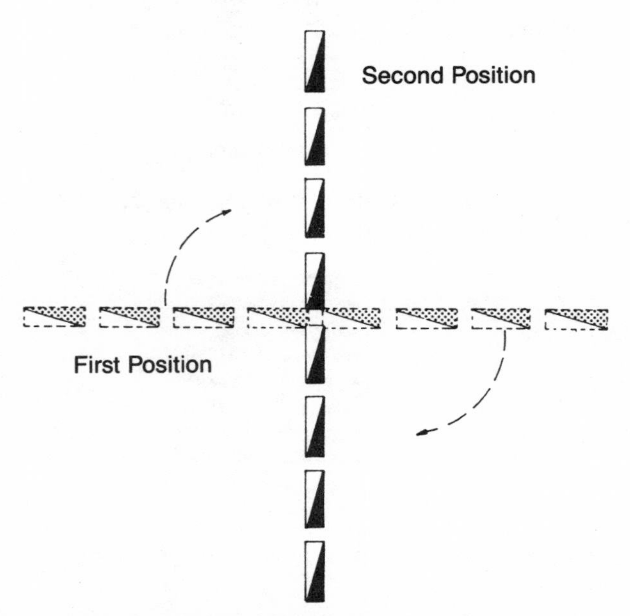

Soldiers in the right half of battalion about face, quarter-wheel, and then about face again to face the new front.

#7A Performing a Countermarch (first version)

The object of this maneuver is to have the battalion face the opposite direction.

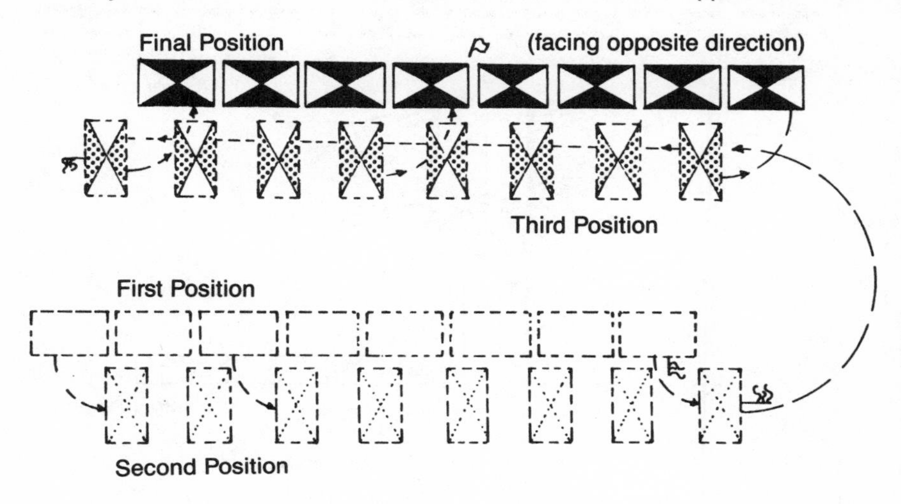

#7B Performing a Countermarch (second version)

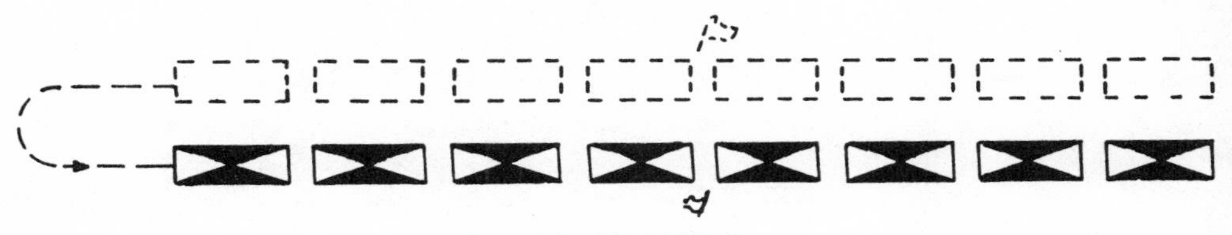

#8 Battalion Crossing Bridge

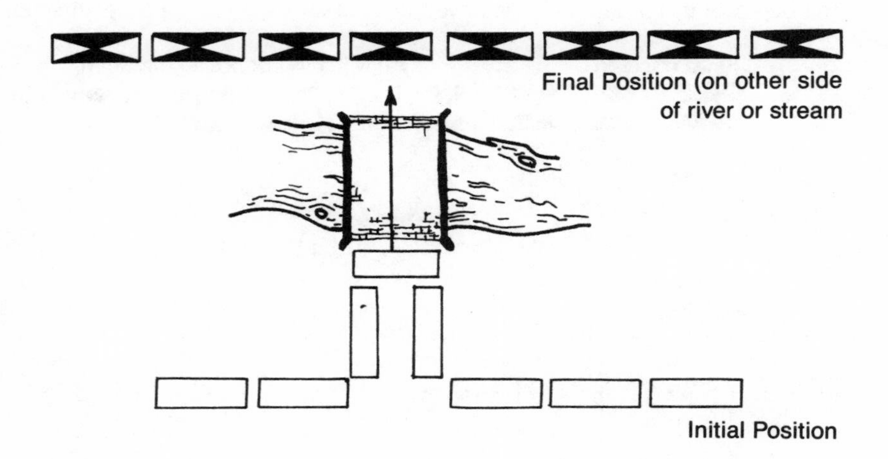

#9 Types of Squares and Their Formation

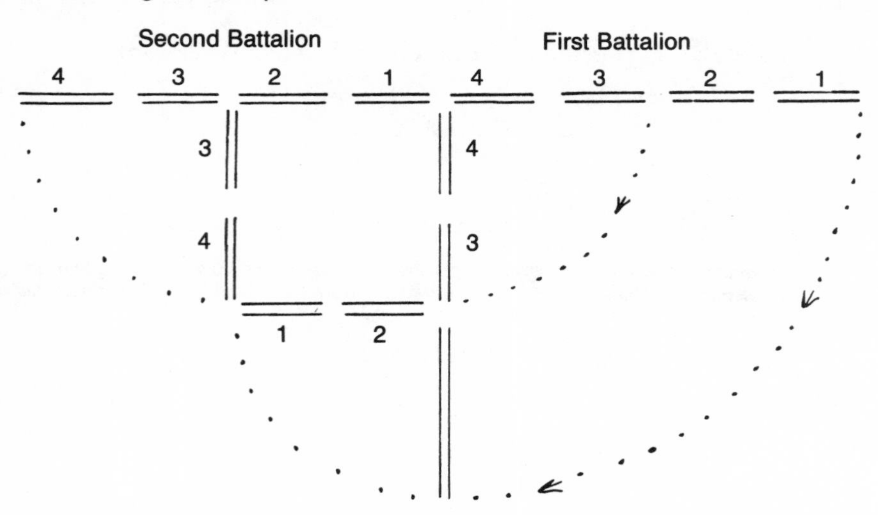

Each face of a square is a division made up of two platoons.

"Quick" Regimental Square

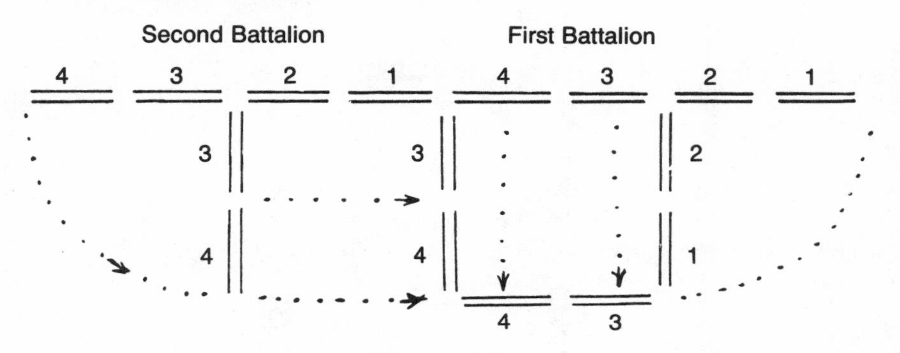

Forming a Three-Sided Square

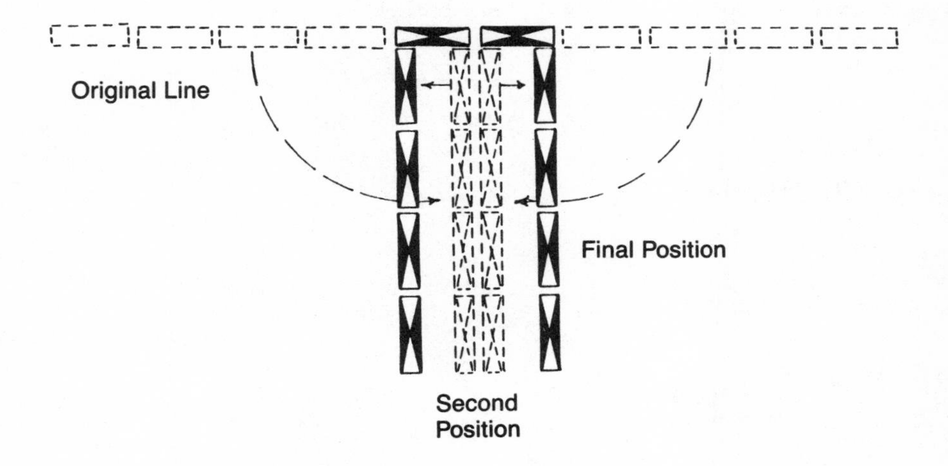

#10 Oblong Square

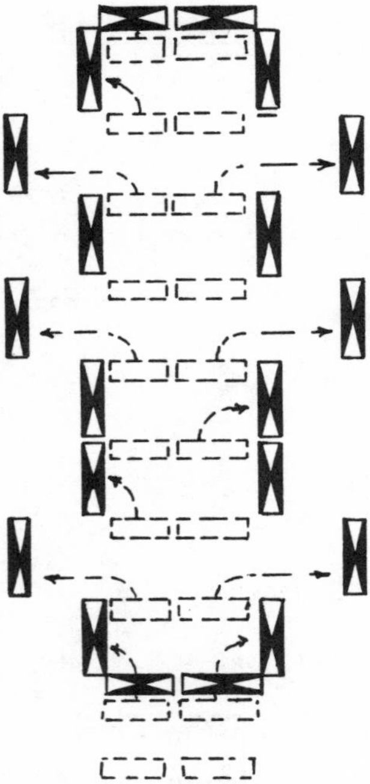

Alternate sections have advanced out of square to platoon fire.

Initial Position in Column.

Chapter 14

#11 Organization of French Battalion, 6th May, 1755

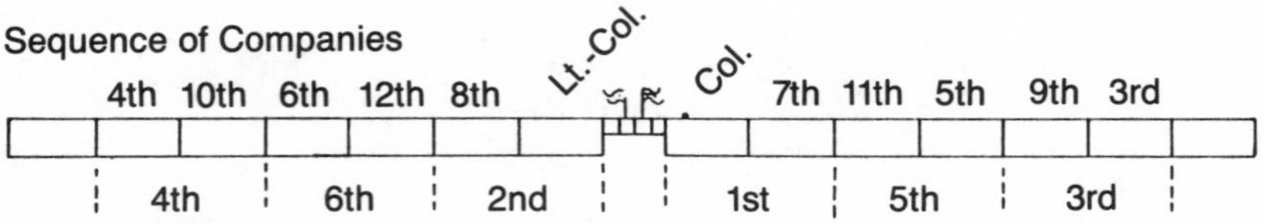

Sequence of Companies

4th 10th 6th 12th 8th Lt.-Col. Col. 7th 11th 5th 9th 3rd

4th 6th 2nd 1st 5th 3rd

Sequence of Platoons

#12 Types of French Infantry Columns, Circa 1754

Column by Platoon

Column by Thirds

Column by Half Rank

#13 Changing Width of Column

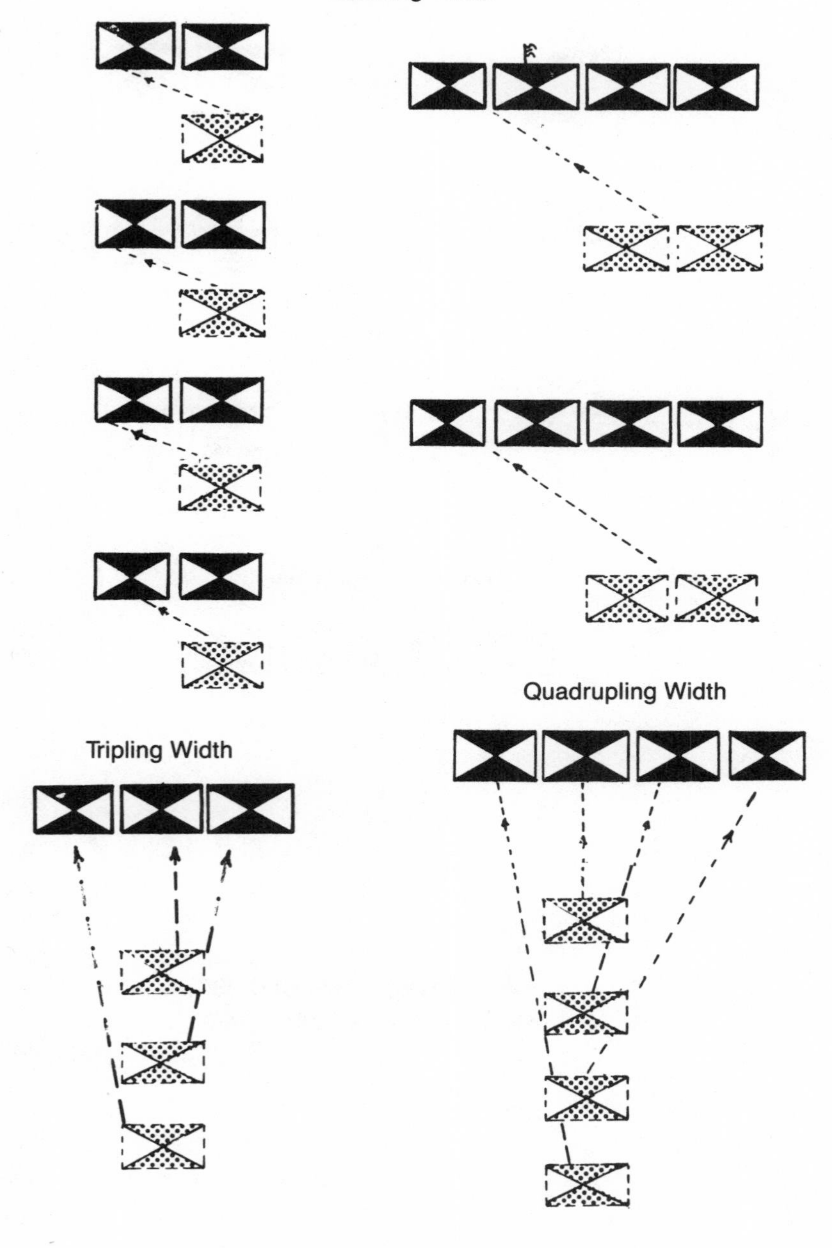

#14 Forming Column of Attack

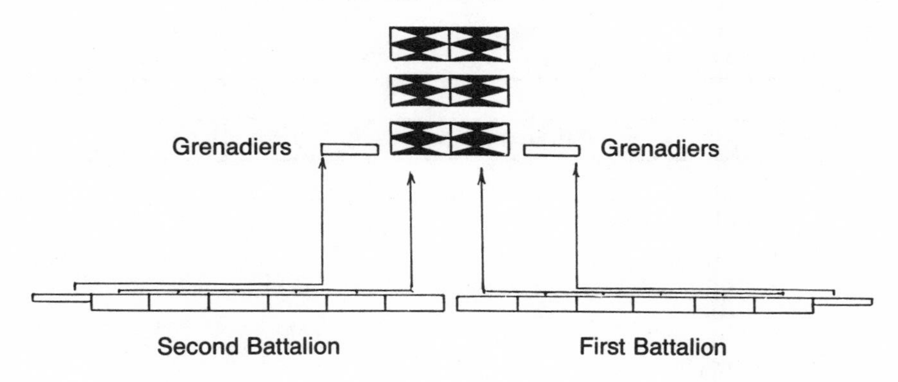

#15 Forming Column of Retreat (to the front of the line)

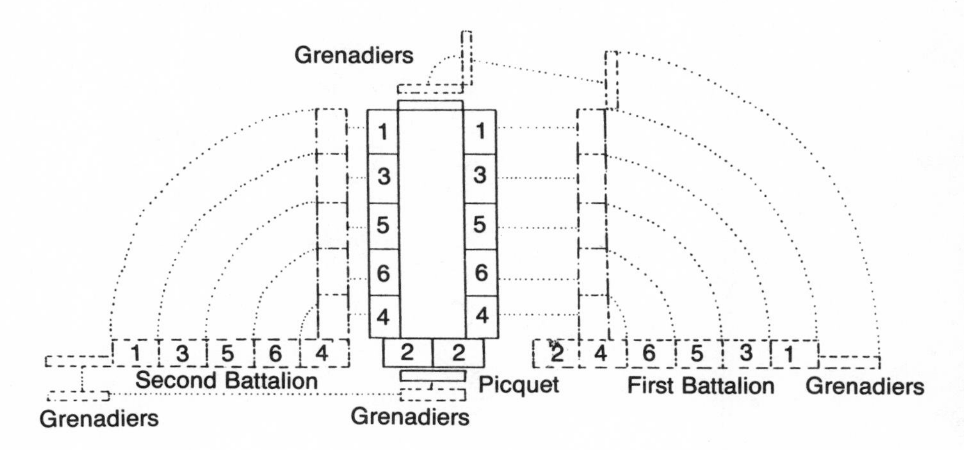

Numbers represent platoon numbers.

#16 French Platoon Firing, 1755

Sequence of Fire	8	4	6	2	1	5	3	7
Company Number	Picquet	2 & 8	4 & 10	6 & 12	11 & 5	9 & 3	7 & 1	Gren
Platoon Number		2	4	6	5	3	1	

Chapter 15

#17 Typical Advanced Guard, Circa 1756

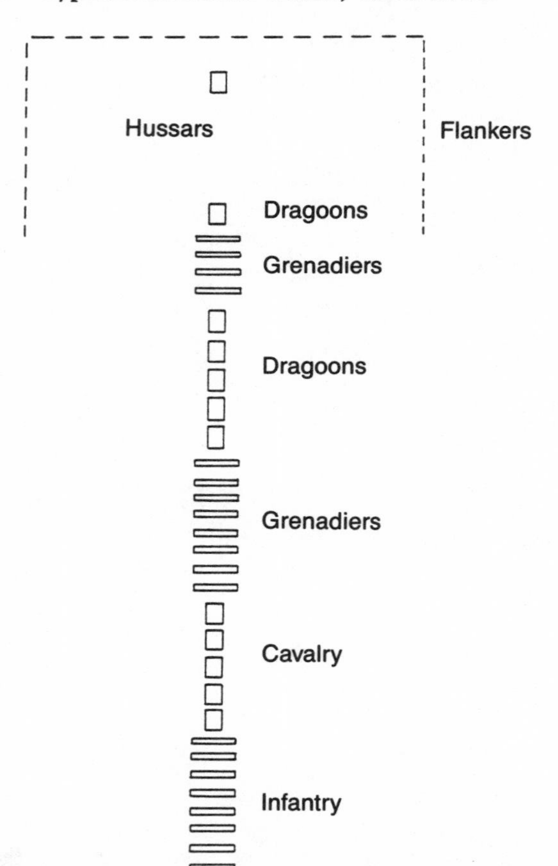

#18 Prussian Practice of Deploying Cavalry Squadrons between Columns of Route to Guard Against Enemy Attack

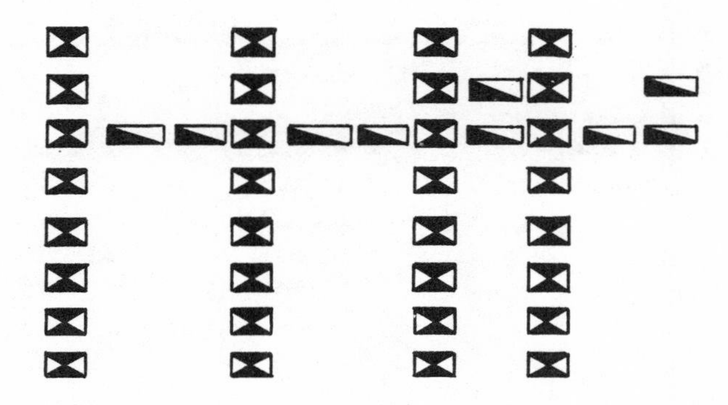

#19 Typical Prussian Battle Order Prior to Battle

Corps de Reserve

#20 Arrangement of Cavalry on Wing (July 25, 1744 Disposition)

Hussars

Cuirassiers

Dragoons Dragoons Dragoons

Hussars

#21 Prussian Methods of Placing Cavalry in Echelon on Wings

A. If army is deployed on a wide plain:

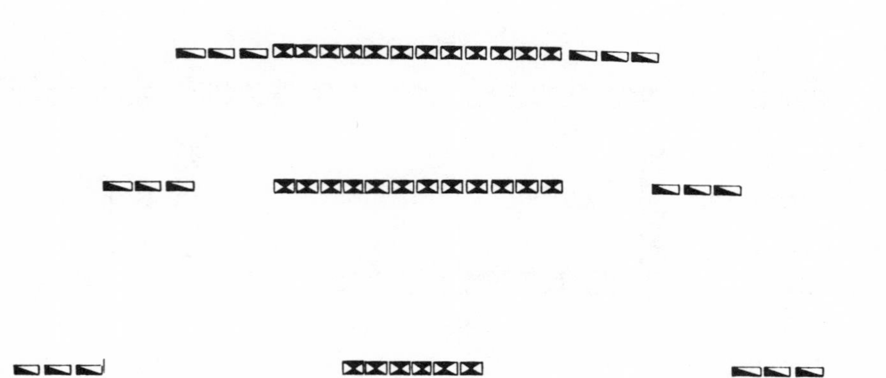

B. If cavalry is protective flank using echelons:

C. If hussars are used to protect flank using echelons:

#22 Position of Prussian Cavalry Relative to Infantry (varied according to circumstances)

A. Cavalry placement when flank is also protected by interline infantry facing outward:

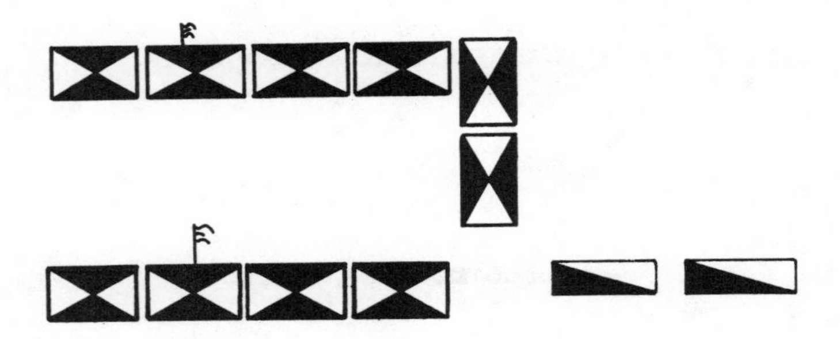

B. Cavalry placement when no infantry faces outward:

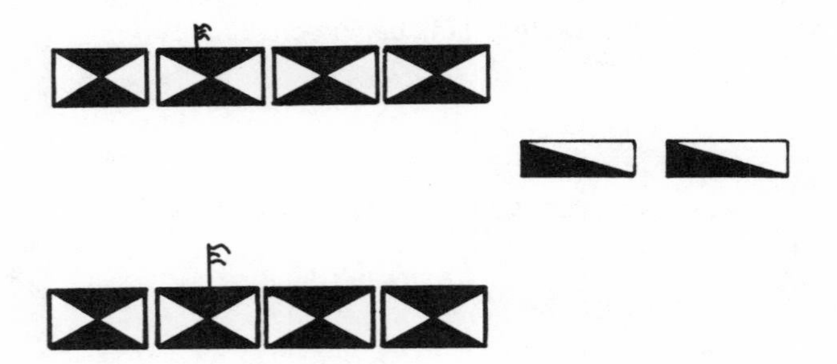

C. Same as in B, but there's an abundance of cavalry:

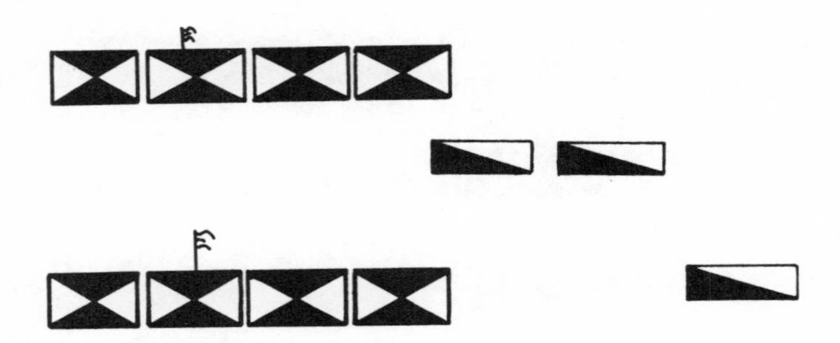

Index